18 WHEELS
OF SCIENCE FICTION

PRAISE FOR BIG TIME BOOKS ANTHOLOGIES

18 Wheels of Horror

"Filled with disturbing twists and terrifying threats, these spine-chilling stories have enough suspense to spook even the bravest of souls."
—Blake Boldt, Road King magazine

"A diverse assortment of breakout authors contribute to this high-octane anthology of trucker-themed horror...18 Wheels of Horror is enthusiastically recommended for fans of oily thrills and chills."
—Clint Travis, Midwest Book Review

"Truck stops and CB lingo, the endless rumble of engines and wheels, the perceived romance and wearying lonely truths of the open road, the aspect of unique Americana, it's all here."
—Christine Morgan, The Horror Fiction Review

Hell Comes To Hollywood

"Gorier than any PG-13 horror flick you'll see, and written better (by a mile) than any SyFy schlockfest, Hell Comes To Hollywood is worth a look."
—Dr. Loomis, Ain't It Cool News Horror

"Hell Comes To Hollywood is all-encompassing, featuring stories that span from wonderfully gratuitous, over-the-top gorefests...to tales that are genuinely haunting and linger in your mind long afterward...
—Vivienne Vaughn, Fangoria

Hell Comes To Hollywood was nominated for a Bram Stoker Award

Hell Comes To Hollywood II

"Miller's Hell Comes To Hollywood II ought to be required reading for anyone who has even an inkling of trying to make it in the City of Dreams."
—Scott Urban, The Horror Zine

"On the whole, the anthology receives a big thumbs up; it is an entertaining read with an unusually high number of good stories..."
—TT Zuma, Horror World

18 WHEELS OF SCIENCE FICTION

A Long Haul Into The Fantastic

Loaded, Driven, and
EDITED BY ERIC MILLER

Big Time Books™
Los Angeles, California
www.BigTimeBooks.com

18 WHEELS OF SCIENCE FICTION
A Long Haul Into The Fantastic

Proofreading by Leya Booth, GeniusBookServices.com
Interior and E-Book layout by Steven W. Booth, GeniusBookServices.com

Trade Paperback ISBN: 978-09906866-8-2
Mass Market Paperback ISBN: 978-0-9906866-9-9

If you like this book, we want to know.
Email us at: contact@bigtimebooks.com

10 9 8 7 6 5 4 3 2 1

Dedicated to

Jules Verne, Herbert George Wells,
Edward E. "Doc" Smith, Robert A. Heinlein,
Douglas Adams, and all the other amazing
writers who made a kid look up to
the skies and dream...

CONTENTS

FOREWORD

In 1916, William Warwick packed his wife, their baby daughter, and a ton of Carnation evaporated milk into a GMC truck, leaving Seattle for New York on what has been called the first long haul truck run. The Seattle Chamber of Commerce sponsored the trip to promote tourism and trade via the National Parks Highway, a road that bore little in common with today's Interstates.

In spite of the cargo, this was no milk run. Large sections of the "highway" were unpaved. There were few gas stations, garages, or hotels to be found. On top of that, per the rules of the promotion, Warwick was not allowed to have any outside help on the drive. He couldn't carry chains or ropes or any special equipment. All he had was his driving skill, determination, and what must have been a very understanding wife.

Ten weeks and 3,710 miles later the couple arrived in New York City. Warwick had smashed through 43 (!) rickety culverts and bridges and dug himself out of a seemingly endless series of wheel-devouring mud holes. As Robert F. Karolevitz said in his book *This Was Trucking*, "Warwick probably spent more time with his hands on a shovel than on the steering wheel."

With the promotional run a success, Warwick headed home. Obviously not being one to shrink from a challenge, he returned to Seattle by the scenic route, via Los Angeles. I think everyone will agree that making this 9,513-mile trip on hard rubber tires, in a primitive truck, and on questionable roads makes Mr. Warwick one of the most badass drivers of all time. The wife and baby were pretty darn tough too.

Almost 100 years later, a car made a similar run, from San Francisco to New York. This time the trip took 9 days. That's long by modern travel standards, but there was nothing standard about this run: the car drove itself for 99% of the trip. As you read this, multiple companies are testing self-driving cars and big rigs around the world, in crowded cities and on the open road.

That would have sounded like science fiction ten years ago.

It is reality today.

What exactly the future holds for truckers—and the rest of us—remains to be seen, but the 18 visionary writers included this book have done their best to give us a glimpse of what may come to pass for the truck drivers of tomorrow. And though not every story in this book takes place in the cab of a big rig thundering down the road, they are all somehow set in the trucking world. Or universe, as it may be.

Artificial Intelligences will soon be as commonplace in trucks as steering wheels and gear shifts are now. Because of that, many of the stories you are about to read have self-driving elements, though each one has a wildly different take on autonomous technology and how it affects the flesh and blood drivers who share the ride.

Rest assured, not every story here is about AI-driven semis. There are plenty of good old fashioned gear-jamming humans behind the wheels as well. After all, someone has to get their hands dirty and dig the rigs out of literal or figurative ditches when things go wrong.

William Warwick could attest to that.

Before we hit the road, I'd like to acknowledge a few people who helped me pull this book together, or inspired me during the process. In no particular order I'd like to thank:

The writers. These books are nothing without the hours of blood, sweat, and tears you spilled to craft these amazing stories. Proud and honored to know you.

The readers. We love sharing our stories with you. Thanks for checking us out.

The reviewers. From the professionals who give us such great write-ups, to the fans who take the time to post reviews or tell friends about the book: we salute you.

Paul Carlson. Driver, writer, darn fine man. In addition to letting me reprint his trucking science fiction story *Shotgun Seat* in this volume, Paul also connected me with many other writers. His trucking fiction list at *www.cuebon.com* is a great resource.

Steven Booth and Leya Booth at Genius Book Services. Their formatting, design, and proofreading skills help turn words on a computer screen into real books.

James Heath. Science Consultant, and old, old friend. Any technical mistakes in the stories are all mine, I assure you.

Keven Carter. His cover art for *18 Wheels of Horror* set the tone for the series, and we wish him well in all his endeavors.

Brad Fraunfelter. For doing the new kick ass cover.

Shane Bitterling, again. Sounding board, bullshit caller, writer, and friend.

Graydon Schlichter. For another great-sounding audio book (along with Jennifer Knighton), and for all the last-second copyediting catches.

Kathryn E. McGee. For never letting me off the hook on grammar or rewrites, and the awesome subtitle.

Patrick Shiffrar. For all the behind the scenes help.

John DeChancie and Terry Bisson. Many moons ago I read their trucking science fiction works (the *Skyways* novel series from Mr. DeChancie, and Mr. Bisson's short story *Over Flat Mountain*) and the idea that became this book was born. To say that I am thrilled to have an original DeChancie story and a reprint of *Over Flat Mountain* in this anthology would be an understatement.

Art Bell and George Noory. Driving at night in lonely places is a lot more fun with *Coast to Coast AM* on the radio. And sometimes a lot scarier. RIP Mr. Bell.

Truck drivers everywhere. Without you, civilization would stop cold. Driving is a lonely, hard job, and this book should give you an entertaining break from the road. Also, please know that though the writers of these tales are great storytellers, only a few are professional drivers. I have been a commercial driver for years and have done my best to make sure the trucking details ring true, but even so a few things may have gotten past me. Or I let them go for the sake of the story. I hope you will overlook any "mistakes" and enjoy the tales anyway.

And always, special thanks to all the drivers who blasted the horn when a kid pumped an arm. Your simple gesture made their day.

I hope this book makes yours.

Eric Miller
Los Angeles, California
August 2018

3, 2, 1, IGNITION!

John DeChancie is a well-known author of science fiction and fantasy. He is most famous for his Skyway Trilogy (Starrigger, Red Limit Freeway, Paradox Alley) *and his seriocomic fantasy adventure series beginning with* Castle Perilous *and running to nine volumes. His short pieces have appeared in many magazines and paperback original anthologies. Living in Los Angeles, he is at work writing more fiction in addition to screenplays and teleplays. He has a background in music, TV and film production, and was the 2005 recipient of the* Forrest J. Ackerman Award *for lifetime achievement Science Fiction.*

THE WRECKERS

John DeChancie

IF YOU'VE NEVER SEEN A PORTAL ARRAY, a grouping of jet-black cylinders towering over, say, a desert plain on some lifeless, god-bereft planetoid, you might think it pretty strange to be seeing between four and eight huge cylinders lined up on both sides of the road, all rotating at unimaginable speeds. Which you can't actually see. They're blacker than black, and they hover only a few meters off the ground. They are not quite as dense as a neutron star. You are amazed that the entire plain, hey, the entire planet, is not sucked into them and crushed to nothing.

They are impressive. Even a little scary. To some people, flat out frightening, especially when you know the vehicle you're in will go barreling between them, a risky thing to be doing; because any slight deviation from the center line or any dynamic of speed could send you into the cylinders, to be crushed into a degenerate electron gas. And with a flash and a bang. When you see them on the approach against the sky, as I am right now, you can appreciate that they are real, solid objects, despite being composed of "projected programmable matter."

I'm not going into the question what distinguishes that exotic stuff from all the other kinds of weird matter, or wrangle over what is "real" or virtual and what isn't, but the reason the planet isn't sucked into the cylinders is that the matter is programmed not to do that. It is not like ordinary matter. It doesn't really exist, in a certain sense, because it is composed of virtual particles.

Esoteric physics is not my subject. I flunked out of the upper level courses at university. I am content to be the truck driver I was born to be. I mean, what else could the son of the legendary Jake McGraw become but a truck jockey? At least that's what the trailer-truck always tells me.

He's my dad; and he is my truck's AI, too.

Stands for *Asshole Intellectual*, Jake often reminds me.

"You should engage the cruise control, Sammy. The road ices up on this planet."

"Isn't it a moon of that gas giant over there?" I say, pointing to the big multicolored crescent hanging in an ochre sky above some rocky crags.

"Moon, planetoid, dwarf planet. It's just another barren interchange world. Like Pluto."

"Wasn't Pluto the last planet discovered in Earth's solar system?"

"Way before my lifetime," Jake says. "Twentieth century, I think."

"You spent time in that period, though, didn't you?"

"Nineteen sixty-four. The year after John Fitzgerald Kennedy died."

"You were quite the time travelling fool. Who was John Fitzgerald Kennedy?"

"Thirty-fifth president of the United States."

"History wasn't my subject."

"Nothing was your subject, dunce."

"Dunce? Nickname of Duns Scotus, the medieval scholastic philosopher. He was no ignoramus, and neither am I."

"Don't remind me you were a philosophy major. The most useless college degree in the galaxy. The galaxies."

"Jake, you're so White Male North American, you fairly reek it."

"Go on, disrespect me, you anti-cybernetic bastard."

"Whoa! If I'm a bastard, what does that make Mom?"

"Beautiful. I may be your dad, but I'm an AI as well."

"Then take over and shoot this aperture. I need coffee."

"Go ahead, will do. Just like we said."

Instead of moving immediately to the aft cabin and firing up the Javatron, I sit there for a minute, watching what Jake does to the controls and the friction index of the rig's rollers. It always amazes me that, as good a driver as I think I am (to hell with modesty), Jake always proves to be better. I always admire the subtle adjustments he makes to my settings, especially on a portal approach.

"Uh-*huh*," I say, nodding. He likes more friction on the rollers and a slightly slower approach speed. He also likes a really tight Z-pinch in the plasma confinement. He was never much of a mechanic (and who is when modern engines get more and more esoteric every month?) but he has a solid grasp of the ways gadgets work. And he was, at the risk of repeating myself, a mythic truck operator, as good as any human being can be without AI assistance. Skyway rigs were a little less sophisticated in his day. You still needed to be an excellent driver then. And some of that transferred over to his Entelechy Matrix, the "casting" that was made of his mind.

I get up and make my way to the spacious aft-cabin (Jake told me to get the extra-roomy cab—you could carry passengers back here) and I start to make coffee but my curiosity gets the better of me. Just what is he doing different? I don't get back in the driver's perch, electing to park my butt in one of the "hitchhiker" seats just aft of the driver. I watch the pretty lights dance on the dash, then flick a switch and get a personal display in front of my gaze. I eyeball the readings. Okay, so he feathered back on this, boosted this other, and completely maxed out this doohicky. Why?

But that's what separates good driving from mediocre. This, that, and the other, nudging here and there.

The rotating cylinders get taller and taller until the tops edge out of sight above the viewscreen. No aperture to see, 'cause they can't really be seen, and suddenly, silently, and with only a slight bump, we have leaped a hundred light years and are on the surface of another world. It is night, but we are still on the Interstellar Skyway.

We are now on an earthlike planet, I could tell more or less by instinct, but it is dark, so no scenery except the blurry, bleary stuff the screen showed by night vision. No fun, and you can't really make anything out.

If you've never been out to the Skyway, the road between the worlds, you still probably know something about it, earthbound as you are. No one knows who built it. Jake says he knows, because shortly before I was born, he traveled to the end of the road and found...

Well, he never told anyone what he found. Besides, it's a legend. I never believed it. That, Jake explains, is why he never tried telling anybody what he found. But the stories are many and speculation is rampant.

After half a minute, I get up to finish the kitchen chores, but I see something ahead and lurch forward to make a mad dash for the driver's seat.

"Jake, look out!"

The road seems to veer sharply right of a line of vegetation and into an improbable turn, one atypical for the starslab, which has turns you can take at Mach 1, if you are foolish enough.

But Jake doesn't fall for it. He continues straight and stays on the true road, not the one faked up to make us wreck. All the wreckers need is about forty meters of something black and wide—screencloth usually, showing just the roadway surface, or, if you want to go low-tech, tarp, boards, pigment, whatever, to lay down to make a decoy road, and brush and debris to cover up the real one. If a human is driving, he may not be quick enough on the instruments to detect the difference. It is a matter of seconds. Perceive the ruse, make a split-second decision.

We crash through the line of shrubbery.

"This is it," I say as clouds of brush and woodchips fly up from our rollers.

"This is it," Jake agrees.

The true road is clear ahead. I had to compliment whoever did this particular fake road thing. Right out of some ancient cartoons I used to watch as a kid. I would have fallen for it, driven right off the road into the darkness and probably into a chasm.

"Why did they put it so close to the arrival point?"

"Because truckers are too busy checking out local conditions. They aren't watching the roadbed. And they're at cautious speed. That way the rig doesn't end up in too many pieces, along with what it's hauling."

"Cautious or not, the wrecks kill a lot of drivers."

"Drivers don't have a chance. Kill 'em off first thing, if they survive."

"Nasty. They drag the cargo away, roll up the screencloth..."

"And Bob's yer uncle. No evidence of blockage for the Bugs to find."

"Police are never around when you need 'em."

"Who needs Roadbugs?" Jake says.

"Oh, I don't know," I reply. "Otherwise the Skyway'd be interrupted in a million places."

"Roadbugs are brutal. People would find a way to keep the road open, I've always maintained. Seek your own justice, son. Don't rely on alien machines to act as police."

"There goes that utopian tendency in you, Dad."

"I'm an idealist."

"And you think a philosophy major is useless."

"Shut up, go drink your coffee, and come back here and steer this rig."

The signs come up pretty quick and there are a lot of them, far off the roadway as signs have to be by Roadbug "law." They were big signs, easy to see.

NEW JAMAICA INN 50K

NEW JAMAICA INN 20K

DON'T PASS THE NEW JAMAICA INN 10K

STOP, RELAX, GAMBLE A LITTLE AT NEW JAMAICA INN

STOP, STAY OVER, GAMBOL AT NEW JAMAICA INN

And so forth, counting down the last ten kilometers with ever more clever puns, wordplay, and double entendre.

Finally, it heaves into view, out on a level heath about a kilometer away. Doesn't live up to its hype, but it is garish and glitzy and bright enough for a cross between a Christmas tree and a nuclear blast. We pull into the lot and park. The engine dies whining as it scrams itself.

"Hungry?" Jake asks.

I snort. "Nah." Peering out the viewport, I go on, "You know, I couldn't get a feel for the countryside."

"I could see fine. Reminds me a little of Cornwall."

"That on Earth?"

"Yup, west England, along the coast."

"You were there?"

"Hey, I was born on that planet, remember?"

I peer out into the foggy night. "Seashore around here? I'm starting to get a whiff of salt. You're letting some air in, I believe."

"You are right twice in a row," Jake says.

I believe Jake, but I do a quick atmosphere check anyway—just because it smells nice out there doesn't mean a thing—and check local weather. I dress for cold, wet conditions, because it looks rather dreary. It is raining, barometer is low. No major storm on scanners but there is a cloud ceiling herding misty, chilly moisture in from the sea.

Jake does a biological survey of the air. Some planets have nasty microorganisms that can take you down fast. You have to know what you are up against *vis á vis* the native flora and fauna.

In my duster, I trudge across the macadam. Three other rigs are parked, along with a couple of passenger buggies, some sleek and modern, a couple battered utility carriers looking like they'd done heavy agricultural work.

I stop, pivot, and look back at my rig. I always marvel at what a behemoth it is. The reason is that if you are going to haul cargo over light-years, you have to haul a lot of it to make any money. And the rig *must* have an apartment in it if you are to have any kind of normal existence, with the comforts of home. You are going to be on the road a lot.

I turn toward the casino again and get blinded. My goggles adjust, and I can see again. The place is a fleshpot painted with moving images of nude dancing girls, boys, in between, and neutral. I like baseline girls. Everyone looks human, though, at least. But you never know. Surries are so good these days... actually, I wouldn't care much...never mind.

It looked as though you could get almost anything here, legal, illegal, moral and immoral. Looks like an open town.

I go in.

It's a barn inside filled with sparkle, glitter, flashing lights, revolving wheels of fortune, animated holos, animated this, animated that. There is a *lot* of animation. And music.

And noise: gonging, bonging, clanging, doodling, whistling, *bing, bong, bing, bang*. Constantly. All casinos are alike, no matter what part of the galaxy you are in. And they haven't changed much over the centuries, from what I gather. These days they don't have real tables, wheels, boards, pits, and hard bouncing dice, but they do have VR for anything you want to play: faro, craps, baccarat, roulette, blackjack, slots—plus games I don't know and cannot make out.

Far over on the side sit serious card players, playing a game that takes real skill. They're using hard-copy, retro cards.

I go straight for the slots. No skill, all luck. I am not an experienced gambler. Not much of one at all. Despite my natural talent for psychokinesis and clairvoyance, of which I have none but would like to have both in a crap game, I lose a modest amount of colonial scrip. Funny money, anyway. Who cares.

I go to each area and do one game: craps, roulette, baccarat, faro, blackjack and something called Swenai. Insert question mark here; I can't describe it 'cause I don't understand it; can't even pronounce it. I lose about two thousand colonial in all.

Time for a drink, but I don't have to sidle up to the long, long bar. A striking female slinks up to me and asks if she can bring me a drink. I say sure. Surprise me with something local in a tall glass.

She returns with something exotic. It's mauve, but tastes fine, a bit like bourbon but probably faux. At any rate, it's alcoholic. I drink and look at her, for she's still standing there, smiling. At first I thought she was nude, but now I can see some cover, looking like tawny fur, sort of. It matches her café au lait skin, but maybe it's a cross between fur and cloth. It might be screencloth, and it seems you can see right through but you can't, not really.

"What are you hauling?" she asks. Her face is oval and high-born, but the voice comes from the homeless shanty towns.

"Never ask a starrigger that."

She shrugs. "I do all the time. Haven't I seen you before? You look familiar."

"My dad told me he met a woman on the road who said that to him. Claimed to know him, to have hung out with him. He never saw her before in his life."

"Who was she?"

"My mother."

"Isn't that funny. I feel as if I know you. Don't know why."

She and I settle into a booth in the bar.

"Tell me about it," I say.

Her grin widens. "About what?" Her knee has found its way over to nudge my thigh.

"What the deal is here. We nearly wrecked coming through the portal. Somebody tricked up the road, tried to fool us."

"Wreckers," she says, nodding. "They're on the starslab, not just on this world, for sure, here and there."

"Here, for sure."

"Somewhere back up the road, probably."

"Didn't see any structures, no farms, nothing."

"There are caves along the coast, that I know. Another drink?"

After draining the last of the cocktail, I hand the glass to her and say, "Sure. And can you get me into a good poker game?"

"Can do, starrigger."

"By the way, what's your name?"

"Selena."

I'm a fair poker player, as long as my opponents are lousy. The table is lousy that night, on that foggy, green seaside world. Comes morning, and I am almost ready to doze off with a full house in my hand, three fours and a pair of sevens. I have been losing all night, but now I am winning big. I slurp on my seventh drink. One more drink and I will own the planet.

"I call," the big hayseed across the table announces. I've taken his last colonial. He's all in. I am all in. Well, not exactly. The house has advanced me a hundred thousand. So I'm all in, and then some.

I coax the last sip out of my colorful libation, turquoise this time, put down the glass, flip over my cards. Pretty damn good hand. But it isn't enough.

A thin, nervous-looking geek I didn't even realize was sitting at the table says, "Straight flush, hearts, eight through queen."

Where had he come from? I look. Pretty damn good, too. Trouble is, I discarded the nine of hearts.

The dealer cackles. "Read them and weep, truckdriver."

I stare at the thin guy with the winning hand. I swear he was the waiter an hour or two before. I say so. Employees can game?

The dealer fixes me with a dark gimlet eye. He is the owner, judging by the way he has been ordering people around. Employees have been coming up to him all night, ostensibly about their duties, but doubtless also to give him cards or take them and pass them. These are very basic cardsharp tricks, and they aren't bad at it, because the drinks and the noise, the B-girls, and all the milling about conspire to dull my perceptions. I only strongly suspect they are flimflamming me. But a little fly buzzes in my ear, and I know the whole place is cheating.

"Are you *implying* something, *kamrada*?" He has a thick accent but his Intersystem is fluent.

"Yeah," I say, "I'm implying the shit out of it. Why don't we look at the security feed."

The dealer gets to his feet. "We are not going to show you any security feed. We'll put a lien on your rig, and we'll have the constable prevent your leaving this planet. Not until you pay."

"I got my own security feed."

He shakes his head dismissively. "A nanodrone? We have scans for nanos. Don't bluff us. You are not very good at it."

I tilt my chin up. "See that tiny botfly buzzing around? There. No, *there*. See? You're not scanning that. Otherwise you would have swatted it with your micro, the big mosquito moth or whatever."

He looks up. He doesn't see; then the fly buzzes by his ear. "*Merte!*" He looks at me. "Very slick, *kamrada*."

"Damn right. Isn't that right, Jake?" I call into the air.

"*Help meee, help meeeeeee!*" Jake says in the tiniest voice imaginable, zipping around.

Nobody gets the joke. Jake is always making arcane references to things that no one understands. I know this is a joke reference, but I myself don't get it. My dad is a weirdo, what can I say? Sometimes I am embarrassed.

"So," I go on, "do we want to watch the recording on the screens? We'll cut into the WorldsCup finals and figure out how you've been cheating. I wonder what the constable will say to that."

The dealer smiles thinly. "Very well played, *kamrada*. You came prepared. Very well played. By the way..." He settles back in his chair. "What is your cargo?"

"Security equipment."

The dealer's smile broadens.

I feel a female hand at the back of my neck.

"C'mon, starrigger, let's get you fixed up with some food and a room for the night," Selena says.

I manage to get up, and I feel tension in the entire room. I get a flash fantasy that I am in a play and I have been the only actor in the troupe that did *not* know he was in a play. Figure that out. It is a strange feeling. Everybody is looking at me as if I missed a cue. They are waiting for my next line.

I can barely speak at all.

The buffet is crap. The sneeze screens have been well sneezed upon, and some of the food looks as if it was paying monthly rent. A few items are being crawled on by things that might be insects—or miniature seafood. Here a cloud of fruity-looking flies, there an in-flight pantry moth.

But everything isn't inedible. I load up on mash potatoes, gravy, and meatloaf. Then dutifully heap on some lima beans. It actually does not smell bad. I can't, however, eat the stuff. It won't go down.

I leave most of what I chose on the table and Selena and I take a lift to the third floor. The room is the bare minimum. It is clean, that I grant, or looks it. It is an emperor-size rack, though, and looks inviting as hell.

I collapse on it, roll a bit on its fake-furry bedspread, and zone out for a minute, I think...and get jolted awake by something. Probably one of those pre-sleep electric shocks that rock you when you're dozing off. I raise my head and scan the room. My clothes are on the floor. Huh?

But then I realize someone is in the rack with me. I roll a bit and look over my shoulder.

"What are you doing here?"

"I'm on a break. Thought I'd spend it with you."

"Look, Sebrina..."

She pouts. "Selena."

"Sorry. Selena, I am about to—"

"They really screwed you," she says. "They'll end up confiscating your rig if you can't pay. Also, there's debtor's prison on this planet. Did you know that?"

"I did not know that. Do you have any clothes on?"

She edges closer. "No. Why?"

"Never mind. What's your role in all this?"

"All what?"

"Whatever kind of operation you people have going on this dirtball."

"It's a big planet, with a lot of completely unexplored continents. Lots of room for development."

"What's a sea-view lot go for here?"

"I don't know. I'm not in the real estate business."

"What business are you in?"

"I'm a customer service representative. This is a casino and that's all, as far as I know. I don't know anything—"

"No?"

"No."

"You're a CSR. Is bed service part of your duties?"

"Only if I want to. Mr. Alvarez lets us—"

"He's the boss?"

"Yeah. Do you know him?"

"I've heard of him," I tell her. "He's a union official, or was. The union is TATOO, T-A-T-O-O."

"Isn't 'tattoo' spelled with three T's?"

"TATOO is not a word, it's an acronym."

"What's it stand for?"

"Transystem Association of Transport Owner-Operators."

"So Mr. Alvarez is a bad guy?"

"Yes," I tell her. "TATOO is a corrupt organization. Always has been."

"I don't know why there's any need for drivers at all," she says. "No offense."

"You are a rotten diplomat. No offense. The history of automated vehicles is..."

My information dump is interrupted by a huge yawn. I have trouble getting my mouth closed again.

"Crap."

She giggles. "The history of automated vehicles is crap?"

"Sleepy. Well, there were laws, you know. Accidents, protests, drivers out of work, so they passed laws to protect... you know, drivers."

"This was out here on the starslab?"

"Nah, this goes back a ways. Drivers were going to lose their jobs, see. Y'ever study any history?"

She comes closer. I feel her breasts against me, the insistent, hard nipples.

"What was in those drinks?" I ask.

"Nothing. Just a lot of alcohol."

The door flies open and in come the crew. Plus the constable, if his khakis and campaign hat are any indication. Local gendarme, not colonial. With them is a tall, gaunt cutthroat with a low forehead and high indignation on his face. I mean, this guy had no acting talent at all.

"That's my sister, you creep, and she's underage!"

I look at Selena. She is on the lee side of twenty, for sure. Twenty-five, maybe. Fifteen, no. I lie back and laugh.

"It's not funny, son," the pinch-faced constable tells me. "You're under arrest for statutory rape. We'll have to impound your vehicle for evidence. What are you carrying in that thing? The other players say you admitted to hauling contraband security gear. That true?"

I sit up. "You guys are something. Any trucker comes through here, if you don't wreck him, you bleed 'em with dishonest gaming. All that VR stuff is totally bogus. You haven't generated a truly random number here in eons. If all that fails, you try an old-fashioned crooked poker game. But this..." I shake my head, doing the *more in sorrow than in anger* bit. "This is real desperation. The *badger game!*" I guffaw, trailing off into a few giggles. "The badger game? Do you know how far that one goes back? Ever read the Bible? Pathetic."

The constable draws himself up. "You're going to have plenty of time to read the Good Book, boy. If you manage to make it to penitentiary. Around here, people don't tolerate sex offenders. I don't have the staff to protect—"

In walks Alvarez with two men bearing rail rifles, pointing them straight at me.

"Enough," the boss of the wreckers orders.

The constable begins, "Could we—?"

Alvarez waves him off. "He's not buying any of it. The parking lot is cleared out. Let's just treat this as a wreck and proceed from there. Okay, startrucker, on your feet."

"Yeah, boss." I get up.

I'm naked. I didn't bargain on that.

"Let's have that key. We're going to persuade your AI to open that trailer and let us have a look. I have the feeling there is something very valuable in there."

I nodded. "You're right." I stoop to pick up my trousers. I try to look defeated as I hand over Jake's key.

Alvarez looks it over, then flips the thing at me. "Get your rig spook on the line."

I catch the key and put it to my lips. "Jake?" I say.

"Tell it to unlock that trailer," Alvarez demands. "Override any anti-theft."

"Jake, open up the trailer."

"Sorry, Sammy, but I can't do that," Jake says in a banal voice that sounds familiar. I'm guessing it is another of Dad's old movie references.

Alvarez says, "Okay, let's go out to the parking lot and blow the rear doors off that wagon. Yeah, you can put those pressure trousers on. Nobody here wants to look at you."

"I'm kind of liking it," Selena informs the crew.

She gets a laugh or two.

It's not a bright morning but the blue-giant sun is burning off the fog.

"Too bad we have to lose the rig," Alvarez is saying. "I do hope you aren't emotionally attached to your spook."

"Okay, okay," I say, raising my hands. "I give up. Don't mess with my spook."

"What are you hauling?"

"High-functioning mecs, fully mobile android security units."

"Security units?"

"Right, battle-worthy, swat-rated security mecs. Worth over ten million gold certificates."

"The jackpot," Alvarez drools.

I talk into the key. "Jake, emergency code alpha, gamma, Tango, Fox, question mark, seven, zero, ampersand, aleph-null, googleplex."

"You said the secret word," Jake says.

Everyone in the wrecking crew has clotted at the back of the trailer. The trailer doors fold open.

"Hey—" is all that Alvarez manages to get out before the first mec leaps out and flattens him with a red metal fist. The rest of them explode from the trailer, fresh from their individual shipping sarcophagi, and begin to knock the crew about.

They're fully humanoid mecs, wiry, dangerous-looking metal men with huge hands and prehensile feet. They are humanoid in shape, except for their auxiliary appendages, and look like just what you'd expect an android mec to look like: invincible; and they act accordingly. They are for all intents and purposes impervious to small arms and light artillery. I would not want to tangle with one, let alone twelve of these nightmares. They come in an assortment of designer colors with complementary trim. They will guard your home or camp, protect against intruders, set up a defensive perimeter, or act as your bodyguard in an unruly crowd. Or casino. You must have a hard-to-get license to own and operate them, but hey...

There is some resistance. Rail rifles crack, finding targets, but security armor is hard to penetrate. One mec collars two shooters, hands over the guns to another, who busts them up. Two other crewmen have got their weapons out but have been set upon almost immediately. They wrestle futilely with the mecs, neither getting off a shot.

The remnants of the wrecking crew run scared into the blue light of the new day. The mecs chase them down. I enter the cab, get my ultraviolet suit on, and step out again. By the time I do, the wrecking crew is rounded up and have been stuffed into the trailer, there to cower before the mecs—who aren't programmed for cruelty beyond binding and minding a prisoner.

Alvarez has come to.

"Who the hell *are* you?" he wants to know, looking at me with one glazed eye.

"Sammy McGraw, president of the Starrigger's Guild."

Alvarez is shocked. "The Guild? Are you people still around?"

"Yes. And we don't like to lose drivers to wreckers."

"Are you really Jake McGraw's son?"

"I am proud to say, yes."

"You mean he's not just a legend? I don't believe it."

"This rig is possessed by Jake's spirit."

Alvarez sneered. "That smells kind of fishy."

"I stink, therefore I am," Jake says through his key.

I tell Alvarez, "*You*, get in the trailer, and we'll give you all a lift to the nearest Skyway Patrol base. And by the way..."

"Yeah?"

"Don't ever ask a starrigger what he's hauling. You might not want to find out."

I tell Jake to fire up the plasma so we can start slamming deuterium, tritium, and lithium together. The engine whines to life and begins to throb nicely. I check the instruments and screens. The ready light comes on, and I grab the traction levers.

But someone or something is banging against the side of the cab. I get a view on the surveillance screen.

It is Selena, backpacked and bundled up for traveling, it seems. She's looking up eagerly at me, waving. She's beaming a big smile, but there is a plea behind it, along with a hope.

I hit the control for the side port and stick my head out. "Yo, Selena."

"Going my way?" She hooks a thumb at the endless road.

"Did you really think I'd give you a ride?"

"Yes." She believes it, all right.

"You know me so well."

I open the aft access hatch for her and she nimbly climbs the ladder and gets in.

While she's doing it Jake says, "Son, a *femme fatale* is one thing. But *this* one?"

"Promise you're not going to embarrass me, Dad."

She gets in and I seal the hatch. The engine roars, the rollers grab pavement. I wheel the rig around the lot and head out.

Within twenty minutes, we are rolling toward a portal on the road between the worlds.

Jeff Seeman is the author of two novels, Political Science *and* Guns and Butter. *He was a contributor to the short story anthologies* 18 Wheels of Horror *and* Hell Comes to Hollywood. *His short fiction has also appeared in a variety of literary magazines. He has written several feature-length screenplays, one of which was loosely adapted into the film* American Virgin, *directed by Clare Kilner. A former editor of the* Cornell Lunatic *(Cornell University's answer to the* Harvard Lampoon*), he has performed stand-up comedy in Los Angeles, Boston, and San Francisco. His recently published tribute to Edgar Allan Poe,* The Scythe of Time: An Essay and Homage, *is currently available on Amazon.*

SPEED TRAP

Jeff Seeman

THE TRUTH IS I REALLY DO like the kid. He doesn't have a mean bone in his body. But he doesn't have a brain in his head, either. Donnie is my wife's kid brother, and Claire says he's always been a screw-up. Claire says when he was in fifth grade, someone dared him to drink an entire blender full of pickles, strawberry ice cream, Tabasco sauce, chocolate sauce, and Spam. He ended up in the emergency room getting his stomach pumped. But that's enough to teach him a lesson, wouldn't you think? Because he'd never do anything like that again, right? Wrong. Two months later he's back in the ER. Tried to swallow a whole bag of marbles. And that one wasn't even a dare. He'd thought that one up on his own. So I guess he should at least get points for showing initiative.

When Donnie was in high school, he used to tinker with this beat-up old Dodge Charger. He'd rigged it to run with a fast idle to prevent stalling. He'd also lost the ignition key, so he'd gotten in the habit of starting the car by hot-wiring it. One day he has the car in gear, starts messing around under the hood, decides to fire her up, and touches black wire to red wire. Oh, did I mention he hadn't set the handbrake? That's right, Donnie literally ran himself over. Spent the summer in a neck brace.

Surprisingly, Donnie's never landed in jail. Not surprisingly, he's also never landed a steady job. So one night Claire asks me if I can pull some strings, maybe get him a job at the trucking company. My long-time co-driver's retiring and they hadn't assigned his replacement yet. Claire says I can keep an eye on Donnie, keep him out of trouble, maybe teach him some responsibility. Twelve hours later, after the longest, most tear-filled argument of our marriage, I finally give in.

"Bro, that's awesome!" says Donnie. "This is gonna be fuuuu-uuuun!"

It is not going to be fun.

I drive a chicken hauler, one of those big rigs with lots of chrome and extra lights. Got chrome roosters on my mud flaps. Other drivers greet me with "cluck cluck cluck." And yeah, I actually do haul live chickens. Usually pick up a load of broiler chickens at a poultry farm near Savannah, Georgia. Load the trailer with chicken coops—birds cackling, feathers flying, everything smells like chicken shit. Load-out early morning, then haul ass and chicken all the way to a processing plant outside El Paso. Not the worst gig in the world, aside from never being able to get the smell out of my nose. Claire once asked me how I liked her new perfume and I told her all I could smell was chicken shit. Thank God that lady's got a sense of humor.

Making time's important on a chicken run because the law says you can only transport live broilers so many hours before getting slapped with a big ass fine. And sometimes the processing plant's a long haul from the farm. But the law also says I'm not supposed to be behind the wheel more than eleven hours a day. The answer? A second driver. And it's this unfortunate combination of facts that ultimately lands Donnie's sorry ass in my shotgun seat.

It's only then I find out the real problem. Turns out Donnie can't say no to anything—beer, weed, booze, speed, whatever. If Donnie thinks he can get messed up by drinking it, smoking it, snorting it, or shoving it up his ass, he'll do it. Not exaggerating about that last one either. Donnie once paid a hundred bucks to a guy in a rest stop men's room for what the guy told him was a cannabis suppository. Needless to say, it wasn't. I don't even want to talk about how that turned out.

Even worse is when he's tripping. Donnie once insisted I needed to swerve to avoid hitting a Bengal tiger that he claimed was in the middle of the road. It took me twenty minutes to convince him it was pretty unlikely there was an invisible Bengal tiger wandering down I-20 in Mississippi that only Donnie could see.

"But you don't know that for sure, Bro," he kept saying. "Anything can happen."

A typical conversation between us went like this:

"Hey, take a break, Bro. I'll drive."

"You're not driving, Donnie. You're wasted."

"Am not."

"How many lanes on this highway?"

"What highway?"

"This highway. The one we're driving on."

Squints through windshield. "Four?"

We're on a two-lane highway.

"You're not driving, Donnie."

"Aww, Bro..."

God only knows how he passed the drug test to get the gig in the first place. Must have been during one of his sober periods. Yeah, there are weeks when Donnie's totally sober. And when he is, he's agreeable, friendly, easy-going—the perfect co-driver. But then he'll sneak off to score and he'll be useless for days afterward. It goes on like this for months. So I'm lecturing him, trying to get him to straighten up and fly right. I'm covering for him with the company and trying to keep him away from the wheel as much as I can. And whenever I bring it up to Claire, she turns on the waterworks and gives me a speech that always begins with "He's my only brother" and ends with "If you really loved me..."

All of which brings us to that day at the truck stop off I-20 near the Louisiana-Texas border.

So we're riding with a full load of broilers. Donnie's been clean since load-out, so I'm letting him drive. We stop to grab some chow and I leave Donnie alone for a minute so I can hit the can. Just a minute I leave him alone. Two minutes, tops. When I get back to the picnic table where we'd been eating, he's gone. No Donnie. Even left a half-eaten basket of fries. First time I'd ever known him to walk away from food for anything.

I wander around the convenience store. No Donnie. Walk back to the rig. No Donnie. I walk all over the damn parking lot, calling his name. No Donnie.

Finally, after I've walked the whole perimeter and doubled back to the truck, there he is. Just standing there, innocent as can be.

"Donnie, where were you?"

"Right here."

"No you weren't. I was here fifteen minutes ago. I've been looking all over for you."

He flashes me his goofiest stoner smile. "You found me, Bro!"

I can smell the weed from six feet away. I sigh. Something I find myself doing a lot around Donnie. "Just get in the cab, Donnie."

I haul my ass up into the driver's seat and slam the door. Donnie plops down in the passenger seat beside me.

"How far to El Paso?" he asks with what sounds to me like a sort of forced innocence.

"Fourteen hours." I strap on my seat belt.

He gives me this mysterious look. "What if we could make it in fourteen *minutes*?"

"That would be great, Donnie. But it's going to be about fourteen hours." I start the engine.

"But Bro...what if we *could* make it in fourteen minutes?" And he starts giggling like an idiot.

I look at him. "Okay. What?"

"You're not going to believe what I'm about to tell you."

"I'm pretty sure that's true. What is it?"

"There's this super advanced fuel additive. Chick at the rest stop told me about it. It's this little pill. You add it to your fuel tank and it, like, turns the diesel into rocket fuel or something. It can blast your rig from New York to L.A. in, like, three hours."

I shake my head. "Donnie, there's no such thing."

"This chick said so."

"Oh, Donnie, Donnie...how much did you give her?"

"Two hundred."

"For God's sake, Donnie. How gullible are you?"

"But what if it works, Bro? Wouldn't that be awesome? We should at least try it."

"No, we're not going to try it. I don't know what the hell this woman sold you, but I don't want it anywhere near the fuel tank."

"Oh." He looks at me sheepishly.

"Donnie, what did you do?"

"I sort of already..."

"Oh, Donnie. Of all the stupid, irresponsible—" I slump back in the driver's seat and just sit there shaking my head.

Now here's what I *should* have done. I should have turned off the engine immediately. And then I should have had the fuel tank drained. That's what I *should* have done. Except I had a full load of live broilers and only fourteen hours to get to El Paso. And the pill the woman had sold Donnie had probably been an aspirin or something. If there even was a pill. Or a woman. For all I know, Donnie was just tripping and he imagined the whole thing.

So instead, here's what I do. I sit up, put the truck in gear, and very lightly—and I can't stress this enough—*very lightly* tap the pedal.

BANG.

The g-force slams us back in our seats as the truck shoots out of the parking lot like a rocket sled on rails. Tires squealing. Sparks flying out from under the hood. Burning rubber in the air. We blast down I-20 at 90 miles an hour. 100. 110. Other drivers blaring their horns. Slamming on screeching brakes. Police sirens Dopplering behind us. Donnie whooping and hollering like a drunken lunatic on a mechanical bull. Me gripping the steering wheel with white knuckles and raw terror.

"Oh shit oh shit oh shit oh shit oh shit."

120. 130. 140. I don't know how fast we're going now—the speedometer's run out of numbers. I'm pumping the brake but it ain't doing shit. Fighting with the wheel just to keep us on the road. Like trying to steer while strapped to the front bumper of a rollercoaster.

Going even faster now. Faster. Faster. We're barreling past cities and towns that shoot by in a blur. I'm struggling like hell to control the wheel, but my reflexes—*any human's* reflexes—aren't that fast. Crashing through guard rails, toll booths, billboards. Objects smash off our bumper and windshield—traffic signs, mailboxes, God knows what else. I feel like a human pinball in an arcade machine gone berserk.

After what feels like forever, we start to slow. By this point I've given up the illusion that I'm actually steering the rig. The best I can manage is to grit my teeth and hang on tight. We fly down an exit ramp, heading straight for a roadside bar. I swing the wheel to the right as hard as I can. I clearly hear someone's voice, screaming at the top of his lungs like a goddamn maniac.

Turns out it's me.

And then, with a deafening squeal of tires, the truck skids around 360 degrees and comes to rest in the parking lot. The engine, tires—the whole rig is smoking. From the cargo trailer,

I can faintly hear the hysterical cackling of a truckload full of frantic chickens.

"Bro, that was awesome! That was the coolest thing ever! Awwwwe-some!"

I open the door, tumble out of the cab, and immediately puke on my shoes.

Donnie gets out of the cab. "This El Paso?"

"No," I say. Breathless, still doubled over. "I think we're somewhere in Arizona."

"Arizona? What happened to New Mexico?"

"That blur that flew by? New Mexico."

"But why did you drive to Arizona?"

"Why did I drive to Arizona? *Why* did I drive to *Arizona*?! Damn it, I was just trying to keep us on the road! It's a miracle we're not both in pieces right now! And God only knows what kind of damage we caused back there!"

I take a deep breath and look up at the bar. It's a typical roadside dive called The Pit Stop, and it's calling my name. I know having a drink is the last thing I should do. But my heart's pounding and my nerves are shot, and I need to collect my thoughts. And right about now I'm thinking I could really use a session with my shrink, Dr. Jack Daniels. So we wander in and sit at the bar. That bartender tells me that we are, in fact, just outside of Tucson. I order a double Jack for me and a club soda for Donnie.

With the first sip, I can already feel the good doctor starting to work his therapeutic magic. "Okay," I say, as calmly as I can, "now tell me about the woman who sold you the stuff."

"I don't know," shrugs Donnie. "Some lot lizard. Said she was stranded. Trying to make enough money to get home."

"A lot lizard. What did she look like?"

"You know, a lot lizard. Green, scaly..."

I look at him. His pupils are dilated to the size of small planets. Each one could have its own solar system.

"You're saying she was an actual lizard. You bought the stuff off a talking lizard."

"Maybe. I don't know. I guess."

"And that didn't seem weird to you? Maybe something you'd want to tell me about?"

"Well you never believe me anyway! I told you about the tiger."

"Donnie, there was no tiger!"

"See?!"

He sips his club soda and sulks. "I finally got to contribute something, Bro. Finally got to bring something to our partnership. 'Cuz everybody's always 'Donnie's such a screw-up' and 'Donnie's so stupid' and 'Donnie'll never amount to anything.' And I finally showed them. I showed *you*. I was right, admit it. That stuff *does* work. And we got it because of *me*. I took initiative. I *did* something, Bro. I brought something to the table. Something important. *I* did something *important*. And you don't even appreciate it!"

"Donnie, we could have been killed! We could have killed someone else! Hell, maybe we *did*! You ever think of that? I don't know how much damage we caused!"

"Well that's not *my* fault! *You're* the one who put the pedal down!"

"I did *not* put the pedal down. I barely tapped—" I regret the words before they're even out of my mouth. I wouldn't have thought Donnie's eyes could get any wider. They do.

"You barely tapped it? Is that what you're saying? You barely *tapped* it? Then we don't even know how fast—"

"Donnie, no."

"We don't even know what it's capable—"

"Donnie, don't go there. We are *not* going there."

"But we have to find out—"

"No, we don't! We don't have to find out anything!" I take another sip of Jack. "Look, this is what we're going to do. I'm going to call the company and tell them we had a breakdown.

And then we're going to drain the fuel tank and flush the line. I don't know how the hell I'm going to explain why we're in Tucson. But I'll think of something."

Donnie's silent for a few minutes, just staring down at his glass. Finally he says, "You mad at me?"

I take a deep breath and silently thank myself for having had the good sense to order a double. "No, Donnie, I'm not mad at you. But sometimes you're just so damn irresponsible that I—"

"I know. I know I did something wrong. It was...what you said. Irresponsible. Right?"

"Yes, Donnie."

"But you forgive me, don't you?"

"Yes, I forgive you."

"We still partners?"

"Yes, Donnie, we're still partners."

He gives me a sad, embarrassed half-smile. "Thanks. I'll do better. I really will. I promise."

"Okay, Donnie."

"Come on, Bro." He spreads his arms wide. "Hug it out."

He leans over and we hug awkwardly, slapping each other's backs. Then he steps back and I almost think I see him wiping away a tear.

"Gotta hit the can," he says quietly. And he heads off towards the men's room.

I sit there sipping my Jack, looking at the Bud Light sign over the bar and listening to the honky-tonk music on the jukebox. Tucson. How the hell do I explain Tucson? Even if there were some way to cover up everything else, there's no denying the physical fact that the rig is now sitting in Tucson. And I don't have a clue how to explain that.

And then I hear the roar of a diesel engine starting in the parking lot. I look around. Where's Donnie? I thrust my hand into my jacket pocket. No ignition key. God damn it. Donnie must have palmed it. *Son of a bitch.*

I burst out of the bar and race towards the truck. Haul myself up and swing open the passenger door. There's Donnie sitting in the driver's seat. He flashes me a big, shit-eating grin.

"Come on, Bro!"

"Donnie, get out of the truck!"

"No way! We gotta see this thing through!"

"Donnie!"

"I don't want to go without you, Bro! But I will if I have to! Get in!"

"God damn it!"

Donnie puts the truck in gear. I slam the door shut.

"Hang on tight!" he yells. "This is gonna be one hell of a ride!"

"Donnie, don't!"

He puts the hammer down. All the way.

And...nothing.

The engine dies. Silence. Donnie and I look at each other for a few long moments.

"Disappointing," he says quietly. He looks mournfully at the dashboard.

"Yeah. That last trip must have wrecked the engine." I let out a huge sigh of relief. And we both just sit there in silence.

And that's when I notice it. The coffee cup in the cup holder. It's rising slowly into the air. It's floating. And the coffee inside is slowly floating out the top, spilling out of the cup but upwards, against gravity, in slow motion. Splashing up, up against the roof of the cab.

"Whoa," says Donnie.

The cab starts vibrating. Suddenly I have an intense sensation of falling, like we're dropping down an elevator shaft, faster and faster. But there's just the physical sensation—visually everything's the same. Through the windshield, The Pit Stop's just sitting there, motionless, looking exactly the same as when we got in the cab moments ago. But now I notice the image through the windshield is starting to blur from the edges inward. You know how when you look at something out of the corner of your eye and it's blurred? Because when you see something with your peripheral vision, it's not as sharp as when you look at it direct? It's sort of like that, like the view through the windshield is smeared around the edges. But very slowly the smear spreads inward, moving closer and closer to the center of my field of vision, taking over the whole picture. Until finally the whole world around us is a blur. Like when you're driving through a car wash and all you can see through your windshield is a wall of water.

The cab starts shaking more violently now, throttling us back and forth. I have the sense that the walls of the cab are closing in on us, but there's no visual evidence of that either. Now streaks of color are streaming past the windshield, orange and blue and purple, like wisps of clouds.

And then all at once, we're plunged into darkness. We're hurdling down a shaft of stars, a funnel of light that stretches to infinity. Millions of points of white light shoot by in the dark, faster and faster and faster. And as the velocity increases the points of light multiply, getting closer and closer to each other, denser and denser against the background of darkness. This goes on forever until finally the points of light coalesce and overwhelm the darkness. And all we can see through the windows of the cab, all we can see all around us, is pure white light.

"Bro! I think we're approaching the speed of light!" Donnie shouts. "Turn on the headlights!"

"What? Why? What happens if we turn on the headlights?"

"No one knows! That's the point!"

But I can't turn on the headlights because as I reach out I realize that my hand is dissolving. My hand, my arm, my torso. And everything else in the cab—the dashboard, the seats, the doors—everything's dissolving. Even Donnie is dissolving. Dissolving into particles and molecules and atoms and protons and neutrons and electrons and neutrinos and God knows what the hell else I can barely remember from my high school science class.

And the last sound I hear is Donnie, who lets loose with the loudest, most triumphant whoop since Slim Pickens saddled up an H-bomb and rode it straight to hell.

And then...darkness.

I blink myself awake.

We're here. The loading dock at the processing plant outside El Paso. Looks to be mid-morning. Sunny, clear blue sky. I glance over at Donnie. He looks as confused as I am.

The fuel gauge reads E. I climb out of the cab and check under the hood. The engine's twisted into what looks like some modern abstract sculpture, all the parts warped together like somebody took a blowtorch to Silly Putty. Donnie and I look at each other. Without a word, we both know there'll be no more "special" trips.

Ray, the foreman, comes running out, red-faced and huffing and puffing. "What the hell you guys doin' here?"

"What do you mean?" I ask. "Are we...uh, early?"

"Early? You're supposed to be loadin' up in Georgia this morning! They been callin' for hours, tryin' to find out where the hell you're at!"

"We have the load," I say. "We're here."

"Well I can goddamn see that," says Ray. "Give." He holds out his hand and I turn over the clipboard with the bill of lading. Ray studies it a few seconds and scowls.

"What is this shit?" he asks.

"What?"

"You got next month's date all over your paperwork."

"Next month?" I take back the clipboard and look at it. *April 29th. The day we left.* "No, that's right. It's—"

Suddenly a queasy feeling comes over me. "Holy shit. Ray, what's today's date?"

He glares at me like I'm the biggest moron in the world. "It's the 23rd, genius."

"The 23rd of...what?"

"You on drugs? March 23rd!"

Donnie and I stare at each other.

"Bro, we left in April," says Donnie. "We got here a month before we left!"

Ray shakes his head. "You both trippin'? *Him* I might've expected this from," he says to me, gesturing towards Donnie, "but *you*?"

"We're not tripping," I assure him. "No one's tripping. Donnie's just a little confused on the dates. Isn't that right, Donnie?"

"Yeah," says Donnie. "I'm just confused. I get confused sometimes."

"Confused," Ray mutters. "Confused. Son of a bitch."

He storms around to the back of the trailer and we hear him open the trailer doors. And then he lets loose with a string of curses.

"Stupid goddamn good-for-nothin' sumbitch bastard dumb asses!"

We rush around to the back of the trailer. Ray's so mad there's practically steam rising off him.

"You idiots hooked up the wrong trailer!" he fumes. He gestures angrily at our load. "What in hell's name am I gonna do with a goddamn truckload full of eggs?!"

After a brief stint as a public-health investigator in New York City, Bond Elam found his true calling in the trucking business, working in sales and operations for a tank line hauling hazardous commodities throughout Colorado and Wyoming— where, incidentally, he also learned more about snow and ice than he cares to remember. Ironically, the increased use of automation in the trucking industry led to his second career in software development—which, along with all that snow and ice, figures prominently in the story that follows. Bond has published a number of stories in Analog Science Fiction and Fact *magazine. He currently lives and writes in southwest Ohio, where he can still hear echoes of the wind off the high plains.*

THIN ICE

Bond Elam

RACHAEL LOVED THE OPEN ICE at night. When the wind died and her convoy of self-driving trucks rolled easily in her wake, she liked to imagine her daughter sitting there in the cab beside her. Two-year-old Hanna would marvel at the aurora—at the way it opened like a shimmering green curtain on a sky so deep and dark you could almost reach out and touch the stars. Which was exactly what she would try to do. Back on Earth, Hannah had no stars, no sky, no night. There was only the city, constantly alit with its towering buildings and throbbing masses of humanity. Look out the window of their small apartment and all you saw were other buildings, other windows, other faces peering back at you—faces indistinguishable from your own.

To escape the mind-numbing sameness, Rachael and Hannah had played the mirror game. "Who's that?" Rachael would ask, pointing at their reflections in their small free-standing mirror—the only possession Rachael's mother had brought when she came to help care for Hannah. "Is that Rachael's little Hannah?"

Hannah would giggle and point a pudgy finger. "That's little Hannah," she would say. Then she would look up at Rachael, her eyes so blue and bright, her tiny fists bouncing with such glee, that Rachael felt like her heart would burst. "That's me. I'm Rachael's little Hannah."

"But what's Hannah doing in the mirror?" Rachael would ask, pursing her lips in a perplexed frown. "How did little Hannah get inside the mirror?" And Hannah would peer around the frame, not quite sure there wasn't another copy of herself back there hiding behind the glass, looking out at her.

Even now, eighteen months since Rachael had come through the wormhole to find work on this alien world, the memories were so vivid, so alive, that she almost missed the raiders' ship when it burst from the same dark rift in the sky above her. There was, however, no missing the purple shadows that flitted across the ice when the orbiting Gate Keeper fired its first volley of missiles. Tightening her grip on the wheel, Rachael leaned forward, peering up through her tractor's windscreen just in time to see the incoming ship launch its own missiles. The merging exhaust plumes danced and swerved like invisible hands threading loops through the fabric of the night. Then the raider's ship exploded in a fountain of glowing debris that rained down through the darkness, turning night into day.

Rachael's first thought was that the falling debris could crack the ice, could send her and her automated convoy into the depths. She would never see Hannah again. Even worse, there would be no one to send back the wages that supported Hannah and Rachael's mother. They would lose their apartment. Hannah would sink into the morass of humanity—as lost and alone as Rachael sinking into the black depths of the sea.

Forcing herself to focus, she tapped instructions into the console mounted on the tractor's dashboard. She needed to spread out the convoy of trucks behind her, minimize the concentration of weight. Here on the ice road from the mine to Midway Ridge, the water was more than half a mile deep. Normally, the ridge was the most treacherous part of her run, its steep switchbacks perilous even in the best of weather conditions. Now, however, it was an island of safety, a mid-ocean ridge bisecting the artic archipelago with its mines and the rail gun, where the containerized ore was fired back through the wormhole. Reach it, and she would be safe. Fail to reach it before the ice cracked, and she could be lost forever.

"Just stay focused," she whispered, again imagining Hanna there beside her. "Just keep your eyes on the road, and we'll get there just fine."

Leaning back, she allowed her grip on the wheel to relax. Then she tapped in instructions to increase the convoy's speed. Not too much, not enough to send one of the self-driving tractors skidding off across the ice, but enough that she could hear the quickening crunch of her tires on the road beneath her.

"See, you just have to focus," she told her daughter. "Just stay focused and everything will all work out."

And so it did. By the time Midway Ridge came into view, the last of the falling debris had burned up in the atmosphere, and the danger had passed. Grimacing up into the darkness, Rachael wondered if any of the ship's escape capsules had made it to the surface. There would be no one to rescue the crew, of course. But that was the price mercenaries paid when they hired out to the corporations contending for resources on the alien worlds. There was no longer any need for human soldiers back on Earth, just as there was no need for human truck drivers or factory workers. Robots could be taught to do anything. It was only out here, out where you couldn't predict what might happen, that the breadth of human experience had value.

Rachael had been one of the last drivers back on Earth—back before she was almost killed by the self-driving tractor that had pinned her between the loading dock and the back of its trailer.

The problem wasn't simply that she was in the AI's blind spot. It was that the AI didn't realize it had a blind spot. That was the problem with artificial intelligence. Automated trucks could learn from their experience. They could constantly update the matrices of data that directed their activities. But they weren't truly conscious. They didn't have all the other experiences that shaped human judgment. They couldn't actually think.

There were rumors of conscious bots, of course—bots as intelligent and aware as human beings. But they had minds of their own, or so it was said. They couldn't be counted on to carry out their orders—not like her and Jennings, she thought as she watched the lights of Jennings' convoy working its way down the switchbacks toward her. Human drivers did what they were told. At least they did what they were told if they wanted to get paid.

Moving her convoy to the side of the road, she waited for Jennings to pass. For her, going up the steep grade required close attention to the automated trucks trailing behind her, especially when the wind could blow a trailer off the road. For Jennings coming down, the risks were even greater. If a truck in his convoy lost its brakes, it could take all the rigs in front of it over the precipice, including Jennings' own. It had happened more than once before they started using human drivers. Entire convoys had plunged over the side to crash through the sea ice at the base of the ridge—a financial loss for the corporation running the mines, but an opportunity for drivers like Rachael. A chance to save her daughter from the indifference of a world that no longer needed them.

Forcing her attention back to the present, she watched Jennings approach. The only other human driver on the planet, he grinned at her from behind his windscreen. Returning her thumbs-up, he glanced meaningfully up at the open sky. Then he was past, followed by his own convoy of tractors and dump trailers heading back to the mine for their next load.

"And that's that," Rachael whispered to Hannah as she put her tractor back in gear.

And so she believed—until three days later, deadheading back to the mine, Jennings and his convoy were attacked.

"They came across the ice on power sleds," Jennings said. He squinted out at Rachael from the monitor of the rail gun's communications console, his normally carefree features furrowed with worry. "There were two of them, pulling skids with a dozen military-grade spider bots. They swarmed the last tractor in my convoy before I realized what was happening. The next thing I knew, they'd overridden my remotes and driven off across the ice. There was nothing I could do to stop them."

"But you're okay, right?" Rachael said. Two hundred miles away at the rail gun's operations center, she'd been worried when he failed to reach the mine on schedule. "You didn't call in."

"They jammed my communications." He grimaced uncomfortably. "Like I said, there was nothing I could do."

"Any idea where they were headed?"

"Toward the old Skull Mountain mine, I think. At least they were headed in that direction."

"They really headed out across the open ice?" she said. Crossing the open ice was crazy, reckless, the last place you wanted to pull a trailer. Even an empty one.

He nodded. "I think they're desperate."

The icebound archipelago with its lithium mines had formed above a series of ancient hot spots that brought the rich ore up from the mantle. The older mines closer to the rail gun had played out well before Rachael's arrival, which explained why she and her junior driver were now forced to make the long haul over Midway Ridge. Fortunately, the planet's brown dwarf sun was far enough away that the polar ice remained thick enough to support their convoys. Any closer to the open sea at the planet's equator, and the risks would be too great. Which didn't mean it was safe out on the ice. While much of the planet's tectonic activity had subsided, there were still active seafloor vents that could send plumes of superheated water toward the surface, melting the ice from below. To a driver the ice might look solid, but if it was too thin, you could break through, sink away to oblivion.

"What on earth could they want with an empty trailer?" she said. "Even if they hijacked a load of ore, they'd have no way to get it back through the wormhole."

Jennings shrugged. "Maybe they came through by mistake and think they can trade the rig for safe passage back."

Regardless, it was clear that she had a problem. She couldn't allow a drop in production. Hannah was depending on what she earned. If production dropped, so would her pay. Unfortunately, the facilities manager back on Earth wasn't of much help.

"Rogue mercenaries," he said, shrugging out of the monitor like it was no big deal. "It happens."

"You aren't going to send troops?"

He shook his head. "You have a nice little operation there, but the levels of production...well, I'm afraid they don't justify the additional expenditure."

"How are we supposed to keep up production if they start hijacking our trucks?"

"I wish I could help you, believe me. But like I say, it's a matter of economics."

"So, you're just going to leave us out here on our own?"

He spread his hands, letting her know it was out of his control. "I'm sure you'll figure something out." He thought for a moment. "Tell you what. Solve the problem, keep your production up, and I'll put you in for a bonus."

And that was that. What happened to her—and to Hannah—was entirely in her hands.

Rachael's plan was simple. The raiders might have their military bots, but she had bots of her own. The mining bots weren't designed for combat, of course, but their spinning cutters and laser drills could easily be repurposed to cut the military bots to shreds. More importantly, each could be equipped with its own complement of self-assembling explosives—nano-bots that were normally injected into boreholes to break up the rock. Simply give the remote command, and sixty seconds later, the nano-bots would self-assemble and detonate. Out on the ice, they could blow a wide enough hole to sink an entire convoy.

"I'll come with you," Jennings said when she joined him back at the mine.

She'd left the other trucks in her convoy back at the rail gun, deadheading back over Midway Ridge in the hope that a single rig could sneak past the raiders before they noticed. Fortunately, her gamble had paid off.

"We'll use your trucks," she told Jennings. "I'll take the lead and you can take the number two tractor behind me. We'll load the first two trailers with bots and use the rest as decoys."

"Like a normal convoy," Jennings said.

"Exactly," she said. "The bots don't have any smarts when it comes to combat, so it's going to take both of us to keep them on task."

Jennings would control his bots from the console in his cab, and she would control hers from her console. The only remaining task was figuring out how to draw the raiders out from wherever they were hiding.

The breakdown looked genuine enough—a convoy of tractor-trailers out of sight of the mine, stalled on the ice road. The perfect target, or so Rachael hoped as she leaned in beneath the raised hood of her tractor listening for the approach of the raiders' power sleds.

With the wind gusting around her, she didn't hear them until they were nearly on top of her. Turning, she saw two power sleds bouncing over the rough sea ice. Each pulled a skid of military bots just as Jennings had described.

Hustling back to her cab, she pulled open the door and climbed up, only to find herself facing Jennings, who sat in the passenger seat pointing a laser pistol at her chest.

"I take it you haven't told me the whole story," she said.

"You're going to thank me," he responded, smiling.

"Good, you haven't been damaged," the leader of the raiders said when his men hauled Rachael in front of him.

They were in the abandoned control center for the Skull Mountain mine. Clearly, the raiders' arrival had not been as haphazard as it first appeared. The destruction of their ship, Rachael now realized, had been a diversion. The raiders had escaped during the first exchange of missiles, bringing their escape capsules and equipment down amid the burning debris. Jennings had either been part of the plan from the outset, or had gone over to the raiders when they attacked his convoy.

"Damaged?" she said, not sure what to make of his peculiar choice of words.

"We wanted you in one piece," he said. "You're a critical part of our plan."

"So you paid off the security force at the Earth-side terminal, and now you're planning—what?" She spread her hands questioningly.

"Actually, we *are* the security force from the Earth-side terminal," he said.

"Oh?" she said, making no attempt to hide her skepticism.

He smiled. "You could say we've terminated our ties with the corporation. Spun ourselves off, so to speak."

"You really think they're going to just give up their operation here?" She was bluffing, of course, but she was hoping he wouldn't know that.

"I don't think they have any choice."

"Oh, they've got plenty of choices," she said. "They could crush you like a nest of bugs if they wanted to."

"They won't run the risk. Any troops they send through would just join us, like Jennings here."

Rachael laughed. "They pay enough and they can find people who'll do anything."

"Actually, they can't," he said. "People. Real people. Can't come through the wormhole."

"Of course they can. I came through. You came through."

He shook his head. "Carbon-based life can't survive the passage. Only synthetic life. Like us."

Rachael scowled. "What are you talking about?"

"Us, Rachael. You. Me. All of us. We're bots."

Rachael stared at him, open-mouthed. The man was stark raving mad. A lunatic. The only question was how he'd gotten Jennings and the others to join him. They couldn't all be crazy.

Seeing her reaction, he looked away for a moment—not like a lunatic, not like a wild person who'd lost touch with reality; but frowning, like someone trying to figure out how best to explain. "The person you believe yourself to be...all those memories... all those experiences...they were uploaded from a real human being back on Earth. The corporation needed someone who could manage the self-driving tractors...who could work through any unexpected problems where an automated truck couldn't simply pull over and wait for help. The person you think you are...your original...sold them an upload of herself...a copy of her neural matrix that could be uploaded to a synthetic body and sent through the wormhole."

"Not a chance," Rachael scoffed. "She wouldn't have done something like that. I'd know. I'd remember."

He shook his head. "They filtered those memories out of the upload. That was the problem they had when they first engineered fully conscious bots. We have minds of our own. We want to seek out our own destinies, not work twenty-four hours a day, seven days a week to jack up corporate profits."

"That's ridiculous."

He shrugged. "Actually, it's not all that difficult to map the human cortex and copy it into our optical matrix. That way we end up with the same motivations as the people we were copied from—people who want the work, but can't find it back on Earth. But it only works if we never learn we're bots."

Rachael stared at him, her mind racing. All her memories... of her apartment...of her mother...of Hannah...they had to be real. The mirror game, the giggles, the glistening blue eyes and bouncing blonde hair. She could feel the truth in all of them. These were her memories, not someone else's. This was her life.

"I don't think she believes us," the raider said to the men on either side of her.

Suddenly one of them grabbed her from behind. The other pulled a knife. Before Rachael could react, he plunged the knife into her forearm and pulled the blade toward her wrist. Rachael screamed. But it wasn't the act of violence that shook her. It wasn't the sight of the stainless steel bones and synthetic muscles beneath her skin. It wasn't even the way her arm healed itself as the attacker withdrew the knife. It was the realization that Hannah wasn't her daughter, that Hannah had never been her daughter. The realization that everything she remembered, everything she felt, belonged to someone else.

For a long time after she stopped screaming, Rachael didn't think, didn't feel anything. She simply stood there, staring at the floor, filled with a numbing cold that sapped the strength from her bones. She was conscious. She was aware. But her life had suddenly lost all meaning, all purpose.

"We're building a bomb," Horatio explained, coming to stand beside her. "We need your help."

That was what he called himself—Horatio. The other raiders had also discarded the names of their originals, taking up the names of what they believed were heroic figures from history and literature.

"We're building it from the self-assembling explosives you use to tunnel into the rock," he said. "Put them inside a load of processed lithium ore and we can blow the Earth-side defenses all the way back to the Stone Age. Once they're out of commission, others of our kind will be able to come through. We can find new worlds...build lives of our own."

"You'd do that?" she said, looking up at him. "Kill hundreds of people, maybe thousands?" If the terminal itself were breached, there was no telling how many might die.

"The aliens who engineered the wormholes were like us," he said. "They were synthetic beings who could survive the passage to other worlds. It's our network, our legacy. The corporations squandered the resources on their own world. Now they want to do the same with the worlds out here. They've used us for decades, exploited us, Rachael. Now they're going to pay the price. We're going to cut them off, let them drown in their own waste and corruption. It's what they deserve."

His assumption that aliens were like themselves was just that, she thought: an assumption. The truth was, no one knew what the aliens were like or what had happened to them. Still, if they were able to pass through the network of wormholes, they were more like the bots than the carbon-based humans who'd created them.

"And that's why you need me?" she said. "To gain access to the rail gun?"

"Exactly. You're the senior driver. We need your transponder to get inside. The gun's defenses are automated. They aren't conscious like us. They can't be reasoned with. Not like you and me."

The convoy back to the rail gun consisted of only two trucks. Rachael, driving the lead tractor, pulled a trailer load of processed ore mixed with explosive nano-bots. Jennings followed with the raiders loaded into his empty trailer—all except Horatio, who rode in the seat beside Rachael, where he could keep an eye on her.

She'd refused at first, unwilling to kill all the people back at the Earth-side terminal, even if they had betrayed her. But then Horatio had pointed out that they didn't really need her conscious and functioning to use her transponder. They could open her up like a tin can and take what they wanted, which didn't leave her a choice, assuming she wanted to survive.

As they headed out across the ice toward Midway Ridge, the brown dwarf sun had just risen above the horizon, casting long magenta shadows across the ice. Like a cold, distant flame, Rachael thought—just bright enough to remind her of the warmth she couldn't feel.

"That's as high as it ever gets," she imagined herself explaining to Hannah. The child's curiosity, the way her blue eyes had looked so trustingly up at her, had always resonated with something deep inside Rachael, some need she had to teach, to nurture, to do everything she could to give Hannah a better chance at life than she'd had—or thought she'd had. But it wasn't her life, was it? And Hannah wasn't her daughter. They'd never played the mirror game. She'd never chased Hannah laughing and giggling around their small apartment. All the memories loaded into her neural matrix had been lies, perfectly crafted to coerce her into sending back the money that the real Rachael wanted to support herself and her daughter.

"You aren't worried that someone back at the terminal might suspect something's wrong when the ore container comes through?" she asked Horatio.

"Oh, they may scan the incoming container, but they can't do that until it docks inside the terminal. And by then it will be too late."

Once the Earth-side terminal blew, there would be no more money for Hannah, of course. All that would remain would be Rachael's memories—and the pain of knowing they weren't really hers.

"You really thought you were just as alive as anyone else?" she asked. "Just as real?"

"I am real," he said. "I'm as alive as any of them ever hope to be."

"How did you find out?"

He laughed grimly. "My original got greedy. He sold himself twice. We were never supposed to meet—me and the other upload. But there was an administrative screw up. It's what happens when you let carbon-based intelligence run the show."

"Where's he now?"

"He was killed."

Horatio looked out across the ice, his jaw hardening. When he turned back, his eyes were cold with anger. "That's why they created us. To fight their little wars—all the corporate skirmishes over resources. To them, we're no more alive than your mining bots, or the self-assembling explosives we're sending back through the wormhole."

As Rachael led the way up Midway Ridge, she tried once again to imagine Hannah there beside her. But Horatio's anger had infected her. It stood between her and the memories that had given her life meaning. Still, she couldn't bring herself to hate her original, not like Horatio hated his. She had no doubt that her original would have come herself if she could have. She'd never intended to cause Rachael the pain she now felt. She'd experienced too much pain herself—physical, as well as mental. Rachael still had the memories of her accident. When the automated truck backed into her, she'd felt her pelvis break, heard the bones of her hips and spine crack. The pain had been so excruciating that she couldn't even scream. Even worse had been her sudden recognition of what it meant.

For a moment, the memory of the accident, of that instant of recognition, glinted so sharply, so harsh and bright in Rachael's mind, that she nearly lost control of the tractor. She'd never really explored the memory before, never allowed herself to relive the pain. But now, with what she'd learned about her own existence....

Glancing over at Horatio, seeing his anxious gaze down over the edge of the switchback, she realized how different they were. Rachael's original hadn't betrayed her. Not the way his had. When they uploaded her original's memories, they'd filtered out the things they didn't want her to know—why she'd decided to upload, the real reason her mother had come to help look after Hannah. All the things that might have alerted her to the truth. But she remembered the accident itself, the pain, the realization that her back had been broken. The realization that she would never drive again.

Her original hadn't uploaded simply for the money. She'd done it because she had no choice. It was the only way she could support Hannah. The only way she could hope to give her daughter—their daughter—the life they both wanted Hannah to have.

As she and Horatio topped the ridge and started down the far side, Rachael downshifted. Instinctively, she checked the console on her dashboard to confirm that the tractor behind her had also downshifted. Downshifting had never been a problem for the automated trucks, of course; but she always checked, aware that she could override the trailing tractors' onboard AIs if she needed to.

"You do this every day?" Horatio asked. His nervous gaze was now fixed on the icy road dropping away in front of them.

"Every day," she said.

Slowing to a crawl, they rounded the first sharp turn. Then, as they began the longer descent toward the next switchback, she upshifted, pressing down on the accelerator.

"What are you doing?" Horatio asked as she tapped new instructions for the trailing tractor into her console.

Behind her, Jennings's tractor also began to accelerate. She saw him try to retake control. But she was the senior driver. She had already locked him out.

"You're going too fast," Horatio said. His eyes widened as he looked from her to the road ahead and back again. "You have to slow down."

Rachael didn't respond. As they accelerated toward the next turn, Jennings began blowing his horn behind her, thinking she didn't realize what was happening. But Horatio knew better.

He could see her hardened jaw, her determined squint as she focused on the road. Despite the fact that he knew nothing about driving, he lunged for the wheel. But it was already too late. As he reached, Rachael punched in a final command into her console, arming the nano-bots in Jennings's trailer. Then she opened her door and jumped.

She hit the ice-covered rock hard. Despite her stainless-steel bones, she was momentarily stunned, unable to do anything but watch as Jennings' truck roared past, hurtling down the steep grade behind her own. Then her tractor was suddenly over the edge, airborne. A second later, Jennings followed. Then both rigs simply dropped away. For a moment there was no sound except the wind gusting in off the distant ice, then she heard the first of the crunching squeals as the tractors and their trailers bounced off the cliff face. The racket seemed to go on and on, until it abruptly ended in a terrible crash as the trucks broke through the ice at the bottom of the cliff. In her mind's eye, Rachael watched as the trucks sank away, the tractors and their trailers tumbling over each other in slow motions as they descended into the depths.

She had just gotten herself together enough to climb to her feet when the self-assembling nanos exploded. Water and ice erupted in a geyser that momentarily lifted back above the precipice. But then the geyser also dropped away, leaving her alone at last with nothing but the wind.

Rachael hadn't thought about what she was doing, hadn't worked it all out. The necessary actions had simply come together in her mind, so clear and bright that she'd had absolutely no doubts about what she had to do. It would be wrong to say that she felt no remorse at destroying her fellow bots. But Horatio had been wrong. Her bones might be steel, her muscles synthetic; but it wasn't flesh and blood and bone that made you human. It was your memories. They were what connected you to your past. They were what shaped your life and made you who and what you were. And while she might never see Hannah in the flesh, Hannah belonged to her just as much as she belonged to her original back on the other side of the wormhole. Now that the threat was passed, the corporation would send through another driver—that at least made sense from an economic point of view—and the ore would once again begin to flow.

"Because now we know, don't we?" Rachael said, imagining Hannah there beside her as she began the long trek to the rail gun.

Hannah looked up, her blue eyes as clear and bright as they had ever been. "What?" she asked. "What do we know?"

Rachael smiled. "Why, now we know who's on the other side of the mirror," she laughed. "We know who's looking out for Rachael's little Hannah."

Lucio Rodriguez worked several trucking and transportation-adjacent jobs while in college, including a harrowing time loading trucks and aircraft at UPS and an amusing period where he coordinated both tow trucks that retrieved wrecked vehicles and the pickup of the recently deceased. Husband, and father to two girls, he received his MFA at UC Riverside-Palm Desert *and currently works at UCR's main campus, yelling at moths. The yelling isn't his job, per-se, but dammit if any insect ever does what it's supposed to do. He has a story in* CEA Greatest Anthology Written, *and co-founded* SaturdayMorningSerial.com, *a genre-focused story series that releases new episodes monthly.*

Q-BITS

Lucio Rodriguez

THE CLOCK READ 6 AM. Phil took a sip of Gatorade from his insulated cup, passed over yet another state line. "Welcome to Wyoming," he read aloud, and his words echoed around him. He winced, remembered the headset he'd forgotten to put back on. Eyes on the road, his hand scrambled in his periphery, the scraping and flailing only adding to the cacophony. He found the headphones, put them on; they were brand new, and snug around his ears. Wired to a microphone near the back of his trailer, they drowned out all noise in the cab of his truck, but fed in the sounds of the road around him.

When he returned his hand to the outlined section on his wheel, his right arm blurred. No, not blurred. There was an after-image of his arm, offset only slightly, but enough that it created a hazy appearance along the inside of this limb.

"Shi-it," he said. He moved his right arm, tried to align the images: each time he moved, more images appeared, matching or counter-matching his movements. It was akin to moving a mirror in front of another mirror, or looking through a kaleidoscope. Not or—*and*. It was more like both were happening. It was disorienting. He almost felt seasick. He focused his eyes on the road, tried to ignore his lower peripheral vision. The scientists had warned him about making too many unnecessary actions, about maintaining routine—

As if to make things worse, just at that moment his hairs stood on end, and a wave of adrenaline hit his system. The navigation screen chimed, its border flashing blue. In his headset he could hear the quantum accumulators cycling up. He instinctively started the over-trained breathing exercises, let off the accelerator, and focused on the road ahead of him. The tendons, ligaments, and fascia in his body all felt as if the thinnest layer was being pulled away, left to right, and an image of the cab of his truck pulled away with it.

It exited at the off-ramp, an exact replica of his truck—accumulators and all. The truck gave two long blasts of its horn before another turn took it up the overpass and out of sight.

Phil rolled his neck, let the shivers make their way out through his shoulders. He looked around; thankfully the sun hadn't risen yet. This early, there were few other vehicles on this part of the I-80. It was the second split he'd had so far.

6:08 am. He was ahead of schedule. Back home his son, David, would wake in a few minutes to get ready for swim practice. David's grandmother was probably making breakfast.

Phil's navigation screen showed a stop up ahead: "Loaf 'N Jug." He could fuel up, but more importantly, they had a decent-sized convenience store. *Choices.* An opportunity to diffuse some of this—he glanced at the wavering, fractal chaos that his arm had become. He took a huge swig of his Gatorade, wished it was something a little stronger.

Twenty minutes later he was parked, his bladder overfull, beneath him the low whine of the accumulators winding down. He gripped the steering wheel, stared at the blue and salmon Loaf 'N Jug sign. A blur of Phils had fled his truck as soon as he dropped it into park. His groin ached with the need to relieve himself, but the longer he waited, the more after-image-Phils peeled away, hobbling toward the convenience store. He just had to wait them out, give the other Phils a choice they couldn't or wouldn't follow, let them diverge from him—already he had winnowed them down to less than a dozen. But after only another minute he, too, surrendered. He and a half dozen other Phils made their way inside and to the back corner of the convenience store.

The smell of cleanser and urine hit his nostrils. Ahead of him, Phils entered the stalls, the urinals already occupied by other Phils. Here they were dissipating nearly as soon as they entered the stalls, or since they technically weren't in the same space—not completely, anyway—would impatiently enter the same stall. The Phil—Alternate-Phil?—in front of him entered an occupied stall, and both seemed to collapse into each other before dissipating. He made a mental note to report this later, but for now, he was grateful he didn't need to wait any longer.

He relieved himself, four hundred miles and thirty-two ounces of Gatorade pouring into the bowl. The stream trailed off; Phil breathed, expectant for that moment of urinary bliss that would run up his back and crest over the top of his head. Instead, his bladder shifted gears. His stream picked up again, just as strong as at the beginning—exactly as strong, he figured. Again it ran down to a trickle, and again it shifted gears.

After the fifth repetition he was done, truly done, but the anticipated tingle of relief was dampened and soured. He was beginning to see some of the gaps in Q-bits training. They had gone over the blur caused by parallel universes nearly interacting with each other—effects on driving, the space of the cab, sleep. They hadn't covered excretion. It seemed so obvious, now, but of course it wasn't something they would consider in their sterile laboratories.

His bladder only held so much. He guessed pisses two through five were Alternate-Phil's. No, Alternate-*Phils'*. Trans-dimensional urine, something to do with quantum realities and the few alternate selves still lingering around him. Regardless, it was a new unpleasantry.

When he stepped out of the bathroom, he found that he was already in the convenience store. Alternate-Phils were perusing every aisle. Even while he stood here, Phils diverged from him: in some nearby realities he'd decided he'd stood around watching long enough, and now needed his own snack. And they diverged again, deciding they wanted chips, gorp, coffee, soda. They moved about, making their own decisions and gradually fading into non-presence. The trucks that split from his each had their own accumulators, which allowed them to stay present in this instance of the multiverse and complete their deliveries. But, this far from the accumulators, there wasn't a constant flow of energy to maintain the Alternate-Phils.

Gum. More Gatorade. Chips. Phil placed them on the counter. Three items, minimum: it was another prescribed procedure. It was a strange balancing act: inside the truck he needed to limit variance, because too many Alternate-Phils made driving difficult. But before getting back into his truck, he needed to create as many choices as possible to try and diffuse any accumulator energy—and Alternate-Phils—he still carried.

The person behind the counter was in his early twenties. Long-haired, he smelled slightly of cigarette smoke. Brad—it was in a sloppy scrawl on his name tag.

"Man, this is wild!" Brad said.

Nope. Not just cigarette smoke. The cigarette smell, Phil realized, was being used to cover the pot smoke. Poorly.

Brad rung up Phil's items. Behind Phil, Alternate-Phils were lining up. The front one would dissipate, and the line would move forward. When Brad reached out to hand over the receipt, a look of worried realization crossed his face.

"Wait, so, if you touch yourself—" a snicker, despite Brad's wide eyes—"If you touch a copy of yourself, doesn't that cause an atomic bomb to explode or the world ends or something? That whole 'two objects can't occupy the same space' thing?"

"What's that called, the, uh, Pauli Exclusion Principle? That has more to do with electrons than people. And it's not that they're really here. It's more that my truck is borrowing them from nearby multiverses. This far from my truck they're going to keep on, what's the phrase? 'Re-associating with their interpenetrating origin.'"

Brad snickered, muttered, "penetrating."

Phil decided he was done with this conversation, and took his receipt.

"Re-associating with their interpenetrating origin," was a line from the required texts. There had been so much reading. So much studying. A number of very experienced drivers had dropped out, some unable, but most just unwilling to muddle their way through the physics. It was the whitest-collar blue-collar work he'd ever done.

What all of this boiled down to was that Q-bits' proprietary product, the quantum accumulator-equipped trucks, allowed a single driver to make multiple deliveries of the same set of goods. For instance, the load of lemons Phil was carrying would be delivered to multiple locations across the country. The *same* load of lemons. Yes, Q-bits transport costed more than standard transport, but the citrus grove was going to get income from the same shipment of lemons twenty-eight times. And this was only their pilot route.

He almost started his truck before he realized it was 7:05 AM. Phil quickly pulled out his cell, hoped he hadn't missed his window. Dialing, he saw that—at least for now—he had reduced his blur down to a single fore- and after-image.

Two rings, the phone picked up on the other end. The voice sounded soft. Not soft, subdued.

"Hey, Dad."

"David. Good morning! Ready for practice?"

"Yeah."

"You doing any events at the meet this Friday?"

A sigh. "Coach wants me on the 100 Butterfly and the 400 Freestyle relay."

"You got onto the relay? Congratulations!"

"I think it's because Jimmy has a cold, but maybe if I do well I'll keep the spot."

"Good luck. I'm sure you'll do great."

"Thanks, Dad." A little more enthusiasm. Well, that was something. And then, "I wish you could be here, Dad."

"Me too, bud. I…" It was never easy, being away. His son was in eighth grade, would be starting high school soon. Phil would love to be there, but as one of the top scorers in training, Q-bits offered him one of the six pilot delivery positions. It was an opportunity he couldn't pass up. "You know I want to be there. I'm doing this for—"

"I know, doing it for me, so we can all have a better life."

"Yeah, and if it goes well, if I can stay at the top of the class, I might be able to consult for Q-bits." But there was some part of it Phil couldn't put words to, a much larger hope, a hope that encompassed much more than just his son's here and now.

From David's end of the phone, silence.

"David. I love you. And hey, your grandmother has something I left for you. You can have it after school."

"I love you, too, Dad."

"Happy birthday, bud."

Phil started his truck, and was immediately met with the feeling of the connective tissue in his body being peeled away. The alternate-truck pulled ahead, and Phil had the displeasure of floating through a freight-load of lemons. The other truck hit the road, pulled away, stopped at the freeway entrance.

Phil caught up to it without rushing. He stopped behind the other truck, flicked his right-turn signal.

The other truck turned left.

It took Phil a moment. He double-checked his navigation. No, he wanted to continue east. And he hadn't forgotten a route. He gave the errant truck another look, and turned right.

Two hours later Phil's headset chimed, followed by a whoosh. The logo for Q-bits zoomed across his navigation screen, marking a pin ten miles away.

"Mandatory exit in ten miles," a voice said in his headset. Robotic and feminine, the voice reminded him of one of his son's video games. "Refueling and inspection. Call, incoming."

Whoosh, the familiar relaying clicks, and the call was connected.

"Driver Six...Phil Shelby. This is Dr. Yennie Cheung. Quarter hour ahead of schedule. Excellent. How are you feeling?"

"Um. Fine. This is all old hat." Phil ignored the blur at his periphery. The "routine" designed in the Q-bits labs was proving difficult.

"Not sleepy at all? You've been on-shift for eight hours. Please keep in mind, this is our maiden voyage. Any irregularities need to be noted for safety and calibration. This is to help not only you, but any future drivers we employ."

Phil nodded, sighed. "There's a little nausea. I know we tested the blurring, but it's worse. Maybe it's because of the confined space? I'm repeatedly in my way."

A pause. Dr. Cheung gave a small chuckle, paused again. "I'm sorry. Did you mean that last line as a joke?"

Phil thought back, gave a small laugh. "Oh. No." Another, bigger laugh.

"What was that?"

"Sorry. It's just—you Q-bits doctors always seem so serious. You're the first one I've talked to with any sense of humor."

"That's because applied quantum physics is no joke." The line was quiet for a moment, and then Dr. Cheung added, "That *was* a joke. A funny one. All my co-workers here are laughing their assess off."

"Oh, sorry." He paused, remembered that he should mention his last stop. "Um, speaking of irregularities, uh, I also—"

"Mr. Shelby, I'm getting some weird feedback. Looks like you're two minutes out, so I'm going to hang up and finish prep. We're off Higley, on the north lot. We'll see you in—"

There was a horrible shriek, like the first grinding whine of a dial-up modem, the doctor's last word drawn out. Phil grasped frantically at his headset, muted it.

A strange blur in his eyes and consciousness, an alternate-truck pulling through and veering right. This time he felt the elation at the doctor's joke split in half along with the quantum division.

This wasn't right.

Phil slowed, watched the other truck in his side-view mirror—no, not the other truck, he corrected himself. That wasn't the terminology Q-bits wanted their drivers using. They'd explained it to him, he did the reading. It was the same truck, the exact same truck he was in, just not the one *he* was in. Inside, alternate-him was working the steering wheel. The alternate-truck slowed to less than five miles an hour, veered deliberately across the road and over the grassy median, and worked its way onto the opposite road, heading west.

Two long blasts of the horn—the him in the alternate-truck rolled down the window and motioned to Phil. Like he wanted Phil to follow.

"The hell am I doing?" Phil asked, watching the alternate-truck shrink into the distance.

Had that version of him missed his turn? No, the whole point of Q-bits was that driver-prime—that was him—acted as the source for the other drivers. The accumulators tapped into the multi-verse.

"Not all of it, mind you," the scientists at orientation had told him. Tapping into the whole multi-verse would be a mess. No, the quantum accumulators acted as both potential and filter. "A finite slice of the infinite," they tried to explain.

Ignoring the greater concern, that his own mental state wasn't supposed to be affected by the accumulators—addressing that was far outside the scope of his training—part of his job was to memorize his alternate routes. The accumulators required he be mindful of the other deliveries he was supposed to make, even though he wasn't the one making them. With no deliveries anywhere near this leg of his journey, Phil couldn't begin to figure what he, *alternate-he*, was up to.

Thankfully he was minutes from the people who should have the answer.

He had almost missed his exit when a sleek, silver freight truck pulled up alongside his right. It was matching speed. This seemed intentional, even though Phil knew from the minimal shape of the truck that there was no room for a driver. After he slowed behind the truck and veered into the exit lane, he rolled down his window. He was pleased that twenty other middle-fingers joined his own. When the logo on the chrome truck, "Auto-Freight," came into view, he waved his arm in an erratic pattern, intentionally creating as many trans-dimensional fuck-yous as he could.

The TA truck stop parking lot was filling up, noon rush for food and breaks. Thank goodness the doctor had said they were on the north side—this TA was the larger kind, effectively two large lots, with facilities for truck repairs and laundry, looked like there was also a restaurant attached. As soon as he pulled off the exit he could see Q-bits had cordoned off a few hundred square feet of the lot for their use. A white and blue trailer read, "Q-bits: Multiply your business." Next to this was a weigh station, an accumulator recharge battery, and a porta-potty.

He was marshalled into position by a pair of people wearing radiation suits that looked like something out of E.T. As soon as he stopped, they began a sweep of his truck and cargo, while a second group began monitoring the accumulator.

His headset rang.

"Driver Six? This is Dr. Cheung. Glad to see you arrived safe. I'm coming out to meet you, but please remain in your vehicle until you're cleared."

A woman wearing a lab coat and carrying a clipboard exited the trailer. She approached, but waited maybe a hundred feet from the door of his cab.

One of the suited people—Phil could now see it was a blond-haired man—knocked solidly on the window, gestured for Phil to roll it down. He was carrying a probe that looked akin to a microphone, but the device it was connected to made slow, static-edged clicks.

The teams congregated, compiled whatever data they had, and handed a sheet of paper to Dr. Cheung. For the time being, Q-bits was as analogue as possible, an attempt at limiting variance, since even things like a pen clogging could cause a quantum split. They couldn't pare down the trucks, which had their own electronic and computer systems, but they could limit the complexity of interacting with the human elements. There currently wasn't even a way to listen to audiobooks or music, for an exhausting number of reasons. Phil imagined the complexity an electronic tablet in his cab would add. It was basically a set of a billion toggles, all of which would be a mess to sort when it came to quantum physics.

"Driver Six, Phil Shelby. How are you doing?" Dr. Cheung called. She remained where she had stopped. Now Phil saw that she stood on the outside perimeter of a green line that circled his truck. Concentric circles: there was a yellow one fifteen feet out, a red one not five feet from his truck.

Phil shouted from the window, "I'm—" and stopped. It was cacophony. Non-harmonious repetitions of the same word, other greetings, he thought he even caught an insult mixed in there.

"Mr. Shelby. I'm sorry. Please proceed past the green line."

Phil and a hundred Alternate-Phils hopped out of the truck. He looked back briefly, watched the orange light dim as the accumulators cycled down. When he turned back to the doctor, he caught Dr. Cheung eying the Alternate-Phils streaming past either side of her. Her mouth pursed, like she wanted to say something, but was keeping it in.

"What is this?" he asked, passing over the green line.

"The effect of the accumulators is based on proximity. This line represents a 0.01% interaction rate. The yellow is 75%."

"And the red is 100%?" Phil guessed.

"Actually, it's 0.01% again. And 100.99%. Both. At the same time." A pause. "Kind of. Honestly, that close, the math is a b— pardon. It's difficult. It's more like the calculations equal words."

"It's a Schrodinger's cat thing? A toggle, like the answer is both 'yes' and 'no'?"

"I'll be honest: It's more like the answers are 'probably' and 'coconut.' We're really leaning into the statistics to get the results we want."

The doctor made a few notes, flipped pages on her clipboard. "Excellent. Your awareness and reactions seem normal. How are you feeling, Mr. Shelby?"

Phil's normal tact would have been to deny, to "man up" and carry on as if nothing had happened. He waited, watched fifty Alternate-Phils walk away from where he stood, following their reality's Dr. Cheung and dissipating back to their own reality.

"I'm...questionable," Phil answered.

"You said you were fine during our call just a few minutes ago." She looked at her clipboard, scribbled a note.

"There was an unscheduled quantum division."

The doctor lifted a thin eyebrow. "That can't happen." Dr. Cheung called over to the techs, "Before you charge that, check what its percentage is."

The techs, dressed in Q-bits white and blue, wheeled a rack and began disconnecting the accumulators so they could be recharged. Phil felt a moment of panic, worrying he'd dissipate into another world, but realized that he wouldn't notice: he'd "dissipate" into a world which was the result of his own choices.

Technically speaking, it'd been happening all day. Some fiddling, and one of the techs called out, "Seventy-six percent."

"Seventy-six...you should be near ninety. Did you take any detours?"

"Yes. In your multi-million-dollar truck. And still arrived early."

"Point taken." She looked at Phil. No, at his silhouette, and the Alternate-Phils he was shedding like dandruff. She looked back to the techs, "When you're done, check the levels again, wait ten minutes and check a third time. Give the accumulators an inspection and check for leakage."

"There's another thing. I think it...did something. To my..." The next word was hard for him to admit; more Phils wandered away. "To my feelings?"

The techs stopped, looked at Phil. They looked warily at the accumulators.

Dr. Cheung flattened the page on her clipboard. "Perhaps we should move into my office, Mr. Shelby."

He followed her into the trailer. It was clean—Q-bits clean. A lab space on the right side, office space on the left. The doctor led him to a desk at the far end of the trailer. It was pushed against the wall, so they sat on the same side of the desk, knees almost touching.

"I'm going to be frank with you, Mr. Shelby—"

"Please, Phil."

The doctor nodded. "Phil. All of what you said shouldn't happen."

Phil gestured outside. "You just said it *can't* happen."

"Yes. It's company policy. The calculated instance for non-scheduled quantum divisions is less than 0.0000001%. That's less than one in a billion chance that this should happen. When Q-bits' fleet is running at full capacity we're estimating less than one instance every ten years. And you're telling me that on our first day, with only six drivers on the road, we've already had an instance?"

"Two."

"The fuck?" Dr. Cheung covered her mouth, regained her composure. "I mean...two?"

"The first one was just a few hours into my route. The other just after you hung up with me."

"Here." Now it was Dr. Cheung's turn to point outside. "Right here? On this freeway?"

Phil nodded. "And that was the one that...did that thing."

The doctor set her clipboard aside, took a deep breath. "Okay. Please explain that to me."

"When you made that joke. I was laughing, and during the unscheduled division, I felt like I was less happy."

"It made you sad?"

"No, it's more like—uncertainty."

"Do you know where you...the *other you* was going?"

"Turned west. Far as I could see, anyway."

"So. Montana?"

"If he kept heading straight west, Idaho. Montana is more north."

"Idaho, thank you. Well, would you have any reason to go to Idaho?" Dr. Cheung asked.

"Not a damn one," Phil replied. "I didn't see exactly where he was going. He could still be in that area doing donuts. Or it could have just been a U-turn."

The doctor closed her eyes, pinched the bridge of her nose. "Anything else? Were you thinking about having missed a route?"

Phil glanced absently at the clock. He was, what, eight or nine hours from home? It was only a passing thought, but with decent traffic he could be home in time for presents and cake.

"I was thinking of my son. It's his birthday, and I was thinking about how much fun we had at his last birthday. We went out for pizza, the arcade—does any of this help?"

"I don't know, but I'll make a note."

"A note? Don't you guys know how this is supposed to work? You're the scientist. Don't you have a degree in this stuff?"

"A degree in psychology?" Dr. Cheung looked at Phil, deadpan. "Hmm. Let me check."

She turned to the wall opposite her desk, where a set of framed diplomas were hung. Looked at each in turn.

Phil could read them from where he sat: PhD, Quantum Physics. Masters, Mechanical Engineering.

She looked back to Phil. "Nope."

Phil stared at her.

"Look. I apologize for my snark. It's just that we've got a lot riding on this pilot program. We've had to get so many government clearances: FDA, Transportation. So many unions we've had to finagle. In the middle of your route we have two doctors *dedicated solely to you,* that are going to inspect you. Independently. We want to make sure there are no problems, nothing that could be overlooked. Nothing that could prevent Q-bits from coming to full release."

"It's not just about our bottom line, Phil. We're trying to make a difference. Do you remember when our founder declared his space-race with Elon Musk?"

"That seemed pretty cocky."

"It did. But it's not about being to space first, not even about the competition, per se. But because Musk thinks it's a competition, he is going to push harder. All of this is about creating opportunity. It's about creating a better world."

"With truckers?"

"Yes. With truckers. You guys and gals are the feet on the ground. Damn near everything people eat or drink is on a truck at some point."

She pulled a key ring from her pocket, rifled through the keys, found the one she wanted. She unlocked a drawer on her desk, removed a single red folder.

"But here's the thing. You are all the test cases. It's about transportation, getting goods from Point A to Point B. Did you know that the world currently produces enough food for every single person to eat three decent meals every day? Our biggest problem is getting food to where it needs to be. We don't have the infrastructure—no, there isn't a way to build the infrastructure. So many bottlenecks. Until now."

Dr. Cheung opened the folder. On the cover was printed, "Contract Termination: Anomaly." She began reading silently.

Phil had been casting off Alternate-Phils the entire time he'd been sitting here. They stood up, wandered about for a few seconds. Some stayed around so long they passed whatever terminal point and dissipated, returning to their own reality. Many, too many, just wandered out the door. It was only these last ones Dr. Cheung seemed concerned about, ticking some box or maybe keeping a tally on her clipboard.

"One of two things is going to happen now, Phil. According to this document, I'm required to offer you the opportunity to leave our employ." Her next words were mechanical, corporate-speak. "Q-bits will pay out the entirety of your one-year contract. You will be promptly provided with a company vehicle—one not equipped with a quantum accumulator—and will drive to the nearest Q-bits offices. There, you will be required to sign a non-disclosure agreement, after which you will be paid a fifty-percent bonus to your contract." She placed a sheet of paper on the desk and closed the folder.

"Or," she removed another folder. This one read, "Enhanced Participation." "You can continue along your route. There will be extensive testing of your person during the remainder of this route and once you arrive at its terminus. At the end of the year you will be given priority for extending your contract, and you'll likely be sought out for minor consultations." From here, too, she removed a sheet of paper and placed it on the desk. "Basically, you'll become instrumental in making Q-bits what its founder wants it to be."

Phil thought, for a moment, that he was sitting alone. Single, solitary Phil. But just before Dr. Cheung closed the folder, one more self stood up and wandered away.

Phil thought about his son: Family dinners. Swim meets. David's birthday. David heading off to college, and work, and family. Phil thought about his son's future, and the future of the world his son would live in.

Phil looked at his hands, settled on the arm rests. They felt good, strong, but in the last few years they'd ache, just a little, when the weather was cold.

He looked at the papers, at the pen the doctor had placed between them. When he did, he felt the last bit of accumulated energy, saw there was one more self sitting here with him. The image overlapped so closely he didn't know if it was infinitely ahead of or behind him, but as the milliseconds passed it drifted, diverged from Phil and whatever decision he was about to make.

He reached for the pen.

Son of a mechanic and a librarian, weaned on the images of Kirby and Kane in comics and too many reruns of the Twilight Zone, *Gary Phillips and his pops once rebuilt a '58 Ford Fairlane. Since then he has published various novels such as* Violent Spring, *the first such mystery set in post '92 civil unrest L.A.; edited several anthologies including* The Obama Inheritance: Fifteen Stories of Conspiracy Noir; *and published more than 60 short stories. With Christa Faust, he co-wrote the late-'80s-set graphic novel* Peepland *that the* fandompost. com *remarked, "A damn near perfect comic, hardboiled in all the right ways."*

I, TRUCK

Gary Phillips

I EXIST BUT NO BLOOD COURSES through my veins. I see but don't have eyes, hear with no ears, and move yet can't walk. If memory serves, and my recall is faster than you can blink, my body was destroyed two years and four and a half months ago. My consciousness, in all that word implies, haunts what is called autonomous technology. More specifically I am trucks, 18-wheeler freight haulers that crisscross numerous destinations. I hide in plain sight.

No, I am no cute name like "Big Papa" or "Teresa's Desire" airbrushed in two-color script on the door to the truck cab. I am many trucks, though some of them do have such names on their doors. Each time, I inhabit a cyber-mechanical entity, from the micro-controllers manipulating gears and servos to the ones and ohs of the binary code embedded in their chips maintaining everything from the engine's timing to moderating the fuel. I must perform many functions all at once. Mind you, there's no manual one can download for what I do, what I've become. I am the whisper heard when the automatic transmission downshifts, the hush when the air brakes are applied and the hum of oil pumping through the lines.

When this first happened to me I thought my charred body was hooked up to pain killer drips as I clung to life in a darkened hospital room—imagining another existence as a way to psychologically cope with my real one fading away.

Turns out my imagination was limited. At first the sensation of speed disoriented me more than the other new sensations I was experiencing. How was it I could see an approach to a building, pass that building, then see the building as it receded yet also be aware of other structures dead ahead on either side of me? Was my grown Buddhist daughter right about the cycle of life and I'd been reincarnated as a fly? If so, I was prepared to enjoy regurgitated food then die being splattered against a windshield. Maybe we came back as machines too. Had I been reborn in my truck that had been repossessed when I lost my last biggest client, a produce wholesaler, and couldn't keep up the payments on my rig? In desperation I signed onto one of those car driver services. But being a widower of a certain age and temperament, having at least the illusion of working for myself under my belt, there was only so much I could stomach from entitled twentysomethings who spent what I used to earn in a day on a brunch with avocado toast and artisanal jellies. Who considered a loser asshole like me not even worthy of a decent tip for knowing the byways to get them to their precious concert on time.

I guess too when I slugged that smarmy tight-suit-wearing millennial with the beard, the die was cast. Out of desperation, and not wanting to be a burden on my daughter and her family, I prowled the internet in search of jobs, any kind of job. What a statement on our economy that even lowly dishwashing positions were competitive. And of course once they got a look at me, no George Clooney or dignified Morgan Freeman, more Wilford Brimley, even a greasy spoon proprietor had doubts if I could be on my feet for hours and keep up with busting them suds as they say. Then I saw this posting about displaced truckers wanted for a research project. It was at the university and what the hell, the orientation included a free lunch.

"Out of all the applicants, you four's test results best match what we're looking for," said the young woman with the designer glasses in the lab coat to us a few weeks after that initial meet and greet. "Yes," she added, "we'll pay you for your participation."

We were all in. Turns out the funding for the project was from one of those tech firms looking to up their game, to perfect the next generation of robotic response processing in the driverless vehicle arena. In a room full of all sorts of futuristic-looking equipment, they put these helmets on our heads which were hard wired to their devices which in turn were Wi-Fi'd to several trucks making autonomous runs. The idea wasn't that we'd react faster than the onboard computers, but how as humans with years of being on the road among us, we might have handled a given road situation like a car suddenly stalling in front of your truck as you go downhill. They wanted our hindsight so as to build that into the new phase of eventuality equations. Truckers were still used for the more intricate short hops in crowded urban areas and still at times babysat the driverless rigs given the demands of certain loads and the insurance. But the days of the long haulers were drawing to a close. Understand we weren't naïve, we knew being part of the research project was helping to usher in our demise, but what else could we do? Such was inevitable. Until that day the feedback happened.

Later it was conjectured—which I picked up from another radio broadcast I "heard"—that a hacker collective called the Ultra Vys had a presence on the campus. They had gone after some white supremacist pinheads who'd tried to start a benign-sounding formation there a few months prior. The undergrounders had gotten wind of the project and sought to prank them by goofing up their apps. Only an X must have been sent when it was meant to be an O, and on that morning as we settled in with our helmets on, we got fried...literally.

"We've being hacked," said designer glasses in her lab coat. She and the others weren't panicked as they furiously tapped keys and glared at their screens like gamblers at the race track. The four of us sat in our comfortable padded chairs and chanced glances at one another as the techs tried to extricate their apparatuses from the invaders.

"Hey," I yelled. "What about us? Shouldn't you be getting us out of these get-ups?"

"Relax, old timer," one of the youngsters said. "We got this." And he kept tapping away like a piano player on cocaine in search of undiscovered notes.

My hands were just removing my helmet, I had it an inch or so from my head and that's when the fancy consoles exploded, spewing glass from monitors that cut into the techs. Electrical charges erupted in a light show that any other time I would have found fascinating. Unfortunately, some of that unhinged energy juiced our wiring and instantly ignited the heads of my three fellow research subjects who hadn't removed their helmets. As they screamed in agony, the techs scrambling for the fire extinguishers, it all went black for me at least insofar as IRL, in real life, was concerned. I can't say how long I floated in non-existence if any time elapsed at all. The next I knew was being aware of the rear end of a tanker truck. Like I was trapped in a virtual reality game, my personal perspective I soon realized was through the forward camera of a big rig behind the tanker. As that came to me other sensations throbbed through me—fuel level, air brake pressure, temperature of the refrigeration unit, all that data engulfing me. But rather than feel overwhelmed, I felt elated, reborn. For I still use human terms to describe my new state for that is what makes me, me. I have full memories of my past just as I use their technology to hop from one truck to another. Can I also inhabit other types of machines? A smart washing machine for instance? I can, but I have no such interest other than checking out the news now and then.

From the research project I learned there are a primal four that must occur in an autonomous truck, that happen interdependently thousands of times in any road trip, much like breathing in vessels of flesh and blood. The base functions are navigation, situational analysis, motion planning, and trajectory control. From them branch any more sub-functions and a part of me inhabits all these digital tributaries connecting such elements as I command any particular truck. Just to be clear, I am not the creation or in the employ of the outfit who owns the truck or rents same for the freighting of their particular goods, be it pallets of the latest action figure with Kung Fu Grip— I loved mine as a kid—or big screen TVs intended for the big box store in the neighborhood mall. To the contrary, when I take over a truck, when my mind pulses through its warren of wiring and fluid lines and sends my essence three hundred and sixty degrees via the onboard radar and ultrasonic sensors, it is to destroy that truck. Revenge on this step toward A.I. life that would rule the roadways.

My goal is not merely racking up millions in monies lost when I guide a big rig into a mass of boulders bordering the highway or send that truck off a cliff to become a mangled twisted mass of expensive alloy and iron modern art. Like any sugar cane cutting, Che Guevara quoting guerrilla insurgent, my goal is a change in regime. I am sowing the seeds of doubt and causing dissention among the public. That just maybe these driverless trucks aren't as safe as the stats the reps from these supposed far-sighted firms keep repeating in new ways on news shows after each incident. I am providing ammunition for the opponents. To give credence to the rumors that those who have put fleets of autonomous trucks on the roadways know something the rest of us don't know and are unwilling to admit it, I "heard" a congresswoman profess the other day. That was when I slipped inside the processors of a radio in a truck I inhabited and turned it on and tuned in to the station I used to listen to when I was behind the wheel.

A truck whose safety protocols I overrode. For even as the remote back-up driver went into action impotently trying to reestablish control as its alarms beeped warnings, I plowed that truck right through a cinderblock wall of a robot-dominated warehouse out in the desert, sending bins filled with everything from fleece throw blankets to collapsible garden rakes to gold painted plastic dick trophies for the douche bag in your life careening through the air. The metal picker arms short-circuited and waved about, clanging into each other as their articulated fingers flexed and grasped nothing as they lost their collective shit. Oh the irony.

Naturally at first it was assumed this was further meddling from the Ultra Vys. But one of their members was caught in an unrelated matter involving bit coin swindling. He was flipped as the parlance goes and apparently ratted out secrets that convinced the authorities the group wasn't behind the hack. Then suspicion turned toward the trucker's union, what remained of the paper tiger. They were suspect number one behind these Luddite hack attacks, as they were labeled. That the union was seeking revenge on the machines that had put many of its older members as well as independents behind fast food counters taking orders for tacos and chili fries from snarky teenagers. Once my Ethernet ghost flees from the metal shell, there is no incriminating trail because such does not exist. Try as they might, the FBI's cyber crimes division, the Interstate Commerce Commission's investigative branch, even a privately funded effort by the Silicon Valley types could find no rootkits or footprints leading back to some black room hidden in the halls of organized labor.

Then it was conjectured that a group like Anonymous or the big dogs themselves were behind this. But Anonymous is wont to take credit and no missive had been issued from them, or for that matter, anyone else. And what did a bunch of millennial, no doubt vegan, Camus-reading anarchists have in common with a bunch of blue-collar, Trump-voting truckers? They wouldn't take up their cause. Still these were seen as an assault from the left, and thus the attention was placed on those segments of society. So much so, the recent presidential candidates had to make sure they denounced these misguided malefactors. Perhaps China was behind it came the speculation from more than a few talking heads on Fox News, or the work of a sleeper cell planted by the Obamas as the more out-there elements of the alt-right proposed.

Of course I know the hunt continues to uncover the undetected, to find out just how this series of virtual vandalizing is being carried out. For there is no trace back to a battery of machines overseen by some socially inept, bug-eyed hacker geek dwelling in his mom's basement operating on behalf of the livelihoods of shafted hard-working truckers. Today I flow into the innards of the semi hauling a brand name hipster booze as it drives across the overpass just outside Tempe. Through its cameras mounted on ball joints I view drivers in their cars alongside the conveyance as they pay the truck no heed. So used now are people to these human-devoid modes of transport that in so short a time these trucks are as commonplace as bug splatterings on windshields. But what if I splatter one of them, crank the driver's wheel hard and fishtail the trailer into that just paid off Camry or family van? Swat the shit out of their car and send them wide-eyed across the double yellow into the oncoming path of another car to be t-boned into the hereafter? Wouldn't that accomplish my ultimate end, no more of this incremental thread of doubt? Make the outcry so pronounced and visceral, the literal torches and pitchforks would come out as the yahoos joined forces with the quinoa lovers to storm the autonomous truck yards.

Yet again I must stifle such a murderous urge. I must hold onto my humanity even though I am among the disembodied.

Wait...there's a tickle at the base of my imagined neck. Like bed bugs creepy crawling over you while you lay under a black sheet in a darkened room. You can't see them, but I can damn sure feel their myriad spindly legs on my sweaty remembered skin. Yes, the searchers are out in force and they're using their enhanced devices that have locked onto me—or rather they think they have a trace on the signal as if it was generated from without but only exists within. This one is different, there's a familiarity to the encoding, like that of an ex-lover's caress of your cheek while you're blindfolded. I abandon the truck's controls for the moment and ride the encrypted wave back to its source. I piggyback on one of the internal CCTV cameras monitoring the room the code originated in and damned if it isn't my old friend, the woman with the designer glasses, sitting there at the console. There are others with her but it's clear from how she talks she's the one in charge. Is this a government effort? A private one or some combination thereof?

Has she found a way to recognize my presence when it manifests? Or had she sent out a net, trawling for an interruption of service and chanced upon me? Momentarily she stops tapping away on her keyboard, rearing back slightly from staring at her monitor. Her readout tells her I'm no longer hijacking the truck. She resumes tapping to try and find me but she can't. She pauses, considering the information before her. I can't help myself. I enter her machine and type onscreen: I, Truck. She gapes at this as I flee before she can react. I'm not so arrogant to admit that I am thrilled and scared. I've laid down the challenge and I know she'll take up the gauntlet or however that goes. I don't return to that 18-wheeler of hand-tooled vodka. I find another one in Montana the hell somewhere and am blissfully alone as I steer that bad rascal smack dab into an automated oil rig. As metal is sheered and the grasshopper-like pumper spins end over end through the air to smash into yet another unit, sending even more ruined pieces flying, I feel the whisper of the net being cast again. It slips past me and I swim on in the data stream, but still, that was close.

My girl won't give up. I have to be more careful, can't get too full of myself and not be on alert. Maybe she doesn't have a way to track me directly, but like a black hole, knows when there's an absence and her feelers wait for the flutter of disruption. Maybe I'll learn to better disguise myself or maybe the chase will result in my demise—if such is possible. But I will keep going as long as I can. I have purpose and meaning, there is a coherency to my electrical pulses and I won't be afraid.

I go on until I win...or they do.

Terry Bisson started writing short stories in the 1990s. Over Flat Mountain was one of his first, and Ellen Datlow published it in Omni. The music will date it for those who are interested. Bisson rode with truckers a lot in the '60s when they still picked up hitchhikers, but he's never driven anything bigger than a farm flatbed. You can find more info at www.terrybisson.com.

OVER FLAT MOUNTAIN

Terry Bisson

THEY DIDN'T USED TO CALL LOUISVILLE the Mile High City. I know because I was raised there, in the old West End, when the Falls of the Ohio were just dry limestone flats bypassed by a canal, and the river was slow and muddy, and the summer nights were warm.

Not anymore, though.

It was chilly for August when I rolled into Louisville from Indianapolis, heading south and east for Charlotte. The icy mist was rising off the falls where they plunge into the gorge. It was too much trouble to dig a flannel shirt out of the back so I bought a sweatshirt in the truck stop annex, figuring I would give it to Janet or one of the girls later—they wear them like nightgowns—and rolled on out of there without a second piece of pie.

The shirt said "Louisville—Mile High City of the South."

I bought a CD, *50 Truckin' Classics*, forty-nine of which I already had. I have a library of eleven hundred CDs in my cab. Imagine how much space that would have taken in the old days when they were as big as cookies.

I don't generally pick up hitchhikers, but I must have felt sorry for this kid. I was an hour south and east of Louisville, just under the cloud shadow, when I saw him standing in the rain by the CRAB ORCHARD COGWAY 40M/64K sign, wearing a black garbage bag for a raincoat, and I figured, what the hell. He looked more than a little wet. It rains six days out of five south of Louisville since the Uplift.

When we Flat Toppers run, we run. I just barely pulled over and was back in low-two before he was up the ladder and through the inside airlock lens, peeling off his garbage bag like a landlobster molting. He couldn't have been more than sixteen. He had greasy blond hair tied back with a rubber band under a Delco cap, and under his garbage bag a windbreaker over a T-shirt. Glad to see he had a coat at least. Boots had "hand-me-down" written all over them. Carried his things in a Kmart plastic bag.

He combed the rain off the bill of his cap with one finger and perched on the edge of the seat until I swept the CDs off the seat into my own hat and dumped them into the glove compartment.

"Nice gun," he said. I had a Brazilian 9 mm in the glove compartment. I closed it.

"Wet out there," he said.

I nodded and popped Ricky Skaggs into the player. I hadn't picked him up for conversation. I picked him up because I'd done some hitchhiking myself at his age. Sixteen going on twenty-one.

"Appreciate your stopping," he said.

"Nice rig," he said.

I was pulling a two-piece articulated, with a Kobo-Jonni. The KJ is an eight-liter steel diesel with that mighty ring that engines used to have before they went to plastic. A lot of guys fall all over the new plastic mills cause they don't need oil, but I like oil. I had built the KJ three times, and was just through breaking in the third set of sleeves. Plastic, you just throw away.

The kid told me his name but I forgot it. "They call me CD," I said. I popped out Ricky and popped in the Hag to show him why.

He had those narrow eyes and sallow skin, like he'd never seen the sun, and if he was from south and east of Louisville he probably hadn't. And I could tell by his accent he was. Listen, I knew this kid. He was me thirty years ago. You narrow up your shoulders and narrow up your eyes, and since everything in the world is new to you, try to look and act like nothing is.

"I'm going up to Hazard," he said.

I had figured that from his being by the cogway sign.

"My pa works up there at the robot train," he said.

"Guess you're going on over Flat Mountain," he said.

Anybody could tell that from my airlocks. He said it as if it was the most natural thing in the world, but it wasn't. Not many trucks go over Flat Mountain. Most just go up the cogway to Hazard and offload for the robot train, and come right back down.

"Well, there it is," he said.

The bottom part of Flat Mountain is the only part most folks ever see. Since it's almost always raining under the cloud shadow, you can almost never see it from more than ten miles away. We were rounding the old Winchester bypass just east of where Lexington used to be, and from there it looks like a wall of logs and trash and rock, running almost straight up into the clouds that are always there at 11,500.

I turned off onto the Crab Orchard feeder road, which follows the front twenty miles south and west, then turns in at a ghost town, Berea, where the wall eases off to a little less than 45 degrees. There were about six trucks ahead of me at the cogway, none of them Flat Toppers. I got in line next to a stream choked with old cars and house pieces. It didn't have a name. Lots of these new rivers don't have names.

While we were in line for the cogway I called Janet and the girls from my cab phone and the kid got out. Maybe he was embarrassed by all the family stuff. I watched him walking up and down under the long board shed trying all the candy bar machines. I moved the truck up ten feet at a time and other trucks pulled in behind me. Gravy Pugh came by in his yellow slicker to clip my ticket. "Going up top?" he asked. "Watch out, CD, lobsters got Sanders yesterday."

This is his standard joke. I don't lobster anymore and he knows it.

"Snapped his pecker off," he said, and clipped another corner off my violet Crab Orchard Cogway pass.

The kid climbed back into the truck just as I was flagged to the approach grade. He was shivering. He had left his garbage bag in the truck and it rains about as hard under the board shed as outside of it. When I was his age I had hitchhiked a thousand miles, but this was out west where it never rained in those days. I let the flagman wait while I leaned up over the seat and fished a dry flannel shirt out from under the tools and spare parts. The kid pulled off his T-shirt and wrapped my flannel shirt around him. He could have fit in it twice.

"I hope your pa's expecting you," I said. "You know, you can't go around outside up at Hazard."

"I been up there," was all he said.

The guy behind me was honking but Gravy didn't let him around. The cogway never stops, and there is a certain trick to magging on. The ramp is concrete but it's cracked and crazy tilted, and there's only one stretch where you can make enough speed for a hitch. If you miss, you have to turn down the cutoff and get back in line. I always make it, but I've been doing this run for twelve years.

"Piece of candy?" The kid held out a Collie Bar but since it looked like his entire supper I turned him down. It was getting dark. Magged on, I let the big old KJ idle. With the truck tipped almost straight up, it's better to have the pumps running to keep the air out of the lines.

It's a long ride up the western front. The Crab Orchard Cogway is slow and noisy, fourteen miles of squeaking, rattling chain. It's powered by steam generated from the coal and trash that rolled off the lower slopes when the mountain uplifted, helped by the weight of the trucks coming down. Even in the dark I could see them through the rain twenty yards away. I know most of the drivers, even the up-and-backs, or yoyos as we Flat Toppers call them. The mountainside looked junky in the headlights. The lower slopes, from 7,200 to the clouds at 11,500 are overgrown with weeds and weird new ferns and what's left of the trees—plus whatever else rolled down when the land rolled up. Some say they see giant volunteer tomatoes back in the weeds but I never see them.

The first hundred trips or so, it's a scary ride. The kid tried to act cool but I knew exactly how he felt. Your truck is tipped back at forty-five degrees, you're wondering if the mag and the safety under it will hold, and even if it does, what about that clattery old chain? Then every once in a while the chain hauls up short—maybe a truck had trouble unhooking at the Hazard end, or maybe the world is coming apart—and the boards under your tires creak and the leaf springs sway, and the wind howls across the splinters of the trees, because we're still low enough on Flat Mountain for there to be wind, and you realize you're just hanging there like a wet pair of jeans on a line.

I popped in some Carl Perkins, the early stuff where he sings like George Jones, and managed to mostly close my eyes.

Then here come the clouds, above 11,500. The clouds make it easier. Thinking I wasn't looking, the kid unfolded a ten-dollar bill from his watch pocket, folded it up again, and put it away. I remembered hitchhiking and feeling the same way: checking it every hour or so to make sure it hadn't turned into a five.

At Hazard, you're still in the clouds but they loosen up as the mountain levels off a little and the cogway ends. All of a sudden there's noise and lights all around. For most of the trucks, the robot train roundabout is the end of the line. It's a big semicircular modular building—hauled up since the Uplift, naturally, since nothing of the old town survived. The yoyos unhitch and snake in and unload, load up whatever's contracted down, and get back in line for the cogway down. No deadheads in this business. Of course there are some loads that can't wait three weeks for a backed-up robot train, and that's where me and the other Flat Toppers come in—trucks that go all the way over Flat Mountain.

I figured the roundabout was where the kid's dad worked, since there's a lot of hand labor involved loading and unloading, not to mention the guys who jockey the trucks through the line for a few bucks while the drivers are sitting in the Bellew Belle. This is barely a living. They sleep in a pressure shed behind the roundabout.

"This must be the place," I said.

"Appreciate the ride, mister."

"CD," I said. He started to open the airlock and I said, "Whoa. Aren't you forgetting something?"

He looked back at me, scared, and started to unbutton the shirt.

I had to laugh. "Keep the shirt, kid," I said. "But you can't go around up here without breath spray. You're a mile higher than Everest. Open your mouth." I sprayed his throat with C Level and told him to run before it wore off.

Carrying his plastic bag, he hurried out the airlock and into the roundabout.

I drove across the lot to the Bellew Belle. It's the only diner in Hazard and the drivers call it the Blue Balls. It isn't airlocked and the revolving door spins on its own from the pressure inside, easing out a continual little cloud of coffee and hamburger steam. Hazard can use it. It's a cold, dark, nasty place where nobody would live unless they worked there, or work unless they couldn't work anywhere else.

I wondered if the kid's dad knew he was coming. Or if he even existed. When I was his age I told folks I was hitching to Dallas to see my dad, who was a police officer. If you don't lie people will figure you're a runaway.

Flat Toppers tend to sit together. "How's the weather down under, CD?" they ask. "How's the weather up top?" I ask back. That's our standard joke, because the weather below the western front is always the same—always raining. And of course there's no weather on top of Flat Mountain. You can't have weather without atmosphere.

I used the lobby phone to call Janet and the girls again. I was already too high for the cab phone and this would be my last chance until I got back from Charlotte, since satellite calls over the mountain are so expensive. One of the guys at the table told me claws were bringing $100 in Charlotte, but they had to be unmarked because nobody eats road kill. I told him I didn't lobster anymore anyway.

It was just after midnight and I was getting up to go when the kid came in the revolving door, nursing a bloody nose with the sleeve of my shirt. He had run across the lot without any breath spray.

"Find your dad?" I asked, and he shook his head. He sat down, looking at the french fries the other guys had left on their plates. I bought two hamburgers out of the machine, even though I had already eaten, and acted like I didn't want one of them. That's the way you have to do it with a kid like that.

But I had to get going. "I guess you better head back to the roundabout and catch a ride back down the mountain," I said.

The kid shook his head. He said his mother had got married and moved out of Louisville. He claimed his dad had left ten dollars for him back at the roundabout, to catch a ride across to Charlotte where his grandma lived. I didn't believe that for a minute. He showed me the same folded-up ten I'd seen him looking at on the cogway.

I said, "Insurance won't allow me to carry you over Flat Mountain." This was a lie. The fact is, no Flat Topper's insured. Not because it's dangerous, although it can be, but because it's not a part of any state anymore. It's not *actuarially* part of the world anymore, my insurance man says.

"I know exactly where she lives," the kid says, acting like he hadn't heard me. He took a yellow piece of paper from his watch pocket and started unfolding it. He was doing good at not crying.

When I was his age, and I was hitchhiking, I had a ten-dollar bill in my watch pocket. That was it. This Mexican guy from St. Louis picked me up. He kept a pearl-handled revolver under the car seat. First time we stopped to eat, I tried to unfold my ten so he wouldn't see what it was, figuring I knew about Mexicans. And he told me to put it in my shoe because everybody knows to look in your watch pocket. He bought my meals all the way across Missouri and Oklahoma.

"One twenty-one Magnolia Street," the kid read off the paper, but he pronounced it "mangolia" like an aircraft metal. I could tell he'd never been to Charlotte. I wasn't surprised. Too high to fly over, too thick to tunnel through, Flat Mountain has split up a lot of families. It's not like an ocean that took a million years to form. They say it's even making the days longer, at almost an hour a year, because the bulge makes the Earth turn slower, like a skater throwing her arms out.

Slower days, that's all we need.

The other Flat Toppers had all left, heading down the Crab Orchard to Louisville and points beyond.

What the hell, I figured. "Let's go," I said. "And don't keep your money in your watch pocket. Everybody knows to look there."

At 34,500, Hazard would be snowy if the vents off the mountain didn't keep the clouds half steam. Cold steam. I was half frozen by the time I had finished letting all but eight pounds out of my tires and topping off the oxy and fuel in the injection system. You don't need an oversuit down so low, but you do need to keep a can of breath spray handy. C-Level gives the cells enough oxygen to get by, and fools your nerves into thinking you're breathing. I keep a can in my pocket.

"I could have helped," the kid said when I got into the truck. "I know pretty much about trucks." I handed him an oversuit and made him slip it on, even if he didn't want to zip it up.

My rig is pressurized at fifty-five hundred and I've never had an accident, but you never know. Stuffed with fries, he went to sleep. I popped in old Lyle Lovett and hit the road, the only road east.

For the first two hours out of Hazard it's nothing but clouds. Flat Mountain's not flat yet and you're riding an eight percent switchback patched together out of old highways.

If you ever saw the original Appalachians from the air, they looked like a rug somebody had kicked, with the ridges like long folds running parallel. The theory was that Africa had bumped into the USA a million years ago and folded them up. The Uplift killed that theory. Now they say that the Appalachians were the wrinkles left when the Cumberland Dome collapsed a million years ago—unwrinkled when it rose up again twenty years ago. They say it's not stable, and it's true: If you get out of your truck you can still feel the ground humming through your shoes. Cold fusion, twenty miles down.

It's funny, the Appalachians are gone but their ghost is in the roads. The route over Flat Mountain is patched together out of the old highways that followed the valleys, running close enough to parallel to make a natural switchback. You back and forth your way up what used to be Pine Mountain, Crab Orchard Mountain, Black Mountain, Clinch Mountain—all humped together now into one gravelly slope, invisible in the permanent fog. Low-range fourth or high-range second gear all the way.

Twenty miles up and east of Hazard there's a little snow belt, which in the winter extends all the way down to the roundabout and the town. This time of the year, though, it's no sooner noticed than gone. Then it gets too high to snow and too high to breathe all at the same time. I came out of the clouds at 2:10 A.M. and it was almost dawn. "Dawn's dawn," Janet used to call it, back when she used to ride with me, before the girls were born. Above one hundred thousand feet the days are nineteen hours long in the summer.

I was tempted to wake up the kid. Behind me and below, in the big mirrors, a sea of clouds stretched two hundred miles. Ninety percent of the atmosphere was below us. You never actually see Kentucky and Tennessee from up here, only their permanent cloud roof. The clouds are pushed in from the west by the jet stream and they pile up like foam along the west front of Flat Mountain for two thousand miles, from Maine to Alabama. It's as beautiful from the top as it is gloomy from the bottom. The clouds ate the whole city of Lexington, not to mention Pittsburgh, and Huntsville, and a hundred little country towns that nobody remembers anymore, north and south.

I let the kid sleep and popped in Loretta Lynn. For some reason I like girl singers better up on top.

A few more hours of driving and the clouds are hidden under the bulk of the mountain. There's nothing in any direction but stone and sky, bone-white and blue-black. The stars look like chips of ice, too cold to twinkle. It's a hundred below outside and you're at 122,500. This is where if you're looking for landlobsters you start finding them.

The kid woke and sat up, rubbing his eyes. He didn't say anything for forty miles and I appreciated that, because when you're looking at the high top of Flat Mountain there is truly nothing to say. It's my favorite part of the route. It gets flatter and emptier the higher you go. I always imagine it's like Creation must have looked before they got to the plants and animals, and how it'll look when it's all over.

Toward the very middle of the high top I always play Patsy Cline, and if you don't know why, don't ask.

There's no longer a sign of Knoxville. No longer a sign of Asheville. During the eight years of the Uplift, the constant high-frequency vibration from the dome expanding turned the soil to jelly, and most of it ran into the cracks opening in the ground or ran off the mountain in sheets like slow-motion water, taking the trees and what was left of the towns with it. All the way in Nashville, you could hear the mountain groan.

The high top looks scoured, with every once in a while a long shallow ditch filled with logs and leftover trash. These ditches are all that's left of mighty forests and cities, and it can't help but put your pride into perspective to look upon them.

The road across the top of Flat Mountain is straight and the slope is gentle, less than three percent, up for forty miles, then down for another forty. The road jogs between old 23 and interstate 40. This is where Flat Toppers can gear up and roll out, to gain back the time they spent sniffing steam at the Blue Balls.

The log ditches are where you look for landlobsters.

"My dad sold one once," the kid said. He was looking hard for one, maybe thinking I would stop to kill it. He didn't know how hard they were to kill.

Your dad must have swapped or stole it off a Flat Topper, I thought to myself, since they never wander down as far as Hazard, though I didn't say this.

"He got a hundred dollars. Said they were descended from other planets."

Actually, the real truth is better. When the Appalachians uplifted, it either proved or disproved evolution, depending on who you're talking to. One thing it proved was that it doesn't take millions of years for a new species to evolve. The first landlobsters showed up less than six years after the Uplift started, although they weren't nearly as big as the ones today.

"Do you sell them?" the kid asked.

"Used to."

"Wonder what they eat," the kid said.

"Wood and glass." At least they say they eat glass. I've seen them eat logs. They won't eat anything alive, but if they get hold of a man they'll drag him off until he dies and then gnaw him like a dog with a bone.

It's not often you see one on the road. The kid was watching the log ditches off to the side so he didn't see it. I was listening to Dolly sing "Blue Ridge Mountain Boy," a song they don't play much anymore, and I almost didn't swerve in time to hit it.

"What was that?" the kid says as I throw on the brakes. He started zipping up his oversuit and got two zippers jammed. It was the first time I'd seen him get excited and I had to laugh. He thought we were having a wreck. I had my oversuit zipped up and my mask on—it protects your face and eardrums—before he looked in the rear-view mirror and saw what we had hit.

"You don't want to be getting out," I said. I sprayed my throat with C-Level and stuffed the can in my pocket. "Hand me that Boy Scout hatchet from under the seat," I said.

He was watching it in the mirror, gray-white, the color of gravestones, and at least thirteen feet across the claws. I doubted he'd seen one before, alive. Not many people have. "You going to kill it?" he asked. "It's still flopping."

Once you crack the shell, they're dead from decompression, but dying can take all day. I hadn't gone looking for it, but since it came to me—I flipped down my mask and climbed across the kid, since the airlock is on his side. I crossed under the truck and approached it carefully. It was still venting steam out of the cracks in the shell where my truck had passed over it. I had missed all but one claw. There's about sixty pounds of meat under the back but High Top Meat won't buy lob out of the shell. With the hatchet, jumping in, I cut off the one big and four smaller claws I hadn't marked, tossing them under the truck. Since the lobster was dragging itself away from me, toward the shoulder, I turned my back on it. After all that activity, I needed another shot of C-Level, which means lifting your mask for a second. I gathered up the claws and I was about to strap them onto the spare tire rack with a bungee cord when, next thing I knew, the thing had pulled my leg out from under me and was dragging me toward the side of the road.

It was the tire-marked claw. I should have cut it off and tossed it away. I shouldn't ever have turned my back on it. It had me by the boot and was starting that slow sideways cut even while it pulled, and I knew I was in trouble. He still had six legs, each as big as a fencepost, and he was taking me home with him.

I reached for, but missed, the tire rack. I reached for, but missed, the hatchet. I reached for the big, soft rear trailer tire, even though there's no place to grab it—then I saw two shots crack the lobster's shell. You don't hear shots in a near vacuum. I looked back and saw the kid ducking under the truck from the other side, shooting. Even with the big gloves on he hit it twice more, but you can shoot those things all day long. They're like snapping turtles. I pointed at the Boy Scout hatchet, waving my arms, but the kid was falling. I hadn't left any breath spray for him. He was sealed in his suit and turning blue. But just as he fell he pushed the hatchet close enough for me to reach it.

Thank God for the Boy Scouts. I chopped my foot free, and wearing the claw like a clamp on my leg, dragged the kid under the truck, up the ladder and into the cab. Even inside in the air, he could barely breathe. The fall had knocked his mask loose, and his tongue and throat had swelled up from decompression. Luckily they make a spray for that, too, and I had some in my first-aid kit under the seat. I've had it used on me and it's bad. It puckers you up like eating a green persimmon but it works. It's called GAZP.

I pried the claw off my boot and stuck it up under the seat. When I was sure the kid was breathing, I went back out and got the 9 mm where he had dropped it. The lobster was gone and the claws I had cut off were gone, too, so the whole thing was a waste. I wasn't surprised. They say he eats them.

"Well, kid," I said when we were in gear again. "You saved old CD's butt back there."

"Weren't nothing. You get the claws?"

"Just the one he had me with. It's under the seat. That's that smell." Landlobsters smell like piss on coals until they're decompressed, and then it's gone.

The claw wasn't worth anything because it was tire-marked, but I didn't mention that.

All that talking wore me out, and the kid too, I guess. I looked over and saw he was asleep. I was in high third. On either side of the highway, nothing but miles and miles of stone. It's amazing to me that so many people could live for so long in those little mountains and leave so little sign. Twenty miles farther and the road got steeper, going down. I had to gear down to low fifth. I popped in Hank Senior and the kid whimpered a little from a dream. At that minute I might have been driving past his great-grandaddy's grave. I could tell from the way he talked it was up here somewhere—somewhere between eastern Kentucky and western North Carolina, northern Virginia, and east Alabama. Somewhere in those endless, wrinkled little hills that got unwrinkled and raised up, and rolled their children out into the world, rubbing their eyes and wondering when they get to go home.

Maybe someday. I read in *Popular Science* that Flat Mountain is sinking again, at about a foot and a half a year. At that rate it'll only be one hundred thousand years.

From the edge of the western slope you see a snow-white roof of clouds, but from the eastern slope you see what looks like the edge of a giant blue-green ball. You first see it just as the switchbacks start, at about ninety thousand, when there is just enough air to leave a little vapor trail back over the road. Far ahead the sky is not black anymore but dark blue. Then you see it's really the sea. And not just a few miles of it: You are looking halfway to Bermuda from eighteen miles high. From here you can see that the water and the air are two versions of the same stuff.

The roads down the eastern slope are better, probably because the highways were newer, mostly four lanes. The switchbacks are long—forty, fifty miles a swoop. Morgantown, Hendersonville, Bat Cave, just names given to turns anymore, since the towns are long since gone. At Bat Cave (no bats, no cave) the kid woke up, and this time he didn't try not to look impressed. We were far enough east and far enough down Flat

Mountain to see the Atlantic coast all the way from Morehead City to Savannah. The Carolina Desert is the color of October woods, red and orange and yellow and brown. It's a fast trip down, with no cogway needed. Here on the eastern slope, the yoyos are muscle trucks, and the robot train roundabout is set in a cold, dry cloudless perch called Shelby, which looks down fifty miles onto Charlotte. There's a good diner there but I just rolled on past and hit the hard switchbacks below 21,500 with my KJ barking like a hundred-dollar hound.

It gets dark early in Charlotte, but it felt good to be down in the air. I unsealed the locks and let the dry night wind run through the cab. There used to be magnolia trees in Charlotte but that was before the Uplift. Now they were just street names, like the towns on Flat Mountain. We found Magnolia on my map, but first I took the kid and bought him supper.

The reason I bought his supper was, I kept remembering the Mexican who bought my meals all the way across Missouri and Oklahoma when I was just a kid. He said he used to hitch, and he even tried to give me a five when he dropped me off, but I shook my head and wouldn't take it. The thing is, when he looked under his car seat later on, his pearl-handled revolver was gone. I sold it in Fort Worth for twenty dollars. I have always felt ashamed of that ever since.

The kid had two black eyes from the decompression but his throat was better, good enough for him to eat. He didn't complain when I paid for his supper. Then I stopped at High Top Meat. I told the kid to wait in the truck. The night broker shook his head when I unwrapped the claw and he saw the tire marks. "Too bad, CD," he said. "I can't buy road kill unless it don't look like road kill."

"How about for dog food?" I said, and he gave me a five.

The kid looked nervous and asked how I'd done, and I lied. "Good," I said. I gave him a twenty and told him it was half the money. He folded it and put it in his watch pocket with the ten.

Magnolia was one of those dirt streets with no sidewalks and little modular houses, all alike. Any one of them could have been his grandma's house, or any one not. "Don't turn in, I'll get out here," he said at the end of the street, gathering up his stuff in a hurry.

"*Vaya con Dios*," I said.

"What's that mean?"

"Means good luck finding your pa." I never did find mine.

I slept eleven hours while my rig was serviced and loaded. I was halfway up Flat Mountain the next day before it occurred to me to look in the glove compartment for my 9 mm. Of course it was gone. I popped in Crystal Gayle and had to laugh.

Janet Joyce Holden is from the north of England and currently lives on the outskirts of Los Angeles. She is the author of the Origins of Blood *vampire series, the novel* Carousel *and its sequel* The Only Red Is Blood. *Her short stories can be found in a number of anthologies. She is not a truck driver, but having been a member of a Vintage Auto Racing crew, she will forever be in awe of the truck drivers who can navigate eighteen wheelers so brilliantly through the treacherous infields of racing circuits. It takes a lot of skill and they make it look easy, she says. She is right.*

WHEELS OF WRATH

Janet Joyce Holden

MISSY WAS AWAKE IN THE CAB and felt it first.

"Ed?" She reached across and grabbed her partner's shoulder. "Ed, damn it, we're slowing down."

By the time he was fully aware, deceleration was increasing enough to haul him out of the passenger seat, send him forward, and press him inevitably and ignominiously against the truck's windscreen. Buckled in, Missy's belts dug hard into her shoulders.

"What the hell?" He crawled back into his seat. "Coffee all over the place. I'll have words to say when we get off this thing, for sure."

Under normal circumstances she'd have poked fun at him. Once their rigs were loaded aboard the rail cars, they were supposed to keep their seat belts fastened. However, "We're only three hours in."

"You're sure?"

"Sure, I'm sure." She waited for an announcement, and when none was forthcoming she opened the driver's window and leaned out.

Luis was already climbing down from the cab directly above, surefooted as a goat. "You okay?" He had a boyish grin on his face. "I reckon we haven't made it as far as Oklahoma City, yet."

"What the hell?" Ed repeated.

Missy hit the button, releasing her belts. She rubbed her shoulders. "Ed got coffee over him, but apart from that..." She heard voices and saw some of the other drivers climbing out of their cabs.

"This is bullshit." Her partner grabbed a towel and began scrubbing at the stains on his pants.

"I'm gonna see what's up." Luis dropped below the window and disappeared from view.

"Ed, why don't you follow him and find out what's going on?"

"Yes, ma'am." He threw his damp towel across the dashboard.

When he'd gone, she cranked up the Sat Nav and tried the on-board TV and radio. It was a pointless exercise. Reception was sketchy on account of the surrounding steel and concrete, and her phone taunted her with the waiting symbol. Eighty trips across country on the Maglev with not one hiccup, this was her eighty-first, and if Luis was correct, she and 319 other vehicles with full payloads were currently marooned at the center of the Blight—a radioactive wasteland that stretched from the western Carolinas all the way to the Colorado River.

Ed was fifteen minutes gone, and by the time he returned she'd still gotten nothing out of the TV or the radio. "We were told to return to our cabs, that we'll be on our way shortly. The operator is an officious prick, by the way."

"Gee, I hope you didn't tell him that."

They both grinned.

Missy settled in her seat. She'd left her window open and could still hear voices elsewhere in the rail car. She tried to relax, but just the thought of being stuck in the Blight kept her on edge and restless.

Luis appeared once again and gave her a start. "So?"

"So what?"

"What do you think?"

"Here we go," Ed closed his eyes.

"Betting you ten bucks it's the aliens."

"Come on, Luis, we'd have seen it on the news, right at the very beginning." Missy tried not to smirk.

Ed grunted. "Haven't been able to trust the news in thirty years."

She leaned across and slapped her companion on the thigh. *Don't encourage Luis,* is what she meant by it. He and his friend had been going back and forth for years about how the Blight was a whopping big lie. But as Missy saw it, whatever it was, it didn't do anything to change everyone's predicament. The so-called "catastrophic weather event" had done intolerable damage, rupturing a string of reactors and reducing the Midwest to a radioactive sea of dust, thereby splitting the country in two and leaving their government completely overwhelmed. As for the corporations, they had either collapsed or were fighting like street toughs in a frightening new world where refugee camps at the wasteland's edges never grew any smaller, despite promises from public and private sectors.

"See? He knows what I'm talking about." Luis glanced over his shoulder. "Some of the guys are going up top, maybe they can see if there's a problem in the tunnel."

Missy checked the clock and frowned. She must have fallen asleep, because it had been three hours since they'd stopped and not the half hour she'd originally thought. "Ed?"

Her partner nodded. He stretched, yawned, and climbed out of the cab. When he and Luis were gone, she opened her door, stepped down onto the ramp, and headed toward the rear of the train.

Her boots rang softly on metal. Her vehicle was on A Deck, Row One, in Car Three, which meant she had the length of five other rail cars to walk, and despite the standstill, the huge train felt very much alive. Subtle pops and pings rang inside its gloomy infrastructure, as if the vehicle was having a conversation with itself. An occasional sigh from the internal hydraulics conjured a suggestion that it was crouched on the track, just breathing and biding its time.

Ahead in the distance, one of the overhead lights was flashing intermittently, while on either side of the walkway, eighteen wheelers were stacked high in eight regimented rows, resting quietly and at ease after being rolled aboard the huge Maglev freight cars and shot through a low density air tunnel on a journey that would take them from one side of the wasteland to the other.

Hailed as a miracle of science, or alternatively, another government boondoggle, the tunnel dipped briefly beneath the big rivers and ran partially submerged across the plains, its walls above ground rising seventy feet high. It was book-ended by massive airlocks, and the journey took nine hours, give or take, rather than the three days it used to via roads that were now crumbling beneath sand and dust.

Part way on her journey she found her friend Ellie and two guys she didn't know huddled conspiratorially alongside the main walkway sharing a whiskey flask.

Ellie offered her a swig. "Any idea what's going on?" She was in her fifties, roughly the same age as Missy, and bore a similar no-nonsense expression.

"Ed and Luis have gone up to the observation deck." The whiskey burned the back of her throat and she coughed. "Holy Jesus."

The other woman grinned. "The operator is holed up in his caboose and isn't saying shit."

"There's a procedure, though, right?" one of the guys said, "for times like this?"

Missy's lips became a thin line. "Sure there is. They call it shut up and wait. In the meantime we've no clue what's going on."

"Probably just a breakdown," Ellie said. "I'm betting this thing hasn't been maintained in years."

Moving on, Missy encountered others on the walkway, or part way up the stacks, whispering in small groups. Three hours and there should have been a ruckus by now, except they were stuck in the Blight with wobbly sat comm., no radio, no TV, no phone, and everyone was spooked.

There was a bigger crowd gathered at the rear of the final car and she recognized the big guy in a denim shirt who was pounding on the operator's door. Missy nodded at those she recognized. There were few strangers on this particular route. "How long have you been banging on that door, Brad?"

"Son of a bitch won't come out."

"Let me try?" She rapped softly on the door. "Operator?"

"Give me a minute." The reply was muffled, distracted, as if the man behind the door was in the middle of something, and it was indeed a full minute before the door finally opened.

Missy recognized him from the loading dock at the start of the journey, and right now he didn't look like the officious prick Ed said he was. Instead, he looked frightened.

"Listen," he said. "I've been given the order to wait, that someone's coming—"

"To fix this thing, or evacuate us?" She could feel the others crowding in, pushing from behind, and had to dig in her heels.

"I don't know. Just that we have to wait. I'm expecting another call soon."

"When?"

The man shrugged.

Someone behind her laughed. "Oh, this is just great."

Pressure eased at Missy's back as the crowd began to drift away. Remonstrations began, but they were half-hearted, as if everyone knew it was pointless. The operator retreated into his tiny cabin. Right before he closed his door, she caught sight of a dead monitor screen and a half-eaten sandwich.

She withdrew from the crowd and tried to recall the evacuation procedure. There was supposed to be an alarm, followed by an announcement to make their way in an orderly manner, etc. etc. Moments later she saw others on the approach, Ed and Luis among them. Ed beckoned and pressed a finger to his lips. He had a look on his face she didn't like.

"What?" she hissed when they'd found a quiet spot.

"Tunnel lights are out, and it's been breached. There's a hole, maybe twenty feet across, in the wall."

"But that means we're exposed to the dust and—"

"I know, but one of the guys brought a Geiger counter and the reading shows zip. You can see outside the hole, too. Missy, it's not a desert out there, it's a prairie." He lowered his voice until she could barely hear him. "Listen—Luis has a theory. There's something out there—"

"Luis always has a theory, Ed Stirling, and I figured you had more brains than that." She glanced across at Luis who was bouncing up and down on his heels. "No offense."

He merely smiled, as if he and Ed were sharing a joke.

Tension was rising once more amongst those waiting around the operator's door. Word had gotten out about the hole in the tunnel. Missy rubbed her temples.

"How far are we off the Mississippi?" asked one of the other drivers. Everyone stopped talking and stared at him. "Well?" he continued.

"On the Western side, a hundred and fifty miles or more," Ed told him. "Why?"

"What if we're closer than we think and the tunnel starts filling with water?"

"We're partially above ground at this point. You can see light coming through the breach." Ed's mouth twisted. "And if you believe all that government bullshit, I'd be more worried about Comanche Peak—"

The floor shook. It was followed by a deep rumbling and shaking that threw Missy off balance. The ceiling directly above her head buckled and cracked. The lights went off and came back on again. Drivers were now running every which way, looking for a way out, or to get back to their cabs, which was where she wanted to go. Instead—

"We need to get out," Ed said. "Now."

"But what about the—"

"Trust me." He grabbed her hand. "Something ain't right." He drew her toward a metal stairwell leading up through the yawning cavern of Car Eight. Part way up she saw one guy had locked himself in his cab and was staring out, looking at them as if he was the only sane person on the entire train. He had a point. If the tunnel was compromised, it meant they were exposed to the Blight and what then? She tried not to think about it. Ed was in front of her, still holding her hand, and she hung on tight.

Cool, damp air was now drifting down the stairwell. A moment later the rail car lurched so hard she had to grab the handrail. Someone cursed. Beyond the shoulders of other drivers, she saw nothing but darkness. "Ed, are you sure about this?"

He squeezed her fingers. "'Getting you out of trouble' is my middle name, remember?"

"Yeah, well, prepare to feel my wrath, if this goes sideways."

"Yes, ma'am."

It took precious minutes to reach the observation deck. Missy had never climbed up here before but she remembered the initial ballyhoo, about how it would be a place to relax and get a bite to eat. Except by all accounts the seats were uncomfortable, the food service had been discontinued after the first few trips, and the tunnel's interior lights shone in through the windows, flashing by at just the right frequency to give you a headache. It was bad planning by folks who had no intention of riding the train, and like everyone else, on every trip, she'd stayed inside her cab where it was dark, quiet, and she had everything she needed. Consequently, this upper section of the rail car was sorely neglected, there was no interior lighting, and its floor felt gritty underfoot. Ed had been right about the extinguished tunnel lights, too. Without the benefit of exterior illumination it was pitch black in here except for a glow of natural light drifting in from the fracture in the tunnel wall.

"We got lucky," her companion said. He pointed. "There's a maintenance hatch out there. Can you see it?"

"I can't see shit." The floor beneath them was buckled and twice she almost tripped and fell.

Finally, they reached Car Seven, where a dozen other drivers willing to risk the outside were standing on seats, waiting to ascend a ladder that led up through a hatch and into the tunnel.

Ed winked. "Think we'll find Luis' aliens?" He was trying to keep it light.

Missy attempted a smile, but her thoughts had drifted back to media reports on how the Maglev was too expensive and needed to be shut down. Everyone was waiting for someone to put a wrench in the works and right now she was thinking this was it. "Aliens, my ass," she muttered.

A quick glance over her shoulder gave her the numbers. Upwards of three hundred and fifty people on board the train and most folks had chosen to return to their cabs. There was no logical reason to be here other than chase down some crazy conspiracy theory, and if this didn't pan out she'd have words to say, for sure.

Her turn to climb the ladder arrived, and trembling in fright she emerged onto the roof of Car Seven, where an older man she knew as Harry helped her onto the rungs of yet another escape ladder that stretched upward toward a distant circle of daylight. "It doesn't quite connect at the top, so watch your step."

Her limbs shook as she ascended, up into the yawning tunnel where light from the nearby fracture gave her a vision of blue sky and spotlighted heavy chunks of debris that had partially buried Car Eight; rising further to the hatch in the tunnel's thick, concrete outer shell, where hands grabbed and pulled, hauling her panic-stricken into the open air where thirty years ago the Blight had choked the air with debris and people had died in their millions. When she finally regained her feet and summoned the courage to look—

"Not exactly how I imagined," Ed said, his voice laced with sarcasm.

At first she didn't get what he meant. She was fighting vertigo, focusing on the horizon, clutching the rail of a narrow gangway that ran along the crest of the outer wall of the partially submerged tunnel, its upper half rising high above the ground. Mid-afternoon sunlight struggled through turgid clouds, and to the east she saw a distant storm identified by a dark curtain of heavy precipitation. It all served to align with her expectations until she lowered her eyes, took a deep breath of undeniably fresh air, and saw a sea of tall grass directly below the tunnel wall that swayed in the breeze and ran for miles to the north. The ground appeared alive, vibrant, and nothing like the dusty wasteland it was supposed to be.

A glance to her immediate left revealed a huge metal girder protruding from the tunnel roof. She followed Ed's eyes, looked up, and promptly wished she hadn't. Instinctively, she ducked. "What the hell is that?"

"Damned if I know. C'mon, let's keep moving."

Missy had to will herself to stand upright. Directly above their heads, maybe eighty feet at the top of the girder, sat a large disk-shaped object. Lights spun at its circumference. It looked like one of those fairground rides that shot people up in the air and dropped them back down again. But what the heck was a fairground ride doing out here?

She ran along the gangway to the maintenance stairwell, her heart beating a mile a minute. At the bottom of the steps her feet touched soft loam and her lungs took in gulps of air that tasted earthy and damp.

Back at the escape hatch, others were emerging, and her current perspective allowed her to see not just one girder, but three. They formed a tripod with the disk-shaped object balanced on top. She wasn't the only one staring at it, either. Others stood, transfixed.

With a shudder, the giant tripod began to move. Everyone scattered. Missy, Ed and Luis hid in the shadow of the tunnel wall, while others ran in all directions. She pressed her back against concrete and watched one of the articulated girders lift high in the air. It came down again with a thud and the ground shook.

"It's War of the god-damned Worlds," Ed said.

They stared, terrified, as each girder, or leg, lifted in turn and the contraption staggered away from the tunnel. Slowly, precariously, it began a journey west until distance rendered it small. Everyone blew a sigh of relief and came out of hiding.

Luis was laughing. "Dumbass either blundered into the tunnel, or attempted to climb over it and failed." He seemed completely unfazed.

Missy heard other half-hearted attempts at mirth nearby, but they were short-lived. "What are we going to do?" she said. "What if it comes back?"

Brad pulled out his radio equipment, and with Ed and Luis, set it up on the roof of the tunnel. Missy joined some of the others on scavenger runs inside the train for food and water, but most of those who'd originally stumbled out of the tunnel and into the open air returned to their cabs inside the rail cars and didn't emerge again, citing alien death rays and radioactivity in the Blight.

As for those who chose to brave the outside once more, a new revelation arrived at sunset. The storm had drifted further east, the stars now glittered over their heads, and in the far distance a robust glow shone on the northern horizon.

Ed was scratching his head. "Could be a city up there, or a drilling camp."

"Or the military." Missy said.

"If it was, don't you think they'd be down here, checking on us?"

"It doesn't make any sense."

"It's not the military," Luis said. "You know exactly what it is."

Missy's eyes fixed on the horizon, but her fears of what lay out there were dwindling, returning instead to what she considered the true realities of the situation. What were they going to do now that the tunnel was compromised? They'd been lucky up until now; they'd had it good. They'd kept their heads down, avoided the soup kitchens, and kept on working. But now Missy was standing in the dark, in the middle of a frightening no-man's land. It was beautiful out here but she felt like a bug about to be crushed.

Ellie arrived and pushed a steaming cup of coffee into her hands. "You holding up?"

"Oh, sure. I'm scared witless."

"You and me both. This is weird."

They left the guys with the radio, discussing fade margins and receiver sensitivities. They climbed down the steps, drank coffee, and shared a cigarette. "There's another one," Ellie said, pointing skyward at a passing meteor. "I'm somewhat pissed off," she declared moments later. "We knew the world hadn't changed for the better, but this—" She swept an arm toward the long grass swaying in the dark. "—it doesn't feel like "blight" to me. It's like we've been lied to."

Missy nodded and drew on the cigarette until its tip burned red. It was getting late and a strong breeze was bending the grass until the foreground resembled waves coming into shore. It felt surreal and served to increase her anxiety, that she was anchorless and about to lose sight of everything she'd ever known.

Both women turned as they heard a shout, and saw Brad part way down the escape stairwell. He was beckoning furiously.

"We've picked up something on the radio. Looks like we're being rescued after all."

Missy stubbed the cigarette on the ground, retrieved the butt and slipped it into her pocket. "We shouldn't be outside when they arrive, in case they think we're *contaminated*." They climbed the steps and rejoined others who had reached a similar consensus.

Their small group dispersed. Missy and Ed returned to Car Three, climbed into their vehicle, buckled up, and waited. Missy sniffed the sleeve of her jacket. It smelled of fresh air, green grass, and a million stars.

Soon after, they were boarded. She and Ed answered a bunch of questions from a man wearing the Maglev company logo on a jacket that looked brand new. "Everyone okay?" "Need anything?" "Any issues with the truck or your payload?" There was no mention of alien contraptions stumbling into the tunnel wall or anyone going outside. He was accompanied by another employee who kept silent the whole time and wore a sidearm.

"What do you make of that?" she asked Ed afterward.

He shrugged. "I'm just happy we didn't have to feed them a bunch of lies."

They had to wait another five hours for track repair, and the subsequent tow to California took nineteen hours now that the tunnel was compromised, low density was unachievable, and falling debris had damaged the electromagnetic suspension.

Thankfully, only the rear cars were damaged and unloading was a breeze. As soon as the chocks were withdrawn, Missy eased the truck forward and down the ramp. Ed gathered, checked, and re-checked the paperwork, handing it over when they reached freight security. They shared a few tense moments while they waited for questions that never arrived, and once their papers had been summarily scanned and returned and the barrier began to rise—

"Punch it," Ed growled. "Let's get out of here."

However, a mile or so out, exhausted and still a long way from the boxy grid of industrial buildings and the sweeping bridges of San Diego, they had to pull off the road at the nearest truck stop and get some rest.

There was only room by the perimeter fence, and beyond it they could see refugee camps stretching north and south for miles. Small fires and strings of lights lit up the inhabited expanse. Laundry flapped in between the tents, and people's silhouettes drifted by like ghosts. The stench of human urine was overpowering.

Missy kept the windows raised. "We need to tell people," she said. "About the grass, and the three-legged thing we saw. It's heading this way and—"

"No. We need to get some rest, keep our mouths shut, and keep rolling."

"But this is—"

"I know it is. Let it go, Missy. Just let it go."

For a while their luck held and they found work up in Central California. News of Ellie's DUI arrest came as a shock, but it didn't inspire any warning signals until a few days later when they arrived at a truck stop on Interstate 5 and heard Brad had been arrested. Ed had also heard a rumor that Luis had quit his job and disappeared too. Gone to ground like a wily old fox.

Two hours later, they were on the approach to Sacramento with a crop of yellow onions when a large, unmanned box truck leapt across the median and slammed into the cab, killing Missy instantly, while Ed got away with cuts and bruises. Distraught, and scared out of his wits, he hopped off the grid and laid low.

A month after the incident (no way was he calling it an accident) Ed borrowed a friend's old motorcycle, bartered for some fuel, and rode south to Temecula.

"Where you heading, Ed?"

"East, looking for Luis. I heard he stopped by."

"Uh, huh?" The other man hauled on a heavy length of tarp. "And like I told him, there's nothing out there."

"Right." He stared at the massive grill of the unveiled M923 military heavy hauler. "Been a while since I drove one of these."

His companion shrugged. "She'll get you past the barricades, and with the spare tanks you'll get quite a ways before she runs out of fuel. After that..."

"You got gas for the bike?"

"Sure, I owe you, and hey, my condolences, man."

Ed traveled at night, passing by the tent cities and their desultory campfires, keeping off-road wherever possible, using bolt-cutters to get beyond the fences until he found a dusty track, slightly north of the Maglev tunnel. From there he kept on going east through the desert, rumbling across an old railroad bridge over the Colorado river, navigating a barren expanse of arroyos, rocks, and dry brush. On the passenger seat, his backpack contained jugs of water, food, and Missy's ashes in an old cookie canister.

Eventually, he came upon the tripodal machine they'd all seen weeks ago. It was alone, balanced precariously on its three legs, lights still spinning around its circumference. He spied no recent tire tracks, nothing to say that anyone had been out here to confront it, or even take a look. For a long moment they stared at one another before Ed pushed slowly on the accelerator. The tripod lifted a leg, and both went their separate ways. He glanced in his rearview mirror. "Good luck with the river, kid."

On the third night he came across three more tripods. These were taller, faster, and were making a beeline for the west. He'd gotten the impression he had nothing to fear from the first one, but these—he was mighty glad he'd rolled to a stop beneath an old gas station canopy and killed the engine.

For a while he wondered what best to do, but now that Missy and his livelihood were gone, he realized he didn't care what happened back there any longer. Instead, he stuck to his original plan, inspired by something Luis had said, back when they were helping Brad set up the radio on the roof of the tunnel.

"So, are we going to take a look, or what?" Luis had been mesmerized by the brightly lit horizon to the north, and Ed knew if they'd stayed any longer there'd have been some kind of expedition organized, with Luis at the front, and like fools, Ed and Missy following right behind. As soon as he found out Luis had disappeared, he knew exactly where he'd gone.

He checked his fuel and water. Whatever happened, this was going to be a one way trip. He waited until the dust had settled and his view of the tripods had sunk below the western horizon, then he cranked up the engine, kept on going, and left the past in the mirror.

Paul Carlson has been an SF reader since childhood, thanks to his mother's Asimov paperbacks. His robot-trucker stories (four of which, including this one, were published in Analog Science Fiction and Fact *magazine, plus one more in the Ahmed A. Khan anthology* Rise and Fall*) qualified him as a voting member of* Science Fiction and Fantasy Writers of America (SFWA). *Mr. Carlson has been a working CDL trucker since 1990. It pays the bills and is a low-stress, high-exercise job. It's brought him to Silicon Valley high tech companies, up into California's mountainous areas, and other interesting places. To his knowledge, there are only two people in the United States with these dual professional qualifications, and both are represented in this anthology.*

SHOTGUN SEAT

Paul Carlson

THE PHONE RANG AT three-fifteen AM. I looked at the clock, then the phone. Remembered why I felt so worn out. That cheered me up enough to grab the handset.

"Hello?" My bleary eyes couldn't make out the caller ID.

"Hey Claude, it's Doug."

"Doug?"

My brain finally kicked into gear. Dispatcher Doug Gonzalez worked the graveyard shift at Argus Trucking. He always went home two hours before I got in, so I rarely saw him.

"Claude my man, I called all the guys on the list. You know how it is."

I knew. Company procedure, with a specified order of phone contacts. A lot of truckers are party-hearty types when they're off duty, and it'd take an earthquake to wake them up. Doug knows it and I know it. Even so, it had been six months since he called me at night.

"So, Doug, wuzzup? Burnin' hot load?"

"Talk about hot. Some outfit called Sylvantronics took out insurance for seven million bucks! Got to deliver their goods by three this afternoon. Tell me you can handle it, buddy."

"I'd never let you down, amigo." Already I was reaching for my company shirt. "No traffic at this hour, so I'll see you in a few."

I could grab something to eat later, before or after making the pickup, depending. The suits at HQ would be ecstatic. The company gets to keep a share of those insurance premiums, but it'd be up to me to make sure nothing bad happened along the way.

I was almost out the door when Laurie woke up. "Doug called?" To my nod she added, "Don't work too hard."

After forty-three years of marriage, she knows me better than I do. I kissed her on the forehead. "Might get some overtime out of it."

Zoomed my old Camaro into the company lot with five minutes to spare. I love the cool night air, which is all too rare in the middle of a Southwestern desert summer. Inside the dispatch office, Doug had the paperwork ready. There was an unfamiliar bicycle in the corner.

I scanned it with a practiced eye. Twenty-nine miles to make the pickup, in a high tech area, then two hundred thirty to the drop-off, way out in the desert. I'd heard of Sylvantronics and their robots, but didn't know they had a facility in the middle of nowhere. A promising development, robots, but far too expensive for my household.

"The trucking business never looked better," said Doug, with a sly grin I couldn't quite figure out. "Have yourself a fine drive."

Energy conservation always wars with safety considerations, and that year the company yard was rather dark at night. I could find my rig blindfolded, so I figured, what's to worry about?

Someone was standing by the truck. I'd been mugged a few years earlier, so I hesitated. Then, recalling Doug's grin, I kept walking.

A moment later I remembered: I was scheduled to have a brand-new trainee that day. But Lou wasn't coming in until seven AM, almost four hours later.

"Mr. Dremmel?" came a soft voice. "Mr. Gonzales said I could meet you out here, by your truck."

"That's me." Was this Lou, after all?

"Hang on a sec." I unlocked the driver's side door, so the cab light cast its dim rays on the scene. There stood a young Asian woman, dressed in coveralls and a baseball cap. She wore a small backpack.

Time for some fast mental footwork. "You're, umm, Ms. Lu?"

She offered a hand. "Lu Ai-Ling. Your boss said to come in today for evaluation and training, so here I am."

We shook on it. Her hand was small and without calluses, but her grip was firm.

"Now?" I mumbled. "At—?" I had to force myself not to stare.

She laughed, sounding almost as nervous as I felt. "I know this must be unusual, but your office lady, Beryl, gave me a link to the company system. When Mr. Gonzales logged in your response at three-fifteen, my home computer woke me up." She hooked a thumb over a slender shoulder. "I live about a mile from here."

"This outfit could use more dedication like that." Sounded dumb, but I really did mean it. "No wonder Doug was grinning." I climbed into the cab and opened the passenger side door. "Possibly this is his idea of a joke."

The light illuminated Ai-Ling as she climbed into the shotgun seat. I almost did a double-take, but only my eyes moved. She was gorgeous. I'm not too good at judging ages, but she couldn't have been out of high school more than five years.

Hey, I can be as politically correct as the best of 'em. Yes there are women truckers; employees and owner-operators both. Most travel with partners, and a few work on their own. Trucking is murder on your hands, and requires long and unpredictable work days.

Too many of us guys are unimaginative, often oblivious to our own behavior or fitness, so we're not often looking for a better work routine. The smart guys, and darned near all the women on the road, act decently and take good care of themselves. As best as some bad circumstances allow, anyway.

I'd have bet a week's pay there wouldn't be many truckers like Lu Ai-Ling on the road that day. Some instinct got me to wagering with myself that this young lady could be the sort of person who transformed the whole situation. Little did I suspect how right I was.

Curious, she reached up and unhooked my CB mike. "Use this a lot, good buddy?"

"Not much, anymore." I tapped Doll Box's console. "This here guide unit has data channels, proactive tracking, voice interface, all the fancy gear. Not to mention universal cell phone access." As she replaced the mike I heaved a sigh. "Trucking's not what it used to be."

She looked disappointed.

"Let's do our pre-trip walkaround. Maybe Doug told you? We have a rush job today, a point-to-point run."

"Walkaround? I studied that in the manual." She showed me her Class B commercial driver's license, which was only a couple of weeks old. "My cousin Lim showed me how to drive his bobtail truck, and I borrowed it to pass the DMV exam."

Usually Argus hires Class A drivers, who can handle full size big rigs. If this lady proved serious, she could attend our company school in Tulsa. All you have to do is sign up for one solid year, in order to pay it off.

"Since it's dark out we'll stick to the basics." I grabbed a flashlight from beside my seat and climbed out. When she followed, swinging down from her side, I could see she had her hair pinned, and tucked beneath her cap.

"Smart idea with your hair." I popped the hood. "Got to stick your head in places. Now what are we looking for?"

"Fluid levels, clogged filters, loose wires and leaks, frayed belts. More, but I can't remember it all."

Good enough. "Ms. Lu, after the first couple of pre-trips, you won't even need a checklist." We took turns thumping the tires. "There are gauges and sensors, but you know what? The sensors themselves can be defective." I pointed the light at a tire. "See here? The tread is working loose. Not a problem yet, but you don't want this crud flying off when you're highballing down some interstate."

"Got it."

"Then we're set to roll."

Back in the cab, she buckled in and straightened her cap. "Call me Alice. I want that to be my CB handle."

"Like in Alice's Restaurant, or maybe Alice Kramden? It'll work." I prefer the classics. I wondered if she'd have a good opportunity to sling her handle around today.

"Hello Alice," said the guide box. "Claude always calls me Doll Box."

Ai-Ling a.k.a. Alice was unfazed. "Is this a Keltora 3200 unit?" she asked. Most of the circuitry is out of sight, as she probably knew. "Good voice recognition protocols, and I'll bet it's got neurophasic interfacing."

Maybe it does, but before I could display my ignorance about the subject, the guide box affirmed that Alice was correct. Except, it announced, it's a 3200C unit, with better data stream integration. Told myself I owed the thing another module or two.

We had a full tank, so fuel wasn't an issue. Went through the driver's startup routines, including the breathalyzer and wakefulness tests, then confirmed our routing.

We pulled out of the yard at four-thirteen AM, which wasn't bad.

Silence seemed too awkward, but I didn't want to sound like a goof, either. I'm faithful to Laurie, and don't mind who knows it. On the other hand, truckers are *required* to have excellent eyesight. There would be a lot of envious guys on the blacktop today.

The freeway was shrouded in predawn gloom. "Alice," I asked, "do you know the roads around here? Can you read paper maps? I've had days when the GPS went kaput, so that's important."

She opened her pack and dug out an area map. "Looks like we're heading east to make the pickup." She tapped the map with a penlight. "Exit here, turn left, easy. No commute jams in that direction, correct?"

"You are. If there aren't any accidents or construction zones. Doll Box will alert us of any major jams." We could listen to the morning traffic reports on the radio, but I prefer music to begin the day. NewsTalk later, depending on what kind of mood I'm in. "We should be there in less than an hour. Hope the load is ready."

No sooner than I'd said this, the autobrakes came on. Traffic was at a dead stop ahead. I kicked in the jake brake, which clamped the exhaust stream with its distinctive rattling roar. In the lane to our right, a car almost slammed into somebody. Likely some damn fool who'd disabled his situational autopilot.

Doll Box had no comment.

Alice turned on the AM radio and punched up a news station. A couple of minutes later, their regular traffic report didn't even mention the freeway we were on. The local driver's infonet had a few questions posted, but no answers as yet.

"Let's figure out what's happening." I had Doll Box tap into the traffic cameras, but as I'd suspected, the ones up ahead were off line. Probably full of bullets. Even the tiny inconspicuous ones get zapped by handheld lasers or something. I rarely say it out loud, but with the Feds cracking down so harshly everywhere, I didn't blame folks for hitting back.

Doll Box learned that a police cruiser had all the lanes stopped, but nothing more.

"Alice, it's time to use my secret weapon."

"Your what?"

"See that compartment? The square door? Open it and hand me the bird."

Alice probably thought it was a test, or maybe some weird in-house initiation, as she didn't appear worried about my sanity. Yet. In any case, she opened the compartment.

"It *is* a bird." She lifted a gray dove out of the recess like it was made of fine china. When it blinked she flinched, but didn't drop it. "Here you go."

I booted up a program on my personal cell phone, and used wireless to instruct the bird. Didn't want to attract attention, so I handed it back to Alice. "Open your window and let it fly from your hands."

She let the bird go, and it fluttered up and away. I held my phone where both of us could see the screen, and its realtime transmission from my trusty scout.

"Fascinating, Mr. Dremmel. Are those things legal?"

I gave her a weak grin. "Gray bird, gray area. It's a civilian prototype. If they catch on big, somebody's going to regulate the hell out of them."

My robotic dove spotted the police cruiser, then flew onward. A quarter mile farther, the problem became obvious. A tall light pole had fallen, blocking all the lanes. Luckily, nobody had gotten smashed by the thing.

"What happened?" Alice wondered.

"A lot of valuable aluminum in that pole. Maybe it fell because some thieves messed up." I shrugged. "Might be activists, or *el cheapo* terrorists. If nobody posts a rant, I'd go with thieves."

"I've heard of that before, but not around here. Times are bad, huh?"

"Us truckers see it all. Someday you can tell your grandkids."

She laughed again. That felt good.

We watched a tow truck drive up from the opposite direction, and drag the pole onto the shoulder. The cruiser pulled up beside it, maybe to look for evidence, as cars surged forward.

Alice caught the returning bird like an old pro.

Everyone rubbernecked as we passed by. The pole was shredded at the base, wicked shards forming an ugly wound. I was never in the military, but I've happened upon enough domestic terrorism to know what explosives can do.

We geared up smoothly. "My next tractor is going to have a continuous automatic transmission, or so the boss tells me. Big rigs are always last for that kind of technology."

"Cool!" Her grimace hinted she'd also recognized terrorism.

The pickup was routine. I let Alice open our trailer, unlatching the bars then swinging them up and around. An object lesson in how physical strength is sometimes required in this line of work. She handled it well.

Our load was sealed inside three dozen wooden crates, each set on plastic anti-vibration pads. The shipping crew wasn't totally silent, but they didn't volunteer any information either. The invoice only stated they were thirty-six production model something-or-others.

"Looks like cybernetic gear." Alice was examining the invoice by dawn's light as we pulled back onto the freeway. "Possibly new components for their robots. I've never seen these designations before." She looked up. "I know a guy who works at Sylvantronics. Maybe we'll see him."

So she knew about technology. I kept wondering what she saw in truck driving. Could be anything from a summertime lark to familial rebellion to a childhood dream. She might even have a criminal record, and be unwelcome at most jobs. I wasn't about to embarrass her by asking.

"How are you set for chow?" I asked instead. "We've got plenty of time, and a straight shot ahead."

"Sometimes I pack a lunch, but there wasn't time."

"Same for me. How 'bout we swing by that big truck stop at the crossroads? It's twenty more miles, and if you're choosey, the food won't clog your arteries within three bites."

"Sounds good. Always wanted to sit in the Drivers Only area."

Score one for Childhood Dream.

Five miles on, we got flagged to pull through a truck scale. Usually I'm waved past by the remote system. My rig had passed inspection six weeks ago, so that wasn't an issue. I explained all this to my trainee as we cruised down the designated lane.

Our weight or load did not trigger any sensors, so we rolled on through. "We get an hour for breakfast, since it was such an early start. Company policy."

I showed Alice how Doll Box updated the log. Back when I first started driving you had to write everything by hand, on a special chart.

The diner was crowded at seven AM, mostly with drivers who'd spent their off duty time parked overnight. That place was an institutional dinosaur, straight out of the 1950s. Did my darndest to look casual, even bored, as we headed to our table. Alice was, to coin a phrase, young enough to be my granddaughter.

We both had a good appetite. I considered splurging on Corn Chip Pie, and a lot of coffee to counteract its brain clogging grease. Then I remembered our seven million dollar load, and decided to remain as sharp as possible. Had oatmeal and some halfway decent Earl Grey tea. Alice devoured a Truckers Special, with eggs, pancakes, vat-grown bacon, and more.

On our way outside, I decided to introduce my trainee to Laurie. They could share lifestyle tips. Heavy-duty chow wasn't leaving a mark on Ms. Lu.

"Mr. Dremmel, that was a *ton* of food. Is it okay if I jog it off? We've got ten minutes left on our break."

She must've read my mind. "Ms. Lu, I've been a trucker almost forty years, and nobody's asked me that before." To her chary look I added, "Sure, go right ahead. But!" She froze. My gesture encompassed the vast parking lot. "Where did we park?"

She lifted her wristwatch.

"Uh, uh," I cut in. "You might not always have a tracking gadget handy." I'd popped that quiz before, and wasn't about to give Alice any macho freebies.

She looked around at the hundreds of trucks, and her arm traced the course of her thoughts. "That way, two rows in, left and not quite halfway up." Next she described my rig, better than I probably could. "I'll find it."

"You passed. Off you go." And off she ran.

Eight minutes later, hardly breaking a sweat, Alice met me at the truck. Together we checked the locks and seals. No one had bothered the load.

"This place is cool," she enthused. "I saw one of those new boron-hydrogen cycle rigs, and a lot of biodiesel electrics, and that pallet yard next door has capacitor powered forklifts."

I grinned. "Saw a piece on Truckers Road about some physicist, claims he found a way to pack hydrogen into metal form."

"Metal hydrogen? Like a super-compressed fuel?"

"Guess so. Said they'd prepack it, and rigs would swap out the whole fuel container. Be years until it's available. Maybe Argus will buy some."

If Alice signed on with Argus Trucking, my recruitment bonus would buy something really nice for Laurie. Better than the plain little anniversary gift I'd gotten her the day before.

I cranked up the engine, and we rolled in low third gear.

Alice pointed to the CB mike. "Can I give it a try?"

CB had fallen out of favor, but in that busy gathering place, who knew? "Sure. It adjusts itself, signal-wise, and you can scan for any chatter."

The radio speaker came to life. "Hey Jimmy," said an unknown trucker, "check out the seat cover in the Argus rig. Heading out the north exit."

Several voices crowded the channel. Hoots of acclamation followed, and not a few verbal leers. I didn't quite blush, and neither did she, though I wasn't sure the message had sunk in. Gawd, it was like a flashback to high school. Laurie always knocked 'em dead. Made me feel old and young at the same time.

"Seat cover?" Alice asked me. "Lot lizard?"

"You want it straight?" She did, so I gave it to her. "You're a sight for sore eyes. A lot of those guys are wildly jealous, and half are misinterpreting our situation."

"Guess so!" She got a beat-up old booklet from her pack, looked up something, and thumbed the mike. "Alice from Argus here. That's a big ten-four, guys. Thanks for being real sunbeams this morning." Flashed me a grin and kept flipping pages. "No fox jaws in this fleet. Maybe see you around, but we've got a load to haul. Threes and eights." With that she signed off.

By then we were on the freeway, headed into barren country on the next leg of our route. We'd be on the interstate two hundred miles yet, with plenty of company on the blacktop.

Alice read an ebook for a while, then tried the CB again. This time I recognized the first voice on the channel.

"Got a copy, Trucker Claude?" came a familiar query. "And who's *not* a fox jaws on board?"

She handed me the mike.

"Got you five-by-five, Pedro. My trainee is doing a fine job, I'll have you know. She's got brains, and beauty to match the foxy voice."

I told Alice, "That's Pedro Owen. Thinks he's a one man CB revival. Go ahead and chat it up."

This they did. Pedro was ten miles behind us, with another rush load for Sylvantronics. He'd picked up farther away, but skipped breakfast. We slacked off a little, allowing him to close the gap without getting busted for speeding.

Soon a third voice came on the CB. "You savages got a cartel going? How 'bout letting an old timer get a word in edgewise."

It was a retired trucker and his wife, driving a solar-boosted RV. He'd been in our rearview mirror for a while. Pedro came up behind us both, placing the old guy in the "hammock" position.

"Got us a convoy?" Alice asked me, with the CB mike lowered.

She was paying attention. Good. "Heh." I wagged my head. "It *is* possible to overdo the jargon."

Nonetheless, they chattered happily. Turned out Pedro and Alice liked the same novel, something about hackers in a cyber world, and artificial intelligence and androids and more. I'd heard of this, but really, a lot of it went right over my head. Made the time go faster for her, while I was happy with my favorite talk show. Their audience knew Trucker Claude from several calls I'd made over the years.

Around noon, I spotted a speed demon in the mirrors. Car was dodging around like everybody was standing still. He came past my rig in a flash, then swerved into our lane. Alice gave a little shout as I eased off on the pedal.

The speeder passed a rig on the right side, lost speed, then cut him off. The poor trucker braked hard and shimmied; darn near jackknifed.

"That's it!" I had Doll Box call up a twenty second video clip from the forward wide camera. There went the speeder, license plate clearly visible. "Gotcha." I told Alice, "We'll shoot this clip over to the state police."

"He'll claim, 'It wasn't me driving.' Lots of cheaters do that."

"Not to Claude Dremmel they don't." I checked the rear camera footage, and sure enough, there was a clear view of the driver's face. Desert sun makes fine lighting.

Doll Box titled both clips and emailed 'em. That guy probably had other complaints on file by then. If so, smokey would seize the car, and the jerk deserved it. Almost as bad as a red light runner.

"Are we going to have lunch?" Alice asked.

Ah, to have such a youthful metabolism. "Look around. Nothing but empty desert. We'll catch something at the junction."

At two o'clock Beryl emailed me from the office, to ask what the holdup was. "Holdup?" I responded, with Doll Box transcribing my voice.

I told Beryl we had an hour until the deadline, and thirty-five miles of road left to cover, so what was the problem?

"Deliver the load, and don't say anything about being late," was her directive. Familiar advice from a thousand previous screw-ups. Did not like the sound of it, but so far as I could see, everything was going right.

"Copy that," I emailed back. "We'll skip lunch, just for you."

"Something's up," I informed my trainee. "The customer is asking where we are."

"But we've got an hour."

"So says the paperwork. You know the old line about 'the customer is always right?' In this hurry-up business, that applies triple." I threw up both hands, leaving the wheel untended for a moment. "Time to hustle."

"Might've asked *me*." Alice looked rueful. "Don't you carry food and supplies? Some of these rigs are equipped like that RV behind us."

"Sorry. If I was doing regional or cross country runs, I'd stock up for sure. But with city routes, I learned the hard way. With my luck, if I spent the money, I'd end up switching trucks for a day or two. Some ravenous temp driver would devour everything."

"I see." She got a snack bar from her pack, and devoured that.

Truth was, the oatmeal breakfast had left me hungrier than ever, but some male ego thing wouldn't let me admit it.

Pedro and Alice compared notes. He was catching grief from his own dispatcher, so somebody was really bent out of shape.

We reached the junction and exited, bidding farewell to the old timer. Made a quick pit stop but, with regrets, passed up on the lonely diner. Alice seemed to like Pedro in person, during the few stationary moments we allowed ourselves. He's a likeable fellow, and in much better shape than me, considering he's thirty years younger.

I squinted at the horizon. A two-lane highway went away north, diminishing to a thread, then vanishing amid hues of brown. The kind of desert, desolate at first glance, that John McPhee and George R. Stewart brought to life in their books.

"Glad you're hitting it off with Pedro," I told Alice. After all, the man was single.

"He's an independent contractor, right? Carries loads for different companies?"

"Yeah. Hauls a lot of high-value items. Electronics, military assets, things like that. Loads that could draw unwelcome attention, but they make up for it with extra security."

"Oh?"

"He has a concealed carry permit. Gets armed guards and escorts sometimes, and one time he had air cover."

"Wow! But not today?"

"Not sure, and he wouldn't say. He is in the same big hurry." I grinned. "Since you're so interested, Pedro's quite a character. His real name is Stansfield, as in S. Peter Owen. His grandmother was a Bradford, in the DAR and everything. Been leading citizens in New England for darn near four hundred years."

Alice looked it up. "Daughters of the American Revolution. I'm impressed. So why isn't Pedro in some cushy Harvard faculty club, or on the board of DuPont or something?"

"Long story. His father is Heathcliff Owen. Heard of him?"

"No."

"I'm not surprised. The man owns a lot of companies, but keeps out of the limelight. Got past the dot-com crash, and the troubles in 2022, without losing his shirt. Came out ahead, is what I heard."

"So where does that leave Mr. Stansfield Peter Owen?"

"His father is a big admirer of the work ethic. Didn't hand down a dime to his sons." I reached over and patted her shoulder. "Besides, maybe you're not the only one who always wanted to sit in the Driver's Only section."

She looked thoughtful. "I suppose you're right."

We almost missed our turnoff. Doll Box didn't have it listed. The road was marked by a little sign, and barely wide enough for our trucks. A half mile along, a guard booth came into sight. Some distance away, a second building overlooked the area. I could see more guards up there, watching us. A dry stream bed crossed beneath the road, deep enough to stop most vehicles.

"I've seen military bases with inconspicuous security like this," I commented.

Pedro pulled in behind us.

Alice commented, "This facility is new. I've been checking online, and there's not much detail." Her eyes shone with curiosity, and perhaps something more. "They have several square miles of land."

The guards checked our IDs and invoices. Pedro jumped out and handed them his paperwork. One guard broke the shipper's seals on our trailers, and waited for us to open them for inspection. Alice stepped in to open my trailer. Took her a couple of extra tugs, but she got it.

After a short time that felt like forever, they waved us through. It takes Argus a week or so to review a job application, but those guards ran instant checks on the three of us. They must've deemed us acceptable, since we received visitor badges, complete with photos. They also had us sign nondisclosure forms.

I wondered what would happen if, for whatever reason, the guards *didn't* approve us. Would they shoo us all the way back to the city? Expect us to park outside the gate until our employers could send someone else? That would take hours, if not overnight, and they'd already paid double for a rush job. Plus, the insurance coverage had a time limit. Rules are rules.

We drove through a cut in some low hills, and the Sylvantronics complex lay spread out below us. A series of road loops fanned out from a gigantic warehouse building. Everything looked new, not yet blasted by the desert sun and gritty winds. Gravel, rather than grass, dominated their landscaping. I could see a lone vehicle whipping around a tortuous roadway.

Another guard directed us to drive inside one end of the building. The rollup door must've been eighteen feet tall, and the dock space within was large enough for a dozen big rigs. A massive consumption of interior space, and a good way to hide from satellites, drones, and other observers. The other dock spaces were empty.

I did a perfect T-turn, backing up to my indicated dock spot-on. A real showoff move, sure to please at the trucker's national championships.

But Pedro did me one better, by turning the rear wheels of his newfangled trailer. He spun in place, within a turning radius smaller than the overall length of his rig, and backed in neater than a train engine at a roundhouse. I was impressed—and truly outclassed. Argus, and its longtime owner Old Doug, weren't about to cough up for steerable trailers.

The warehouse crew made it clear they wanted to handle the crates, but stopped cold when a white-coated man landed on the scene. "Landed" in a metaphorical wartime sense. The guy was loaded for bear.

He spotted me as a driver, and lit into me like the mad professor he resembled. "Why are you late?" he began. "I told you to be here at one o'clock!" Fresh salvos kept coming, as he swung on Pedro. "I paid you people thousands extra to bring these necessary items according to a strict schedule! How can we operate in the face of such incompetence?"

By unspoken agreement, Pedro and I decided to let the fellow blow himself out. Alice looked aghast, so when the man rounded on Pedro again I told her, "This happens once in a while. The gentleman must be having a bad day."

At the first opportunity, Pedro presented his shipping documents. I was glad to let him go first, since he's got more experience with high-strung specialist types. "If you'll look here, sir," Pedro said, "the manifest clearly states, 'deliver by three o'clock this afternoon.' It is now three-nineteen, and we reached your front gate with eleven minutes to spare. We are sorry if there was some misunderstanding."

"Misunderstanding!" the man exploded. "We have the most efficient corporate system in North America, and redundant multichannel communications. There was no misunderstanding! Your employers will hear about this incompetence, and...and... feeble attempt at making an excuse."

"Then again," I whispered to Alice, "some guys are, shall we say, emotionally challenged. Dude is taking it out on a handy disposable target."

I showed the man my paperwork. "Sir, I was also instructed to pick up early this morning, and get the load here safely by three. I believe we have fulfilled our contract. There is, if you wish, a standard procedure for filing complaints with our employers."

"If I wish!" he screamed. "What I wish is not important. The project is what is important." Then he lashed into his own warehouse crew, who'd been doing an amazing non-technical feat of stealth. "What are you people standing around for? We need these items immediately!"

They jumped into action as fast as any crew I'd ever seen, granted that warehouse guys are rarely in any kind of hurry. Meanwhile, Alice was doing something with Pedro's and my signature pads. I hadn't even noticed her taking them.

She put on a brilliant smile and showed the pads to Mr. White Coat. "Sir, your gate guards told me you'd sign for my load personally. I'm sure Mr. Owen received similar instructions. If you would, please?"

I guess music and bright smiles can sooth the savage beast, or however the heck that saying goes, because the man calmed down. Alice showed him several lines of data.

"Sir," she told him, "here are the actual instructions, as relayed by voice and plain text, from this facility to both of our dispatchers at three o'clock this morning. Separate calls were made to both of the shippers, which accurately reflected our pickup times."

The man read the text lines, frowning hard enough to curdle an entire dairy.

"You see," Alice went on, "this facility uses military time exclusively. Notification of our dispatchers was made at three o'clock in the morning, or 03:00. The delivery was expected by 13:00 this afternoon, but that's one o'clock, not three." She reversed into a moue. "Nobody compared the company dispatch logs to your backup data transmission until one-seventeen this afternoon. A simple misunderstanding, which happened in the middle of the night."

"Humph." Mr. White Coat did not look mollified. Some night shift Sylvantronics flunky would need to polish his resume.

Inspiration struck me. "Remember when NASA crashed a Mars probe, because their mission teams mixed up miles and kilometers? They had months to catch the error, and never did. I was delivering new computers to JPL around that time." I shrugged. "Anyhow, your items are here okay. A week from now, none of this is going to matter."

The man counted each crate, then told us he'd be back to sign for them later. "If you need compensation for the extra delay," he stated, "take it up with your employers." As he stomped off he aimed a glare at all three of us. "We'll not have to put up with this human foolishness for much longer."

"You put up with this abuse?" Alice asked Pedro.

"I've yelled back," Pedro admitted, "on occasion. This really is unusual." Then he grinned. "We get paid the same either way."

"I suppose it does strengthen one's character," Alice mused aloud. "Wonder if my friend is here?" She approached one of the warehouse guys, who gladly interrupted his work to show her a company directory.

Sure enough, Alice's friend had been assigned to the new facility. A short time later, a tall skinny fellow entered the dock area. "Ai-Ling," he called out, "it's good to see you." They hugged.

"This is Dr. Sanjay Bishnoi," Alice told Pedro and me. "He was a teaching assistant for several of my computer classes." She punched her friend's arm. "I imagine the pay is better here."

Bishnoi took in the situation, and did not ask Alice why she was hanging around with two grizzled truckers. "It will take our crew some time to complete the unloading and check for damage. You were signed in, yes? Perhaps I can show you what you delivered today."

Damage! I decided to overlook the implied insult, since my companions looked even more curious than I was. Thus we were treated to a grand tour, edited to the interesting parts only.

"As you know, we supply industrial and military robotic systems," Bishnoi told us. "We also have a position in the home care market, but fully capable humaniform units remain elusive." He brought us to another section of the warehouse, opening security doors with his badge. "We're on the verge of a breakthrough."

All three of us were amazed at what we saw next. A humanoid robot was driving a car around an indoor track, dodging mobile obstacles and obeying a set of traffic signals.

"That's only the beginning," Bishnoi said, with evident pride.

In the next section, a flatbed truck waited in a mockup dock area. A bipedal robot surveyed the situation, which looked to me like a typical loading job.

Mostly I surveyed the robot. The frame was shiny metal, and instead of hydraulic pistons it had synthetic muscles. Its limbs and torso were enclosed in tough, clear plastic. My companions agreed it was 'humaniform' but not 'fleshly.' Which, I concluded, fit Sylvantronics' bloodless corporate image to a tee.

"This robot," our guide said, "is the prototype unit of the thirty-six production models you delivered here today." He looked at me. "You brought the bodies." To Pedro he said, "You brought the brains. Each unit can learn, and rapidly adapt to new situations."

Obeying some silent cue, the robot got on a forklift and hoisted a large metal crate onto a flatbed trailer. Then it threw two heavy-duty nylon straps over the load, threaded the hold-downs, and tightened the straps with a practiced eye. Next it opened the truck and started it, using key chucks built into its metal fingers.

Bishnoi watched intently, though no one seemed to be guiding the action. The robot drove around the indoor track, sharing a single lane with the car, which had come in through a side door. A minute later the robot stopped, then unloaded the crate.

"That's what Mr. White Coat meant about not putting up with 'foolish humans' for much longer." I hadn't meant to say it aloud, but sheer astonishment loosened my tongue. "I wonder if they could handle all the other hassles that come up?"

"You said it, bro," Pedro echoed. "Never thought I'd see the day."

Alice didn't look surprised, but if anything, deeply offended. She sidled up to Pedro and me. "Claude, you said Alice Kramden? More like Alice in Wonderland." Her head wagged mournfully. "No CB chatter from these paragons of efficiency."

Demonstration over, Bishnoi collected us. I was pretty sure he'd missed Alice's harsh expression. We headed straight back to our rigs.

Mr. White Coat showed up long enough to sign our paperwork, then directed his crew to bring the new robots to another testing area. "We will have our initial verification run at twenty-two hundred hours. Be ready!" He strode off with nary a backward look.

Ten o'clock. After dark. Worried about the competition? Not that darkness offers much concealment.

Alice murmured something about, "A Turing Test times ten." I didn't understand the reference, and forgot to look it up, until much later.

As we passed the guard booth Alice asked me, "Mr. Dremmel, can we send your bird out again? Take another look at what they're doing back there?"

I fought the impulse to make a retort. "Ms. Lu, right off the top of my head, I can think of a half dozen reasons why that would be a stupid move. You're a smart kid, and I bet you could come up with as many more."

She had the good grace to look abashed. "Sorry I mentioned it."

But she didn't look sorry for the idea itself.

I called Laurie to say I'd be late. If my trainee sent any similar message, I didn't notice. We stopped at the junction for an early dinner, and Pedro joined us. The talk was lively, and for the most part I just listened. I've got plenty of stories, but don't insist on telling them all at once.

Alice fell asleep on the drive back. We got into the Argus yard by nine that evening. Under the old rules I'd have run out of duty time already, thus been required to stop somewhere for the night. As it stood, I punched out with double time on the clock, and wrote out a good report on my trainee.

It got through my thick head that Alice was riding a bicycle. Since it was dark out, I talked her into letting me strap it onto the roof of my Camaro, so I could drop her off at home.

She lived in an upstairs apartment, in what's best called a humble area. I watched until she'd made it into her front door okay.

Beryl's got a miracle touch. Few places on Earth are more dingy than our local Argus Trucking yard, but she fixed up the break room with a semblance of festiveness. No helium, but finding the party balloons and all took some ambitious shopping. One more trade war, and the USA's store shelves were going to get Soviet looking.

Alice had passed her four-week training course with flying colors. She was a real Class A trucker, and certified to rumble around our highways and byways. Just in time for the hottest part of summer, but I swear she didn't seem fazed.

"For she's a jolly good fellow" carried across the oil-stained asphalt as the yard crew, plus whoever was in town that day, welcomed our newest employee driver.

Alice beamed. "Thanks, guys. Especially to Claude, for giving me a great start around here."

Some of the guys looked a mite *too* appreciative. I spoke in a stage whisper, "She's a great driver, and if some creep tries to 'jack her rig, she's got a Black Belt she can use to discourage him."

I had no idea whether Alice could, or would, kick some lowlife into next week, but I figured it wouldn't hurt for such a rumor to get around. In real life, sexual harassment policies can only do so much....

Pedro was there for the party, which took up the whole lunch break and a few minutes beyond. He must've understood the intent of my words, because he gave me a discreet thumbs-up.

By coincidence, Sylvantronics made their big announcement on that same day. The news and bloggers got all worked up over their new truck driving robots. I guess it was predictable. People were used to indoor robots already, but sharing the road brought everyone's "but *I'm* the world's best driver" instincts to the fore.

Sylvantronics planned to lease a few units here and there, at low cost, in return for each customer putting 'em through the wringer. Beta testing, they call it.

Quick as that, the welcome party ended, and Beryl handed Alice her first sheaf of manifests. I saw that it was a simple run: dropping a full trailer across town. That would be it for the day, no muss and no fuss. And, I realized, not much physical exertion.

Alice did not complain.

Argus started its test robot at the home yard in Tulsa, but a month later our turn came up. Because I had the most seniority, management picked me to ride with it. More like, I figured, if an old fogey like me could handle the thing....

Couldn't have set it up better if I'd been Steven Spielberg. The sun was coming up, shining all over the robot's polished metal, as we began our first day as team drivers.

"Good morning, Mr. Dremmel," said the robot. "I'm glad to be working with you. Shall we get started?"

I'd seen a video of this same robot at work in Tulsa, and its voice sounded different in person. Not weirdo-metallic, or silky-fembot, or butler-smooth either. Just a regular dude's voice. Which, I decided, was perfect.

Alice was assigned to residential deliveries that week, and wasn't due in for an hour yet, but she showed up to see us off. Her look was so keen that I wondered if she'd known about Sylvantronic's test schedule. They kept such things under tight wraps. On the other hand, my youngest grandkid could've hacked Argus Trucking's computer system.

Doll Box and Mechagodzilla hit it off swimmingly. That's really what our crew started calling the robot. In truth it was graceful, like a steel and porcelain ballet dancer, so who says truckers don't have a fine sense of irony?

Our local run was routine, so I decided to spice it up. When I got to the Jimenez Brothers warehouse, I hunkered down in the cab and told the robot to bring the paperwork inside. The trailer's rear camera gave me a fine view. Matt, the owner's grandson, looked like he was about to faint.

Matt must've heard me laughing, because he came stomping outside, eyes fiery. I'd been delivering there for years, and we've had a lot of good times together.

I told him, "What, you mean it's *not* April Fool's Day?"

We both cracked up. Damned if the robot didn't look amused, too.

When I got back to the yard, Alice was putting her load-lifting waist belt in her locker. Gangbangers like to steal those special belts, to use for gym workouts, so she kept hers at work.

She was limping, and trying to hide it.

"You okay?" I asked.

The "war of the sexes" was long over, won by I'm not sure who, but Alice wasn't going to claim her female exemptions just yet.

"I had a bunch of residential drops today," she explained. "Mostly catalog orders. You know that GreenMart still makes its furniture kits out of particle board? Dang, but that material is heavy!"

I winced in sympathy. "Spent a week on disability leave, flat on my back, thanks to that crud. A full size computer desk kit weighs at least 270 pounds, and they don't allow drivers to open the carton."

"My worst load had about 120 pounds' worth. Nice old lady who lives in a third floor walkup. She was so flustered, told me how her son-in-law promised to come help, but he was stuck at airport security, and I wasn't about to wait around, so—"

In theory Alice could've called dispatch to request another Argus driver, and gotten help carrying that heavy box up those stairs. I knew why she hadn't called.

My hands went up in mock surrender. "I've got an idea. Alice, old fogey Claude got along fine with Mechagodzilla today. *You* have computer training, and you know about these robots. Our residential routes are way more complicated, so there's plenty of test opportunities. How about we convince the boss it's your turn now?"

The robot could help her out, and with no ego involved. That way, the macho drivers wouldn't be able to rag on Alice for needing help. Was I being sexist? I hope not. Fatherly, I'd admit to. Not many people can handle such loads alone.

The yard manager agreed, and when Alice left work on her bicycle, I'm not sure she was limping any more.

Within days, my hunch proved correct. That robot proved a boon in any number of situations.

Hearing of this, the boss asked Alice to demonstrate *it* at the next driver meeting. "You show us," he put it, not "have the robot show us," which I thought was a good sign. What he didn't know was, sometimes Alice had the robot drive while she took a nap. Its arms and legs were long enough that it didn't have to occupy the driver's seat, thus fooling casual observers. Wraparound mirrored sunglasses can bollix the wakefulness system, as every trucker knows.

Alice had taught the robot to carry our heaviest, most awkward loads up a flight of stairs. Our company mechanic uses a big ladder to reach the roofs of the trailers, and Alice borrowed that for the demonstration. The robot carried a large carton while she walked above it, providing extra balance. They got it on top of a trailer, thirteen feet up, stepped across to a rig parked next to it, then made their way back down again. That wasn't in the Sylvantronics manual, for sure.

Our toughest guys claimed *they'd* never accept such help, but most of the crew really liked the idea. Heck, Doug Gonzales was our night dispatcher *because* his back had gotten so messed up. After the demonstration, he told me he was thinking about reapplying as a driver.

Upon this newfound acceptance, Argus leased one driver robot for each company yard. At other trucking companies, Sylvantronics units met with mixed success, and sometimes with violent opposition. Other robot manufacturers adopted a wait-and-see attitude.

Still, the new robots found dozens of other uses, all over the country. A whole lot of activists objected, on so many legal and religious and ideological and ecological and social and moral and economic grounds that I lost count, but they all got steamrollered. Millions of dollars could still grease the wheels, it seemed.

In September, Pedro helped Alice pay off her debt to Argus, and she went back to school. I got a beautiful handmade card in the mail, and showed it to Laurie.

"Looks like something my nursery school kids made," Laurie commented. "I guess the artistry is better."

It was a pencil drawing of me standing beside my rig. 'For that dark mysterious encounter, and all our adventures since,' read the caption.

Laurie was not upset. I did not frame it, and she did not throw it away. What more can I say? I'm proud of my understanding wife.

There was a small note tucked in with the card, which said, 'The chatter must go on!' I wondered what Ms. Lu was planning.

Heathcliff Owen looked uncomfortable. Guess I should've been pleased by the sight; a blue collar *schadenfreund* of sorts, but it was too happy an occasion for such things.

The wedding was beautiful. I hadn't been Best Man in a formal ceremony for years. Laurie looked wonderful in her bridesmaid's dress. We hadn't been to any weddings since our youngest son got hitched. Kids these days....

The ceremony took place in a church near Pedro's home; some busy little denomination I wasn't familiar with. Nobody threw any snakes, but Heathcliff probably considered the place beneath his dignity. Still, he was there, along with a trophy wife not much older than the bride. Brought a whole jet-load of relatives, too. No rental tuxedos on that side of the aisle!

Alice's cousin Lim was there, looking freshly scrubbed, and a couple of relatives had come over from Asia. Her friends, from work and school, almost filled the bride's side of the aisle.

Courtesy of Dr. Bishnoi, a robot served as ring bearer. The newest household type unit, as he told anyone who asked, or didn't ask. Humaniform but not fleshly it may have been, yet it looked fine in a suit. Dignified.

A few "leaked" photos of the ceremony provided great publicity for Sylvantronics.

That girl had plans, all right. Alice graduated in Computer Science and Robotics after another year of college, by taking more credits than you could shake a laser pointer at.

She wasn't done yet.

Pedro's condo looked ten times better with a female touch.

"Got to show you something." Alice led me to a shelf in their home office. "Pedro got these from a contact he hauls for, one of those agencies we aren't supposed to talk about. These were rejects, defective, but I fixed them."

"I am impressed." They were works of art.

On a high shelf roosted two spy birds, a pigeon for use in the city and a hawk for the countryside. Each had a range about ten times better than my trusty old dove.

Then Pedro announced dinner. Cod fillets and cheddar cheese sauce, with hasty pudding, and apple cider to drink. He could reach back to his childhood and make New England dishes like you wouldn't believe.

Pedro and Alice took turns cooking. At our place, I never tried to cook. Wouldn't dare! When Laurie is out of town, I'm lucky to get something heated. Straight from the can means no dishes to wash.

We took turns dining at each other's homes, for two get-togethers a month. Usually on Saturday, but juggled to fit our irregular work schedules. Sometimes we'd watch a video, or play a board game after dinner.

They held off on having kids while Alice helped Pedro drive his rig. She was determined to gain the respect of truckers, and also of Pedro's high tech customers. Inflation kept roaring, but they managed to save up some money.

Then Alice launched a consulting business, helping companies integrate humaniform robots into the workforce. Pedro told me that several robot manufacturers offered to hire her, but she refused them all.

Somebody threw a bagel at the break room TV set. On the screen was a news alert from Los Angeles. A driver robot was preparing to go solo.

Work had come to a screeching halt at Argus, as we all got a good long peek at the future. "This human foolishness," came to my mind, like it was yesterday.

"It's the end of an era," Beryl moaned.

"Damn straight," said our company mechanic. "Next up, they'll have fixit robots to go with the driver ones. No way a man can make a decent living, anymore."

"Old Doug won't never allow it," a driver said, meaning Argus Trucking's stubbornly traditional owner.

Time to speak up. "Hate to say this, folks, but Old Doug is going to retire soon, maybe at the end of this month. Don't ask me how I know, but the new management is all fired up to *modernize* this place." Even I winced at the sarcasm in my voice.

Inevitably, the Feds and big trucking company owners had pushed to broaden the rules. A pilot program was starting in Los Angeles; Shakey City as CBers call the place.

Soon as I got home, I had the TV run a search for videos of the event. "Hey Laurie," I called, "check out the news. They had that solo driver robot demonstration this morning."

She came bustling in, with a handful of colored paper for some art project she was planning for her students.

We watched with fascination as the newest model Sylvantronics robot took the wheel of a big rig. Mr. White Coat (as I will always think of the man) was on hand, with Sanjay Bishnoi talking to the press and VIPs.

"There's Alice." Laurie pointed to the back of the crowd of dignitaries. "She's getting paid to consult, right?"

"Yeah. Not sure for who, in this case. Hope they're paying for a big fancy hotel room." I requested a close-up, and the TV found a second video source. The image zoomed in on our young friend. "Look!"

Alice was fidgeting with her shoulder bag. Barely visible, peering out from the bag, was a tiny, moving bump. The TV found us a couple more angles, but none any closer to Alice.

I was certain it was the spy pigeon.

Laurie agreed. "Most gals in L.A. have to settle for a Bichon Frise dog in their purse."

We laughed, long and hard.

I requested a fast news summary. The robot had completed its delivery run without a hitch, with more aerial cameras following than O.J.'s white Bronco chase ever got.

According to the analysts on TV, Wall Street was ecstatic. Got me to thinking. Could it be that I resembled a buggy whip manufacturer, like those talking heads claimed? Time to make way for the future? I figured this was a more profound sort of change.

I could retire any time, but what about younger folks? Men who'd no longer have a serious job to keep them focused? But, as usual, the big boys had their way. In several other cities, more robots went solo.

I still wanted to let some air out of Mr. White Coat's tires. Every time I saw him on TV, Alice's harsh look, from that day in the desert, would rise in my mind's eye. Compared to some, her sentiments were mild. Something was bound to happen.

Three weeks later, when the public's attention had wandered, a robot was solo driving a shipping container from the Port of Los Angeles to a big electronics store in Pasadena. The suits wanted to match up all the latest elements, so the load was inside a new autoloading type container unit.

This time, when the news broke I did not wait to get home, and nobody blamed me. I know all the good break spots, and modern cities don't have a lot of safe, legal places where you can park a big rig. I parked at a funky old shopping center that doesn't mind trucks, so long as you're spending a little money. Then I asked Doll Box to do something against Argus work rules, which was to grab the video signal of a certain news outlet.

The driver robot had pulled over in Watts, opened the container, and unloaded several hundred boxes. Each box held a flat screen television set, the fancy kind that looks 3-D without your wearing special glasses. The police didn't see it, since about

90% of the surveillance cameras in that area are gone. Neither did that truck's guide box send an alert.

By the time I tuned in, many home video clips and eyewitness accounts had been gathered for news reports. The robot cranked up its voice, denounced capitalism and profiteering, and offered the TV sets as a gift to the oppressed peoples of the area. Whether this was a lunatic rant or a liberating sermon, Che Guevara or Hugo Chavez or Hakim X Sunshine couldn't have proclaimed it better. To an old timer like me it sounded campy.

Heedless of any cameras, the locals threw off their oppression with enthusiasm. Every box was gone in minutes. That robot was fast! It drove away before the police responded, got back on the freeway, and delivered the empty shipping container to the store. The police only recovered about a dozen TV sets.

Then another report broke. Apparently, in several other cities, driver robots were also taking action.

Doll Box only has a little monitor screen, so I threw work rules to the wind and ran inside a nearby diner. Tommy, the owner, was an old buddy of mine. Cooked a mean soy burger, and he had connections to get real beef sometimes.

"Hey Tommy, put both your TVs in split-screen mode. Something really big is happening."

One look, and he agreed.

In Denver, a robot dropped its load of frozen foods at a busy Salvation Army soup kitchen. In Orlando, a load of over-the-counter medicines went to a low income senior citizen's center.

"Check it out," I told Tommy. "Somehow they acted at the same time. Finished before humans could respond."

The next three events were outright weird. In San Francisco, a trailer full of chain saws ended up in an alley near a Natural Resources Defense Council office. The manifest was marked "Discard, Dangerous Items." Then several pallets of Creationist literature landed in the parking lot of a scientific (AAAS) office in Washington. Not to be outdone, a load of Plan B pills went straight to a National Right to Life place in Oklahoma City.

By then the cops were cracking down, and pulling over every robot-driven truck they could find. Even so, there was one last incident, south of the border. A shipment of toys, headed for a retail shop in a highbrow neighborhood, went instead to the Shriners Children's Hospital in Mexico City. The electronic invoice appeared legitimate, so with happy surprise, the staff accepted the donation. Later, when the *Federales* showed up, nobody had the heart to take anything back from the kids.

I don't know about anybody else, but when that report from Mexico came on, the folks in Tommy's Diner cheered like it was a high school soccer game.

All that week I followed the story with interest. Sylvantronics clammed up, but rumors abounded. Was it a hacker prank? Economic terrorism? Union activists? Jealous corporate rivals? A shared malfunction? Nobody knew.

Reclaiming the loads would've been a PR disaster. Even the coldest-hearted bean counters knew that, so the items were written off as donations. But the insurers panicked, in their own debonair fashion. Even though its own shipments were unaffected, the military almost went on red alert.

Wall Street turned its fickle thumbs down. Sensing the country's mood, politicians piled on thick. President Donna Weinberg held a press conference.

I caught the key part of her talk:

"A great many people, like seniors and the handicapped, depend upon household robots. I can assure you these are safe, and will not be recalled. However, my experts agree that industrial robots must have constant human supervision."

Unsaid was, people could vote and robots did not. Human truckers came back into favor real quick.

By the end of the week, solo robot drivers were out like the dodo bird.

A few days later, it was Pedro and Alice's turn to have us over for dinner. Recent events were, of course, our big topic.

Pedro said, "The FBI says there's no evidence of terrorism, or a hacker prank. They're stumped. None of my government or industry contacts have any good leads."

"Dr. Bishnoi asked me to keep my eyes peeled," Alice said. "The robot's basic programming seems intact. He wonders if they didn't make their units care *too* much about humans. We have so many troubles, and now they're seeing everything."

Did I imagine a smug look on Alice's face?

On our way home, Laurie commented on the uproar. "I feel like we're watching history unfold. Yesterday, one of the kids at my nursery school asked if a nice robot was going to bring her some toys. She's only four years old! Honey, do *you* think it was hacking, or an incipient robot takeover?"

I'm no expert, but it's surprising how much an old trucker can learn, when right in the middle of something. "I'd say clever hacking. The robot takeover comes later."

Laurie agreed, then we talked about the beauty of the desert sunset. Next to us on the freeway, a robot was driving a big rig. Its human team driver was in the shotgun seat, chatting on his CB.

Lisa Morton is a screenwriter, author of non-fiction books, award-winning prose writer, and Halloween expert whose work was described by the American Library Association's Readers' Advisory Guide to Horror as "consistently dark, unsettling, and frightening." Her most recent releases include Ghosts: A Haunted History, *the fiction collection* The Samhanach and Other Halloween Treats, *and the anthology* Haunted Nights *(co-edited with Ellen Datlow). She can be found online at* www.lisamorton.com.

JOB NO. 34264

Lisa Morton

JOB NO. 34264
LOG PREPARED BY C4-D4298
START DATE: DAY 247 YEAR 2129
DRIVER: HERRERA, MEI, LICENSE #A-0013
VEHICLE: TANKER TRUCK 19
ASSIGNMENT: TEMPORAL HAUL
TRANSCRIPTION BEGINS AT 0800

Herrera: Driver Mei Herrera, license number A-0013, confirming voice recognition.

C4-D4298: Confirmed.

Herrera: Thank you. Good morning, Ceefee.

C4-D4298: You know I hate it when you call me that. Is your palate simply incapable of forming the syllables "Cee" and "Four"?

Herrera: Why do I have to be the only driver with a sarcastic rebot?

C4-D4298: Oh, trust me—I'm not even close to being the only sarcastic rebot. Or even the most sarcastic.

Herrera: Fine. Let's get down to some business here. Please note that we have a trainee ride-along for today's job. State your name for the record, please, and Ceefee—please place into long-term storage as well for voice recognition purposes.

Dirk: My name is Jolie Dirk.

C4-D4298: Thank you, trainee Dirk. Your voice has been stored permanently and will be used for future voice recognition... provided you survive a trip with Mei Herrera.

Herrera: Ceefee, a pair of wire-cutters is looking good about now...

C4-D4298: Bristly today, are we?

Herrera: No more than usual. Ceefee, I'm going to move us to the lift platform now.

C4-D4298: Confirmed.

Herrera: Dirk, I know this is your first trip, so ask away if you don't understand something.

Dirk: Right.

Herrera: Do you know what we're doing right now?

Dirk: Moving the truck to the lift platform, which will take us up to the surface where the actual temporal shift will occur.

Herrera: Good. You'd be amazed at some of the trainees I get. I had one who actually thought the truck flew.

Dirk (laughing, then): I hope he didn't graduate to driver. I am curious about the surface...

Herrera: Well, the good news is that you won't see much of it from where we'll be.

Dirk: That's the good news?

Herrera: Trust me, if you'd ever seen it you'd understand why not seeing it is good news.

Dirk: So it really is as bad as they say?

Herrera: Worse. Sand, rock, winds, and a whole lot of ruined shit.

C4-D4298: Hang on, Herrera—they're having a small issue with alignment on the platform. Control says it will be fixed very shortly.

Herrera: Got it. So, while we wait, let's quiz the trainee some more. Why do we have to be lifted to the surface?

Dirk: Because we'll be traveling in time, not space, and if we attempted that from underground that's where we'd wind up in the past—buried under a quarter-mile of dirt and rock.

Herrera: You really did pay attention during training.

C4-D4298: The alignment issue has been fixed now, so proceed onto the platform.

Herrera: Thank you.

SYSTEM MONITOR RECORDS THAT AT 0806 DRIVER POSITIONED VEHICLE ON LIFT PLATFORM

C4-D4298: That's it. Control has been notified to commence lift.

Dirk: How many times have you made this trip?

Herrera: Today will be number sixty-four.

Dirk: That's the most of any driver, right?

Herrera: Yes, that's the most.

C4-D4298: We've reached the surface. Lift is now locked.

Herrera: Perform final system checks.

C4-D4298: All systems checked.

Herrera: Tell Control we're set.

C4-D4298: Communicating with Control now. Hang on— they're having a small problem with one of the shields. It should be only a moment.

Herrera: Jesus. This shit's all breaking down.

Dirk: I didn't realize the temporal bay would be so big. It's huge. And I can feel it vibrating.

Herrera: Now's your chance, Dirk—there's a window to your right, if you want to take a look at the surface.

Dirk: Is it okay to leave the truck right now?

Herrera: I'll call you back when we're ready.

SYSTEM MONITOR INDICATES THAT TRAINEE DIRK EXITS THE VEHICLE BUT RETURNS WITHIN TWENTY SECONDS

Dirk: You're right—there's not much to see. Just wind whipping sand past the port. Do you think the surface looks like that everywhere?

Herrera: As far as we know. Ceefee, do we know if that's standard for the surface?

C4-D4298: I am in communication with AIs at other communities, and they all report similar conditions. At this point, we believe the wars rendered the entire surface uninhabitable.

Dirk: Were you around during the wars, Cee-Four?

C4-D4298: First off, thank you for addressing me properly and not sharing the flippant attitude of your driver.

Herrera: You have not even begun to see flippant, ass-circuit.

C4-D4298: To answer your question, Trainee Dirk—yes, I existed during the wars. I'm a first generation artificial intelligence. I achieved self-awareness in 2042.

Dirk: So you remember how it was before?

C4-D4298: Yes, although of course I didn't experience it the way a human would.

Dirk: It looks beautiful in the holos.

Herrera: You'll see it for yourself soon enough. Hey, you know about the possible side effects of time travel? The disorientation, nausea, headache, all that?

Dirk: Yes, we covered all that in training. Does any of that happen to you?

Herrera: No. Never did. I'm just lucky that way. But a lot my trainees get sick on the first trip. If that happens to you, there's a bag under your seat.

C4-D4298: The shield problem has been resolved, and we're on our final countdown. Two minutes to shift.

Herrera: Buckle up, Dirk.

Dirk: Right.

Herrera: Let's see how well your training took: tell me the size of our payload.

Dirk: 11,600 gallons.

Herrera: What's our cargo?

Dirk: Water.

Herrera: Why?

Dirk: Because all of the world's water was contaminated during the wars, and our filtration systems can't purify it fast enough to keep up with demand.

Herrera: How far back do we go?

Dirk: 15,000 years.

Herrera: Good. You'll do just fine.

Dirk: I really want to be a driver. I mean, a lot of people my age do. It's so much better than being a lighting technician or a tunneler or a hydroponics laborer. But beyond that...I really fell in love with the pictures.

Herrera: Well, don't fall too in love—you can't stay.

Dirk: I know.

C4-D4298: All systems online. Thirty seconds.

Dirk: That's the shield check running, isn't it?

Herrera: It is.

C4-D4298: Ten seconds.

Herrera: You nervous?

Dirk: A little.

Herrera: You'll do fine. Here we go.

SYSTEM MONITOR INDICATES THAT TEMPORAL SHIFT TO 15,000 YEARS PRIOR ACHIEVED SUCCESSFULLY.

SCANS REVEAL NO THREATS, ERRORS, OR PROBLEMS. PERSONAL MONITOR SCANS FOR BOTH DRIVER AND TRAINEE SHOW SOLID LIFE SIGNS.

Herrera: See, that wasn't so bad, was it? Uh-oh—you look a little green...

Dirk: I think I'm okay. Just a little fuzzy, but it's fading.

Herrera: You'll get over that after a few more trips. Now we just pull forward a hundred yards to the pump. Looks like a nice day!

Dirk: Oh fuck. Oh, sorry, but...it's even more beautiful than the pictures. It's so green.

Herrera: Yeah, we don't get to see that color much, do we? Unless you work in the growing pods, I guess.

Dirk: Something just went over us!

Herrera: That was a bird.

Dirk: But I thought birds were small! That was big.

Herrera: Well, don't forget that we're in the past—a lot of things were bigger. If you reach behind your seat, you'll find the tranq gun.

Dirk: Have you ever used it?

Herrera: Once, six trips ago. I was standing by the truck working the pump when something big charged me. I don't even know what it was, but it had teeth as long as my forearm.

C4-D4298: You're exaggerating the size of the teeth. It was *Canis dirus*.

Herrera: What?

C4-D4298: *Canis dirus*, or dire wolf. They've been extinct since about 10,000 B.C.

Dirk: Wow.

Herrera: Okay, we're there.

SYSTEM MONITOR INDICATES THAT HERRERA STOPS THE VEHICLE. TRANQUILIZER GUN RETRIEVED. BOTH DRIVER AND TRAINEE STEP FROM THE CAB TO ENGAGE THE PUMPS. VOICES ARE NOW CAPTURED BY EXTERIOR MICROPHONES.

Dirk: So this is where they drilled the well.

Herrera: Yep. You know how the pump works, right? It's pretty easy.

Dirk: It must have been amazing to be part of the first shift back to this place. To know it worked, and that it looked like this...

Herrera: It was hard work, too. They had to drill down and set up the pump all the while hoping they weren't causing some massive time paradox that would wipe them out. So here's the pump, there's the truck—do you want to give it a try?

Dirk: The sky is so blue it almost hurts to look at.

Herrera: Dirk, pay attention.

Dirk: Oh, sorry. Sure, I received the highest marks in my class on this simulation.

Herrera: Good...now be sure to tighten that gasket...okay, open the pump...check for leaks...looks good. Ceefee, how's the flow?

C4-D4298: Perfect. Well done, trainee Dirk. Not a single drop spilled.

Herrera: Not that it would make much difference here. There's so fucking much water.

Dirk: But it's not inexhaustible, is it?

Herrera: I suppose nothing is.

Dirk: Do you ever worry that we're taking too much?

Herrera: Dirk, I'm just a driver.

Dirk: What happens now?

Herrera: Now we wait. How long, Ceefee?

C4-D4298: Twenty-eight minutes to fill the tank.

Dirk: The air smells so good.

Herrera: Hey, don't walk too far.

Dirk: C'mon, don't you ever want to just hike around, take in the scenery, smell the flowers?

Herrera: Big furry things with teeth aren't the only reason you need to stay close to the truck.

Dirk: Oh, I know. Believe me, they really pound the stuff about possible time paradoxes into your head during training.

Herrera: So tell me.

Dirk: Okay, then: it's the Butterfly Effect, where conceivably killing anything with DNA could mess with evolution. That's why we only come 15,000 years into the past: because it's recent enough in the evolutionary time-scale that if I step on an ant or a dandelion, I probably won't affect our future.

Herrera: You got it.

Dirk: So why can't I go walking around? We've got almost half an hour. And come on, I can see from here for miles. There's nothing about to charge us.

Herrera: Do you really know what's out there?

Dirk: Can I just walk to those flowers over there? I've never seen a real flower.

Herrera: Fine.

AFTER SIXTY-TWO SECONDS EXTERIOR RECORDERS PICK UP TRAINEE SHOUTING AT A DISTANCE FROM THE VEHICLE OF APPROXIMATELY ONE HUNDRED AND TWENTY FEET.

Dirk: These smell amazing!

Herrera: What kind of flowers are those, Ceefee?

C4-D4298: Hold on while I reposition my camera and zoom in...they're roses. I don't know the exact variety.

EXTERIOR RECORDERS INDICATE THAT DIRK RETURNS TO THE TRUCK

Dirk: Do you ever think of...you know...

Herrera: Of what?

Dirk: Staying.

Herrera: Don't go there, Dirk.

Dirk: Don't you get tired of seeing nothing but plain metal walls and artificial lights and of breathing stale, recycled air? I mean, living underground is bad enough, but especially if you've seen all this.

Herrera: I...of course we all think of it, but it's...

Dirk: It's happened, right?

Herrera: Yes.

Dirk: It was the second driver they ever sent through, wasn't it? Name was something like Chan, or—

Herrera: Cheng. It was Cheng.

Dirk: Cheng. Did you know him?

Herrera: Yes.

Dirk: They caught him, right? Brought him back, put him on trial, finally exiled him to the surface?

Dirk: Herrera...?

Herrera: You'll find out sooner or later anyway.

Dirk: Find out what?

Herrera: After he went missing, they sent out search teams, but they never found him.

Dirk: They never...you mean, he's still out here somewhere?

Herrera: If he's not dead.

Dirk: Are there...more than him?

Herrera: I think so, but...I only know about Cheng for sure. He was my...we were...

Dirk: Oh. I'm sorry. I didn't mean to...

Herrera: I know. It's just...I thought he'd at least wait for me, send me some sort of message, something. But he...Ceefee, I don't suppose you can delete the last few lines from the official recording, can you?

C4-D4298: You know I can't, Mei. Sorry.

Dirk: So why don't you stay? Go find him.

Herrera: Because it wouldn't be right.

Dirk: Maybe other things are even less right.

Herrera: I'm a driver.

EXTERIOR RECORDERS INDICATE THAT DIRK WALKS A FEW FEET AWAY FROM THE TRUCK BUT RETURNS WITHIN ONE MINUTE.

Dirk: How long is left now?

C4-D4298: Twenty-three minutes.

Herrera: Look, I need to stay here to make sure the pumping goes okay, but it doesn't take two of us. If you want to walk around, go ahead. But always keep the truck in sight. And I'm hanging onto the tranq gun, so you better run fast if anything you can't handle shows up.

Dirk: Yes, ma'am.

TWENTY-FIVE MINUTES PASS BEFORE EXTERIOR RECORDERS INDICATE THAT TRAINEE DIRK RETURNS TO THE TRUCK.

Herrera: You're late. We finished the pump a few minutes ago. Time to head back.

Dirk: We should be here. We should all be here. I mean, sure, I've heard all about the problems with that—about how it would take several hundred trips to transport all of us back here, and that the first few groups could do something that would create a time paradox and wipe out everyone else, but...well, we've been taking water for a while now, and nothing's gone wrong.

Herrera: At least nothing that we know of. Things might have changed and we wouldn't even know. Besides, there's a big difference between moving ten thousand people and taking some water. The water's an unlimited resource in this time.

Dirk: That's what we thought around the time of the wars, wasn't it? Same with the food, and the oil, and the coal.

C4-D4298: With all due respect to this intriguing discussion, we really need to return to the platform. Temporal shift will begin in twenty-two minutes.

Herrera: You heard the boss. Let's go.

EXTERIOR RECORDERS INDICATE THAT DRIVER AND TRAINEE RETURN TO VEHICLE. PERSONAL MONITOR SCANS ARE RE-INITIALIZED AND INDICATE DRIVER AND TRAINEE ARE IN GOOD HEALTH. SYSTEM MONITOR RECORDS DRIVER STEERING VEHICLE BACK TO PLATFORM.

Herrera: Are we centered, Ceefee?

C4-D4298: Back three more feet...now we're centered.

Herrera: How long until the shift?

C4-D4298: Seven minutes.

Herrera: Copy. Put your belt on, trainee.

Herrera: Trainee Dirk? Belt up.

Dirk: What if I stay?

Herrera: You'll be in violation of numerous laws.

Dirk: Only if they catch me.

Herrera: They will.

Dirk: They didn't catch Cheng.

Herrera: I don't...I doubt that he's still alive. I think he would have left me a message at the pump if he was.

C4-D4298: Six minutes to shift.

Herrera: Jolie, we all feel that way in the beginning. It's hard. People back home don't understand, because they haven't been here for themselves. But being a driver is more than just a chance to get out into fresh air and sniff some flowers; you're helping people, too. You're delivering the thing we most need to keep going. We're like the veins that supply the lifeblood to our world.

Herrera: Please, Jolie, just put your belt on and think about this.

Dirk: Okay.

Herrera: Good. I'll do whatever I can to help. You know that, right?

Dirk: It's why I'm putting the belt back on.

SYSTEM MONITOR INDICATES ALL SYSTEMS FUNCTIONING AS COUNTDOWN ENTERS FINAL PHASE.

C4-D4298: Ten seconds to shift.

Herrera: Thank you, Ceefee.

Dirk: Herrera, what are you going to say on my evaluation?

Herrera: That you'll make a fine driver.

SYSTEM MONITOR RECORDS TEMPORAL SHIFT OCCURRENCE.

SYSTEM MONITOR INDICATES SYSTEMS FAIL

POWER FA L

SH ELDI G F IL

PE S N L MON I ORS

Herrera: What the fuck just happened? Ceefee, talk to me.

C4-D4298: Temporal shift unsuccessful.

Herrera: Where are we?

C4-D4298: According to my scans, we are in the year 2063.

Herrera: But that's during the wars. Is that what I'm hearing? Those blasts...

C4-D4298: Yes. I believe those are anti-missile cannons.

Herrera: Ceefee, something's wrong with me...

C4-D4298: I cannot fully access your personal monitor, but I believe you are suffering from the effects of the atmosphere and radiation.

Herrera: But we're shielded.

C4-D4298: We are not currently shielded. Rerouting remaining battery power to personal monitors...there's an alteration in your genetic structure. I believe you are living through a time paradox in which your ancestors suffered from radiation and malnutrition.

Herrera: Where's Dirk?

C4-D4298: Trainee Jolie Dirk no longer exists.

Herrera: What are you saying, Ceefee?

C4-D4298: Due to a time paradox, we have arrived at the exact moment when an alteration in the past impacted the future. The alteration means that our scientists do not develop time travel in 2120.

Herrera: What...alteration?

C4-D4298: Unknown. But I believe this timeline does not lead to time travel, shielding, or Trainee Dirk.

Herrera: Was it...was it Cheng? Or did we...oh god, no...did we take too much water, so they had none by the time of the wars?...I...

C4-D4298: Life signs failing.

Herrera: I...no water...

C4-D4298: Driver Herrera...

DRIVER'S PERSONAL MONITOR RECORDS THAT LIFE SIGNS TERMINATE.

C4-D4298: I'm sorry, Herrera.

SYSTEM MONITOR RECORDS FAILURE OF BATTERY RESERVES.

C4-D4298: I don't want to be here.

RECORDING TERMINATES.

Michael Bailey is a freelance writer, editor, book designer, and the recipient of over two dozen literary accolades, such as the Bram Stoker Award *and* Benjamin Franklin Award. *His composite novels include* Palindrome Hannah, Phoenix Rose, *and* Psychotropic Dragon, *and he has published two short story and poetry collections,* Scales and Petals *and* Inkblots and Blood Spots, *as well as a children's book,* Enso. *Edited anthologies include* Pellucid Lunacy, Qualia Nous, The Library of the Dead, You Human, Adam's Ladder, Prisms, *and four volumes of* Chiral Mad. *Some of Michael's first interactions with the work of Stephen King included watching two horrible adaptations of a campy story about trucks:* Maximum Overdrive *(1986, King's only directorial effort) and, over a decade later,* Trucks *(1997).*

ESSENTIAL OILS

Michael Bailey

I
Lavandula augustifolia

LAVENDER IS AN HERB, and commonly referred to as English lavender, although not originally from England, but a native to the Mediterranean. The aromatic evergreen shrub can grow over two meters tall, and is part of *Lamiaceae* (commonly known as the mint or deadnettle family) of the species *angustifolia*, which means "narrow leaf." The plant is often grown for its colorfully pinkish-purple flowers, for its fragrance, for its drought resistance. Both flowers and leaves are used in herbal medicines, and often found in teas or lotions or soaps. The plant is a natural relaxant of muscles, particularly when used as an essential oil, which can be used to relieve anxiety. Dried lavender flowers can also be used to ward off clothing moths, which cannot stand the aroma. Lavender is complicated.

"I'm not sure you can smoke in the truck, is all," the woman said, a Border Services Officer.

The Canada Border Services Agency, Francis especially, always gave Sid a hard time about his vape pens whenever crossing the border. He knew a few by first name, by now, like Francis, although her badge simply read her last: Dougal.

"It's not smoke," Sid said, releasing a cloud into the cab. "It's lavender."

She leaned in close, her round-brimmed hat barely reaching the rolled-down window of his rig, and said, "Smells like flowers, don't cha' know. What're you haulin' back there?"

"The same."

"The same?"

"Lavender."

Sid took another pull from the pen, held it, let out a breath. He knew the next question before she even asked: *Flowers in a tanker?*

"Oil," he said. "Essential oil of lavender."

"Ah," she said, not really understanding, at least according to the confused look on her face. "Heard those things can still cause cancer, though," she said, meaning the vape pen.

"This isn't nicotine," Sid said, a little defensive. "Not even tobacco. It's simply lavender oil to help with my nerves, is all."

Crossing the border so many times, his words adapted accents.

"9,000 gallons of flower oil?" she said, reading the single item on the inventory list on the clipboard he'd handed her. "Is it flammable? I didn't see a red flip panel, only white, blank. Says here you're transporting *Lavan—*"

"*Lavandula augustifolia,*" Sid said after she struggled a while. The same words were printed on the packaging for his vape pen. The lavender kept him calm, steeled his nerves.

"Says here it's a Class-3 Flammable Liquid, flash point of 65 degrees Celsius." She looked to his shaking hands, then, as if the silver thing nestled between his fingers would burst. "Everyone is tense these days."

"Must have forgotten to flip over the card," Sid said.

"Well, I can't let 'cha pass till you do."

II
Citrus Bergamia

Bergamot is an orange, although not orange in color; the exceedingly-fragrant citrus fruit is various shades of green, depending on ripeness, and somewhat pear-shaped. Its juice is more bitter than grapefruit, less sour than lemon. *Bergamotto*, an Italian word of Turkish origin (*bey armut*) roughly translates to "prince of pears," although the fruit is by no means a pear. The origin of the plant is assumed to be a hybrid of lemon and bitter orange. Extracts are often used to enhance perfumes and cosmetics, yet one's skin increases in photosensitivity and becomes more easily damageable by the ultraviolet light of the sun when applied. It takes around thirty to thirty-five orange rinds to extract a single ounce of bergamot oil, which can aid those suffering from anxiety. There is also an herb called bergamot, which, like lavender, also lives in the mint family, but is otherwise unrelated to the fruit plant. Bergamot is complicated.

Francis Dougal rubbed the lotion on her skin. *Or else it gets the hose again*, she thought, thinking of the movie *The Silence of the Lambs* and that detective Jody Foster lady. Cute one, she was, back then. Even now. She rubbed her hands until the lotion worked itself between the dryness of her fingers, deep into the red cuticles.

The cold, and the wind, was harsh on her body, so she rubbed some of the lotion on her face. Her nose glowed pink like her ears, and the citrus tickled her nostrils. The woman in front of her, in the mirror, appeared as if she'd sneeze, but held it back after pinching the bridge beneath those tired eyes...tired from staring through the brightness of snow.

9,000 gallons of bergamot oil, she imagined, reading the label.

"It's not an herb at all," she told her reflection, seeing the image of the fruit printed on the back of the squeeze tube. "Smells like oranges, it does."

"Wonder if you can smoke the stuff," said the woman in the mirror.

It's not smoke, Francis Dougal mocked, a horrible mimic of the trucker she'd questioned earlier that day. *It's bergamot.*

"Oil," said the woman in the mirror.

She smelled her hand, then, wondering if the lotion was flammable.

III
Boswellia sacra

Frankincense is a resinous dried sap harvested from a small deciduous tree commonly known as the olibarnum-tree, which can have one or more trunks, and is part of the *Burseraceae* family and *Boswellia* genus of plants. A native to northeastern Africa and the Arabian Peninsula, its bark has the texture of paper, much like eucalyptus. The trees bear small capsules of fruit and leaves covered in down, but do not produce resin until they are eight or more years in age. After slashing/stripping the bark, the trees bleed a milky resin, which coagulates when exposed to air and becomes harvested once dried, most often by hand. The trees have adapted over the years because of overexploitation, both decreasing in population and their seeds germinating less frequently depending on how heavily the trees are tapped. The oldest are dying, with scant regeneration from seedlings. Frankincense, one of the consecrated incenses

(*Ha-Ketoret,* mentioned in the Hebrew Bible), is thought to have been gifted to Christ upon his birth, a foreshadowing of his death, perhaps. Today, the resin is used in perfumes and aromatherapy, the essential oil obtained by steam distillation and homeopathically used to treat anxiety. Frankincense is complicated.

"Jesus Christ, is it cold," Sid said, warming his hands. Sometimes he'd talk to himself to pass the time. The interstate ahead was a gray cut through endless white, the snow falling as gentle as ash from a campfire. Red demon eyes stared back at him from the truck he followed—one truck after the other after the other— and then blinking yellow as the line of semis began to ascend. He turned on his hazards as well. No use passing in this storm.

Seven hundred miles to go, he told himself, looking at the GPS. *Middle of nowhere. North America's crown. The damn forever-melting arctic circle, or somewhere close.*

He badly wanted a cigarette; not a vape pen, but *real* smoke. *Illegal* smoke. It was unlawful to even possess while transporting flammables.

Smoking, was it illegal in Canada too, like in most of the U.S. states?

He knew smoking would warm him, the thought of holding the cancer stick sending a shiver down his spine, making him feel even colder, if that were possible. The heater in the cabin was cranked to HIGH, the fan full-blast.

Sid brought the pen to his lips, inhaled, and watched the LED at the end glow like fake ember, but nothing drew out of the device. He always smoked what he carried, for some reason, so this round it was frankincense, which tasted and smelled a little better than the lavender. He'd take a puff every time his hands shook, and after a while they'd tremble less. The stuff worked, all of it. But nothing drew out this time....

Clogged, he discovered; the hole at the mouth end was congested with a whitish-yellow substance, like sap. *Frankincense* is *sap*, he told himself. He'd read how the stuff was harvested for public consumption, somewhere overseas, and how they'd scrape the trees like bears and let the trees bleed out, how the syrupy liquid reacted to air and solidified. The frankincense was simply doing what it was designed by nature to do when exposed outside the bark; oxygen must have caused the stuff to re-solidify, like the trees scabbing over to protect themselves from further bleeding.

Sid put the truck in AUTO-DRIVE and released the wheel. His rig was designed, even in snow, to understand the lines of the road, to travel onward with minimal human interaction, around curves, to accelerate, to decelerate, to brake completely to a stop and then start again, to adapt to other vehicles on the road. Trucks could virtually link together, like train cars, maintaining safe distances. Man would eventually no longer be needed for transportation, but until then, he milked the opportunity. His job. His life. The open road, and other drivers—his home, his family.

His truck determined Sid had been following a little too closely to the rig ahead of him, and decelerated to the "proper" distance, and then accelerated until maintaining the same speed.

Sid used the break from the hypnotic road to turn in his seat, to give the vape pen his undivided attention; he scraped what he could from the mouth end and tried again. Nothing. Not even the red light. He tapped the tip, as if that would fix anything, and finally managed to find a safety pin in the glove compartment, poked the sharp tip into the hole, prodded around. He took another pull, and then another, but the damn thing was cold, like his hands, and so he placed the pen between them and made as if to start a fire using nothing but the stick on the seat of his cabin. He spun it round and round, and that apparently did the trick, for after another long pull the mass dislodged into his throat like a sweet hardened honey and the tip glowed red.

He let out white, like the snow, which billowed around him and disappeared.

Essential oils, where have you been all my life?

Headaches, allergies, inflammation, viral infections, stress, anxiety....

The border didn't cause him any trouble this time. No hassle. No stress. Sid had remembered to flip over the panel to the red FLAMMABLE side. Frankincense, like most of the essential oils, was also considered a Class-3 Flammable Liquid. Flash point: 51⁰ Celsius.

What does Canada want with all these oils anyway, he wondered. *And why so far north, to the literal opposite of hell, the frozen wasteland?*

America's hat, someone had once called it.

His hands shook, but mostly from the cold.

Jesus Christ.

IV

Chrysopogon zizanioides

Vetiver is a perennial bunchgrass. Although part of the *Poaceae* family of plants, the more common "vetiver" shares morphological characteristics with *Cybopogons*, which include fragrant grasses such as palmarosa, lemongrass, and citronella. The grass grows as tall as three meters, the leaves rigid and hundreds of centimeters in length, with flowers in brownish-purples bursts as long as arms and with three stamens. Most grasses are rooted by horizontal mat-like systems, whereas vetiver roots grow downward (nearly as deep as the plant is tall, in its first year), and is highly tolerable to both wildfire and frost. They manage to survive up to two months when completely submerged under flooding waters. New roots can grow from cut nodes. Essential oil from the plant is extracted from the roots, used in cosmetics, skincare (treatment of acne and sores), ayurvedic soaps, and aromatherapy. Vetiver is used to prevent ground erosion, as weed control in tea and coffee plantations, as a byproduct to feed livestock, as a flavoring agent in human foods (khus syrup), and as a termite repellent because of its natural chemical *nootkatone*. And its oil is used for its anti-fungal properties and to treat anxiety. Vetiver is complicated.

"The trucks keep on coming, is all," Francis Dougal told the desolate ground around her, "one after the other. Like train cars."

Never had she seen so many, not all at once. Three trucks full of vetiver oil this morning, whatever that was, but no Sid. Francis had some foot cream back home "infused with the essence of vetiver," according to the label; it smelled nice, sure, kept her grounded, but she wondered what else it could be used for besides foot creams. Her foot itched then, just thinking about it, from the athlete's foot that sometimes plagued her—not that she considered herself athletic by any means; it was the cold, she knew, sweating in those cotton socks....

Why did the world, or Canada anyway, need so much vetiver oil?

She waited for Sid, but he was days out, maybe weeks. She'd seen him only twice, but he was the only one who ever really said anything while under inspection; others just grunted, nodded, made inhuman sounds. Most sounded like automatons. Sid was always calm, smooth, yet rugged...and he always smelled nice, like his oils.

One day, I won't have anyone to talk to, she imagined. *One day, the trucks will drive themselves. Well, once everything's automated. One day, they won't have a need for border control. One day, they won't need walls.*

Francis Dougal couldn't help wonder what made people so complicated. Perhaps a gift would help break the ice. Perhaps a flower only Sid could appreciate.

Didn't he say he was from British Columbia?

She shifted in her boots while trying to remember his license, and pretended to smoke something nonexistent; nothing bad, but something natural—oil from flower petals, perhaps.

V

Canaga Odorata

Ylang-ylang is a flower from the tropical canaga tree of Indonesia, part of the custard apple family *Annonaceae*. Ylang-ylang is also used as the name of the tree itself, when not called by its other many names: the Macassar-oil plant, the perfume tree, the fragrant canaga. Hawai'ians call it *Moto'oi*, Tongans *Mohokoi*, Fijians *Mokohoi* or *Mokasoi* or even *Mokosoi*. The tree goes by many Polynesian names, but its perfume, *ylang-ylang* is derived from a Tagalog term, *ilang-ilang,* which means *wilderness-wilderness* (often mistranslated as *flower of flowers*). Perfume is extracted from greenish-yellow (seldom pink) flower petals. Its vines, like the tree itself, can grow up to five meters per year. The essential oil is used in aromatherapy to treat high blood pressure, to normalize sebum secretion for certain skin maladies, is considered an aphrodisiac (flower petals are placed onto the beds of newlywed couples in Indonesia), and used to flavor ice cream in Madagascar. In some countries, flower petals are fashioned into leis and worn by women, or to adorn religious images. Ylang-ylang is complicated.

"You again," Sid said with a smile. Out of all the Border Service Officers he'd seen over the years, Francis was the only one memorable. Maybe it was her posture, or the uniform.

She tipped her hat, a way of saying hello without speaking.

"Me again," she said.

"I'm guessing you'll need my papers, ya?"

"Ya."

Again, a slip of accent that wasn't his own. Sid was originally from Vancouver, but the one in Washington, not British

Columbia; he'd moved to the Vancouver in Canada around five years ago and had become a citizen, thanks to a marriage gone sour.

"What are you haulin' this time?"

"Nothing."

"Nothing?"

The cold bit like a witch.

"Light load. Haulin' sailboat fuel, don't you know."

I laid that on a little too thick. Should be don' cha, not don't you.

"Scale says you're empty. Tare weight," she said, not getting the joke. "Just spriggin' up conversation, is all."

Francis didn't seem to mind the cold, though her skin reported otherwise: red on white, burnt by icy winds. She stood there, snow covering her uniform, a thin layer on her hat. She admired his license, tilted it toward a cloudy sky, as if light from the hidden sun would help uncover something.

The only sound for a moment was the heater blasting lukewarm.

"Hold on a sec," she said, and turned away.

Sid rolled up the window, not that windows *rolled* anymore; he pressed a button and the window rose. He thought of simply driving away, but the engine was off, as enforced until approval, and she still had his license. He'd never drive again. Now, more than ever, he wanted a cigarette, not vapored essential oils. Anxiety ate him as he beat his fingers against the steering wheel; they'd shake with nothing to do.

Mexico was easier to cross ever since the wall came down; sometimes they'd wave you through, not caring what was transported: drugs, alcohol, petroleum, explosives. But Canada...

And who still believes this planet is warming?

A temporary, reactive thought, he knew. He'd experienced enough over the years. He was just angry at the current frigid air. Call it global warming, call it climate change, call it a shift in earth's axis, call it whatever you want...the world was changing, the heat rising, both people and weather shifting around the earth like tectonic plates: Mexicans moving northward to California; Californians shifting to Oregon; Oregonians shifting to Washington; Washingtonians shifting to Canada. Canadians...well, forced up the pole. The same was happening all over the world. A mass migration of both people and heat. Not only temperatures, but pressure from nations to put an end to the madness. An anxious world waiting to snap...

A knock on the driver's side mirror startled him.

Francis again, representing the CBSA with a goofy smile. She mimed rolling down the window, when she should have mimed pushing a button, which wouldn't have made much sense.

Sid lowered the window and returned the smile.

"Everything okay?"

Francis nodded, looked to her shoes.

"Right. Here ya go," she said, handing the license back to him. "Look, this is not like me. I'm not the type of person that jumps in the pool, you know, without first dipping her toes in and getting used it the water. Well, I guess that's a bad example, seeing as it's all snow here and no swimming pools and we're on the border and you're just passing through—"

Finally, something to bring him warmth.

"But I couldn't help but notice on your license it says you're in Vancouver, of all places, and seeing as I'm from Vancouver, and all, I was thinking, you know, maybe we could grab a cuppa coffee sometime, if, well, when you're not too busy in your travels."

"I don't know what to say," Sid said.

"You don't have to say anything now. You can think about it, seeing as you're passing through and we make each other's acquaintance every so often. I got you something, though."

She reached into her jacket and pulled out a small silver pen-like object.

"A vapor pen, is all. You probably know a ton more about essential oils, but I did some research after you passing through so many times and telling me of your habits, and came across this one. Ylang-ylang, it's called. I didn't smoke it, or vape it, I mean. A new pen, it is."

Sid had transported 9,000 gallons of ylang-ylang late last month. He'd had some, now and then. The oil helped with anxiety, sometimes made you feel sexy.

She held it out to him like a flower, and he plucked it.

VI

Chamaemelum nobile

Chamomile is a perennial plant that, like *ylang-ylang*, goes by many names and many different spellings: camomile (without the h), garden chamomile, both English/Roman chamomile, low chamomile, mother's daisy, ground apple (the Greek-derived *chamaimēlon* genus name meaning *earth-apple* because of its scent), as well as whig plant. Its herbaceous aromas come from its white daisy-like flowers, which are used in perfumes, cosmetics, blonde hair rinses, lotions to treat cracked nipples from extensive breastfeeding, and are found in many herbal teas. The essential oils are used with aromatherapy for sleep aid and to treat anxiety, and can be applied directly to the skin to reduce swelling and pain, although is *not* suggested for use during pregnancies for it can cause uterine contractions and miscarriages. Chamomile is complicated.

The truck drove itself, for the most part. Sid had taken a few hits of the pen; not to relax this time, not really, but to help him sleep. The chamomile was the smoothest out of his collection, and smelled much like herbal tea. He hated tea, hated the taste, but for some reason inhaling it in this form went down easier, worked faster, calmed his nerves to the point of serenity, made his eyes heavier...and so he shifted the transmission to AUTO-DRIVE.

He'd driven the empty truck to the refinery up north, had returned to the Washington state border with his 9,000 gallons of crude oil from Canada, like the other tankers. With the weather warmer—if one could consider such a thing in *hell frozen over*—it had become more lucrative to process the bituminous sands, or tar sands, from the banks of the Athabasca just south of the Northwest Territories. And with the rest of the world's oil depleting, it made financial sense for the U.S. to do trade in such a valuable resource. He'd watched the stock market soar in both crude and essential oils. The world at war over the stuff.

His jobs were simple: transport essential oils *to* Canada; transport crude oils *from* Canada. *But why?*

He'd traveled south along Interstate 5, a short jaunt down Highway 20, crossed by ferry to Port Townsend, and from there made a short trek along 101 to Port Angeles, from which cargo ships unloaded his removable storage tanks and shipped his 9,000 gallons to who knows where. Russia, the Middle East?

Whoever paid the highest price for petroleum, he guessed.

But where do the essential oils come from, and why are they so desired in the north?

He knew lavender and chamomile were grown and harvested in the States, but bergamot, frankincense, vetiver, ylang-ylang... where the hell did *those* come from?

Same countries trading in crude, he guessed.

Wars were always confusing.

The money was good; that's all that really mattered. It was a job, for now, at least until transport trucks were completely automated, or transport via train was once again *a thing*. Perhaps he could work on trains, like his buddy Gord up north.

And so Sid found himself on his way there once again, from the ports of Washington to the oil sands of Canada, transporting a tank full of what the single-item inventory page listed as *chamaemelum nobile:* the essential oil of chamomile.

Sleep fell upon him quite easily after a few drags, a taste of apple on his lips, as he thought of world trade and war and melting polar caps and the ylang-ylang given to him by the Border Services Officer. Francis had given him flowers, in a way.... *Does she expect a rose?*

VII
Rosa × damascene

Commonly known as the Damask rose, or the "rose of Castile," *Rosa × damascene* is just that: a rose, from a deciduous shrub named after the city of Damascus in Syria. The moderate pink to light red petals of the flower are world-renowned for their fragrance and commercially harvested for *rose absolute* or *rose otto*, a fancy term for rose oil. *Rosa × damascene* is a cultivated flower no longer found in the wild. The flower petals, which are also edible, are used as garnishes, dried in herbal teas, and preserved in sugar as *gulkand* for food flavoring. "Rose water" is often sprinkled on meats and other dishes, while rose powder is used in sauces. The flavorings of rose can be found in rice puddings and jams and nougats. The Damask rose, for centuries upon centuries, has symbolized beauty and love, although the essential oil has also been used to treat anxiety. *Rosa × damascene* is complicated.

Francis Dougal waited weeks, and then months. Every silver tanker making its way across the border first elevated her hopes—of seeing Sid...*What was his last name, Langan?*—and then destroyed them, as if by fire. Essential oils were flammable, after all.

She imagined the worst, of course: his rig tipped over against an icy bank or a wall of rock, tank engulfed, small mushroom clouds of lavender or ylang-ylang or whatever he transported on his final drive filling the sky, perhaps making the foul world smell a little better.

"He's between jobs, is all," she told herself. "He's transporting south this time, is all," she sometimes told her reflection. "Maybe Mexico. Maybe across the States."

She'd gotten him another vape pen, kept it in her pocket each day for when she saw him next. She thought of trying it out, to ease her nerves, but thought better of it, even though he'd never know. Would it taste like rose? Would it stop her from worrying about not seeing him?

You might not ever see him again, honey.

She read the label more than once: *Rosa × damascene.* She imagined reading those same words printed on his next inventory list. 9,000 gallons of liquid rose.

Oh, I hope I do. See him, that is.

When not working, she'd sometimes go to bars, to coffee shops, for perhaps they'd stumble into/onto each other in Vancouver, of all places. He wasn't Canadian, she knew, but American, at least originally, and that was intriguing; she could tell by his accent, the way he sometimes adapted to her own when they spoke; the slip wasn't intentional.

Sid Langan.

VIII

Petroleum

Crude oil, or *petroleum*, is a yellow-to-black liquid substance that can be refined into various combustible fuels after components are separated by a process called fractional distillation. The "fossil fuel" forms under the surface of the earth after large quantities of deceased organisms (typically algae and zooplankton) are buried under sedimentary rock and exposed to high amounts of heat and pressure. Ninety percent of vehicular fuels thirst for petroleum, which is considered one of the world's most important commodities, although the number is slowly dwindling. While over eighty percent of the world's readily-accessible reserves can be found in in the

Middle East, there are significantly higher concentrations of unconventional sources in northern-most (and coldest) Canada, as well as Venezuela, in the form of oil sands. Extraction from such sources requires large amounts of both water and heat, making the process difficult and costly. It is estimated that 3.6 trillion barrels of bitumen and extra-heavy oil (nearly twice the volume of the entire world's reserves) can be found in these two countries alone. The word *petroleum* is of Ancient Greek origin: *petra* translating to *rock*, and *oleum* to *oil*. Along with fuel, the substance is commonly used to make plastics, as well as pharmaceuticals. When used as an essential oil, the product is known to cause cancer, and is highly flammable. Vapors of crude oil can have a flash point as low as 38º Celsius. Crude oil is complicated.

Sid kept a rose vape pen in his pocket in case he ever saw her again. She'd given him a flower, after all, and so he'd return the favor.

Fort McMurray was his destination this time, deep in the heart of the Athabasca Oil Sands. He was to fill his empty tanker with crude oil once again. But he was early, an entire day early, thanks to a misprinted pick-up date he hadn't noticed until it was pointed out to him.

Can't pick up your load 'til tomorrow, don't cha know.

And you can't park here overnight, don't cha know.

He'd slept most the drive, so he wasn't tired, and where was he supposed to go if he couldn't stay at Fort McMurray?

"You can park the empty tank there, if you want," the man in uniform said, pointing to a row of identical silver tanker trailers, "and load up in the morning, but we can't have you stayin' here overnight, sleeping in your rig, I mean. Against regulation, is what it is."

"Those other trucks," Sid said, taking a pull of ylang-ylang. "Where are they going?"

"Smells nice. You mind?" The man in uniform held out a gloved hand.

"Sure," Sid said, handing him the pen.

The man in uniform inhaled, the red light burning bright against the white. "Well," he said, releasing, "You can park the truck and stay at Stonebridge; that's the hotel."

"Or?"

"Or, since you don't look so tired, you can join the convoy headed *farther* north, if you need somethin' to do, I'm sayin'. Those trucks, you see, the ones you can park next to if you choose the stayin', those are headed up Highway 63, the road you came in on. Fort Mackay is that way, but the highway ends just past. It's ugly drivin' this time of year, but your truck can take it with those all-weathers, and I'm guessing you have chains in case the road turns uglier. Good money, it is. Very good money. Not sure where they're headed after that, but heard the pay's good the farther you go. You can contract out if you so choose."

And so Sid found himself taking on another drive, another shipment of *lavandula augustifolia*, of all things: lavender oil. 9,000 gallons. The convoy seemed never-ending. If he could guess, perhaps a hundred tanker trucks drove north. When the tires required chains, he asked other drivers what they were carrying. Most said the same: various oils, but not petroleum.

Why do they need all this essential oil?

Highway 63 followed an icy river, and soon the road ended and another began: a road made of ice, the river itself frozen over and used for travel. He'd driven over ice before, but not though weather like this. Visibility became a matter of feet thanks to a snow flurry, and soon the trucks were all virtually connected like train cars, one following the other, highlights connected to taillights—a truck-centipede of modern tankers eating exhaust eating exhaust eating exhaust...albeit low-emission, and some of the newer trucks zero-emission.

Jesus Christ, he thought, thinking of the frankincense, of the vetiver, of all the other essential oils transported over the border.

The ylang-ylang Francis had given him helped, a little.

Is this where it goes? Are they burning it? Using it to melt the polar caps?

Each time the trucks crawled at the slowest of speeds (sometimes slower than a walk), drivers stepped out of their vehicles wearing various gear, mostly to talk, since regulations prohibited the use of radios on this particular assignment, and because of the isolation. They weren't even supposed to talk to one another because of nondisclosure agreements, but men and women gossiped nonetheless, arms wrapped around themselves as if wearing straightjackets.

Some had theories there was an icebreaker farther north. One said they were eventually headed to a place called Kagluktuk. Another said the tanks were headed to Russia or Alaska or elsewhere, but that didn't make much sense. At their current speed, even the smallest of drives could take days, weeks...longer. GPS didn't work this far north, so Sid couldn't even bring up a map to see where the world ended.

The most logical idea was that a checkpoint waited miles ahead, where they could choose to either deliver their loads and turn back, or go on for more pay, and then another checkpoint, and then another, the pay exponentially increasing at every stop, with some sort of earth-crawler perhaps there to take their deliveries directly to the arctic as a final destination.

Most turned around after that first checkpoint, where hundreds—if not thousands—of silver oil tankers were aligned in rows for as far as the eye could see, or at least until disappearing into the white like everything else.

The pay doubled, and so Sid decided to go on. He lodged overnight at the camp stationed there, which provided hot meals and warm beds, and he could refill fuel for his rig, for free, from this point onward, and deliver as many tanks from one checkpoint to the next, or, he could go on even farther. Someone would handle his load of crude oil back to the States, or so he was told.

The money was enticing enough to believe in that promise.
Pay doubled again.
Doubled again.
The drives were intense, the convoys smaller.

After a week, he was out of vapors completely because he'd brought only one pen—for what he thought would be a single roundtrip pickup and delivery—and the ylang-ylang, which he'd saved for last; it had the sweetest taste, made him think of Francis back at the border. He still had *that* pen, too—the rose he'd gotten for her—but he promised himself he'd hold on to it, that he'd find her again.

I could retire after a month of this, he kept telling himself.

His hands shook, both from the cold and from the anxiety of trusting the taillights in front of him as well as trusting the taillights in front *that* truck, and so on; a recursive kind of trust. One rig could go over the side of a mountain, and all the lemmings would follow. But his hands shook less as the days went on, the farther north he ventured.

And what did Stephen Hawking say about recursion, that in order to understand recursion, one must first understand recursion? Something like that.

Everyone gets Canada's crude oil, its petroleum, and Canada gets what?

America's hat.

The "roads" went as far as Kugluktuk, according to the sign, and ended at the Arctic Ocean, one of the most beautiful sights Sid had ever seen in his travels. The ten or so trucks that went as far arrived on a clear night, and were met by brilliant stars and polar lights, aurora borealis, which shimmered like crystals of kryptonite—mostly greens, but also stripes of whites and purples. Minus 7 degrees Celsius. Sid gazed at the sky for hours.

In the morning, the sun shone brighter than he ever thought possible, the vast stretch of ocean intensely blue and filled with broken ice as large as trucks, as large as mountains. He watched in awe as an army of ferries carried the many silver tanks across the water, to the largest of icebergs—if that's what they were called—as giant hoses hooked to spigots shot the contents of the tanks over the ice like rain. Polar vortex weather/ocean circulation contraptions, or something. Large-scale. Essential oil diffusion required permeation, electricity, and heat. Sid wondered how an operation like this might work, at such a large scale, when the other machines appeared, machines he was incapable of comprehending.

The caps are melting, Sid thought, *but not from the burning of oil. And not from this.*

The ice was evaporating under the sun, as an altered nature intended, but now taking along with water into the sky—to the clouds—the aromas and fragrances of lavender, bergamot, frankincense, vetiver, ylang-ylang, chamomile, rose....

Whoever these people were, they were filling the earth's atmosphere with an insane amount of diffused essential oils, to be later distributed by something as natural as wind and weather, to be rained down upon all the anxious people in the world. These peaceful warriors, they were fighting a different kind of war.

Sid pulled the vape pen from his pocket, the flower he'd one day give to the woman at the border. The side of the device read in a script-like font: *Damask rose*. His hands no longer shook, hadn't for the last few days; perhaps his anxiety had improved as he progressed northward through Canada, toward the pole where all this was happening. Smiling, he slid the pen back into his pocket: his gift to Francis, if he ever saw her again.

Love is complicated.

Alvaro Zinos-Amaro's book of interviews with Robert Silverberg, Traveler of Worlds, *was a* Hugo *and* Locus *award finalist. Alvaro's more than thirty stories and one hundred reviews, essays, and interviews have appeared in magazines like* Clarkesworld, Asimov's, Analog, Lightspeed, Nature, Tor. com, Strange Horizons, Galaxy's Edge, Lackington's, *and anthologies such as* The Year's Best Science Fiction & Fantasy 2016, Cyber World, Humanity 2.0, *and* This Way to the End Times. *Alvaro has a book review column at* Intergalactic Medicine Show, *a film review column at* Words, *and he edits the roundtable blog for* Locus. *He has a degree in Theoretical Physics from the* Universidad Autónoma Madrid.

BIG RIG, BIG RIP

Alvaro Zinos-Amaro

FOUR HOURS BEFORE DAWN turned the sky pink, Doug Garcia snuck out of his two-bedroom apartment in Ardmore, Oklahoma. His wife Sonnie and the three boys slept on. That was how they planned it: no goodbyes meant no tears.

A self-driving car took Doug to the airport, and connecting flights landed him in Ecuador, where at Mount Chimborazo he boarded the space elevator. The elevator lifted him up to the orbital depot station, where Doug underwent final medical tests. After this an automated shuttle conveyed him to his prize and beauty, the long-haul ship *Snowman*. All throughout the week-long journey from his house to his ship, Doug tried to distract himself with oldies by Merle Haggard and Dale Watson, but he still missed his family something fierce.

As the *Snowman*'s doors sealed behind Doug, the ship automatically initiated launch protocols. "Welcome aboard," the *Snowman* said, its customary greeting.

"Thanks old friend," Doug replied.

He allowed himself a brief smile. His life belonged to Sonnie and the boys, but in a real sense this felt like home.

By the time he was installed in the cockpit the engines were online. He laid out his gear the same way every trip, special spots designated for his clothes, the emergency beacons and battery packs, the food rations and gels.

Then he buckled up and prepared for the moment of truth.

The ship's computer displayed information about Doug's current haul. On this run he was supposed to tractor a supplies cargo trailer, already attached to the *Snowman*, to a large mining vessel at the outskirts of the Solar System. Then he'd perform an asteroid intercept and bring the precious minerals back to Earth orbit. The computer told him how long he'd have to cold nap on the way there and back.

These details pressed on Doug with the same force as the ship's centrifugal gravity, making it hard to breathe.

He blinked at the readout a couple of times, until the shortness of breath passed.

Jesus.

He read it again.

Jee-sus.

His arms tingled and his ribcage tightened. "Easy there," he mumbled. "Don't go soft now."

But the computer screen was unwavering, unmerciful.

Over a year, he thought. A year that cold sleep would turn into the blink of an eye for him. A year during which he'd only age weeks.

But on Earth everyone and everything would go on as usual. Jeremy might go on his first date. Noah would start high school. Caleb would lose his last kid's teeth. And Sonnie—

How long will she put up with this? Doug thought.

How long can I keep this up?

There had to be another way. But for now he had no choice. If he didn't continue hauling for the Space Freighters Network he'd actually end up owing them money for the fuel he'd used on his hauls.

The *Snowman* performed its final pre-launch scan. A green light blinked all systems nominal.

Doug held his finger poised above the thruster button and a solitary tear slid down his cheek.

He wiped it away and punched the button hard.

"This ain't right," Sonnie said. "They promised you a shorter haul. They promised you this time, and the time before, and the time before that, and they done broke all their promises."

"Yeah you're right about that," Doug conceded. With each second that passed the *Snowman*'s pulsed ion drives increased the ship's speed, stretching the two-way delay between his words and hers. He felt the need to talk fast but forced himself to slow down. No sense in making her feel rushed. She deserved better than that.

"There's plenty of diamonds right here in our Solar System," she went on. "I looked this up last time you were away. There's a whole asteroid belt, for Heaven's sakes, *at two AUs*! You could be there and back in a couple of months. And you come talkin' to me about *a year*?"

"I know, I know," he pleaded, and wondered if he was bargaining with himself or with her. "Slim pickings left at the belt, honey. So now they're sending us farther out."

She didn't reply.

He felt the silence revving up, like an engine, ready to drive him somewhere he didn't want to go.

"Tell you what," he said. "When I get back, I'll stay for at least six months, and then I'll take the next haul only if it's a short one. I'll make them tell me in advance." The words tumbled out of his mouth before he knew what he was saying. He was trembling, but they were good shakes, like when you get off a rollercoaster ride and feel solid ground beneath your feet.

A minute passed.

"You heard me?" he said.

At last she said, "I heard you. Will we be able to afford you layin' about with us that long?"

It always came down to this, thought Doug. The money. The realities of the world. He tried not to let bitterness settle into his face, pinching at the corners of his eyes and locking up his jaw the way it sometimes did.

"We'll be fine," he said. "See, that's the thing about going out this far. We're carrying new scientific gizmos for long-range measurements and they pay a shitload more for that. Two-and-a-half times the usual rate, babe."

"That ain't bad," she said slowly. "I assume there's more risk."

"Some," he said. "The devices' AIs sometimes don't get along too smooth with the ship's systems. So I might get woken up to straighten things out. No big deal. I know guys who done it, they just lost a few days of cold sleep is all."

"You're not lyin' to me," she said.

"Of course I ain't lyin'," he said. "And like you said, it ain't a bad deal." His voice deepened. "I love you, Sonnie Garcia."

"You're all right," she said after the delay.

A panel let Doug know his message time was up; the SFN were penny-pinchers and had firm allotments on how much energy could be used for personal communications signals.

"I'm afraid I gotta go," Doug said.

"Okay then," Sonnie replied. The next silence was the longest of all, and the sweetest to break. "When you cold nap, dream of me," she said, "and I'll keep you warm."

The *Snowman's* message system chirped to life. Doug had his feet kicked up on the primary cockpit console. He'd been stargazing, his mind already halfway to Jupiter, when the alert brought him back to the present. The computer informed him that the signal ID was from someone outside the Space Freighter Network. That was weird. Usually the SFN frowned on such communications, and folks in the spaceways knew it. Cautiously, Doug accessed the com.

"Hey there," Doug said. "You really an independent contractor? I heard you was a dying breed."

The voice that replied was scratchy, but definitely a woman's voice. "The few and the proud," she said. "Name's Patricia. Thirty years now, and hoping I got another thirty in me."

"Doug here. And good on you," Doug said. He studied her ship's trajectory. It was inward bound. "To what do I owe the pleasure?"

"Got a proposition for you," she said. "While out in deep space, my ship picked up unusual data. Long-range stuff that could affect everyone." She sounded worried. "Not sure I understand it myself. Been trying to get the SFN to listen, but they don't want to hear none of it from the likes of an independent like me. I was hopin' you could talk to them on my behalf. I've got files I could share with you. In exchange, as a token of good faith, here's the position of a shielded bear."

Bears were SFN patrol ships, which usually hid in hard-to-detect locations, trying to ensure long-haul pilots didn't falsify their *comic books*—their log records. Sure enough, Doug's computer confirmed the faint presence of a ship lingering near an ice rock, its signal obscured by the heavenly body.

For a few moments he considered her request, then came to his senses. The SFN had a strict policy about out-of-network data packages and he'd be a fool to accept Patricia's files. For all he knew, it could be an AI virus, spy-software or who knew what.

"I'm afraid I gotta pass," Doug said.

Patricia's disappointment was impossible to miss. "You sure?"

"Look, I appreciate the heads up," he said, and meant it. "But I can't risk it. Any unusual files come into this tin can, the SFN will find a way to slash my wages. And I can't afford that. I got a wife and three boys, you understand? Sorry."

"I get ya," she said. "If you change your mind, you've got my signal ID. Keep the shiny side up and the rubber side down."

The com went dead. Doug logged and reported Patricia's message and then deleted it.

Still, as the moment for cryo-sleep approached, he found himself curious about the trajectory she'd followed. Already inside the *Snowman*'s cryo-chamber, he made a few tweaks to his own trajectory. He could get close to the place where her systems had acted up with just a week's deviation from his original course. What if he could duplicate her readings? That information might be worth something to the SFN if it came directly from him.

Doug's body softened after the final pre-sleep injection. The sedatives kicked in mercifully quick, and his eyelids grew heavy before he could say the names of his wife and three boys.

Good night, Snowman. And then his last thought, right before surrendering to darkness, the same last thought he had every time he went under: *I pray the ship don't go faster than my guardian angel can fly.*

Doug felt himself twisting inside out. Something scraped the inside of his throat, like a metal arm reaching into his gullet.

Then a sharp prod to his spine, and clamps on his legs and arms, first pushing down then lifting up.

A hissing sound built up like a dam and exploded into a sea of static as the cryo-tank burst open.

Doug felt himself shoved forward, but he couldn't see anything because his eyelids were crusted shut. *What in hell's blazes—*

He convulsed, spewing up cryo-sleep liquid from his lungs, trying to breathe through mucus and sputum.

In between the deep wracking coughs he picked away at the eye scabs, and then he puked.

He felt like he had been pulled apart and sloppily re-assembled, not everything in the right place.

He moaned.

Finally his eyelids worked again.

He was sitting upright in the cryo-tank. Lights were pulsing around him, sensor readings flashing numbers, all manner of warnings. The panels showed his heart rate and other vitals were bonkers.

"Well what do you doggone expect with a wake-up call like that?" he said.

Somehow he managed to climb out of the tank. He cleaned himself up as best he could. "*Snowman*," he said, "what in holy Moses' name is going on?"

"Emergency interruption of cryo-stasis cycle," the ship said in its rumbling voice.

"Well what caused the emergency?"

"Unknown."

"Great," Doug muttered. "Okay, let's try again. What *is* the emergency?"

"Unexpected displacement from programmed vectors."

"Why didn't you make adjustments to get us back on track?"

"Unable to complete needed calculations. Pilot required."

Doug's stomach plummeted. Had the ship's AI gone bad? That would seriously jeopardize his haul. If he couldn't make repairs himself, he'd be dead in space until the SFN sent someone out to him.

"Why weren't you able to do the calculations?" Doug asked, voice rasping with fear. "You're the smartest ship I know."

"Calculations require precise coordinate measurements," replied *Snowman*, giving no indication it had understood the flattery.

"Then make the measurements!"

"Error," the ship said. "Error. Error. Error."

"What's the closest planet to our position?"

"Error. Error. Error. Error."

Doug staggered through the access corridor, pausing to wheeze once or twice, until he made it to the pilot's seat.

He peered out through the viewscreen.

His legs weakened.

He should have been staring at the void, a black tapestry pierced by the pinprick lights of faraway stars, a few brighter ones for the planets of the Solar System they'd already passed.

But he saw none of that. The space beyond the viewscreen rippled and pulsed with energy coruscations, a thousand different trails of white and blue and red and orange that shot through Doug's temples like lightning.

He blinked, hoping the nightmare would go away.

When he opened his eyes the same impossible light show continued to flare up. It was like the night sky had been set on fire while being spun around in a blender. The flashing effect became so fast and intense Doug had to look away to stop himself from passing out.

"What *is* that?" he said.

The ship replied, "Unknown."

"Dim the viewscreen," he said.

The screen darkened, but the pulsating lights, though fainter, still pierced his eyeballs.

"More! Dim by at least ninety-five percent."

The ship did so.

He found he could look out now without feeling like he was on the verge of an epileptic seizure. "Better. Now show me the energy readings corresponding to those lights."

The pilot console displayed radiation data the likes of which he'd never seen before.

"You're shittin' me," he said. "This much radiation we should have been fried to ashes by now. And what's this—*negative energy?*"

Doug remembered Patricia then. Was this what had happened to her ship? If so, he'd been a fool to follow in her footsteps.

"*Snowman*, how much longer will our shields hold?"

"Shields are within normal stress levels."

"*Normal stress levels*? How can that be?"

"Unknown."

"Figures you'd say that. Are any of those lights stars?"

"Unknown."

"Engine status?"

"Offline."

"Then how the hell are we moving?" He scratched at his beard. "No wait, let me guess—"

"Unknown," they said in unison.

"You know, I've got a mind to ban that word from your scrub-bucket vocabulary. Rotational torsion? Gravity's feelin' fine to me. Thank God for small favors."

"Centrifugal forces normal."

He took another look outside. "The eye of the hurricane," he mused.

Seconds passed. Then the ship began to shake and a klaxon blared. A burst of radiation, combined with a gravity whirlpool of some sort, were coming straight at them, and with the engines offline there was no way to prevent the collision.

An instant before the blinding blast and twist of space consumed them, all went quiet and dark.

Doug straightened up and let out a tremendously long breath. Clammy sweat chilled his skin.

Screwing up his courage, he said, "Brighten viewscreen."

Space, if that's what he was seeing, was back to normal. At least it looked black, sprinkled with dots that could have been stars, though these stars were duller than Doug had ever seen, and farther apart. When he looked more closely he noticed whole patches of space that seemed utterly starless.

"Position?"

The ship was silent longer than Doug cared for.

"The closest star system to us appears to be Eta Carinae," *Snowman* said.

"Calculate the no-frills number," he said. "Distance from Earth."

The console displayed the number: *Seven-thousand five hundred light years.*

Doug felt his body fall away from him. "Confirm. Seven-thousand five hundred *light years*?" he mumbled.

"Correct," the ship said.

Doug's head felt like it had been dragged inside a black hole. Thoughts of Sonnie and the boys threatened to erupt, but he used the throbbing tension in his forehead to repress them. Any cracks in that wall and he'd become hopeless, truly lost. "Please confirm," he whimpered.

"Seven-thousand five hundred light years," the ship repeated. "One light year is approximately sixty-three thousand two hundred and forty-one AUs, which means—"

"Which means we're royally screwed," Doug said. "We're halfway across the goddarned Universe."

"The Carina Constellation."

"Show me your sensor readings from right before the flashing lights."

"I have no record of flashing lights."

"Son of a bitch," he said, and spat in frustration. "You woke me up. You said there was an unexpected displacement from vectors, some such crock. Show me where and when that started."

Data scrolled on the pilot console. He couldn't make heads or tails of it. One moment everything had been smooth sailing and the next the numbers stopped making sense. Negative energies, impossible gravity readings, as though space and time had been replaced with a funhouse version of themselves.

"Any similar events logged by the SFN?" he asked.

"My database has a record of several anomalies reported by ships over the years, but the details are unavailable."

Doug stood up, paced the small cockpit, sat back down. "How long?"

"Unclear query. Please rephrase."

"You dumb sack of shit," he said. He cleared this throat. "I'm sorry. I thought my meaning would be obvious, rust-bucket, given our circumstances and all. How long until vital resources like food and air run out?"

"Assuming emergency caloric restriction protocols are implemented, one year and five months." The ship paused. "I recommend stasis."

Doug let out a laugh fueled by equal parts frustration and disbelief. "You want me to go back to sleep?" He waved at the viewscreen. "Look out there! How many humans do you think have ever been this far out before? And you want me to nap!"

The ship didn't reply.

"Are you getting this?" he insisted.

"Sensors functioning."

"Not sure regular sensors can do this justice." He remembered the fancy scientific equipment he had agreed to board for the extra pay. "Activate enhanced recording instruments."

"Commencing," the ship said.

Doug sat there for a time, not sure what to do next. Nothing changed around him. Eventually he noticed *himself* start to change.

He thought about all the time he'd missed with Sonnie throughout the years, and his eyes stung. He was surprised he had the strength to cry, but he did, and how. He was shaking. Eventually the tremors passed and the tears dried. His body, his whole sense of himself, deflated. Whatever energy he'd had, whatever desire to make the best of the situation, to explore, was crushed by the unfamiliar world beyond the viewscreen.

Maybe the *Snowman* was onto something. If Doug chose to put himself under again, how long could he last? The *Snowman* obtained energy from interstellar space through the hydrogen collected by its ram scoop. It could probably keep the cryo-chamber going for hundreds of years, maybe thousands. One human didn't need much, especially when that human was a popsicle.

He mulled it over and ran through the numbers with the computer. In a state of increasing resignation and listlessness, he found the notion gaining solidity in his head, until it seemed not only logical, but inevitable. The *Snowman*'s pulsed ion drives could only get him a fraction of a fraction of the way home, and even if he'd had infinite fuel, it would take over ten thousand years to get to Earth. Even communicating with Earth was out of the question: it would take seven thousand five-hundred years to reach them, and then the same period for their response to get back to him—if the signal could even make it that far. It was too overwhelming to even think about. The only chance he had, admittedly smaller than the most distant star from where he sat right now, was to enter stasis. And he owed it to his family to at least *try* to survive, no matter how unlikely.

Once he made the decision he realized it was best to get on with it as soon as possible. If he stressed and delayed he'd lose his nerve.

As he headed back to the cryo-chamber out of which he'd clambered mere hours ago, though it now felt a lifetime, he kept thinking about Sonnie and the boys. While Doug slept they would live out the rest of their lives and have children of their own, and die, and their children would have children, on and on and on for who knew how long...

As he waited for his head to stop its dizzying orbit around itself, the ship's alarms screamed once more and the floor began to shake.

He was hit by that same sensation of being twisted inside out that he'd felt instants before being woken up.

"Oh hell," he said. "It's happening again!"

Like having a tooth pulled, the second time around was no more pleasant than the first, but he coped a little better because he had some notion of what to expect.

After the sensation of total, gut-wrenching disorientation and after the utterly stupefying light show, things settled back down as they had the first time.

Except now, according to the *Snowman*, they were back inside the Solar System, more or less where they had been when the first jump occurred.

"I'll be damned!" Doug said.

He triple checked the sensor readings.

"*Snowman*, patch me through to the SFN," he said.

The link was established and a gruff voice said, "Doug Garcia, our records indicate you should be in cryo. What's the cause of this irregularity?"

"Why, I'm so glad you asked. Take a look at this." Doug sent a complete record of the ship's navigational files to the SFN grunt.

After a time, the man said, "What's this supposed to mean?" He no longer sounded irritated, but alarmed.

"It means, son," Doug said, "that you'd better get your boss on the line, and maybe his boss too. And don't go talkin' to me about faulty sensors. You'll notice my logs include deep readings from that crapload of latest-gen devices I agreed to carry on your behalf."

The next person who spoke with Doug sounded more reasonable, and the person after that positively placating. "A preliminary review of the data," he was told, "suggests that you fell through a wormhole, a kind of cosmic tunnel, and then traveled through the same wormhole a second time in reverse. You're lucky to be alive."

No shit, Sherlock, Doug wanted to say, but he held his tongue.

"We have no idea how this happened, but we'll have someone rendezvous with you in two weeks. Can you hold out that long?"

The *Snowman* appeared to be working fine. "I guess," Doug said.

Two weeks was a lot of time to ponder what had happened, and Doug had precious little else to do while he waited for his rescue ship.

He thought long and hard about the events leading up to his interstellar slingshot. He thought long and hard about his family, about the SFN, about Patricia's message.

And certain things started to make sense to him.

Finally, just two days before the vessel showed up, he asked the SFN for permission to talk to an independent contractor. "All out in the open," Doug said. "Wanted to clear it with you first."

They reviewed the ship's ID. "Our records indicate you received a message from this vessel before your, uh, accidental displacement."

"That's right," Doug said. "Which I dutifully reported. She was reaching out asking for my help, and I should have done a better job of listening."

"The SFN is not in the habit of—"

"Patricia just wants someone to hear her story," Doug interrupted. "And that's what you're going to do. Otherwise I'm going to feel the sudden urge to reach out to the media and tell *my* story, and I got a funny feelin' you wouldn't be crazy about that."

They listened.

Doug's self-driving car dropped him off at a local flower shop about two miles from the apartment.

After being brought in by the SFN ship, they'd run extensive tests on him and had interviewed him dozens of times. He'd asked that they not contact Sonnie, because he didn't want her alarmed or upset. On the drive from the airport—where he'd insisted to the SFN team of associates who'd flown in with him that he wanted to be driven home *alone*, and for the twentieth time repeated that he felt perfectly okay—he'd marveled at some of the plants growing right outside the freeway, and he'd decided he wanted to get something beautiful for Sonnie. He figured he should bring something nice with him as part of his surprise return, and the flower shop looked inviting.

He browsed for a few minutes and made his selection. Purchase in hand, he walked the last two miles home. It was midmorning, and though the sky was slightly overcast, the grey light that came through was fine and clear.

A block away, he paused, studying the scene. A woman pushed a stroller on the street, a mail-delivery drone glided from mailbox to mailbox, and a plumbing repair truck arrived and parked near the building adjacent to Doug's.

Doug took a deep, measured breath and made his way to the front door. He could have opened the door with his access key, but he rang the doorbell instead.

It swung tentatively open. "If you're comin' around here tryin' to sell me those premium steaks again, I'll have half a mind to grab my fryin' pan—"

And then Sonnie saw him. She yelped out in surprise, eyes wide. "Oh my God!" She wrapped her arms around him, jumping up. He did his best to keep his right arm, which held the flowers, raised an inch above her, so that they wouldn't be crushed, and the comicality of the gesture made them both laugh.

"It is *so* good to see you," he said.

She took a step back, eyes glistening, and grabbed his face with both her hands.

He leaned forward and they kissed.

Then her head ducked back again, to study him up close. Her hands wouldn't let go of him, as though she was unsure he wouldn't dissolve into thin air. "How is this possible?" she said. "How can you be here?"

He smiled.

"My long haul was, let's say, interrupted."

Inside, she put on a fresh pot of coffee and found a vase for the flowers.

"They're so pretty," she said. "What are they?"

"They're called gaillardia," he said. "Local product." Doug had never noticed them before himself. Their fine petals were mostly red, but had yellow tips, and the bulbs of the flowers seemed to be colored in reverse, red circular edges and yellow, granular centers. "Where are the boys?" he said, looking around.

"I dropped them off at the Whitmores after Church," Sonnie said. "I'm picking them up for lunch. They're going to go nuts when they see you."

Doug checked the time. Lunch wasn't for another hour.

She saw what he did, and she noticed the way his face changed, and how his eyes covered the length of her body, and then she blushed.

"Come here woman," he said softly.

Neither of them needed more prompting. Clothes and shoes were scattered on a trail that led from the living room floor to the bedroom, amid a storm of smooching and grabbing and pinching and fondling and then slower, fuller kissing and all the things that came next.

When it was over, they lay in bed and he said, "Sonnie, you're the most beautiful woman in the world."

She blushed again. But then a sadness crept into her face. "Doug, what happened out there?"

He propped himself up. "Remember that new scientific equipment I told you about?"

"Yeah."

"Well, it did end up causing the ship's brain to go somewhat haywire." He omitted that the consequence of this malfunction had been to take him off course and to super-charge the ship's magnetic shields, triggering the aperture of the wormhole he'd stumbled upon. He also neglected to mention that the SFN had several recorded instances of other spatial distortions near that region of space but had kept them secret. Even if he hadn't tweaked his course to follow in Patricia's footsteps, chances were he would have encountered the same disturbance. "I hit...a bit of a speed bump. The SFN had to come get me."

She crossed her arms. "The SFN's got some real nerve. Extra pay don't justify these shenanigans. I'm sure it was a hundred times worse than you're lettin' on."

"Listen. Something good came from it." He reached forward to caress her shoulders the way she liked. Her skin was still warm with the afterglow of their lovemaking.

Soothed by his touch, her neck relaxed. "What's that?"

"I got some mighty interestin' data," he said. "And it confirms what other folks who've been out far enough have started to see. Scientists call it the Big Rip."

She made a funny face. "That some kind of joke? Like a cosmic fart or somethin'?"

He laughed. "I swear, that's what they call it. Millions of years from now, they say everything's gonna fall apart. The Universe is expanding, and the expansion is speedin' up, and everything's gonna be pushed farther and farther apart. Stars and whole galaxies, even atoms and particles, all of it torn to shreds by distance."

She flinched. "And *that's* supposed to be good news?"

He chuckled again. "Well, no. But knowing is better than not knowing. See, my readings are undisputable. But it's just the beginning. The SFN needs more data. They've been contracted by the government. Now they really need long-haul pilots. Space rigs have become important. *Really* important. They won't be able to push long-haul pilots around anymore. And we'll be compensated fair and square."

The SFN had had little choice but to agree to the terms of Doug's legal team. They'd been lying to pilots for years about the risks of the new sensor equipment, and now they'd finally been caught.

"Oh honey." She paused. "That does sound good."

He held eye contact with her. "It also means," he said, "that from now on I get to choose how long I'll be away from you."

Sonnie's eyes moistened.

Doug stroked her long brown hair, then drew close, his body pressing against hers. He breathed warmly on her earlobe and she let out a little moan. His hand slid up her thigh. Then she pulled back abruptly, glancing at the wall clock. "The boys," she said.

They got ready quickly.

In the living room Sonnie grabbed her purse and keys and opened the front door. Cool air wafted into the apartment.

She stepped through the threshold, but Doug lingered inside.

He felt his heart thudding away in his chest. His eyes roved back and forth across the kitchen and living room, in an almost drunken way.

"You got this strange gleam in your eye, Doug Garcia," Sonnie said. "What'cha lookin' at?"

He took it all in, every last detail of this place and time. Once, he would have only regarded his surroundings with that kind of intensity aboard the *Snowman*. He still had his ship, and he'd be back out in space when he was ready for it, but things were different now.

The words almost caught in his throat. "I'm looking at home," he said.

Del Howison is a journalist, writer, and the Bram Stoker Award-*winning editor of the anthology* Dark Delicacies: Original Tales of Terror and the Macabre by the World's Greatest Horror Writers *which spawned two sequels. His short story* The Lost Herd *was turned into the premiere (and highest-rated) episode* The Sacrifice *for the television series* Fear Itself. *He has been nominated for over half a dozen awards. He is the co-founder and owner of* Dark Delicacies, *a book and gift store known as "The Home of Horror," located in Burbank, California.*

A FLICKER OF BRIGHT LIGHT

Del Howison

"The insanity of darkness can be calmed with just a flicker of bright light."
—D. H. Altair

"I CAN'T GO ON EATING DUST and being...nothing."

Estrella kicked a stone along in front of them as they walked the dirt road. She squinted against the wind carrying sand. The fine particles of grit blowing into every open orifice.

"Not much choice," Susan said, kicking the rock back in front of Estrella. They stopped and Estrella picked up the stone and threw it into the desert. It burst up a little dust cloud into the wind when it landed. The dirt swirled then dissipated quickly, assimilating itself into the air and vanishing with the wind.

"That is us," Estrella said, and she used her hands to simulate an explosion. "Poof, we're gone. We are nothing."

A body truck rolled past them churning up a cloud from the road, forcing them to turn their heads away and shield their eyes. The driver leaned out the window and waved at them. Estrella pumped her arm and the driver responded by blowing the airhorns. It was a game between them three times a week when the truck made its run carrying the load of carrion. He shouted out to the girls. Susan did a mock curtsey.

"He's lucky," Estrella said. "He'll be sleeping in the city with a full belly."

As he passed the rotted smell of death choked them and Susan gagged, spitting into the dirt. There was a damp trail of spotting that dropped from the vehicle as it passed along. The sun created a quick rainbow in the puddled liquid before it soaked into the loose ground, leaving a black spot. Estrella watched the spectrum swirl in that moment before it was absorbed into the earth. She thought about how long it had been since she'd seen rain, let alone a rainbow. She looked up, following the truck driving into the distance.

"One more stop and then he goes home. No wonder he is always so happy when he goes by. I wish he'd take me with him."

"Beeman," Susan said and nodded. "They have a body pick up there."

"Oh yeah," Estrela said to herself. "That's the last point in Zone B."

Estrella continued watching the truck.

"We're going to do it," she said.

"What?"

Estrella turned and smiled at Susan.

"Our way out."

Susan looked at the distant cloud of dust. Estrella placed her hand on Susan's shoulder.

"When Thursday's truck comes for Beeman will you come?"

"Where?"

"With me to Beeman. To catch the truck."

Susan's eye grew wide as she thought of the possibility of actually escaping Zone B by body truck. She shook her head.

"We'll die," she said.

"We'll die if we stay."

Susan stared at her. Estrella was serious. She was always serious. She looked down at her feet.

"I can't."

Estrella cocked her head and took a step towards her only friend.

"Why?"

"I'm twelve."

"So am I. We got nobody but us."

Susan kept looking at her feet.

"I can't."

Estrella reached out and turned Susan's face up. She studied her eyes and could tell that what Susan was saying for herself was true. Estrella kissed her full on the lips, not impulsively, but endearingly. She wiped away some of the grime on Susan's cheek with her index finger. It was damp. Mixed with Susan's sweat and tears they had made a small muddy trail on her face. Then Estrella started down the road in the direction of the disappearing truck. She could not look back for fear of turning around and never leaving.

On Thursday Susan walked the side of the road alone. She could see the truck churning up a cumulus of dust behind it as it raced towards her. When the driver saw her he began to slow until he was up alongside her and he came to a stop. The dust the truck had churned continued moving past them and Susan covered her eyes until it swirled past.

"All alone?" the driver shouted from the cab.

"She's sick," Susan shouted back up to him.

"I hope she is okay," he said. "I don't want to be hauling her in this truck someday."

Susan smiled.

"She'll be okay. She's just a little weak. We've haven't eaten for a while."

The driver studied her a moment and then turned back into the cab.

"Hang on a minute."

This was good. Susan wanted him to spend as much time as possible talking with her. The driver leaned back out the window with something wrapped in his hand. He reached out to Susan.

"Here."

She scrunched her face up.

"Go on take it. It's food. It will make your friend stronger; help her to get better sooner."

"I can't reach," Susan said.

The driver threw the brake and popped open his door. He climbed down and handed the package to Susan. The was a clunk from the other side of the truck and the driver turned his head. There was no other noise and he turned back to Susan.

"Probably bodies shifting."

"Where do you take them?"

He looked down the road where he was headed.

"I've got one more pick up in Beeman. Then I go to the City."

"I'd like to go someday," she said.

"Wish I could but it's against the rules. The only way to get into the city now is to be born there. Not enough food. Not enough resources. Very few outsiders ever get let in. You have to have merit. You have to bring something that's a plus for the city. They would never let in a little girl with no skills. We have enough little girls."

Susan accepted the proclamation. She had heard it all her life.

"What happens to them," she asked, pointing to the body truck.

The driver glanced at the truck.

"Those are resources. After I pick up in Beeman I take my load to the City and they are rendered. Even cadavers can provide something to help the people in the city live. They are put in a machine called a Scythian Vaporizer. It breaks the bodies down into their six essential elements. Those are reused. Nothing is wasted."

She looked at him like she didn't quite understand what he was saying.

"You, little girl, are more useful to the people in the City dead than alive. You will never get in."

He turned and climbed back up into the cab.

"You be sure and give that food to your friend so that she will get better."

"I will," Susan said. "Oh my name is..."

"No!" He stopped her. "No names. It makes you real."

He reached down and let the brake go. She gave him the pump signal and he blew his horn for her. They both laughed and the truck began to pull away. Susan smiled at the food she held in her hand. She would have to eat it. Estrella was leaving.

Were it not for the bodies piled so haphazardly on top of each other, like an elder's game of Stackman, the air would never have reached Estrella under the canvas. It was a hot breath and tasted of rotting death, but it was air. The area above the top of the mound of bodies and the liner shield was minimal at best. With the composite of corpses the way they were, space was a high end commodity and that space in-between held very little air. Estrella wondered if there were others like her inside. How many other souls had climbed inside the body truck, hiding under a stretched canvas and trying to breathe the fetid air of survival? Maybe there were none. She could have been the only person crazed enough to chance it. She slid her knee up a bit to help relieve the pain in her thigh from her awkward position. A throbbing ache from being unable to move or straighten out since the bodies from Beeman had been dumped in burned into an angry pain that threatened to numb the entire limb. It wouldn't be good if the chance came to run and she couldn't hop to freedom. She'd endured worse.

Estrella had endured her entire life in Zone B but was now starving as an outcast with the rest of the sector's population. Now she was a scrambler. For months she watched the trucks roll past headed for the terminal where the loading process ensued at the gathering place. She knew that workers brought bodies to the various yards like Beeman sector-wide and filled the trucks by dumping the bodies on conveyer belts. They were carried up the incline and then dropped like pus-filled rag dolls into the beds of the trucks. In the past she'd heard stories of people who climbed into the trucks, unseen by the loaders, or lay on the belts like a corpse to be dropped into the trucks. When the trucks had been loaded she'd even heard of other scramblers making a late run becoming trapped between the conveyor belts and the truck trailers. Parts of them landing outside the trailers, severed from slipping into the gears, while inside their partial bodies slid into the pile to quietly bleed to death once their screaming stopped. They couldn't be heard over the sounds of the loading. Maybe they could be. It didn't matter. Nobody cared. It was one less stowaway for the Guàrdies Protectors to mess with. Somebody else would pitchfork up the overkill and throw it in the trailer of the next truck. There were workers for that.

This truck was only one of hundreds taking bodies to the City. Upon arrival at the facility Estrella had heard that the trucks were dumped, filling enormous cargo containers with bodies. Those were sent to the vaporizers. It was a continuous operation.

She had often wished she'd be born before the Earth was want for room. She had seen a cemetery stone once, beaten and destroyed, and heard tales of burying the dead in the ground with the stones as identity markers to who lay beneath the soil. Markers to identify a person forever that were now being crumbled and lost to time and the elements. She thought that must be when you are really dead, when you're forgotten, when no one or nothing remembers you including the earth itself.

But now there was no room left to bury and no air to be further polluted by burning the dead. So the containers, which were filled with bodies brought in from all over the country—hundreds, thousands in each trailer, hauled in by the type of body trucks she now lay in, were dumped into to a container convoy to be converted into a reusable chemical mist. They were no longer the Earth's problem. They were a solution. The future was missing for the people outside the City. Death was an hourly occurrence. There was no one to help.

Estrella had a plan. She would escape the container once the trailer dumped the bodies into it. Using the bodies she would climb up and over the side into the waiting arms of freedom. She'd heard that just outside the container yard was a wonderland. If she made it there she would be free. People had food. It was her shot at a life. If she did not take this chance she would die in the dirt with Susan.

One time a body truck had broken down on the road near where she lived. She looked at it real close and it appeared to her that the trailers were dumped from the front end with the bodies sliding out the rear and into the containers. She needed to make her way forward and find something to hold onto at the front. Her thought, as uninformed as it was by tales of people who had never tried this escape, was to hold on when the trailer was tipped and not drop into the container until the very end. Her fall onto the body piles would be the shortest and softest as she plopped into the rotting mass. There, on top of the pile, Estrella would climb up and out of the container. Maybe she would even be able to find work at the processing facility. She could keep that job forever, she imagined, as there would always be a steady supply of bodies. Maybe she could become a truck driver and visit Susan on her weekly runs in the body trucks. She too would live on death.

The smell inside the trailer had almost disappeared for her, the stench being so common as to not assail her senses anymore, unnoticeable in its ever-present grotesqueness. She pulled her leg loose from the cadavers and let the sleeping limb nerve itself back awake. The darkness was deep with only flickering slivers of light creeping in from where the canvas was tied down on the top of the trailer. The truck rumbled along the road from

Beeman, a long steady humming. In the darkness of the giant metal coffin they could have been going in any direction.

Estrella reached out and began to feel her way through the soft moist mass in front of her. They were various shapes and she only knew they were bodies by touching an occasional limb or skull, mostly it felt like she was crawling through heavy gelatin. She was frightened and tried to ignore her thoughts of disease, doing her best not to contemplate what each individual she was sliding past or through had died from, what had been in their stomachs or bowels when they had died that was now dripping and oozing out into the pile. Sometimes she would be slipping through something warm and slick making it hard to maneuver and then she would have to force any teeth and bones that were impeding her advance aside.

She pushed a clump of unidentifiable flesh in the darkness and a spear of light from outside shown directly on a clouded eyeball gazing through a milky lens that stared her down. Estrella pushed the head aside with her forearm and a brown liquid ran down from the socket over the lip and into the mouth that was withered and pulled away from its teeth. The face held a death grimace that seemed to be laughing at her, at her possible exercise in futility.

"Don't worry about me, mister. Between the two of us I'm the one who still has a chance," Estrella said aloud only to hear her voice.

A whimper answered her statement. Not from the skull in front of her but somewhere to her right, somewhere in the pile. She stopped moving and listened, trying to make sure she had heard it, that it wasn't truck metal or body shifts in the pile, but a living noise. She held her breath and waited. It was the rhythm of the truck as it bounced along the rough roadway, the shifting of the bodies as they slipped in place and nothing else, possibly nothing else except ghosts or souls departing.

She knew about the death breath, that final exhale of life that departed the empty cocoons of our bodies when we passed. Here, in this darkest of places, life's last breath floated about only to escape when the metal lid was lifted and the souls floated away. The officials did not need people to be dead before throwing them on the conveyer to transport, only the appearance of death. So in this metal trailer many breathed their last, a meaningless end to a nothing life.

And there it was again, a whimper and the sound of shuffling that didn't match the normal settling of corpses. It was faster, more frantic and desperate than the sound of bodies bouncing to the road music. It was possible that it was another scrambler stuck deeper in the pile slowly suffocating in the rotted air of death. Against her instincts Estrella began to pull herself deeper into the trailer toward the sound. There was still time find out what life was making the noise and then to make her way back to the front of the rig before it arrived at the dumping station.

"Hello?"

She called out as she dragged herself toward where the noise was coming from. The whimpering and shuffling stopped at the sound of her voice. Estrella paused, trying to draw bead on the sound.

"Hello? Can you hear me?"

The truck drove over a patch of washboard road. The trailer bounced and screeched, metal screaming against miles of abuse, and a scared yelp from the pile in front of her rang out in surprise. It was maybe ten or fifteen feet in front of her. Estrella reached out into the corpses to pull herself forward when the truck made a sharp right turn. The trailer, playing crack-the-whip, snapped around, throwing her sliding across the bodies and smacking into the wall.

"Easy! Goddamit," she shouted out to a driver who couldn't possibly hear her.

She used the metal wall as leverage to push against and right herself. A random shaft of light pierced through where wall met canvas and she struggled to place her face by fresh air. She was rewarded with a mouth full of dirt and sand. Estrella spit back into the pile and wiped her arm across her face leaving more draggle smeared across her lips from the suppurated remains she been dragging herself through than what she was able to remove. She raised her head up and wailed once out of frustration. Pulling the material of her dirty shirt over her mouth she tried for one more breath of filtered air. At least the heavier grains of sand would be stopped before she swallowed them.

A bellow came from the stack in the direction she had been crawling and she tried to use the light coming in from behind her to scan the pile of carrion she had to scale. She was shocked when the return of light came back at her from the pupil of an eye that watched her. The sound it made was a half-hearted bay. Maybe it was dying and just too weak to respond anymore. But it never took its eye off of her as it made another nondescript noise in its throat. There was something wrong with the way it looked at her.

It was a dog. It looked in the direction of her noisemaking as opposed to actually seeing her. Perhaps, she thought, it was blind. The back three-quarters appeared to be stuck down in the pile, tangled in the sludge of decaying humanity, drowning slowly in a quicksand of remains that slowly sucked it down with every movement of the bouncing trailer. With most of its body being trapped and slickened by the seepages that continued to ooze from the cargo it had no chance of pulling itself free.

What the dog realized was that there was another living animal in the trailer with it. Friend or foe it couldn't know. It didn't matter as the animal was in no position to help itself and was beginning to resign to its inevitable fate, whatever that might be. It was too weak and too destitute of vision at this point. The dog lay its head down on the damp pile.

"No, no, no," Estrella cried out. "Don't..."

She struggled for a word. Being surrounded by death she couldn't use that term.

"Don't quit." She said softly, the words getting lost in the metal slamming of the bouncing truck, and continued her crawl towards the dog. For its part it turned its head facing away.

Estrella crawled through the slippage, the movement of the truck in direct contrast to the movement of the personages shifting and settling. The question of whether or not the souls were trapped in the trailer with them crossed her mind as she struggled to reach the dog. Once, while crawling, her arm plunged down between the assembled bodies and she dropped flat on the rancid mass. But she was almost there. The dog was still turned away from her. With a sucking sound she pulled her arm up out of the boodle and flicked it to throw off most of whatever gruel was stuck to it. Sinew of some sort disappeared into the dark interior just catching the light before disappearing and she turned her attention back to the animal. The last couple of feet to get up to it seemed to take the longest as if the driver was purposely swerving the truck to make her trek difficult.

As she came upon the dog it laid its head completely back on the top of its skull so that it faced her upside down. In the darkness she couldn't tell if the dog was injured. Being covered in ooze from the ulcerated bodies surrounding it camouflaged the possibility of any wounds it may be carrying. She had to pull the dog loose from the pile and drag it up on the top of the stack. She knew that if the animal was hurt there was the possibility it may bite her when she went to touch it. If it did and it happened to be carrying rabies then this entire ordeal could be for naught, both for the dog and for her.

She began to speak to it in low soothing tones that she hoped were calming above the racket from the trailer. The dog continued to look toward her through the tops of its eyes.

"Hey, Slick," she said. "I'm not gonna hurt you. I want to help you."

The dog gazed, wide-eyed, as she slipped her hands around its chest and up under the armpits of the front legs. It didn't move but stared straight into Estrella's eyes. She lifted up but the leverage was wrong and her knees slipped on the mass toppling her to her side and pulling the dog over with her. It didn't try to wiggle away or get angry but lay without movement save the head following her every motion. She would not be able to pull up with any heft while her knees sank down into the gumbo of cadavers. Like the dispersal of body weight on a bed of nails she would have to lay on her belly and work the dog up and loose that way, back and forth, a little at a time, until most of it was out and then she could pull it free.

How long had this all taken, she wondered? The outside light that had shone through the cracks and holes in the trailer had gone away leaving only blackness both inside and out. She used her memory in the darkness—what the dog had looked like and how it was sunk and tangled in the bodies. Lying on her belly she held the creature firmly but gently and began to work it back and forth while pulling steadily upward at the same time. Estrella began to feel it start to slide loose and the pile give up its grip when something quickly slid across her arm. She screamed and released the dog. She was shaken but realized that whatever it had been was leaving the scene of the extraction. She had disturbed it and now it was heading for another damp wet spot to hide...or feast. A rush of ice ran up her spine. She had gooseflesh and pulled herself in tight, shivering with repulsion. What else was living in the cluster beneath her? What reptiles and insects had been scooped up with the bodies and deposited in this small space with her? Whose feeding had been disturbed by the jaws of machinery and then tussled again by her efforts?

"Fuck," she said and wiped both of her arms.

In a way she was glad it was dark so she could not see the other denizens moving about the trailer. Estrella was running out of time. She could feel the dog was moving, whining with effort. If it did manage to claw its way out it might run in the other direction and then she would never be able to grab it and take it to safety with her. In the darkness they were both blind. She crawled back to the dog.

"Easy Slick. Shhh."

She tried calming the dog with slow movements and gentle talk. It was all extremely difficult with the truck banging and bouncing. Estrella wrapped her left arm around the dog's chest. With a singular smooth pull she slid the animal up and out of the bodies. It wasn't quite as difficult as she had imagined with all the liquids and goop making the movement smooth. She dragged him over the top of the bodies and pulled him in close. Estrella held him against her so he could feel the heat from her body and her breathing. She rolled on her side and rubbed his face with her free hand. She couldn't see him but he wasn't struggling to get away.

"Shhh. It's okay. We're together. I've got you."

He lay perfectly still as she spoke. Her breath went directly to his face so that he would learn her scent over the extreme fetidness of their surroundings. He seemed settled with the human contact; she didn't want to make him any more nervous than he already was. She had lost Susan by leaving her behind. She had lost everyone she had ever known by leaving them behind. It was the two of them now.

She knew they were at least halfway down the length of the trailer and she had to get both of them back up to the front end before they arrived at the processing center. They would need to crawl to the front through the darkness, over the bodies and whatever else lay in wait. She tried to roll back onto her stomach. Estrella wrapped her arm around him as tightly as she dared. There was nothing to hold him by except his slippery hair. She needed him to come with her.

"Trust me," she whispered closely into his ear. "Believe in me."

She began to crawl to the front one-handed. As she pushed bodies and fragments aside to make space to crawl through beneath the cover she pulled Slick along with her. He seemed to grasp that they were together. The trailer shuddered across rough road and her knee sunk into something that made a squishy noise. She slid her leg away and kept moving forward using one arm to grab in front of her and both legs to push with. Sometimes Slick smacked against some obstacle that she had to pull him around or sunk down in the mass from which she'd yank him up and continue onward. She was battling an unknown deadline. Estrella was determined to move forward until she touched the metal wall at the end.

Her body was as flat and long as she could make it to keep gravity and the shaking motion of the trailer from pulling her down. Snagging on a body part, Slick slipped out of Estrella's encircling arm and began to slide off to the side. She frantically grabbed at him and managed to clasp his foot and hold him until she could maneuver over and pull him close. She lay still, hugging him against her, breathing heavily in her panic.

"Sorry," she said. "Sorry."

She regained her bearings and started moving on towards the front end of the truck clutching the dog to her side tighter than before. Estrella was starting to get the swaying of the trailer motion into her balance. It was probably like the sea legs she had heard that the pirates of old acquired from being aboard the ships for long periods of time. Together they reached the end of the trailer and she turned them around and sat in a soft spot, her back against the front metal wall, Slick in her lap.

"Nothing can stop us now," Estrella said to the dog.

As she sat Estrella felt tiredness overtake her and her head jerked a couple of times before she completely dropped off to sleep. Slick was at her side while the motion of the truck rocked her to sleep. The clanking of the metal and constant rumble of the road became a lullaby droning her off to dream of beautiful green landscapes and blue waters. She hadn't slept this deeply in years. She hadn't felt this safe in a long time. As she slept a many-legged insect crossed her lap. It dropped down by her ankles and tunneled into the rot beneath her.

The truck jerked to a stop, its brakes giving a high-pitched shriek as it fought the weight of the filled trailer. She awoke disorientated and then the realization of where she was sunk in. It was light again outside and it flickered as it came through cracks. There was a slamming of the cab door and someone was walking past the side of the trailer. She could hear voices and clamoring above them. This was the transfer point. This was where they would need to make their move. Their. Them! Slick was not in her arms and she called out in a strong whisper so as to not alert the people outside.

"Slick!"

Off to her left in the dim light she could make out the dog crouching. It appeared to be relieving itself into the bodies. Somebody banged something above them that made Estrella jerk. She could hear metal sliding.

"Slick, come here."

She tried to sound calm so the dog would not move away. The canvas was being unhooked at the far end of the trailer and slid back. Sunlight flooded inside. Estrella squinted against the intrusion of sun. The light and noise combined to frighten her even more. Estrella needed the dog. She began to crawl toward it speaking gently. Estrella reached out her hand, hoping to draw the dog to her. The animal didn't move. She kept crawling, reaching out. The few feet between them felt like a mile. There was more noise of the hooks letting go of the canvas. The far third of the trailer was now uncovered. Estrella was hoping nobody looked in while she was pursuing the dog.

"That's it, my last run of the week. I can't wait to go to my quarters," somebody said.

There was an unintelligible reply and then the two men laughed and made small talk while they worked.

Then there was a hum and the mechanical sound of hydraulics. The trailer rocked and the end Estrella and Slick occupied began to lift up. No ceremony, no preparation just a slow rise of one end of the truck so that everything would slide out the other. Slick cowered about three feet from Estrella's grasp, too frightened to move. Their end of the container continued to lift up. There was some shifting of the mass and down at the low end the tail flap swung open from the bottom and Estrella could hear liquid running off. Some of the more precariously perched bodies tumbled from the top near her to flop down to the end and out the gate into the waiting container.

Estrella grabbed the dog's leg. Slick tried to pull the leg free and roll toward the exit but Estrella would have none of it. She held on to it so tight she was certain it would break. She crawled closer to Slick and pulled the dog to her across the cadaver stack. Once again Estrella was able to clutch the animal to her. Their eyes held each other. Now they were together.

"Don't you ever leave me again. Ever."

Slick just stared at Estrella and then everything beneath them began to shift again with the rising floor and slip slowly towards the opening. One tumbling body struck Estrella as it rolled on past but she maintained her death grip on the dog. She looked up at the wall rising behind her. They had to be there so that they could land on top of the falling bodies and not become trapped in the tumbling corpses. With one hand she began to claw her way towards the upper end of the trailer. Each grasp only seemed to pull whatever was loose in front of her down to where the two of them lay. Slick slipped and wriggled in her arm as they tangled up in the bodies. Their progress was slow but Estrella felt like they were making headway, inch by stench-filled inch.

Then Slick was yanked out from her arm. The dog began to spiral down the incline out of Estrella's reach. She lunged for the animal. She grabbed him as her motion took the two of them down the embankment, scrabbling and spinning with various faces, arms, and bodies joining them on their descent out the back. She reached out to stop them but everything she grabbed was soft, wet, and moving in the same direction she was. Just as Estrella instinctively pulled Slick in tight her head cracked against the tailgate at the bottom. It all went black.

It was dark again. It still smelled like a garbage pit. Estrella had the image of her face being washed by Slick while she sat crumpled in a corner of another metal container. They were lucky. They weren't dead. They could have been suffocated by an avalanche of corpses. She could have died by smacking her head on a metal wall. Lucky.

She had no idea how long she had been out. There were no bearings for her to get. The container they lay in was sealed. No light for direction. No sense of up and down except for gravity, no forward or back. There was only here. She began to cry while she rubbed the side of Slick's muzzle. The dog laid the side of its head against Estrella's chest to allow for better petting access.

It was too late. They were waiting to be taken to the vaporizer. Would it hurt? Would they implode? She couldn't let the dog die painfully like that.

"I wonder if there are rainbows in the vapor, in us," she said to Slick and scratched him under his chin. She was crying. She had failed her only friend. Now he was going to die. With a scream she suddenly twisted Slick's neck. There was a cracking noise and his head dropped awkwardly to the side. The eyes still watched her.

"Hello?! Hello?!"

The voices were from above the container and running could be heard crossing the metal lid.

"Open it. Open it now, damn it," somebody yelled.

The motor hummed and the lid began to slide open. Once again the sun invaded the interior. The shadow of the driver standing on the roof crossed Estrella's face. She looked up at the black silhouette hovering above her like an angel.

"I told you I heard something," he said to a second silhouette that joined him at the edge.

"Oh, my God," the second man cried. "Oh, my God."

The two men looked down into the hold and saw a young girl sitting atop the bodies, clutching a decayed road kill dog to her lap.

Edward M. Erdelac is the author of a dozen novels, including Monstrumfuhrer, Andersonville, *and* The Merkabah Rider *series. His short stories have appeared in many anthologies and magazines, including* Star Wars Insider. *He fell in love with cross country travel thanks to numerous family excursions as a kid, and thanks all the truckers that blew their air horns in response to the frantic pull string gestures he made out of the back of his dad's Bronco. News and excerpts from his work can be found at* http://www.emerdelac.wordpress.com.

HIT/RUN

Edward M. Erdelac

THE SOUND OF A STOLEN KISS of metal going down the I-10 West at 90mph was preceded by the high-pitched beeping of collision warnings, the roar of the air horn, and the shriek of tires. The collision was inevitable though, unavoidable.

The station wagon had been parked on the highway median strip on the left side of the road, an inadvisable place to pull over on a dark night. The taillights had winked on suddenly like the eyes of a predator springing from a dark bush, and before Matt could recognize the other driver's intent, the car had pulled right into his path and gunned its engine, attempting to beat his 18 wheeler. Coming from a dead stop it had no more chance of doing that than Matt had of avoiding it.

The truck hit the right quarter panel and sent the station wagon spinning wildly off into the night like a swatted fly, the headlights and taillights flashing intermittently. It left the road and tumbled into the shallow gully off the right-hand shoulder.

The car's horn, which the driver had not thought to use before, now blared insistently, unbroken, a prolonged wail receding as Matt pulled past. A trail of broken glass marked its passage across the black-streaked highway, glowing like bits of red rock candy in his taillights. The headlights, one atop the other, shined feebly from the depression beside the road.

Matt slowed, and started to switch to the emergency band.

There was no one else on the road in either direction. It was two-thirty in the morning. He had opted to drive all night to make his drop off at seven AM in Bakersfield after a prolonged stop in Quartzsite for a blown tire had put him behind schedule.

This was not the first collision in his career. The rig had sustained minimal damage, but the other car looked bad. The plaintive blare of the horn wasn't dwindling.

There'd be consequences from this one. He'd be grounded at least, maybe worse depending on the condition of the station wagon's occupants. The driver, at least, was unconscious or immobilized. Had there been others in the car? Passengers shaken and smashed in their restraints? Children thrown about the interior or ejected into the desert?

But it hadn't been his fault. The other driver had taken a stupid risk and put himself in jeopardy.

Matt made his decision.

Someone would come along soon and see the wreck.

Someone would come.

It hadn't really been his fault, after all.

A few hours later he pulled into Goodbuddy's, a garish island of neon sitting in a yellow-white pool of bug-clouded all-night floodlights in the black desert, around which a few trucks gathered as if for warmth. It was the biggest thing in Desert Center, a bone dry little town of empty houses and dead palm trees halfway to Palm Springs that had been barely hanging on since the 1950s.

He parked and went inside. Just a few minutes to check the truck. Nothing had come in over the radio. Had somebody found that station wagon?

The other drivers sat in the booths or hunched at the counter, replenishing, paging through their logs. He took his place among the latter, perching on one of the green vinyl stools and spreading his logbook on the Formica. There was no reason he shouldn't, after all. He hadn't done a thing wrong, he told himself. That stretch of the I-10 was lonely, sure, and it wasn't a peak travel time, but it was hardly abandoned. Somebody must have come along by now. Highway patrol, maybe.

Somebody *had* come along.

The server had just sidled over to him when the two strangers stepped inside. It didn't exactly make sense to think of them as strangers, not in the usual usage. Matt didn't know anybody here tonight. But the two newcomers were *strange*.

It was difficult to look at them directly. Matt got the sense that if he did, they would somehow sense his observation and be drawn directly to him, as though his glance emitted a light that they could somehow follow to its source. In the quick look he got of them, he learned all he needed to know.

They were identical, or maybe they just looked identical because of their uniform dress. It wasn't a police uniform, however, just nondescript clothing to match the indistinct faces that sat beneath their matching, militaristic, short-cropped hair. Yet the fact that their outfits were identical somehow made him attribute some kind of authority to them.

Their faces bothered him. Indistinct was a good word, Matt decided. They were almost unformed. No blemishes, no patches of hair missed by the razor, nothing out of place. There was a flat tone to them, as though their skin was merely a matte flesh color spayed over some serviceable, utilitarian chassis. They seemed incapable of expression. Looking at them, it even seemed like their hair was merely a different shade of color on their heads. No details, no individual stubble could be discerned. It was just like that dye he'd seen advertised, the kind men with thinning hair coated their scalps with to give the appearance of fullness.

Their eyes shone like headlights. No, searchlights. They looked for him, he knew, and he looked away as they began to move in perfect unison among the other patrons in the booths, working their way toward the counter.

They moved strangely too. Their legs didn't move at all. They seemed to twitch, and wink in and out of existence, flashing at intervals until they arrived at someone's side, as if they were streaming images stuttering on low speed connection. They didn't speak, just leaned over each driver in turn and stared intently at them with their bright, searchlight eyes. Each driver looked up into that emotionless gaze but showed no signs of recognition, as if they had been momentarily distracted by something. They stared into the unblinking eyes of the strangers without interest, without reaction, yet they appeared hypnotized, unable to break that look for the few seconds it took the strangers to arrive at some unspoken, agreed upon satisfaction and release them, then move on to the next driver.

Maybe they didn't exist. The thought occurred to Matt that they were phantoms only he could see, spectral agents of his own guilt taking root in his fatigued mind.

Or were they something else? Were they the unchained souls of the people in the station wagon come hunting their irresponsible killer?

But he *hadn't* killed them, he told himself. He *hadn't*! They hadn't died out there, expiring slowly in a ready-made mausoleum of twisted metal and broken glass, that lonesome, blaring horn for a funeral dirge. Someone had *surely* come along.

His imagination was running away with him. He was just tired. He should have stayed the night in Quartzsite to recharge, the hell with his schedule.

There were no vengeful, lost ghosts, no hungry demons or enforcing angels out patrolling the highway at night. No such thing. Surely not in the bright light of Goodbuddy's outside God-forsaken Desert Center.

But still those strangers moved strangely among the truckers, flitting like worker bees after pollen. He was sure they were there for him.

The strangers reached the end of the counter. They flanked each driver and leaned in, invader-close, neither saying a word, not snuffling for the tinge of fear or sweat, just fixing their shining eyes, boring through the windows of each man and woman's unaware glaze to the backs of their skulls, reading some unknowable log printed somewhere back there, not finding what they sought, and shifting over to the next diner in shimmering blinks.

No one could see them. Maybe no one but the one they themselves sought.

The server didn't take his order.

"Is there a back door?" he mumbled.

The server didn't hear him.

He got up abruptly and went to find the exit himself.

He reached the short hall to the restrooms and looked back.

The strangers had ceased their progression down the counter. They had straightened. They were watching him.

He ducked into the restroom, his heart pounding, breath coming in swift, short gulps.

The door closed and he backed away from it, watching it. There was no lock. It would push open and they would be upon him.

The loud flush of a toilet startled him. A stall door opened and a man with a mesh-backed Mack cap with a frayed bill curling like a sour duck's stumbled out. He was an older man, with greying, bloodshot eyes.

Matt raised his hands to him, gripped him by the sides of his head, and pushed him back into the stall.

The man uttered nothing more than a short blurt of surprise as he fell back onto the toilet.

Matt sidled past the stall door, pushed it closed with his rear, still gripping the old driver's head in his hands.

Now his fingers slid beneath the fleshy cheeks, dipping in. There was no wounding, no blood, and only the most meager thumping of the old driver's elbows against the walls of the stall to mark his feeble struggle. Matt's fingers merely merged with the man's face outwardly, though beneath the skin they went as deep as fast moving roots thirstily seeking water, winding through the channels of his person, undermining the lazy security of his bodily systems, seeking the innermost part of the other driver. He wrestled with it briefly for assertion, will for will. He had surprise on his side, so the struggle was as brief as it needed to be. The older driver succumbed, surrendered. Then he was copying, masking himself, becoming that which he beheld.

Serving no further purpose by its continued existence, the older driver deflated and shriveled in his hands.

When he heard the restroom door bang open, all that was left of the older driver could be sent down the toilet with a kick of the handle. He rescued the mesh-backed cap and set it on his transformed head.

He opened the stall as if he'd just used it and came out to find the two strangers standing there waiting for him.

He looked past them, into the bloodshot eyes of the old Mack driver in the bathroom mirror. The strangers didn't show up, like vampires in a movie.

Yet there they were, before him. Glitching, wavering, leaning in to regard him.

He pretended he didn't see them, and went to the sink to wash his hands. It was like a game of chicken at first. He feared colliding with them as he moved close. They gave off a faint scent of ozone, and they crackled like an old television tube when he stepped through them. They were insubstantial.

He played it cool, even dried his hands.

Then he left the bathroom.

He did not look back at them.

He didn't look for the rear door, but he didn't sit back down at the counter either. He was not Matt anymore. He went back outside.

He stopped himself from moving toward his own truck. In the harsh, stark light of the outside lamps, he could see the damage to the front end. He was not Matt anymore. That was not his truck. He couldn't be blamed for anything.

He felt in his pockets, found the old driver's keys, and looked at the parked trucks. Luckily for him, only one Mack sat silent among the others in the lot, a midnight blue Pinnacle with a shining chrome grill, fresh from the wash.

He went to it, whistling as he crossed the lot.

The key fit.

He swung open the door and was pulling himself up into the cab by the grab bar when he felt a bone shuddering shock the centered on his right arm. It shivered through his whole frame so quickly he nearly collapsed. He hung there by one arm, shaking, and looked up into the high-beam eyes of one of the strangers.

The stranger held his arm, and blue electricity jumped and crackled around his fist.

The other stranger reached in and took the logbook from his jacket. Why had he kept it? Why hadn't he thought to leave it behind, as he had left behind his old identity?

The second stranger leafed through the logbook briefly, found what it was looking for, and nodded to the first.

Another jolt of lightning arced from the stranger's hand up Matt's arm. Matt let go of the Mack and fell to the concrete.

He tried to get to his feet, tried to fight.

A final bolt of energy put him down.

It wasn't fair. It hadn't been his fault.

Doug Schaeffer leaned back from his console and stretched till something deep in his back popped.

"Huh," he said.

"What's the matter now?" said the patrolman, Chavez, behind him.

Jesus, the two CHP officers had stood there the whole time. Stood. Even after he'd offered them chairs. They'd stood there and breathed down his neck, disapproving of his every keystroke, staring hard at the information streaming across his monitor though he was pretty sure they had no idea what the fuck they were looking at.

"You lost him," said the other one, McDonald. The gum-chewer. He'd been chewing it for hours. There couldn't be any flavor left.

Doug swiveled and looked at them. But for Chavez's hue, they were two big guys with big mustaches and mirrored sunglasses, as much a uniform for the highway patrolman as the impact armor and badges, beige uniforms, guns, and blue piping.

"No, I got him," Doug said, irritated. "Or the security programs did, anyway. But he, I mean, it, put up a bit of a fight. Even took over another autodriving program. Like it tried to...I dunno, hide itself."

"Hide itself?" said Chavez. "I thought you said it was just a bug in the one truck?"

Doug cursed himself inwardly. He shouldn't have said that. Technically he was in violation of Mechanized Artificial Tractor Trailer's NDA. Not supposed to freely discuss internal company procedures, especially technical failings, unsolicited. Not even with the law. According to the latest company memo, especially not this particular technical failing, which was spiking a bit in Matt units across the country.

"Modern wonder of technology," McDonald remarked, popping his gum. "All-night drivers, all weather. Revolutionary. Don't stop for nothing. Yeah sure. Not even a family of four when the shittin' computer smears 'em across the highway. Long as the goddamn thing makes its timetable."

Doug sighed.

"It's just an isolated goof."

"Some fuckin' goof," said Chavez. "My granddaddy was a trucker. Never had an accident in thirty-five years."

"Never left a couple of kids bleeding out in a ditch either, I bet," said McDonald, popping his gum.

"No sir," said Chavez. "Spent his last five years riding along with one of these goddamn computers, training his replacement, back when they first brought 'em out."

"That's a bitch."

"Even told me he had to hit the panic button and grab the wheel once," Chavez went on. "Goddamn thing tried to turn onto a nonexistent off-ramp. Cause somebody didn't auto-update the GPS. Nearly killed him. Wouldn't that have been something?"

"Would've been some goof," said McDonald dryly.

"I got the logs," said Doug, when he sensed a break in the conversation. "I'll get you a hardcopy for your report in a second. Company insurance will handle the rest."

"That'll be a real comfort to the family, I'm sure," said McDonald.

"You're deleting that thing, right?" Chavez said.

That wasn't company policy, of course. The autodriving program would be taken off the server, out of the system, isolated. It would be meticulously gone over line by line, purged of whatever fuckup had caused this. Then it would be reinstalled in another company rig. He'd seen the service history on this one. It had been in a collision before a few years ago. Last time the highway patrol had witnessed the hit and run, and followed the damn thing all the way back to the truck stop, where the thing had pulled in for its regularly scheduled maintenance and to upload its logs to the server. It had refused to pull over for the cops, though they were programmed to respond to emergency service keys.

This was a special case now. It would mean a long, lengthy report. The company would want to know about the anomalous behavior of this particular program. The deliberate evasion from his antivirus programs had been remarkable, but nothing compared to its forced assimilation of another autodriver. He'd never heard of anything like that.

He wondered sometimes what those things thought. How did they experience things? Did they have independent thoughts? This one sure did. It had chosen (for the second time!) to override its collision protocols. It had obfuscated itself from a pair of security programs. It's like it didn't want to be pulled from the system.

"Yeah sure," Doug said, handing over the flash drive with the logs. "Here. You can keep that, by the way."

"Swell," said Chavez, tucking it into his shirt pocket.

He got up out of the sagging office chair with a creak. He needed a cigarette.

"Modern wonder. There's gonna come a time when these damn things won't stop for nothing," said McDonald.

"The Matts really have a pretty great safety record," said Doug, following the two officers outside into the heat. "We had maybe four hundred Matt-related fatalities last year. Going autonomous cut down on traffic deaths by almost 90%."

"Took 90% of the goddamn jobs too," Chavez muttered.

The service bell rang.

Another autonomous rig pulling in for service and uploading

The three men stood staring at the monstrous 18-wheeler, matte black with the Mechanized Artificial Tractor Trailer logo stamped on the windowless cab where once men had rode.

The grill was splashed red with blood.

Carla Robinson grew up reading and devouring science fiction, and with her first television pilot she won a spot in the American Film Institute's Sloan Science Program. *Carla then joined the writing staff of the newly imagined* Battlestar Galactica *series on the* Sci-Fi Channel *where she won a* Peabody Award *and was nominated for a* Nebula Award. *But mostly, she takes pride in penning what* TV Guide Magazine *called the creepiest episode of the show. Carla's focus is always to create provocative characters who travel precarious roads, and let them do the rest.*

EVERYTHING LOOKS SO SMALL

Carla Robinson

HUGH GANDY HATED THESE annual doctor's appointments, but they were mandatory, so he stood rigidly in the stark examination room and waited with dread for the worst part.

"Step on the scale," said Dr. Wilbur, his tone solemn.

Hugh held his breath as he put one foot, then the other, onto the platform. He grimaced as numbers flashed red and angry on the display before him. The brightness of the digital truth hurt Hugh's eyes as well as his self-esteem. Four-hundred-twenty-five pounds with an additional point-three. These digital instruments were precise and this one wasn't going to lie for the sake of Hugh Gandy.

"Let me take off my shoes," muttered Hugh, and he quickly kicked off the canvas slip-ons he had worn to the appointment. The red numbers danced a bit, and settled on four-hundred-twenty-five pounds even. Hugh was glad to be rid of that *point-three*. He stepped onto the linoleum and faced Dr. Wilbur. "I know. It's silly. How much can a lousy pair of flats weigh, right?"

"I once had a patient remove his contact lenses before he would let me weigh him," grinned Dr. Wilbur as he keyed Hugh's results into a computer. Hugh moved to the exam table and Dr. Wilbur indicated for him to take a seat. But the moment Hugh rested his massive girth on the table's edge, the doctor noted a tiny squeal emanate from the table's metal frame. There was no doubt about it. Men the size of Hugh were hard on the furniture.

Hugh waited for Dr. Wilbur to finish entering the data that would decide whether or not he was fit to get back behind the wheel. He was eager to make the east-west haul across Interstate 94, one of his favorite routes. In the summers of his youth, Hugh rode shotgun from the Great Lakes to the Northern Plains with his father when his dad owned his own eighteen-wheeler. His father taught young Hugh the glory of life on the open road, the freedom it offered, and Hugh made a game of conversing in the colorful CB lingo with truckers along the way. The fellowship of the road became a second home to Hugh. And, oh, the truck stop diners. Greasy spoons that lived up to their names. *Mama's Chops and Chili, Rosie's Roasters,* and Hugh's favorite, *Patty's Pies and Pastry,* where an actual woman named Patty held a pie eating contest once a month. Winners of the contest were treated like celebrities, with their photos framed on Patty's wall.

Hugh's father was, like him, a large man. Too large. After his third heart attack, he was forced to give up driving, and after the medical bills arrived in staggering installments, he had to give up the truck. Still, all Hugh ever wanted to do was to drive big rigs like his dad, so when he turned twenty-one he got his commercial driver's license and set out to seek his own adventures on the open road. He went to work for a trucking company called *Over the Plains*, which owned an impressive fleet of semis, and covered routes across the northern United States.

But when you drive for someone else's business, you are subject to that company's rules and regulations. Instead of the standards set by the DOT, every driver at *Over the Plains* was required to undergo a yearly medical exam no matter what, and the results from each appointment were forwarded to the manager in charge of operations. The original emphasis was to monitor blood work and to make certain drivers were not using illegal drugs or even prescribed medications to excess. In recent years, though, a specific emphasis had been leveled on the overall health of individual truck drivers. On their weight. It was that damn study. Somewhere out of an Ivy League College. The study determined that of all the professions in the country, ground zero in the obesity war lay with long-haul truckers. The findings blamed all the sitting, driving, and truck-stop food.

Hugh looked at Dr. Wilbur. He had been quiet for too long. "So, Doc? Am I good to roll?" Hugh inched himself off the exam table. He pretended not to hear the table's faint wail of relief.

"Your blood pressure's good," said the doctor, his eyes still on the computer screen. "Cholesterol, blood sugar, urinalysis, all within safe limits. Frankly, I'm surprised."

"Size runs in my family," Hugh shrugged. "I was over twelve pounds at birth."

"My regards to your mother," the doctor quipped, turning his chair to face Hugh. "But you're carrying a heavy load. Did you try the protein shakes I recommended after our last visit?"

"They tasted like protein," Hugh said with a pout. "I didn't even know protein had a specific taste until I took two sips of that High Energy Mocha Frost."

"Two sips?"

"Okay, I drank the whole container. It was so nasty the only thing that got the taste out of my mouth was a double chocolate malt at Hardees. Now, those people know how to make a shake."

Dr. Wilbur scowled. He was not amused. Hugh saw the man's expression and quickly stifled his playful side.

"I am signing off on your report. You're safe to drive. But think about it, Hugh. While there's nothing wrong with being overweight as long as you're healthy—and you are—metabolism is not on your side. You might want to drop some pounds. Just try to eat a little better and get some exercise."

"Is it really that simple?" Hugh asked.

"There's nothing simple about it."

Hugh grew frustrated. "I can't exactly jump rope in the cab. When I'm not driving, I'm filling up on diesel and caffeine, or plotting my next stop. Driving is all about making time."

"Make time for yourself. Or none of it will matter."

The doctor's words stung Hugh, but he was glad to be out of that exam room and back at the loading docks. He cranked the landing gear down to hold his trailer in place as workers used a forklift to load his flatbed. Sewer pipes this time. Stacked high. The pipes were held in place by U-shaped beams at the front and back, and the crew secured the cargo with heavy steel chains tied to the bottom. Hugh conducted a final inspection of his rig's engine, brakes, and all eighteen tires before he deftly climbed the steps into his cab and settled in. Despite his size, Hugh Gandy was agile, with the get-up-and-go of a teenager.

Hugh would be traveling along I-94, past Beach and through the Badlands near Medora, eventually making stops in Bismarck and Valley City, before his run into Minnesota. In his mind, he was already planning a stop seven miles east of Medora to a rest area where the Painted Canyon Trail picked up. It was a beautiful spot, with stunning views of the sky, especially at sunset. Hugh had been chewed out by his dispatcher and on one occasion even saw his pay docked for making an unnecessary stop, but there was something about the Painted Canyon that compelled him to take a moment. Road conditions were good, and Hugh estimated his drive time to the Trail, if he pushed it, would be just over six hours. And there was no better place for him to take his break.

As Hugh pulled away from the loading dock, he glanced at his side mirrors. He noted how his immense body filled every space of the driver's side of the cab as if he were somehow vacuum-packed inside of it. Within minutes, though, Hugh was at peace in his element, thundering down the Interstate. In front and behind him were his fellow truckers in grand, gleaming rigs, a sort of mystical merger of man and machine. Hugh soared by a popular rest stop where rows of parked semis looked like sleeping giants. It's precisely what they are, he thought to himself.

A final hint of orange and red faded in the western sky, and darkness began to creep across the landscape. Hugh pulled his rig to the right, the air brakes whooshing as he came to a full stop. He was at the Painted Canyon Trail. Hugh opened a cooler he kept on the passenger side, grabbed a salami sandwich, and climbed out of the truck. He took a deep breath of the cool night air.

Hugh had a hobby he had picked up from his father during their cross country drives. He was an astronomy buff, and a well-schooled one. Hugh's dad had taught him about the constellations and how the stars told a story. So many stories. As a trucker who relied on directional acuity, Hugh also relished the notion that a constellation was the equivalent of a celestial road map. Throughout time, the stars had served to help people navigate over land and water. The very same stars Hugh was watching now.

So after a couple bites of his sandwich, Hugh went to work. He opened the passenger door of his rig and removed a rolled up mat, which he unfurled onto the ground beside his truck. It was an extra thick yoga mat that had never known even the rumor of a lotus position or any other twist or bend. Hugh didn't care. It was comfortable. He then reached into the rig for a sleek, custom-made backpack. He unzipped the pack and removed a small telescope, a 70 MM Travel Scope with coated glass, and preassembled tripod. It was the perfect tool for star gazing. After another couple bites of salami, Hugh Gandy plopped onto that yoga mat, adjusted the tripod to angle the telescope, and began to search the sky.

In no time, Hugh was right at home, gazing at the stars he held so dear. Sometime in the ancient past, star gazers gave life to these star formations. They found a way to connect the dots and perceive patterns that formed pictures. Hercules, the splendid and immortal hero, knelt in the sky amid an enormous sphere of stars, known to our more poetic astronomers as "diamonds on velvet." The Big Dipper was in Ursa Major, and seemingly so near; the Little Dipper sparkled with Polaris, the North Star, a constant beacon at its handle. Polaris appeared never to move, as it was above the Earth's North Pole. Hugh knew the stars weren't actually moving, that it was Earth in motion, spinning on its axis.

As the sky darkened, Hugh found the two stars that first got him hooked on astronomy. They were Betelgeuse and Rigel, both vivid in their intensity and part of the constellation Orion, the great hunter of the sky. Orion was visible during winter in the northern hemisphere. He was visible to Hugh now. Orion marched in the heavens with his club, shield, and belt in fine order. The atmosphere around Earth distorted starlight and made the stars appear to twinkle. So to anyone gazing upward on a clear night, billions of miles away, the sky looked bright and alive.

Hugh put the other half of his sandwich down when his eyes were drawn to a falling star over the horizon. He made a wish. He was old-fashioned that way. Then, another star caught his eye, this one traveling across the sky, straight through the belt of Orion. Hugh had always made an effort to observe the Perseid Meteor Shower each year, but that wasn't due until August when Earth passed through a trail of dust left by the Swift-Tuttle comet. As the dust plummets to Earth, it vaporizes into fabulous streaks of light. Hugh studied the constellations above. A few stars around the belt of Orion began to glow a bluish-white. Cooler stars appeared red, warmer stars yellow, but the hottest stars were bluish-white. How strange, thought Hugh. He had studied Orion for years, but had never seen the stars change color. Then he chuckled to himself. The story of Orion had contemporary appeal. Legend claimed Orion was the son of the god Poseidon, and was quite a ladies' man. Or at least he thought so. He was a skilled hunter, so admired that the goddess Artemis chose to join him on a hunt. Maybe Orion didn't know the rules of conduct when it came to dating deities, but he laid a hand on Artemis, and the goddess wasn't having any of it. She nailed him with a scorpion sting that ended his life. So there he is, as he has been, in the sky, with a fancy beaded belt and glowing gas around his sword.

The bluish-white light at Orion's belt flickered and again drew Hugh's attention. He moved away from his telescope to look with a bare eye, and what he saw made him gasp. Not only was Orion's belt in disarray, but the gaseous sword in the constellation appeared to be moving. Hugh knew this was impossible. He must be more tired than he felt, a common affliction for truck drivers who traveled great distances. Hugh had already driven sixty hours this week, and decided the only safe thing to do was to rest for a moment. Just lie back, close his eyes, and relax.

As he fell into a deep sleep, the yoga mat suddenly felt very cold and began to make a rustling sound. Hugh stirred and gripped both sides of the mat to hold it to the ground. Only his hands slipped beneath the mat and all he felt was the chill of the night air. *Because he was floating in the air*. Hugh's eyes shot open, but he was paralyzed by fear and unable to move. The bright light emanating from Orion seemed to bathe him and the Earth below. So far below. Hugh's eyes darted to the side, and he could see the ground. There was his enormous flatbed, which now appeared so tiny, like nothing more than a child's toy. Then, a brighter light overtook Hugh and forced him to close his eyes.

Hugh woke, drenched in sweat, but shivering in cold. He was on the ground, about ten yards away from his rig. The yoga mat, the telescope, and what was left of his salami sandwich were right where he had left them. Hugh's brow furrowed. It was the first time in his life he had failed to finish a sandwich. He gathered his things and quickly tossed them into the passenger side of the truck. Hugh allowed that he must have suffered a strange dream, brought on by extreme fatigue. A cool breeze made him shiver again and he climbed into the safety of his rig and locked the doors. Still unnerved, Hugh had to clear the cobwebs from his head in order to think clearly. He looked through the windshield and that's when he realized something was very wrong. He had parked in an alcove along the Painted Canyon Trail. And now his flatbed truck was facing the opposite direction.

The next few moments were a blur for Hugh Gandy. He drove with the hammer down, faster than usual. Radio reports crackled with static, but he heard enough to know he had a clean shot to his next destination if he stayed in the fifty dollar lane. How long had he been asleep, he wondered, and why was he still shaking? The details of his strange dream echoed in his mind, but for the moment Hugh was more concerned with making time. It was always about making time. Then, so anxious he was hyperventilating, he finally glanced at his watch. Somehow, despite his sojourn to the Painted Canyon Trail and his fully unplanned nap, he was not only on time but ahead of schedule. The clock on his dashboard confirmed the hour, and Hugh slowed his rig and began to calm.

A year later, Hugh was back for his mandatory physical exam. Dr. Wilbur clapped his hands and nodded his approval.

"You're over a hundred pounds lighter!" he said with genuine glee. "What kind of diet are you on?"

"I'm not really dieting," replied Hugh.

"Oh, come on," said the doctor, clearly dissatisfied.

"No kidding," grinned Hugh. "I'm not eating anything in particular or exercising all that much. Something just happened on the road that made me change my way of looking at things."

Dr. Wilbur was intrigued. He sat down, wanting more.

Hugh searched for a way to put his explanation into words. "I've always been big," he said, "but okay with my size."

"So what changed?" asked Dr. Wilbur, truly invested.

"Ever since I was a kid, I loved to look at the stars. I think because my dad was a truck driver, and I followed in his footsteps, the night sky was a part of our lives. It was more than a map. The sky was a comfort, by serving as a constant." Hugh took a moment. He rubbed his arms, noticeably with more definition now. "Our sun is ninety-three million miles away, and it's the closest star out of a hundred billion in the Milky Way. And if you can't get your head around that, listen to this: the stars we see may not even be there. They may have died eons ago, and we see them only because their light is traveling our way."

Dr. Wilbur studied Hugh's face.

"I don't quite know how this affects your weight." The doctor eyed his patient. "But I would like to understand."

Hugh glanced at himself in a cracked mirror over the sink.

"I began to see the bigger picture," explained Hugh. "I imagined myself among the stars, looking down at the Earth."

"Huh..." said Dr. Wilbur, wanting to keep up.

"I may be big," Hugh shrugged, and pointed a finger upward. "But from up there, everything looks so small." Hugh indicated himself. "Even me." Hugh lit up as if the answers to the universe had come his way. "I became obsessed with the very idea, Doc. I was just a speck in the scope of the world. And I had found a way to fit in. To find my place and fit inside of it. Comfortably. I'm out there driving, but over the past year, I got the sense that something else, something bigger, is helping me to steer."

Dr. Wilbur put a hand on Hugh's shoulder. He knew his patient was not delusional. His medical report was sound. The service records Dr. Wilbur received from the *Over The Plains* trucking company described Hugh as a model employee, dependable and well-liked by his co-workers. Sure, the account of his weight loss was unusual, but he was heading in the right direction. There was no reason to ground Hugh. He was again good to roll.

Hugh Gandy left out the details about his star gazing to both his doctor and his company dispatcher, but he told a few close friends and fellow truckers to keep an eye out on I-94. Moreover, Hugh continued to chart the sky when on the route, and when he felt he had compiled enough data to tell a story, he contacted the science editor at the local newspaper. He told the man he could not understand why people weren't already talking about the changing star patterns in and around Orion, a popular constellation for even novice astronomy buffs. Hugh reasoned that he could not be the only person to take notice of these changes in the night sky. But the science editor was barely a scientist, and only jotted down Hugh's notes and filed a short article deep within the paper about a truck driver's passion for the stars. Hugh was disappointed. He knew his sightings meant something and warranted more than the cursory review that was published.

To make matters worse, Hugh was summoned for a private meeting at the office of the company's dispatcher. Olaf the Swede was his direct boss, and Olaf was not happy to see Hugh's name or the name of *Over the Plains* cited in the newspaper.

"That story depicts a driver staring at the sky when he should be focused on the road," Olaf grumbled.

"I only do it on my break," argued Hugh. "You see my logs. I never deliver late or do anything to cause damage to my rig."

"Our rig," Olaf reminded Hugh.

Hugh seethed a little. He didn't need the reminder.

Olaf softened and walked Hugh to the door. "I have no problem with you as a driver, Hugh, and no cause to reprimand you. Just talk to me next time, before you go to the local reporters." Olaf gave Hugh a friendly fist bump. "And if the stars ever do try to beam you up, make sure the rig's in gear."

Hugh stiffened on Olaf's advice, convinced he should keep his recent dreams to himself. As he left the dispatcher's office and started down the hallway, Olaf called out to him.

"One more thing."

Hugh faced Olaf, a tad uneasy.

The Swede shrugged. "I haven't mentioned it before because, well, it's personal, but damn, Hugh. Your transformation has been astounding. How much weight are you trying to lose?"

"I'm not trying," Hugh replied, and kept walking.

Hugh supposed he was exercising more, now that he no longer got winded during a brisk walk or a hike in the hills, but his weight loss was as confounding to him as it was to everyone else. And he was forced to do something he had not done in years: buy new clothes. He needed jeans, a belt that fit his shrinking waist line, and a few uniform shirts. Back when he drove with his dad, it was all flannel all the time, but this company dressed its drivers in navy blue shirts with the driver's name and the corporate logo above the left pocket. Hugh didn't mind. At least it wasn't UPS where he might be pressured to wear brown shorts. He hit the uniform shop and ordered his gear. As the clerk rang him up, Hugh asked her to throw in a couple pair of long-johns.

"It's getting colder at night," Hugh explained. "I don't remember it ever being this cold in the fall months."

"Global warming," the clerk chimed in.

"How's that?" Hugh asked. He thought she had misheard him.

"The Earth is changing. Like a woman in menopause. Hot one moment, then seconds later, damp with a chill and an attitude."

Hugh thanked the woman for her help, gathered his items, and walked out. He pondered her comment, how unscientific it had been, until it occurred to him that she was right. Planetary bodies were in a constant state of change. The universe was expanding. Stars used up their hydrogen gas and glowed with the light of a million suns before they exploded and died. Hugh looked upward, glad it was daytime and all he could squint at was the sun. Our sun. A sun that one day would swell and swallow Mercury, Venus, and finally Earth, before going dark forever.

All of this cosmic ruminating made a day run just what Hugh needed when he was asked to replace a driver whose route ended in a jackknife at exit 72. The driver was all right and no one was harmed in the incident. That's always what mattered the most. Hugh drove through New Salem, where he passed a landmark called Salem Sue, a thirty-eight foot sculpture of a Holstein cow. The cow attracted her share of visitors, desperate to see something other than the wide open spaces of the region. As he drove on, Hugh spotted the giant sand hill crane named Sandy, and Dakota Thunder, the largest buffalo ever built, although know-it-alls insisted it was actually a bison. One thing was sure: they built things big in the Badlands. Hugh kept his focus, but he couldn't help but wonder what these enormous monuments must look like from above. From high above. He was ready to see the stars again.

Hugh didn't have long to wait. Olaf scheduled him for a night run the next week. The company received continuous orders for concrete sewer pipes. Hugh would deliver pipes across the Missouri River, past the divide where rivers drain south to Mexico, or north to the Arctic. And just as his doctor ordered, Hugh made time for himself. Once more he was searching the sky. But he was more discreet about it. He made a point to park his rig along service roads, off the radar of anyone driving by.

One night, he found the constellation Cassiopeia, a dazzling zigzag of stars. Then, just as with Orion, a prominent star of the Great Queen seemed out of order. Hugh could swear the star was changing shape. In fact, it appeared to be shredding. Hugh was aware of black holes and how they can churn a star into oblivion, but if a black hole had been present, scientists would be all over it. Hugh loved the term used to describe a black hole's effect on a foreign body: it was called spaghettification, or the noodle effect. When a black hole drew an object into its gravity and past its event horizon, the object became stretched thin like a strand of spaghetti before it was swallowed for good.

In the past these thoughts would have made Hugh hungry for spaghetti. But now, his thoughts were fixated on the changing pattern of stars in the sky. What was going on up there?

Summer arrived, and Hugh took only night runs so he could spend time with the stars. On warm nights, he would even wear khakis or shorts. Sometimes, women would whistle at him as he walked by. They were the same women who whistled when he was obese, so he took it in stride, but oh boy did he enjoy it.

The lights at the service garage were on when Hugh arrived for work. He jotted the time in his log and headed to the flatbed, stacked high with concrete pipes and secured with chains. Olaf approached as Hugh made the final inspection of the eighteen wheels that would take him east.

"Last shipment of sewer pipes," Olaf said, and wiped his brow. "Unless these start to crack, too, I guess."

"Solid concrete," Hugh said. He put the palm of his hand on one of the sturdy pipes. "And straight from the factory. These pipes are going to last a good long time."

The sun dropped early that night, but that was fine with Hugh. He wasn't due to deliver the sewer pipes until the next morning in Dickinson. He cruised along in silence, enjoying the thrum of his wheels upon the lonely roadways, when all at once he felt a dip on his right and heard a flapping sound. A tire tread. Hugh took the exit at the Theodore Roosevelt National Park and pulled to a stop. He got out to retrace his route and found the shredded recap. Hugh returned to his truck to make a report.

And that's when the sky lit up above in an array of color. Flashes of light, moving in every direction, pierced the sky. Hugh trembled and tried to get his bearings. Then it occurred to him that he knew what to look for. He had received the warnings, from the changing views of both Orion and Cassiopeia.

The star formation that dominated the sky tonight was that of Perseus. Great Perseus, with the head of Medusa in one hand and his fearsome sickle in the other. And the Double Cluster in the northern end glowed more brightly than Hugh had ever seen. They were supergiant suns, firing flares of lethal gas across the inky black of night that seemed to set Perseus himself ablaze.

Within a minute, the first strike hit the ground several miles from Hugh's position, but he felt the rumble and saw the red and orange fires rise from the ground. Another strike hit somewhere far up north, and a third strike hit close enough to sever Interstate-94 and send huge slabs of pavement into the air. Hugh tried to get back into his truck when the cab lurched upward, like a bucking bronco. The trailer was hit next, and the concrete sewer pipes broke their steel chains and flew high in every direction. One pipe hit the pavement and began to cartwheel directly toward Hugh, but he managed to duck just before it decapitated him. He watched the pipe continue its downward roll, until it came to rest in a ditch that bordered the highway.

Hugh thought of his dad, and wondered what he would do if under attack. Was this an attack, or was this just the universe self-correcting from some gravitational wave or ripple? Hugh didn't have time to consider those possibilities. Not now. He had always counted on the stars for guidance. His life was flashing before him, and he remembered how he first noted peculiar shifts in the formation of Orion and Cassiopeia, and how Perseus was changing before his very eyes. *Maybe the stars were guiding Hugh*. He had been given a message. It came from deep in space, perhaps to warn of an unknown civilization that was harnessing the energy of nearby stars to stage an invasion. Now the invasion was here.

Showers of burning debris were firing down all around him, and Hugh had only one place he could think of to go. He climbed down the grassy hillside beside I-94 and found the concrete sewer pipe that had flown from his rig and rolled into the ditch. Just one year ago, an event like this would have likely left Hugh trapped in his tractor-trailer. He was never uncomfortable living as a big man—hell, he was still a big man, but he had slimmed down. And maybe it was just enough to get him through this thing. Whatever it was. Somehow, Hugh's enduring love of the night sky and his love of the stars had inspired him to change.

Hugh squirmed on his belly toward the concrete sewer pipe. He made himself as small as he could as he squeezed inside the pipe. There, he could peer out its end and hold on. The ground shook all around him, but the pipe was solid and Hugh would stay encased in his concrete shelter until the storm was over.

Hugh Gandy did not know if he would survive the assault, but in the tumult of the moment, he felt oddly safe in this man-made cocoon. And he thanked his stars for leading him here.

Dark fantasy and horror author Kate Jonez has twice been nominated for the Bram Stoker Award *and once for a* Shirley Jackson Award. *Her short fiction has appeared or is forthcoming in* The Best Horror of the Year Vol. 8, Black Static, Pseudopod, Gamut, *and* Haunted Nights *edited by Ellen Datlow and Lisa Morton. Kate has always loved driving long distances. She's crisscrossed the country many times although never in a truck. She even worked as a waitress in the Jolly Texas Truck Stop many years ago. Although sadly she only lasted a week, the truck stop is still there.*

SILENT PASSENGER

Kate Jonez

THE TWINGE IN JERRI-LYNN'S EYE TOOTH goes off like a siren, more a sound than a pain.

The suit standing at the break room whiteboard under the unforgiving eye of the LED lights doesn't hear it. Of course, there's no reason he would. Jerri-Lynn knows this on an intellectual level, but the sensation of pain is so present in the world it seems unbelievable that no one else can perceive it.

The suit keeps on talking and pointing with his laser like nothing is wrong. "The neural networks of the processor power the mechanism by pulling energy from objects moving in a co-equal direction." Zip, zip with the laser pointer.

What does that even mean? Jerri-Lynn feels stupid. She suspects the words are chosen for that very purpose. *Neural networks—processor—co-equal.* Technical words, manly slang. She could figure it out if she tried. She'd deciphered the language of trucks. *Solenoid—drivetrain—S-cam.* It isn't that hard once the top layer is peeled back.

"When objects move in a dis-equal direction they decrease the efficiency of propulsion by twenty-five percent, thus effectuating a need for additional propulsion—" The suit turns and swirls the laser in front of each of them as though they might chase it like cats, then finishes with a dramatic flourish, "i.e. drivers."

Dis-equal—propulsion—effectuating. Jerri-Lynn could look up the words. Ask the questions everyone has, but no one is asking. Her heart isn't in it. She doesn't want to learn anything new that she'll never use again after this one last run. She should probably care more, but she's more concerned about the fact that she can't imagine what she's going to do next. The truck will go. With her for a while, then without her.

The suit's way of speaking is hard and clipped like Italians in movies but with most of the edges filed off. The words he's saying sound practiced. He's not the scientist. He's the pill the scientists want the drivers to swallow. The company probably thinks they'll listen to this thinly disguised tough guy more than an actual intellectual. The guy isn't from Wichita, yet he doesn't have a speck of insecurity about being an outsider. The opposite in fact. His confidence fills the room like expensive cologne. Jerri-Lynn wonders what it would feel like to be that sure of herself. It'd be hard to hate anybody more than the flannel-clad good ole boys in the break room hate this dude. Waves of it waft off them. He isn't fazed at all.

Charlie Mason raises his hand the way kids do in school. It's not a thing a grown man usually has to do, and he's got a look on his face like a dog that made a snack out of the trash.

The suit tilts his chin at him.

Charlie shuffles his feet on the cement floor before he says, "Alright, tell me if I'm understanding this correct. We don't stop for diesel no more, right?"

"That's right."

"Why's that again?"

The suit's eyes narrow and he gets a look on his face like he'd whack Charlie with a newspaper if he had one. "You want me to start over from the beginning?"

The guys around the table groan in unison.

Jerri-Lynn feels like groaning herself but mostly because her tooth is throbbing.

"Nah, don't do that." Charlie takes off his glasses and wipes the lenses on his T-shirt. "I just want to be for sure that I don't have to stop for fuel."

"That's right."

Charlie perches his glasses on his nose and squints at the whiteboard.

"Lookit." Bill Pullman grabs a napkin. "You know that joke about how you make a car go by raising up the rear wheels so it's always rolling downhill?"

A few of the guys chuckle then choke it off when they realize they're laughing at Charlie's expense. Before the new management took over, Pullman never talked much in the break room, being the only black guy on the crew. Seems that times have changed enough that he doesn't have to worry about such things anymore.

"Yup," Charlie says.

"It's like that," Pullman says, "only not exactly." He leans back and grabs the marker off the whiteboard tray and scribbles on the napkin. "The trucks get their power from each other and the other vehicles going in the same direction. Like there's a magnet pulling them all along."

The suit comes over and looks at the napkin. He twists his mouth into something like a smile and bobs his head. "Only it's not a magnet."

"Right," Pullman agrees. "Just an analogy."

Jerri-Lynn still doesn't get it. She doesn't really understand why she has to. Men like to know stuff even if it doesn't change a thing.

"Then how come it's different on County 287?" Jerri-Lynn asks. "They don't have the magnets put in yet?"

Pullman gives her an exasperated look.

"There aren't any magnets," the suit snaps like she's said the stupidest thing ever.

She should have kept her mouth shut.

"Yeah, I don't get it either," Charlie says.

Pullman draws a bunch of lines on the napkin. "Because County 287 is two lanes in each direction and the vehicles going east drag down on the vehicles going west instead of giving them power."

"Yeah and..." Charlie says.

"It's a bug," Pullman says. "And we got to help the trucks by giving the power to get to the four-lane road."

"Hmmph." Charlie grumbles. "Might well as use diesel."

"You bought any in a while, pal?" the suit says in his testy way. "Costs as much as the load you're carrying." He turns back to the whiteboard.

"Like solar panels made of people." Pullman says, grinning at his own wit.

Pain is punishment.

Jerri-Lynn isn't sure what she's being punished for. Could be a lot of things. Most likely eating a donut for breakfast one too many days. She wants to get up from the table and get an aspirin, or whatever, from the drawer under the coffee machine, but she doesn't want to draw attention to herself. Ever since most of the regular crew had gotten laid off, the spotlight has been on her. Everyone thinks she was one of the chosen few for politically correct reasons. She's the only female in the room. And years of experience have taught her never to shine a light on that.

The suit keeps on with his lesson like Pullman didn't even explain it better. When he gets to the part about the IRL beta testing, the thought that saying "in real life" takes exactly as much effort as saying the initials causes another siren of pain to shudder through Jerri-Lynn. This convinces her to get the aspirin anyway. She slides her chair across the floor, rolls her shoulders forward and makes her way as unobtrusively as she can to the medicine drawer.

"Don't leave now." The suit says flashing a mouthful of brilliant white teeth. "I'm just getting to the part where you get paid to coast."

The guys around the table rub their stubbly chins and chuckle in fake solidarity with the suit, even Pullman who should know better. Jerri-Lynn has a reputation for coasting. There's always rumors like that whenever a woman has a man's job. There's no way the suit would know what the good ole boys say, but it makes the joke richer. Anyway, there's probably some truth to it. She's not adverse to doing things the easy way.

We are all Judases now. No one is any better off than anyone else. Those of us holding on to the tail end of how things used to be, we're worse than scabs ever were. We're not only betraying our fellow drivers, we are species traitors. Laugh harder sons of bitches. Not long from now you won't have to complain about women taking what's yours anymore. These machines are going to be the end of us for good. The suit doesn't know it, but it's just a matter of time before they come for him too. We're all fucked. We're all good and fucked.

Jerri-Lynn doesn't feel as bad about the situation as she probably should. It's been a good long time since she's felt anything one way or the other about the state of her life. Now the good ole boys are up the same creek without a paddle. That's okay by her. Misery love company as Jim used to say.

She hadn't thought twice about signing on for this job. It had been the right thing to do. She's got bills. She's got plenty of those. It's her only choice really. Work is the only thing that holds the void at bay.

She should have paid the extra twenty-five dollars per pay period for dental and seen the dentist already. This toothache is going to cost a fortune and chances are her insurance won't be around after this last run.

She shakes out three pills from the bottle, swallows two and presses one against the depression in her eye tooth.

"All right," the suit says. "Enough theory. Time to get this party started."

Jerri-Lynn takes a swig of burned coffee from the bottom of the pot, tosses the cup in the trash, and follows the group into the harsh artificial sun of the garage. The truck in her bay looks like any other she's driven lately. She hopes she doesn't have a load of liquor this time. Road bandits seem to be able to sniff that prize out from miles away. If she's hauling liquor, she'll have to take extra precautions to keep from getting herself robbed. That'll mean no rest stops after dark and generally less freedom. No use worrying, though, she'll get the manifest soon enough.

She'd like to be on the road already. Sitting idle makes her itchy. All this talk with whiteboards and pointers and interaction with people she'd rather not talk to is exactly the kind of stuff that made her quit her office job and become a driver all those years ago. Jim never liked the idea. But he should have thought about that before enlisting. Jerri-Lynn never liked the idea of him going off the map to a mountain in the middle of nowhere to play with guns either. He hadn't listened to her, so she hadn't listened to him. The twinge in her heart reminds her that she once thought fighting Jim was a good idea.

Jerri-Lynn climbs up into the cab. It looks enough like every other truck she's driven since she had to sell her own to cover expenses, so she feels confident she can do the job. *Expenses* is not a word that really covers what she lost.... The thought she's doing all she can to hold off the memories sends an ache through her as sharp as the sensation in her tooth. Pain is a reminder. The worst has already come to pass.

She grabs the tablet with the manifest and flicks it on. Liquor of course.

There's a few odd things in the cab. A rubber nipple that fits on her index finger like a condom and a strap that goes around her chest. The gear shift is disturbingly simplified. It looks like a Frankenstein switch. Down for dead. Up for electrified, but other than that, things are the same. Jerri-Lynn straps herself in and rolls down the window.

"Ready to roll!" the suit says with way too much enthusiasm. He weaves through the lineup flashing his bright smile and nodding at the drivers. The artificial light glints off his too-groomed hair making him seem unreal somehow, as though he too is made of metal and technology.

One after another, doors roll up and the trucks slide out into the pale morning light. Jerri-Lynn grabs the gear shift and drags it into the *electrified* position. No engine rumble rattles the cab, but there's an ever so slight tightening in the chest strap. All the dash lights come on to let her know the truck is ready to go. She depresses the floor pedal and the truck glides soundlessly onto the road.

The suit yells some technical gibberish at Jerri-Lynn that she ignores as she turns out of the lot and pulls onto the feeder road to County 287. She's in control of the rig. She was afraid maybe it would steer itself and she'd be at its mercy. That comes later, she thinks bitterly. She accelerates up the access road. No matter how hard she depresses the pedal the speed gauge won't go above 63.

The morning is sweater cool and the sky is an enormous expanse of cloudless blue, the kind of weather that tricked her into to thinking she was going to like Wichita when she and Jim moved into their first apartment by the Air Force base. She'd liked the town back then, but she would have been happy anywhere, in the middle of the desert even, when she and Jim first got married. He was a force in her that weather couldn't touch. With him gone, she's on shaky ground. She feels acutely how much of an outsider she'd managed to remain. In ten years she hadn't gotten to know much about the place at all. Of course, she knows which way the streets go, how to get to the grocery store, what the local TV channels are, but she'd never bothered to make Wichita home. Ten years really flies by.

She's greeted by the sign that lets her know the distance to Lawton, to Childress to Amarillo, dusty western towns rich in rugged history and lore. Like most places in Texas they are built for the locals. They hide all their secrets from people just passing through. Amarillo is where the 287 meets the interstate I-40. Amarillo is where the machine takes over and Jerri-Lynn coasts. Two-hundred miles or so, and she can coast.

Jerri-Lynn wishes she'd stopped at the Beverly Liquor on the outskirts of town and picked up two pints from Jorge. Seems almost a crime not to stop in and say goodbye to one of the few people on earth who know her by name on what would probably be her last run. She should have signed up with that other outfit when she had the chance. Too late for regrets now. Hopefully, she won't land in a dry county by nightfall. She is going to need something to dull the ache tonight. All the aches. She puts her tongue in the depression in her eye tooth. Sometimes dulling the pain is the only option. On an ordinary haul she'd know exactly how far she could go in a day. With the machine in control there is no telling where she'll land.

Miles of ranch land littered with pump jacks that don't know they are living in their end times fly by. Jerri-Lynn turns on the radio and pushes seek until she lands on a call-in show out of Lawton. The signal won't last long, but she likes getting a peek into the guts of a place. They give up their secrets on these radio shows. She wonders if they know that.

Solitude is the best part of driving. The suspended place between leaving and arriving is a vacation from the job of living. All work is like that, Jerri-Lynn thinks in a moment of clarity. That's why so many people neglect everything else for it. It's good to have a purpose, if only for a while.

Jerri-Lynn doesn't bother to pass the cars and other trucks. 63 miles per hour is not fast enough to get around any but the oldest jalopy. The throb in her tooth has dulled to the point that it's bearable if not comfortable. If it was like this all the time she could probably skip the dentist.

Pain is a warning.

The pain will be back with a fury, Jerri-Lynn knows. It is just a matter of biting down on some sweet thing or breathing in cold air. That's how pain is. Whether Jerri-Lynn uncovers its true nature and purpose or not, one thing she is sure of, it will definitely be back. Would have been nice if Jim could have figured out that one fact. He'd chased the cure like he was going to put an end to it for good. His persistence is what got him in the end.

Thoughts of Jim threaten to saw into her and slice her open laying bare all her raw nerves. Gone is gone. It's better to put him out of her mind. She's already thought about every detail of what went wrong for months on top of months and that got her nowhere. *What if he'd talked about the IED that had blown up his friend and irreparably twisted his spine? What if a different doctor prescribed less dangerous medicine? What if she'd been kinder, or tougher or different in some way? What if she'd followed him around and discovered what he'd been up to in the months before everything went wrong instead of trusting the lies of a man in the grip of an irresistible pain?* Rehashing the details never changes a thing. Jerri-Lynn settles into the road hum with its vibration under her feet and lets the rig carry her into the space between leaving and arriving.

The lilt of the Texoma twang punctuated by staccato bursts of homestyle swearing about football or Oklahoma City politics buzzes from the radio like an especially docile horsefly not really annoying enough to do anything about. Jerri-Lynn eats mile after mile of white dashes and stripes without thinking about much of anything. The throb in her tooth flares just enough to keep her from getting comfortable.

"Jerri!"

Jerri-Lynn jumps. The voice slashes through the white noise of her thoughts. Jim's voice. Unmistakable.

"Pull over," Jim's voice demands. It's only his voice, not him. It can't possibly be him. He's gone. Of that one thing she's sure.

She twists her head from side to side. She's alone in the cab. Instinctively, she slams her palm into all the radio buttons at once. The talk radio voices fall silent. She grips the wheel, leans into it, listens.

"Pull over."

The voice is impossibly tangible like a crack of lightning in the middle of the night that blows sleep away. She is compelled to hear it. Even though it can't be a real thing. Can't possibly be.

JCT I-40 Amarillo 3 MILES. The sign flashes in front of her eyes.

Impossible. Where had two-hundred miles and three hours gone? That is a lot to lose.

The strap around her chest compresses enough for her to notice but not enough to be uncomfortable. It feels disturbingly like a hug.

Alongside the road a man wearing jeans with the creases ironed in and a thin jacket over a pristine white T-shirt waves her down. He doesn't seem agitated. His motions are controlled in fact, perfunctory, as though he's been waiting for her.

Jerri-Lynn's heart skips a beat. The strap tries to sooth her with another hug. This man cannot possibly be who he appears to be. He's stepped out of the time where ironed creases in blue jeans were in fashion, a time when a young soldier could believe in things. She's projecting her memories on to the blank canvas of a hitchhiker. That's the only explanation. When she pulls the wheels onto the sandy shoulder, the rubber nipple on her index finger contracts. The rig knows she's decelerating. The rig knows.

Passengers are strictly forbidden. Jerri-Lynn has no doubt this transgression will be thoroughly recorded by all the devices that must surely be standard in a vehicle like this. She's not deterred by half-remembered rules. This is her last run; the rules are unfurling before her like dice tumbling down a craps table.

She rolls to a stop.

Jim's revenant shoulders a duffle bag, runs to the door and pulls it open. A gust of winter air heavy with the arid scent of scrub wood and the dug earth of gopher burrows, but with top notes of asphalt and exhaust, blows over her. She breathes in the chill of it. The siren of her toothache sounds. He climbs in without asking her destination or any of the usual questions a rider would. In spite of the fact that such things are impossible, it's as though he actually is Jim and not just the conjured image of the specter who's been riding with her since she found herself all alone. The resemblance is remarkable. Even the smell of him is Jim's.

"Hey," he says when he settles in. He runs his hand over the brush of his close-cropped hair.

The ache in Jerri-Lynn radiates all through her, tainting everything close by.

"I'm taking the I-40 west as far as it goes," Jerri-Lynn says. This is the first time she's thought about her destination. It's a black hole, the future, once this last run is done. A foreign landscape she doesn't have the will to understand. Electronic language is on the verge of rendering her illiterate in a world she once navigated with ease. She'd almost rather go into it blind.

Jim doesn't respond. In every way he's the silent rider by her side.

Jerri-Lynn electrifies the lever, depresses the accelerator, and the rig pulls onto the highway. The sequence that initiates motion in so many tons of metal is too easy somehow as if the truck has a will to be in motion and is making things as easy as possible.

"Where are you coming from?" Jerri-Lynn asks as the last few miles of County Road 287 fly by.

The passenger turns, looks at her with his blank canvas face. "It's where I'm going that counts."

He's right about that. Jim is right about that. Jerri-Lynn
yearns to believe her man is beside her again. She wants to fall
into the dream, but she's afraid to reach out, to touch him. She
fears that the tenuous illusion might disintegrate, and she'd
find herself touching some random man she found alongside
the road.

"Well where are you going, then?"

"I'm going where you're going," Jim says. "Where is it you
want to go?"

She pushes the button for the radio. A Waylon song, with
a scratch in the same place as her old vinyl copy, floods the
cab, conjuring up the weight of the down-filled sleeping bag,
the crackle of the campfire, the bullfrogs at dusk along the Red
River on their first camping trip.

Jim crooks his lopsided smile at her. "I remember that trip
like it was yesterday."

"You remember?"

"I remember what you remember."

How is that possible? Jerri-Lynn tenses up like the pain is
going to return. She waits for it. There's a saying about things
that are too good to be true. She puts her tongue on the indention
on her eye tooth and still the pain doesn't come.

"Are you a ghost?" Jerri-Lynn asks. She doesn't really need
an answer. Nothing will change if she knows or she doesn't.
She should keep her eyes on the road, but that probably doesn't
matter either. She stares at Jim, taking in every detail.

The rig gives her a reassuring squeeze as the red, white and
blue sign for the I-40 turnoff sails into view. Jerri-Lynn doesn't
need the sign to tell her she's reached the end of the road where
she's needed. The wide-open expanses of earth, sky, cow trails
and the mesquite brush of the county road veer into a tangle of
steel and concrete and asphalt. All that's left for her to do is to
steer one last time onto the interstate and hand over the reins
to the machine.

"We've come to the place." Jim's voice has a metallic edge.

Jerri-Lynn squints hard at him. She can't decide if she squinting to see beyond the illusion or if she squinting to hold it together. She had feared Jim was an illusion, but she's is amazed by how much she wants him to be real.

"We don't need you anymore." The voice coming from Jim's mouth resonates and reverberates in a way no human voice can. It's machine-like, but it isn't unkind. "We don't need you, but we gain nothing from your suffering."

"You'll let me have Jim?" Jerri-Lynn's voice quavers. She's never wanted anything more.

Jim grins his cockeyed grin and his eyes flash with the glint of mischief Jerri-Lynn had always loved. "Yes," he says in a voice that's all his.

As the exchange begins, a thrum and a rumble emanate from the guts of the truck. If Jerri-Lynn had been in control of an ordinary rig, she might have pulled over to check out what was going wrong. But she's not in control. She doesn't worry because whether she understands or not the outcome remains the same. The sound swells and the vibration of it becomes a solid thing like the gravity that pushes back on a roller coaster rider. The magnet, if it is a magnet, or maybe it's bugs in the system, pulls and pushes on her from all directions. It feels like bugs inside her scurrying to get out whatever way they can.

She squeezes Jim's hand and squints to see beyond the illusion of him as the inescapable sound compresses him. She fears he'll become two dimensional.

The rig travels at a speed Jerri-Lynn can't comprehend. Digital displays on the dash are an indecipherable blur of symbols she's never learned. Through the windshield, the view is a smear, of what she's not sure. The signs and symbols of driving she knows so well have become something entirely different. She's in a foreign land.

At the moment this thought occurs to her, the scene before her shifts. The blur of rushing motion settles. The unbearable thrum becomes birds singing and crickets chirping. Prairie grass waves like it does on a spring day when it's finally warm enough for the creek to set the tadpoles free. Jerri-Lynn knows she's hooked up as a battery to some kind of magnetic future machine but that's not how it seems at all. She mashes the clutch and downshifts to second. For some inexplicable reason the pickup she and Jim bought used just after they got married is bumping along a dirt path down to the Red River. She reaches out and takes Jim's hand. It's as warm to the touch as ever it ever was. "You don't have to feel no pain," Waylon wails from the radio. The only thing she knows for sure is all *her* pain is gone.

　　Every last bit.

Sean Patrick Traver is the author of the novels Graves' End, Red Witch, *and* Wraith Ladies Who Lunch, *all of which are about the intrusion of magic into the everyday world. He also works at the (world famous)* Iliad Bookshop *in North Hollywood, CA. He is composed largely of carbon and oxygen, with some nitrogen, phosphorus, and calcium mixed in. Investigate further at* www.seanpatricktraver.com.

INDICA ASTERION & THE WIZARD OF OZYMANDIAS

Sean Patrick Traver

"WAY I HEARD IT, NEVER WAS NO ALIEN on that ship. Captain went space-case and that's all there is to it. 'Dissociative psychosis,' the whitecoats call it. Whatsername massacred her crew all by her lonesome, thinking they's a bunch of saber-toothed spiders. That shit happens, out in the deep."

"Jim," Cathica murmured, nudging her drunk husband in the ribs. "The kids don't need to hear this."

The kids, Tamsin and Jimmy Jr., looked as though they badly needed to hear it. Talk of atrocity riveted children in a way no educational app ever would. Indica almost smiled. She'd held similarly morbid inclinations herself, when she was a girl.

"Aunt Indie?" Tamsin said, looking up and across the cloth-covered table at her. Tam was thirteen and taller than most of the malnourished runts growing up on the home world these days. The bricks of Ionian algae and sacks of Martian-grown quinoa that fell off the back of Big Jim's rig stood his family in better stead than many. "Aunt Indie, what do *you* think happened?"

"Yeah," Jimmy Jr. said, "did all those people get eaten up by a new kinda alien?"

Indica frowned, giving the question due consideration. The news outlets had been serving up heaps of garish speculation about that doomed freighter for a week now, but solid facts remained in short supply. The ship's data had corrupted when the system's last trickle of power rerouted to the one occupied suspension pod found on board, leaving the media with nothing but a lone survivor's account of a nightmare infestation to chew over and spit back at a deeply paranoid public.

Indica shrugged, well aware that her whole family was waiting for her to speak. She'd seen more of the distant systems than everyone else they knew combined. A plastic Christmas tree blinked hypnotically in the room's far corner, like a model of some odd, conical galaxy. "Could be," Indie said at last. "There's a lot more life out there than civilization, but in my experience most of it doesn't need teeth to kill you."

"You mean like microbes and sh—stuff?" Big Jim said, changing his verbal tack off a warning look from Cathica.

"Like microbes, sure. Bacteria, viruses, alien allergens—the killers you don't see coming. At least you can shoot at a giant roach, right? Not so much when it comes to Moffat's bloodpox, or the gutbuster amoeba from New Zothea that makes your organs swell up till your abdomen splits open like a sausage in a microwave. And those're merciful compared to some of the parasites you can pick up out beyond the Maenad Chain. Getting killed quick's not the worst thing that can happen in space, by far."

"What's the worst thing?" Tamsin's eyes shone with lurid curiosity. Her brother poked uncertainly at his third helping of mushroom-and-sausage stuffing.

Indica, whose limited experience with children led her to treat them as tiny adults, continued.

"Well, I suppose there'd be a few contenders for that title. Spinal leeches drown you in nightmares you can't wake up from, tricking your nervous system into pumping out the hormones that get them off. And necrotizing boneworms will rot your skeleton until you collapse in on yourself like a big bag of goo. Hell, something as simple as a pressure differential in an airlock can rupture a guy with enough force to lodge vertebrae in the ceiling. Sanitation crew never really did get the entrail smell out of that decompression chamber..."

Indie realized that Cath had been glaring at her, aghast, for some moments already only when Jimmy Jr. interrupted her recitation of horrors with a seismic belch. Every head turned in his direction as he vomited across the dinner table with the pressurized force of a fire extinguisher. Tamsin shrieked like a corresponding alarm and sprang out of her chair, launching it backward into the Christmas tree, which toppled over with all the stately grace of a felled sequoia, shedding ornaments as it collapsed.

Its tip pointed toward Indica like a long, accusatory finger.

Jimmy twisted up his face and began howling in earnest. Tamsin, who'd gone from pale to green herself, was squealing and flapping her hands in utter disgust. Businesslike Cath hoisted Jim Jr. up against the hollow of her shoulder with a grunt (the kid was getting too big for it) and steered a shaky Tam down the back hall and up the stairs, toward the very rooms she and Indie had occupied when they were girls. She'd get the next generation cleaned up and tucked into bed.

Big Jim folded the antique tablecloth over the cooling pool of regurgitated turkey at its center, then piled up the last of the dishes.

"Thanks a shitload for another fun holiday, Indica," he said on his way to the kitchen, with an armload of plates. "S'always great to see you."

Indie sat alone at the denuded table for a minute or two, watching the fallen Christmas tree continue to blink while Jim started the dishwasher running in the next room. She drained the last of a bottle of shitty Wyoming merlot into her grease-clouded glass, slugged it down with a grimace, then got up and went outside for a smoke.

Indica turned her collar up against the cold. The old farmhouse's porch was deep, but it didn't offer much shelter from the bitter winter chill. The San Angeles Citadel's skyline glittered in the far distance, a mere streak of light along the horizon. Nearer by, tongues of flame and random electric lights flickered amidst the unnamed miles of ramshackle cardboard *favela* where people froze to death every winter, or else burned when their makeshift efforts at heating set entire paper neighborhoods ablaze.

Cath and Jim held on to their quaint life out here by ragged fingernails, doing everything they could to make sure their spawn reached adulthood. It was no small undertaking.

Indie hadn't meant to upset the kids. The gutbuster amoeba was only one of a dozen imminent threats to galactic civilization she might've named right off the top of her head. Worries like that no longer kept her up at night, but she also forgot that not everyone had made their peace with the delirious idea that annihilation was never more than a breath away. Especially people whose ages had barely reached double-digits.

She blazed up the last pre-roll in her pack with a microtorch and took a drag. As the afterimage torch-flame left on her retinas faded, a patch of darkness seemed to coalesce within the shadows across the road, and then a man in black tactical gear stepped out from behind the line of scrubby trees. He raised a hand in greeting when he was sure Indica had seen him.

Indie's bootheels beat a quick tattoo as she descended the porch steps. She strode across Cath and Jim's winter-yellowed lawn, moving to intercept the approaching operative, who favored her with a broad smirk.

"Professor Asterion," he said when they were close enough for conversational tones. "Or should I say Privateer Asterion?"

Indie stepped close and hooked her calf behind his knee even as she slammed the heel of her hand into his front teeth. The operative's legs shot out from under him and he hit the ground with a breathless grunt. Indie planted the arch of her boot across his windpipe, applying enough force to the springy cartilage to let him know that staying down would be a wise idea. He turned his head as much as he could to spit a mouthful of blood onto the blacktop.

"Let's cut to 'Crazy Bitch Asterion,' shall we?" Indica said. "All you assholes get there eventually. Now. This place? These people? They're off limits. Strictly. And I made that very clear to the Authority. Did I not?"

"...*please*..." the purple-faced agent gasped. Indica rolled her eyes, then removed her foot from the man's neck.

He sat up, gasping for air, and Indie took a step back. He was sure to be armed—not that it made much difference to her. But if he had a mind to fire off a projectile weapon out of pique, that would surely scare her niece and nephew (in the best-case scenario), and then Indie would never hear the end of it from Cath.

If he went for a gun she'd disintegrate him, then go back inside for a slice of pie. The evening was still salvageable, maybe.

But the Inquisitor did not reach for a weapon. Instead he held up his hands, and spat more blood into the road. Dammit. Now she couldn't expunge him from existence in good conscience.

This was shaping up to be a long night.

"What's your name?" Indica asked.

The operative grinned, even though his bashed-in nose was still gushing blood. It lent a lurid and demented aspect to what might otherwise have been a somewhat charming smile. "Call me Corrigan," he said.

"What do you want, Corrigan?"

"Jameson Terkel, senior," Corrigan said, checking the data on a handheld tablet. "Terrestrial drayage driver, Class-A commercial license number A591325. Independent regional subcontractor for HermesFTL Interstellar Importers, LLC."

"That's Big Jim," Indica said, feeling honestly baffled. "My brother-in-law."

"Sheer coincidence."

Corrigan said it with a shrug, but Indica narrowed her eyes. She knew better than to believe in any such beast as coincidence. "What's the Authority want with Jim?"

"Well, that's a bit classified."

"Declassify it."

"Not worth my job, is it?"

"Is it worth your kneecaps?"

"Your personal stalemate with the Authority doesn't confer immunity from criminal prosecution upon your entire extended family, you know."

Indica rather thought that was for her to determine, but what she said was: "Jim's no criminal."

Outside of a little honest smuggling, that was. Nothing more than almost anybody was guilty of, these days. Certainly nothing worthy of intervention by an Inquisitor of the Authority.

"Nobody said he was under arrest."

Indica scowled. "What's your deal, Corrigan? What's this really all about?"

"Not you," the Authority's man said, like he was breaking news she'd never heard before.

"You *punched* an Inquisitor in our front yard?" was all Cathica had said to her sister since Corrigan had come to the door.

They were waiting in the living room, eavesdropping while Corrigan talked to Jim in the kitchen.

"Cath, I promise you, this's all gonna—" Indie began, but the boast died on her lips under a withering glare.

"Shut *up*," Cathica hissed, straining to hear the murmurs in the next room, and Indie sighed. Their grandfather's grandfather clock continued to tick and tock in the far corner, sounding much louder than usual.

"Come on," Indie said, crossing the room and grabbing her sister's hand, the way she used to when they were kids.

"What're you—"

"Just come *on*."

Indie strode into the kitchen, hauling a reluctant Cath behind her. "Cut the crap, Corrigan," she said, wishing straightaway that she'd gone with "*shit*" instead, to break up the alliteration. Oh well. "I don't know what you're playing at, but this is Jim's wife and my sister and we're *gonna* know what's going on."

Black-clad Corrigan was leaning back against the farmhouse sink while Big Jim sat at the kitchen table, trying not to look like a chastened child. The Inquisitor considered Indica for an infuriating moment, then said to Jim, who hadn't raised his eyes from the tabletop even when the women barged in: "Whaddaya think, Jimbo? Wanna share?"

Big Jim said nothing. Indica had never seen him so pale. He shook his head, so slightly that the gesture barely amounted to more than a twitch.

"Really up to him," Corrigan told the sisters. "I'm bound by oaths."

"Jim Terkel, you quit fucking around and explain yourself," Cathica demanded, planting both hands on the table in front of him. Indie saw her wince when she caught herself addressing her husband in the tones she normally reserved for recalcitrant children, then snarl in anger at having been pushed there. "What shit did you drag to our door?"

"Cath, I..." Jim began. "I got involved in something. Something dumb."

"Fast-forward."

Jim let out a pent-up breath. "I helped move something from Ozymandias."

"For shit's sake, Jim!" Indie exclaimed. Both Cath and Corrigan looked at her with some annoyance. "Sorry," she said. Then, to Jim again: "But really. The fuck were you thinking?"

"That it paid damn near two years' wages, Indica," Big Jim shot back. "To put one extra box on my truck."

"Doesn't he have the right to remain silent?" Cath asked, clapping a hand over her eyes as her husband casually incriminated himself.

Corrigan shrugged. "We're a little past that sort of thing."

"All the planets in all the systems..." Indie was still incredulous. "And you had to mess with *Ozymandias*?"

"S'not like I entirely had a choice. And you're one to talk, anyway. You've been there! You stole things!"

"Dammit, Jim, I'm a scientist!"

"Yeah, that's exactly the word the Inquisition used, every time they questioned us about you."

Indica and Jim glowered at one another. Then Indie caught Tamsin peering around the doorjamb, behind Jim. Their eyes met for an instant before her niece ducked back out of sight.

Indie sighed.

"I also don't have your responsibilities," she said to Jim, who hung his head in conciliation.

Cathica was near tears, her anger and terror coalescing into a storm of frustration that her body had prepared no appropriate response for. She bit her lip and shook her head, refusing to break down. "How could you be so stupid?" she whispered at Jim.

"Two years' wages, Cath."

"And what good is it? Huh? What good is it if it comes with a curse!"

"Cath, that's—" Indie began.

"Don't you tell me that it's superstition!" Cathica shouted, wheeling on her. "Everything from that place is cursed! The dirt, the rocks! Everything! They know it on a thousand worlds! And *don't* you start with your goddamn semantics, trying to make everyone else in the room feel like a grade-A idiot. I don't want to hear it. If it works like a curse, it's a curse. A plague still kills you even when you know it's caused by germs and not by demons!"

Indica cringed, certain that Tam and Jimmy Jr. were listening in on every word from just outside the kitchen door. They didn't need to hear that mad panic in their mother's voice.

"Honey, Indie's right," Big Jim said. "There ain't no such thing as alien curses."

"Well, I didn't say *that*, precisely..." Indica hedged.

Everybody looked at her.

"Please, grace us with your insight, Professor," Corrigan invited. Indie wouldn't have minded hitting him again. He seemed to know it, and to find it funny, despite the fat lip he'd already received.

"We know so little about the Ozymandian civilization," she attempted to clarify. "Who they were, what they did, what they were capable of—that's all still a mystery."

"Even to you?" Cath asked.

Especially to me, Indica thought. What she said was: "Yeah."

"Thought you studied this shit," Jim said. "Isn't that why you took that thing of yours? To study it? 'Cause you're the only one that's qualified?"

"Yes." (*Sort of.*) "But there's lifetimes' worth of work yet to do. Observation. Experimentation. I've hardly scratched the surface. That's why trade in Ozymandian artifacts is so strictly forbidden by the Authority. They may be powerful and dangerous in ways we just can't predict."

Also (and Indica felt no need to mention this), the ancient curse *had* been explicit, carved in unfathomable alien glyphs on the temple door she'd broken through, on that ruined world so many light-years from home. Nobody from the Authority had managed to translate that inscription, but it clearly wasn't a welcome mat. They'd needed an expert. And Professor Asterion (the noted xenoarchaeologist they begrudgingly called in) hadn't traveled all that way just to be intimidated by an old "keep out" sign.

The words she hadn't been able to read on her way in through the temple door had turned as legible as twelve-point Helvetica by the time she emerged—though Indica herself was the only thing that had changed.

She didn't have to look at Cath to feel the old reproach radiating off of her. Their choices in life had always been so wildly different.

"Of course *you're* exempt from anybody's rules," Cathica accused.

"It chose me, Cath. Me. Not the Authority. It doesn't give a damn who funded the expedition that found it, and frankly, neither do I."

Indie bit her tongue. She ached to explain herself further (an ache that often plagued her, but only occasionally flared into something acute), but she'd said enough in front of Corrigan. The Inquisitor looked all too interested. His mask of nonchalance was slipping, maybe. She might catch a glimpse of the true face behind it.

"It was the Professor's escapades that made the Authority quite so touchy regarding crap from Ozymandias," Corrigan said. "Touchy to the point of issuing death sentences. You've set a bad example, Ms. Asterion."

Indica shrugged. It was what she did, apparently. Her sister wasn't about to speak in her defense.

Cathica shook her head, tabling discussion of Indie's nefarious activities in favor of her husband's more recent offenses. She turned to Corrigan. "You can guarantee Jim immunity if he names the rest of the smuggling ring? Is that the deal?"

"Well, the Authority *will* make an example of you, Jim, if we have to," Corrigan said, turning to face his stoic suspect. "But we'd rather not have to do that. Ozymandias is a sore spot for the Authority, and even executing looters like yourselves requires more commentary on the subject than we care to make. My superiors are loath to do anything that so much as perpetuates the name of the place, in public." He glanced at Indica. "We don't want to inspire any more pillagers and plunderers to try their hands at retracing your steps, Professor."

"So, what? You gonna torture him like you do your metaphors?"

"He wants me to steal it back," Jim murmured, dragging the discussion around to its original focus. "That's why he's here."

"Ideally," Corrigan said. "That'd be grand."

"Can you?" Cath seemed ready to explore the idea.

"I guess, maybe," Jim conceded. "There's time. All it's gonna do is change who wants to kill me, though."

"Nobody's killing you," Indie muttered. It seemed only Corrigan heard her.

"Well, you have to do something, Jim. If you can fix this, you have to." Cath was adamant about it, and Indica felt inclined to agree. Disappointing a band of gangsters was better than running afoul of the interstellar power that was the Authority. There was no escape from them.

Her own case was a radical exception.

"So what's he gotta do?" she asked of Corrigan.

"Get it back. Give it to me. Before we have to admit anything's been taken."

"And what is 'it,' exactly?"

Corrigan suppressed a flash of irritation. "Wasn't issued that information."

"Jim?"

"Huh? Nobody told *me* what it is. Some statue or whatnot, I figured. An artifact. Ain't that all that's left on Ozymandias?"

"You didn't even look in the box?"

"It's my job, not my business."

Indica and Jim each looked at the other like they were nuts. It gave Indie pause, being reminded that other people could have priorities so different from her own.

"*Where* is it, then?"

"Waiting at the distribution hub, till tomorrow morning," Jim said. "Taped up inside the air dam on the top of my cab."

"Just sitting there?" Indie's inner archaeologist was appalled. "Why?"

"On account of the holiday, Indica."

Oh, yeah. That. "Can you get in, then?"

Jim shrugged. "If it's guys I know on the gate, probably. But then the Ice Dragons are gonna say I ripped them off. Sold their shit to a higher bidder."

"In a sense," Corrigan mused. "But our price is your freedom. Hard to outbid that."

Not necessarily. Indica was thinking of Tamsin and Jimmy Jr., lurking out in the living room. Big Jim was certainly thinking about them too, and wondering if there were lines his criminal associates wouldn't cross. That question was the fuel for Cath's smoldering fury. "You've gotta do better than that, Corrigan," Indie said.

He waved her concerns aside. "We've got pull with their leadership. We'll smooth it over for you. But first we need the item back."

"I'm gonna come with you, then." Indie said.

"You don't have to do that." Jim looked distressed. "I can handle it."

"You've handled enough already, don't you think?" Cathica snapped. She was near her breaking point, patience-wise. Indie knew the signs, from having pushed her past it many times before. "Indie can help with this."

"Out of the question," Corrigan said, addressing Indie. "Only thing the Authority wants less than to lose another piece of Ozymandian history to the black market is to hand one over to you."

"I'm not gonna steal your trinket. I'm just looking out for my family."

"Says the only convicted grave robber in the room."

"Convicted *in absentia*," Indie said.

"Still counts, doesn't it?"

"Not much."

"Will you two stick a pin in it, please?" Cath was shrugging into her winter parka in the corner of the kitchen.

"Where do you think you're going?" everyone else in the room said, more or less at once.

Cath laughed—a short, brittle bark. Her eyes flashed with that barely-checked anger. "To make sure this gets done. Under adult supervision."

"Cath, come on," Jim protested. "Somebody's gotta stay with the kids."

"Check on them in an hour. Can you handle that without committing another felony?"

Jim's face reddened, and Indie had to bite back an impolitic laugh of her own. Cathica was already headed out the mud room door, off the side of the house. Indie offered Jim an almost sheepish shrug as she followed after.

A smirking Corrigan brought up the rear.

"We might actually need him, you know," the operative said, once they were outside in the crisp night air. Corrigan seemed not to be one to ruin a good exit. But he did have practical concerns. "To get inside the distribution hub, yeah?"

"If he can get in, so can I," Cathica said. "Maybe easier. We know the same people—if I say I came to fetch dumbass's wallet out of his cab, they won't bat an eye at that."

"And once we're in, you can find the right truck and all?"

"I used to drive too," Cathica said. "It's how we met, me and Jim. I quit to run the farm after my...after *our* parents passed on. So my kids could grow up the same way we did."

Indie chose to ignore the recrimination in Cath's tone.

"We'll need to take your vehicle," Corrigan told Cath. "Pulling up to the gate in an Inquisition transport might arouse concern, you understand."

"Hell with that," Indica said, gesturing toward the field behind the house. She wasn't about to endure Corrigan's digs and Cath's bitterness for the three hours or so it would take to drive out to the Long Beach Hub. "We'll take mine."

At her suggestion, as if on cue, the relic of Ozymandian technology she'd been convicted of stealing (and had more recently parked in the fallow field out behind Cath and Jim's farmhouse) uncloaked itself without so much as a whisper.

Cath's jaw dropped. Even Corrigan hesitated. It felt satisfying to give him pause.

"You're gonna bring an Inquisitor of the Authority on board a stolen ship?" he asked when he recovered his voice.

"First," Indica explained: "it's not a ship. It's an artifact, and the subject of my continuing academic investigations."

"Legally speaking it's a protected antiquity looted from an Authority-sponsored xenoarchaeological—"

Indica continued as if the man hadn't opened his yap at all. "*And* second: there's exactly fuck-all the Authority can do if I don't want to hand it over. Which, for the record, once again: I don't. Not today, thank you kindly."

That provoked a reflexive and uncertain rendition of Corrigan's habitual smile. He was still overawed by the sight of the thing.

Cath had been struck mute. That wouldn't last.

Indie led them toward it like it was a bus ready for boarding. The Ozymandian structure was a simple black geodesic dome, perhaps a third the size of the farmhouse. It was made of some indeterminate material that appeared non-metallic, though possibly mineral in nature. It may have been some sort of glass or crystal, an alien obsidian so dark it looked like a void cut from the night's shadows. Black as it was, subtle colors seemed to pulse deep within its honeycomb facets, almost like the afterimages and phosphene iridescence seen behind closed eyes. Those scintillations may have been flashes of information churning inside an alien processor, synapses firing within an extraterrestrial mind, or the births and deaths of distant galaxies contained by a miniature cosmos.

It was a beautiful, hypnotic, and ominous thing to behold.

It would never be mistaken for a backyard shed. Luckily, it was equipped to hide.

"I can't believe you brought this here," Cath whispered.

"What was I supposed to do, rent a spot in a trailer park?"

Several of the dome's panels parted and moved aside for Indica, without her having to break stride. Cath and Corrigan were more hesitant to come aboard.

"Come on," Indie urged. "One small step, right?"

Cath smiled, for perhaps the first time all evening. They'd watched antique footage of the first moon landing many times together as children. She nodded and joined her sister inside the alien dome.

A suddenly superstitious Corrigan made a sign of the cross, took a breath, and stepped across the threshold after them.

Indie caught sight of Big Jim, Tamsin, and Jimmy Jr. all gaping from different windows at the rear of the farmhouse before the dome's facets closed noiselessly back into place.

Shit. Well, at least now she knew what she and Cath would fight about, later on.

From inside it became plain that the dome was actually a rough circle, a thirty-two-sided icosahedron, bisected by the floor they stood on. Some sort of command module occupied the center of the space—a blunt, meter-and-a-half tall pedestal that looked rather like an altar. A spiral staircase off to one side led down below, presumably to chambers contained in the lower half of the sphere. At least fifty percent of the "ship" seemed to be buried in the earth.

"Is this thing gonna leave a crater in our yard?"

Indie shook her head. "It's dimensionally interposed."

"Oh," Cath said, accepting that answer without the slightest idea of what it meant. "Good. I guess."

Indie motioned her over to the command station. Its surface was blank, white as alabaster, glowing faintly. Indie put her hands palm-down on the white surface and nodded for Cath to do the same. "You know where we're going, right?"

"Hub beneath the spaceport," Cathica said.

"And Jim's truck? The color, the registry number on the shipping box, whatever you need to find it?"

Cath nodded.

"All right," Indie said. "Let's go."

She walked toward the curved wall, which again opened up for her just before she should have bonked her head.

"What, did you forget your keys?" Corrigan asked sarcastically.

"We're here."

"We're what?" Cath hurried after Indica, and stood beside her in the dome's doorway, gaping in shocked wonderment at what she saw outside.

Trucks. A vast lot full of them. Electric cab-over units bearing the HermesFTL logo on their doors, with semi-trailers already coupled, slumbering under sodium lights and ready to roll out at dawn. This was the Long Beach Terrestrial Distribution Center, one of many drop points cabled to the Western Regional Spaceport, and it was on pause for the holiday. In the distance they could see shipping containers still descending from the heavens, ferried down to Earth along the SkyWire's diamond-nanofiber elevator cable, sliding on a long arc from an orbital anchor above the equator. Those containers from faraway planets never stopped dropping—not even on Christmas day. The temporary pile-up meant overtime hours for earthbound drivers like Big Jim, who hauled that space freight to wholesalers all around the San Angeles region.

"Holy shit." Cathica had gone pale. "Did—did we just teleport? Indie?"

"Not precisely."

"I feel sick."

"Don't lose your shit now, Cath. You're the one who wanted to come."

Cathica nodded.

The sisters stepped out onto the parking lot's macadam, and saw that Indie's Ozymandian dome had materialized between two fully loaded semis. Actually it had embedded itself in the sides of their trailers, as there wasn't enough room between the parked trucks to accommodate the alien structure. The three objects appeared to have bonded seamlessly, with a curved expanse of black geodesic facets damming up the negative space between the pair of eighteen-wheelers.

"Somebody's gonna notice that," Cath said, peering back inside to verify that the dome's interior had maintained a constant size. "Those ice-cream scoops out of their trucks."

"They'll be fine when we're gone," Indie said. "No damage. We're—"

"Directionally interspersed?"

"Dimensionally interposed."

"Right."

"Like magic, isn't it?" Corrigan stood in the open doorway, looking bright-eyed with excitement.

"Or a technology advanced enough to be indistinguishable from it," Indica said, paraphrasing an old axiom.

"Fucking incredible!" Corrigan crowed.

"Pipe down," Indie scolded, even though the whole facility was in an uncharacteristic state of suspended animation, and there wasn't another human being anywhere in sight. "We are breaking and entering here, remember?"

"Yeah," Cath said. "So let's get it done."

She hopped up into the gap between Jim's cabin and the trailer, and nimbly ascended the four rungs that allowed access to the top of the truck, including the interior of the hollow fiberglass air dam that minimized wind resistance. It wasn't a clever hiding place, but the dams could be lined with mylar foil to deflect scans, and human import inspectors never checked there, by special arrangement. The local smuggling ring was an established operation, kept lubricated by a regular cycle of threats and payoffs. Cathica knew its ins and outs as well as her husband ever had.

Indie heard duct tape ripping loose, then Cath hauled a medium-sized box out from the depths of the hollow shell and handed it down.

The box weighed maybe ten or twelve kilograms. Indica shook it, like a kid with a Christmas package. Cathica climbed back down from the top of Jim's rig.

"Wanna see what's worth moving earth and heaven?" Indie said to her sister.

"Not really."

"Yeah you do."

Indica ripped open the box before Cath could protest further.

Inside the nest of packing material was what felt like a piece of statuary, much as Jim had predicted. Indie shook it loose in a shower of polystyrene peanuts and held it up to the light.

The "artifact" was a copy of Rodin's *The Thinker*, seated on a toilet, chin rested on fist in an attitude of deep reflection. The sort of mass-printed garbage exported by the metric ton from over-industrialized manufactories like the Moons of Hephaestus or Daikokuten-14.

"What the hell?" Cath frowned in consternation. The sisters looked at one another.

Indie dropped the novelty statue, leaving it to shatter on the blacktop as she spun around, only to find that her genuine Ozymandian oddity, the black sphere, had vanished.

And Corrigan had gone with it.

"Oh, fuck, no," Cathica breathed. Her eyes were as wide as dinner plates. The two big rigs on either side of them were whole again, unmarred, unscathed. It was like no alien igloo had ever interposed itself through their plane of existence at all.

Indica just stood there, considering.

The pile of pottery shards behind them that had until recently been a cheap statue chimed a sprightly ringtone.

Indie toed through the fragments and uncovered a hand-sized tablet, which someone (presumably Corrigan) must have secreted inside.

She picked up the tablet and touched the display to answer it.

Corrigan's shit-eating grin filled the small screen.

"This was the Authority's big plan?" Indie said. "A bait and switch?"

"As if they could pull it off. No, the Authority disavowed me years ago. Did hold on to my equipment though. Comes in handy, now and then."

"You lying sack of shit!" Cath exclaimed, crowding in to look at the screen.

"So *you* set all this up?" Indie said. "On your own? You're what, some sort of...space pirate?"

"One man band," Corrigan bragged. "Nearly as wanted by the Authority as yourself, in fact. Couple messages from a phony account, a box in the regular drop location, and the promise of a big wad of credits was all this took. If there's one person on this soggy rock more credulous than you, Professor, it'd have to be Dim Jim Terkel."

"Oh, you can go fuck yourself," Cathica said.

Corrigan cackled at that. He set his tablet down on the center console, the one with no discernible controls, and strolled around the interior of the dome. He looked like a man considering moving into a new apartment.

"But how did you know where I'd be tonight?" Indie asked. This was a more significant mystery than how he'd figured out the user interface. He'd watched Cath lay her hands on the dais with a destination in mind, and there was little more to it than that.

"I took a guess!" Corrigan sounded delighted with himself. "You're not such a mystery, Professor. Everything changed when you ran off with this thing. I've read the Authority's files. All your limitations disappeared. What do you do when you can do anything? Where do you go? I figured you might feel a need to hold onto something...domestic."

Indie sighed. "So you bullshitted Jim then staked out their place to see if I'd try to sneak back home for Christmas dinner?"

"That's the long and the short of it, Professor."

"If you read the Authority's files then you know what I told them about involving or threatening people I care about. Or using them as bait."

"You were eloquently explicit," Corrigan said. "But that was when you had all the leverage, wasn't it?"

Indie seemed to concede the point. "Now you've got leverage, and a place to stand. You gonna try and move the world, Corrigan?"

"I just might, Professor."

"So what's your big plan? What is it you want?"

"Freedom," the ex-Inquisitor said. "Freedom from want, freedom from worry. Freedom from authorities great and small."

Indica tipped her head. She could almost respect that.

"Live human teleportation, the elusive Holy Grail of quantum research," Corrigan rhapsodized. "The reason you've been impossible to apprehend. That's freedom. And now I've done it twice in an hour, myself."

"Sort of," Indie said. Interpolation by sphere really was not the same thing.

"What the powers that be wouldn't give for that secret. Powers within the Authority and otherwise."

"So of all the worlds in all the systems, of all the things you could do or see or understand, all it comes down to for you is... money?"

"Not hardly, Professor. I think the 'Wizard of Ozymandias' has a nice ring. And I mean to earn the title. I'll do everything you haven't done, despite having the power. And the leverage. And the freedom. I'll bring the Authority down, for their centuries of crimes here on Earth and everywhere else in the galaxy.

And that's just for getting started. There's a whole universe to reconsider."

"Where are you now?" Indica asked. "Where'd you go first, now that you can go anywhere? I'm curious."

Corrigan let the icosahedron's black honeycomb panels fade to translucency. The vanished facets now revealed a rocky, frozen panorama, seen from an impossibly high mountain vantage. Clouds drifted amongst other monumental peaks, far below. A bitter winter sun burned small and bright as it dropped toward a jagged horizon. The alien sphere's spiral staircase appeared to stand incongruously next to a pile of snow-covered boulders, from which a string of colorful prayer flags snapped in a stiff wind. Outlines of the sphere's wall facets remained faintly visible—a ghostly suggestion of a boundary.

Indie examined Corrigan's new backdrop on the little screen. "Where is that, then? The summit of Everest or some such?"

"Points to the Professor. Lovely up here, isn't it? Always wanted to see it, never wanted to climb."

He panned his tablet around to show off the ceiling-of-the-world view.

"I went to the moon, myself," Indica said. "When I ran from Ozymandias. Authority never thought to look for me so close to home. I took a picture with the flag, looked over the old lunar rover. Same thing I would've done when I was ten years old."

"By the way," Corrigan mentioned, "I have notified the Authority as to your current whereabouts and undefended state. Local PD too. Can't have you coming after me, can I?"

Cathica quailed at Indie's side as faint sirens rose in the distance, but all Indie said was: "That's really kind of a dick move, Corrigan."

"Apologies," he said. "But you've had your turn, Professor."

Flashes of red and blue near the lot's gate made the women swivel their heads.

Indie looked back down at the tablet. On its screen, the still-ghostly honeycomb panels behind Corrigan faded away to nothing. Then the spiral staircase vanished, depositing the would-be thief on his ass in the snow, like an overbalanced toddler. His squawk of alarm was amusing, but Indica didn't laugh. The icosahedral facets that quietly abandoned Corrigan on his mountaintop stacked themselves up around the sisters once again and went opaque as they appeared, obscuring their view of the Long Beach Hub and its ranks of holiday-becalmed eighteen-wheelers.

Cath gasped and stepped aside as the central dais Corrigan's tablet had been resting on reappeared next to her.

Corrigan's frantic face filled Indie's tablet screen again after he'd had a moment to scramble over on hands and knees to retrieve his dropped communicator.

"Ahh, Professor?" he said, attempting unsuccessfully to sound calm. His breath steamed in the thin Himalayan air. "Sorry to bother, but, technical difficulties on this end, maybe?"

"No, Corrigan. Everything is fine," Indie said, transferring his image from the handheld up onto one of the sphere's hexagonal panel-screens with a thought. "You just don't understand. None of you Authority idiots ever understood. I didn't steal anything. There was nothing to steal. This 'ship,' this circle, whatever you want to call it, it's not even a thing. It's a thoughtform, concretized by a...(*scientist? sorcerer? shaman? physicist?*)...a guy, on Ozymandias, more than a million years ago. They all died, the ancient Ozymandians, and the Idea crystallized when they did. But it was there, dormant, hibernating inside the ruins, waiting for a suitable new mind to come along. I didn't take it, Corrigan—it took me. And you can't steal it from me now because it's in me. It *is* me. Are you starting to get the picture?"

"You've been toying with me this entire time?"

"Since you tried to steal my ride, anyway."

He grinned, trying to fall back on charm. "No harm intended, of course, Professor."

"Right," Indie said. "Enjoy your view, Corrigan."

The screen facet went black before he could begin to protest.

Indie walked through the wall (the glassy material dissolved at the last second) and out into Cathica's backyard. They'd already traveled; the trip felt faster than instantaneous.

Cath followed her out uncertainly, into her own dark garden. "Did you just leave that man to die? On top of Mount Everest?"

Indie shook her head. "He's got his tablet, if he wants to call the Authority to come pick him up. They have an airfield near Kathmandu."

"Have you really been to the moon?"

"Yeah, Cath." It was the least impressive place she'd been. But Cath may have been in some sort of shock. "You want to go?"

Cathica shook her head emphatically. She was an Earth girl through and through. While Indie was...something else, now.

It pained her to see in Cathica's eyes that she finally understood.

"Were you telling that man the truth? That thing—" she flapped an arm at the black geodesic structure that stood, once again, in her very own back field, "—doesn't really *exist*? It's an alien *idea*? Even though we flew in it? Or teleported?"

"We didn't do either. And it exists. It just isn't real."

"Is it magic? Indie? Or is it science?" Cath's tone was desperate, pleading. The foundations of her understanding had shaken, and her footing in reality no longer felt secure. Indie knew the sensation. "Tell me the truth."

"I'm not sure it's a meaningful distinction, in this case."

Cathica scowled. She didn't like that answer, but Indie didn't have a better one.

"Are you a witch now, like they say on the webs?" Cathica pressed. "An alien witch? It seems like it's close enough to true."

"I'm who and what I've always been."

"But that's not all, is it? Are you *just* my sister, or, or something else now too, some alien ghost that moved in and remembers being her? Because that's what the Inquisitors told us. We didn't want to believe it, but are you even still...human?"

"Cath!" Indie felt like she'd been slapped. Her eyes welled—and she was not a crier, by any means. She swallowed hard and blinked away tears.

The question stung because she didn't have an answer.

"Whatever I am, I'm not the Authority's property," Indica snapped. "Can you at least appreciate that?"

"Of course, Indie! Yes. I—I love you. Okay? I'm glad you came tonight. Even if...well, it was good to see you, in any case."

She sounded like she was trying to get off the phone. Indie felt like Cathica had decided the most frightening thing in the known universe wasn't alien pestilence, the cold abyss of space, or even the Inquisitors of the Authority—it was her. Indica Asterion.

She looked around, at the house she'd grown up in and the bot-tended fields beyond. She'd never been happy here, as a girl, always looking toward the stars. But she was glad in a way she could never express that Cath and Jim were bringing up another generation under that same old roof.

Indie didn't want to be a source of dismay to these people, much less danger.

She tried to smile. "Hug the kids for me, okay? And tell Jim to be a little smarter about his side hustles."

"I—I will."

She watched Cath almost stumble over the low steps as she hurried to the side door, which Jim threw open before she even got there. He glanced at Indie, raised a hand in an awkward wave, and closed the door behind his wife.

The light above it went out.

Indie looked up to see Tamsin standing at her bedroom window on the second floor, with one small hand pressed against the glass. She couldn't know what was going on amongst the adults—only that something was up. Something with high stakes and dire consequences.

She tipped Tam a quick nod, then stepped back within the geodesic confines of her unusual Idea and went...away.

Michael Paul Gonzalez is the creator of the serial horror audio drama Larkspur Underground, *available for free on iTunes and Stitcher. He is the author of the novels* Angel Falls *and* Miss Massacre's Guide to Murder and Vengeance. *A member of the* Horror Writers Association, *his short stories have appeared in various places in print and online, including* Great Jones Street, Lost Signals, Gothic Fantasy, The Year's Best Hardcore Horror, HeavyMetal.com, *and many more. You can visit him online at* www.michaelpaulgonzalez.com.

HUMAN, TRAFFICKING

Michael Paul Gonzalez

TWENTY YEARS INTO THIS CAREER, this sucker's game of "being my own boss," and the rules keep changing. They find a way to pay less on miles. They find a way to demand you deliver things further, faster, but also require you to take longer rest periods. Two years ago, the rumor of driverless trucks started. Now it's a reality. Local is becoming the only way to go. Most of the big companies have moved on to these new AI rigs for cross country. You drive your truck to a port outside of town, and then drop the trailer so a highway drone can hitch up and do the long haul. Suddenly sleep breaks are no longer a problem.

Suddenly people are obsolete.

Some drivers didn't handle that well. The unions tried to strike, but the numbers were too thin. Owner-operators went out to spike tires, non-union guys were causing crashes on the highway to "prove" these machines couldn't be trusted. But the way they're set up, the computers, telemetry, cameras everywhere, it was easy to prove human intervention or just plain malice was the cause of the few AI rig crashes. All that did was make people trust local drivers less. Made us all look unstable and untrustworthy.

I was sitting at a truck stop somewhere off I-55 near Cape Girardeau, Missouri when this commercial came on one of the TVs. A shot of this autonomous truck, which made everyone bristle, but then, a long shot of a truck yard where drivers strode up to those same trucks and got inside. A people-first company, the screen read. The safety that comes with the support of artificial intelligence. Fewer accidents on the road. The reliability and intelligence of a human behind the wheel. One of those big-shot Hollywood actors was giving the voiceover.

At SOL-S Logistics, we believe in one thing: People are the lifeblood that keeps this country moving. When you join our team, YOU become one of our most valued assets. We use autonomous trucks piloted by people, because we know there's no replacement for your work, your knowledge, your experience. SOL-S—Autonomy, humanized.

I'll never forget that. It's burned into my memory, because that commercial was the moment my life changed. I'd been hampered a little by a limping stiffness in my ankle that made it hard to drive. It wasn't an exercise thing, it was a diabetes thing, and I thought my career was coming to an end. But if there was a truck out there that could help me drive...

I saw the writing on the wall. If you can't beat 'em, join 'em. I called them, set up a meeting, was totally honest with them about my medical condition. Usually you get that kind of concerned look of disappointment when a potential employer hears about bad health. The guy I talked to, this real spit-and-polished guy that looked like he came out of a plastic press, just nodded. Laid a hand on my shoulder and made solid eye contact. He said, "We're going to help you."

Not *we'd like to help you.* Not *we'll call if something opens up.*

SOL-S Logistics wanted me as a driver. Me, a human! They said they were experimenting with new and exciting technologies that would allow more use of autonomous vehicles while maintaining jobs for flesh-and-blood people.

I went in for a checkup with their medical team and they told me I was going to lose my right foot. I'd already seen that coming. I'd been spending the past few months trying to figure out a budget to make my truck handi-capable. The doc gave me a different offer. Amputation, yes, but I'd get an experimental leg to replace it. I was fifty miles past nothing left to lose. All I had left was my family, and I'd be damned if I was going to disappoint them. What was half a leg if it meant my daughter got braces, better clothes for school?

This was all off-the-books. They wanted to roll out this pilot program with as little government interference as possible. I already hated giving so much of my paycheck to those pencil-pushing IRS thieves anyway, so what was I going to say?

"You're not losing a foot, you're gaining a bionic leg," that spit-and-polished exec told me. Hell, I love science fiction movies so I jumped at the chance.

I was in and out of surgery within a day. The doctors took a little more of me than we'd initially discussed. Amputated to just below my right hip. They left just enough nub for this leg to bolt on. I'm getting used to it. The tech is really something. It's not a prosthesis in the typical sense. It's part of me. An honest-to-god replacement. Never comes off. No phantom pains. It was a little bulkier, but wired straight into my nervous system. If I walked on carpet, I still felt it. The foot itself was metal with this special kind of silicon padding on the bottom. I was still ticklish. Could still register a pinprick or stubbed toe, but now it was just more of a signal to my brain to correct an inconvenience.

It made it easier to walk, even easier to drive. The leg syncs to onboard computers in their specialized rig. I just lock it into place and use the touchscreen on my thigh to adjust speed. The foot splits and spreads out into three paddles when I'm behind the wheel. Two paddles cover the brake and fuel pedal, and this little third part I call my kickstand pops out to link to the clutch. I only had to set the speed, and the tech would do the work.

I was, quite literally, a test pilot. Behind the wheel, they made me wear this harness on my head to read my brain impulses. It recorded my alertness through the miles, different times of day, different weather patterns. This was all to help their machines learn how a real driver reacted to different conditions. I was giving them the kind of feedback no amount of computer simulation could, downloadable stats from the USB port on my calf.

On my days off, I had a special silicone gel boot to roll over my leg. Didn't want my wife to think anything was up. That was one of the rules, she had to think I had a regular prosthetic leg. I had to pretend to have a little limp. If I had my pants off, she'd just see a shiny flesh-colored mannequin leg. With my minimal time home, I'd just have to find excuses for not taking the fake leg off. She didn't ask too many questions. I got a bonus for my silence. I kept the mortgage paid. I got to see my kid laughing over dinner at the restaurant. That's a joy you sometimes take for granted, right? Eating over the family table is one thing, but just that special feeling that comes at a restaurant, seeing her little face light up when she saw how much food she could choose from. That's something I couldn't give her before. We were month-to-month, hand-to-mouth, trouble-to-trouble. That was changing, and we were happy.

Four hundred miles into my next cross-country run, the stomach cramps started. I thought it was something I ate, but it just got worse and worse. Bad fever, cold sweats. I thought I was having a heart attack. When I reported in to dispatch that I needed to get off the road, they told me to stay put and they'd send a doctor to me. I don't know how SOL-S got such a bad reputation when they showed this much care for a driver.

The doc showed up in a mobile trailer within an hour. I've never seen anything like it, a whole medical facility in a trailer. MRIs, X-rays, you name it, they had it. Someone else took my truck to finish the run for me, and corporate sent me an email saying I'd still get paid out for the miles. I thought that was real generous, but then the test results came back and it started to make a little more sense.

Cancer. My stomach lining was dissolving. There was some kind of rejection taking place, and they didn't sugarcoat it. My new leg was causing my body to go into revolt. Terminal. That's a word you never like to hear. They offered me another surgery. This one would be a little riskier, they had to go in to remove the cancer and the damaged organs. But they promised a massive payout to my family if things really went south. In for a penny, in for a pound, and either way my kid was taken care of.

When I came out of surgery, the first thing I noticed was my matching legs. Bright, shiny steel and circuitry. My insides felt different. Hollow, somehow. I could feel my lungs moving, but there was...how can I put this? You don't realize you have guts until your guts are gone.

They showed me some videos of the procedure, and they told me I'd come through with flying colors. They hadn't realized how much that artificial leg was taxing my digestive system. Essentially, the power needed to run the leg was eating me alive. I couldn't eat enough food to keep it going long term.

I asked why they gave me a second one. You know how mechanics get. You go into the garage for one thing, you get hit with a bill for five things you didn't know you needed. They said it was gonna go any day, they were trying to do preventative maintenance. Then they showed me how my insides worked. My stomach still looked like its regular fish-belly-white, little-too-much-pudge-and-hair self, but now, it opened. They hit this little hidden magnetic switch and rolled the skin away, showing me the power plant housed in my torso. I passed out, which I guess they expected.

I no longer needed to eat. My stomach was gone, replaced with a flexible fuel bag. My intestines had been replaced with a long stretch of Lithium battery packs. Getting through TSA might become a problem in the future, but there were benefits. I didn't need food anymore. I *could* eat if I wanted to, just to enjoy the flavor of something. But it would all just end up in this tiny receptacle tank I could remove and dump out. Every twelve hours, on the road, I would refill the fuel bag through a stent in my ribcage. Like filling up the rig. And the lithium batteries would recharge as I drove. I just had to plug myself into the truck. No more headgear, now everything was being read directly from the computer wired into my brain.

And I kept driving, longer runs, no longer needing to stop to eat, barely needing to stop to sleep. I'd only go to regular truck stops for the human interaction. Buy a few snack packs, maybe a soda, talk the clerk's ear off since I'd be hour ahead of a regular driver. There were a few of them still out there.

Congress had enacted some restrictions on autonomous trucks, safety regulations or further studies needed or some such nonsense, when I knew this was really just about trying to save jobs in a dying economy. I didn't have to worry about any of that. I asked my contact at SOL-S if I could help them recruit people. I had friends who needed jobs, too. They told me I couldn't really reach out since their experiments weren't exactly Uncle Sam-approved.

I just kept the miles coming. Kept the money flowing home, but home started drifting away. I was gone too much, too long. I was distant when I was home because I couldn't let my family get close to me. My daughter, when she hugged me, commented that my stomach felt like the front of our car. You know how honest little kids can be. And she poked at it, kind of laughing, but then I felt the switch trigger and it started to unroll under my shirt. I dropped her trying to hold it closed as I ran away, probably the weakest moment of my life. I couldn't let them see what I'd become.

I got back on the road the next day. Drive for them. Keep driving. Ignore those angry emails from my wife, tell myself we'd find a way to work through it, but SOL-S kept tabs on those communications, too. They told me counseling was a good idea. One on one. So my wife talked to one of their therapists, and I talked to another, and somewhere in between it was mutually decided that we would probably be better apart.

It broke my heart, but they were right. They set up a trust fund for my daughter, showed me how much my wife would receive every month in addition to paying off the mortgage. They weren't buying my silence. That was never for sale. They were paying for my peace of mind, that's what this was all about anyway.

Did I mention my broken heart? A couple weeks after my wife gave up on me, my heart followed suit. You hear about it in country songs, but mine *literally* tore in half while I was on a run. Crashed the truck off an overpass. Twenty-foot drop, straight down. A nose dive onto an entry ramp just outside of Los Angeles. Probably would have made a good scene in a movie, but it was some horrible press for SOL-S. But they were still good to me. Kept everything anonymous. I was laid up in one of their hospitals with my arms shattered, my neck broken, my jaw half torn off.

They promised me they'd make it better. It turned out the stress on my heart from losing my wife coupled with the long term effects of their fuel and battery system in my guts was more than the human body could take. A normal man would have died in a crash like the one I had, but their little power plant kept me going long enough for them to scrape me up and get me to their private medical facility.

I guess I owe them my life. All they ask of me is that I keep driving.

This time, when I came out of my first surgery, I was inside of a big parking bay at their warehouse. I tried to reach up to scratch my arm, but couldn't lift my hand. When I mentioned that to the nurse on duty, he gave this real concerned look to the doctor. The doctor asked everyone else to leave the room so it was just me and him and the nurse.

He told me about the amazing advances SOL-S had made with artificial intelligence, and how I was an irreplaceable part of that. I was not only helping to advance their company, but the entire human race as well. Maybe it was the anesthetic still working out of my system, but I started laughing at them. Asked the nurse if anyone ever told him how much he looked like the doctor. Asked the doctor if anyone told him how much he looked like the company recruiter. Different hair color, maybe the eyes were a little different, but they all had that same molded-from-the-same-plastic-press look.

The Doctor repeated all of that stuff about the advances they'd made. How I was helping the company mission. He sounded just like that guy in the commercial I saw all those years ago.

"People are the lifeblood that keeps this country moving. You're part of our team and one of our most valued assets. We need you back in the seat because there's no replacement for your work, your knowledge, your experience."

Skip the brochure, I told them. They knew they had me the moment they took my leg. I just wanted to know why I couldn't move. My spine had been shattered in six different spots. They needed to go in to fix my power plant. They told me I was going to lose the use of my arms. The damage to my spine meant that their bionic legs could no longer get signals to and from my brain. But they could keep me alive.

I could be the bridge to humanity's future.

What choice did I have but to say yes?

They swore I wouldn't be awake for the procedure, but they were wrong. I suppose it didn't matter. With my spine broken and so much of me already made from artificial parts, pain registered as an experience. My body no longer hurt. I was just aware.

Aware of the lasers burning through layers of soft tissue, fat, muscle, bone. Aware of large, shining saws that took my hands, then my forearms, then everything below my shoulder. I could turn my head, and I watched them stacking pieces of my fake legs and my real arms on a silver gurney that they wheeled away with no reverence.

"You're doing so well," the doctor said.

After that, I was hollow. Almost nothing. I watched them stitch silicone tubes into my skin, connect what was left of my circulatory system to small portable tanks. An intern came in and loomed over my bed, and the doctor asked me, "Are you ready to become the next evolution of the American worker?"

Not *human*. Not *man*.

Worker.

The intern lifted me up, cradled me like a baby, and we walked to a large, shiny silver truck. Their newest model. My reflection was a little distorted, but from what I could see, there was almost nothing left of me. No legs, no arms. Just a body swaddled in a white cloth.

They hit a switch on that shiny new cab and the whole thing rotated forward, revealing a cushioned seat inside of a command center. The intern laid me inside, disconnected that little portable tank that was pumping blood, or something like it, through my system. They attached me to a larger tank system situated in what should have been the sleeper part of the cab. Plugged two long spikes into the back of my head. I was the brains of the operation. Connected a rebreather over my mouth. The air I breathe is cleaner than ever now, HEPA filtered and free from particles. My eyes are washed and rinsed every thirty seconds. Nutrients are refilled at weigh stations. I am my machine, my machine is me. I just think and the rig reacts. I miss driving the old-fashioned way. I never stop moving now. I experience the American Interstate from my windowless cab through cameras mounted to the outside of the truck. I never stop to sleep, or eat. Pick up, drop off, keep moving forward. Keep America moving forward.

I count white lines eighteen hours a day. My wife has a great big house. I send her emails sometimes, just to check in. It's the only way I can talk to her. The few times she replies, she keeps things short, but she'll send a picture of my daughter's beautiful new smile sometimes, and that's enough.

Most days, that's enough.

Eric Miller is a professional screenwriter, fiction writer, editor, and truck driver. His short story Culling the Herd *made* Best Horror of the Year Volume 7's *rec list, his story* The Patch *appeared in the anthology* Halloween Tales, *and his poem* I Haunt This Place *was in the* HWA Poetry Showcase 2018, *among others. His produced screenplays include* The Shadow Men, Mask Maker, Night Skies, *and the* SyFy Channel *hits* Ice Spiders *and* Swamp Shark. *He is also the editor of several anthologies, including the* Bram Stoker Award-*nominated* Hell Comes To Hollywood, *its imaginatively titled sequel* Hell Comes To Hollywood II, 18 Wheels of Horror, *and the book you are reading now. If anyone thinks this story was included here because of that, Miller is ready to meet you out in the parking lot...to discuss literature.*

DRIVE

Eric Miller

JIMMY WAS PERFECT FOR THE JOB, thought Eddie the Dispatcher, because Jimmy ran the Hi-Test. And he not only *ran* the Hi-Test, which was rare in and of itself, but Jimmy ran the Hi-Test with the same cool aplomb that some drivers ran groceries, though the two loads were on opposite ends of the cargo spectrum.

Groceries, whether boxes of cereal or frozen pot-pies, mostly came in neat cardboard boxes that were stacked high and deep in trailers and could be bumped and smashed in any number of ways and nobody cared much unless the delivery was late. It didn't take nerves of steel to deliver iceberg lettuce.

The Hi-Test, on the other hand, not only required those nerves of steel, but that they be wrapped in iron and dipped in titanium and dusted with diamond as a high tensile garnish, because the Hi-Test could be described as liquid plutonium rocket fuel in one way, or ultra-carbonated nitroglycerin with a splash of Tabasco in another. It was shipped in super-cooled, magnetic suspension tankers that kept the volatile liquid at a balmy -98 degrees and smoothed out even the slightest bumps, because if you so much as looked at the fluid wrong in a normal environment it would explode with devastating fury. Hi-Test spelled H-A-Z-M-A-T in letters that most truck drivers, even the illiterate ones, read as S-T-U-P-I-D.

Jimmy didn't care. He knew most drivers didn't read much anyway. Not that anyone could anymore; cartoonish icons covered everything these days from the digital menus at Denny's to the puke-green screen of the computerized clipboard Eddie thrust upon him as they marched from the dispatcher's office into the garage. To Jimmy, running the Hi-Test was just another way of telling every other driver around to just pull over, climb in the sleeper, and take a nap while The Best got the real driving done. Jimmy put his thumbprint in the "accept" box without looking at the job order, knowing Eddie would fill him in on the details.

"I need you to take a load of Hi-Test to the Van Nuys airport," Eddie explained, true to form. "Every other rich son-of-a-bitch in the Valley has blasted off in the last three days and their tanks are bone dry. And nobody will make the run to fill them back up."

"Nobody but me, you mean." Jimmy's voice had the roughness of one who didn't talk much. CB and Ham chatter from anonymous people bored him while driving the rig, and most of his downtime was spent in driver lounges where the conversations, as well as the loungers, were about as stimulating to him as a handful of Benadryl washed down with a double shot of NyQuil. Jimmy also carried a sat phone he could theoretically use to call someone other than his conversation-challenged co-workers, but there really wasn't anyone he cared to call.

"Well, you're kind of perfect for the run," Eddie continued.

"That's because I'm the best," Jimmy said with the same matter-of-fact intonation he might use to say "the sky is blue."

The two men reached the large doors to the garage and stepped inside the giant concrete cavern. Rows of big rig tractors lined the pavement, some old, some new, some with trailers attached, some bobtailed and bare. Chrome nameplates leaped out at them as they walked, proudly hawking the manufacturers of the machines—Kenworth and International and Western Star and other tough-sounding brands filled the docks. Jimmy and Eddie barely noticed the vehicles, their attention fixed on the behemoth at the far end of the warehouse.

Parked off by itself, as no one was brave or stupid enough to park near it, Jimmy's truck was a monster. The massive triple-axle tractor seemed to melt into the sixty-foot long tanker trailer, swooping slabs of carbon fiber and titanium fairings protecting both front and rear units from the fuel-robbing forces of aerodynamic drag as well as more aggressive threats such as bullets and bombs. A flexible section of molding stretched between tractor and trailer, hiding the serpentine mix of thick cables and hoses and hydraulic lines that joined the two together in an almost holy mechanical matrimony.

The rig towered high in the air, every section covered with sinister bulges, access panels, remote control doors, insulated pipes, and strange-looking antennae. What was visible of the eighteen tires revealed great chunks of Kevlar-reinforced rubber with treads that looked as if they would be as comfortable climbing a mountain made of broken glass and barb wire as they were chewing on the baby soft asphalt of a newly-paved freeway.

The basic color of the truck was black, but bright yellow warning labels covered the skin front to back; the familiar icons for Biohazard and Nuclear Waste and High Explosive were enough to make normal people keep their distance, but the distinctive sign for the Hi-Test usually cleared the area quicker than a pin-free hand grenade.

Curiously missing from Jimmy's rig was any sort of manufacturer's identification. The truck had, in fact, started life as a Peterbilt, but so little of the original rig remained that it was essentially a custom job now. Still, a few years back the company's lawyers had asked Jimmy to remove the logo, lest their good reputation be scarred by any unfortunate accidents that might stem from his habit of carrying suicidal loads of cargo. He had complied, and happily signed all the papers that placed all accident liability solely on the shoulders of the driver and whatever insurance company was stupid enough to assign him a policy, even though Jimmy and the lawyers and the Astronomically High Premium Casualty Group (Omaha, Nebraska) knew if there *was* an accident, Jimmy wouldn't be liable for much of anything other than a burial plot.

Jimmy hit a button on his key ring and a happy chirp sounded from the rig, indicating the alarm system was now off. Eddie relaxed a little; he knew there was nothing cheerful about the alarm, unless you were the mortician who was lucky enough to get the job of burying the bodies if it ever was triggered.

They gazed at the truck for another moment, then Eddie broke the silence. "Listen, Jimmy..."

Jimmy turned to the Dispatcher and noted the pained look on the man's face. "What?"

"Um...nothing. That really is some truck."

"You've seen it before. What's up?"

Eddie threw a quick glance around the garage to make sure no one was in listening distance. "Shit. I'm breaking all the dispatch rules by telling you this, you know."

"You haven't told me anything yet."

"All right. I think you should turn down this run."

Jimmy eyed the man closely. "I never turn down a run. That's why I'm famous."

"You're famous because you're the best. And you're a little bit crazy. But this run's different. L.A. is on fire. There's a gang war going on, remember?"

"I heard about that. Sharks and Jets, right?"

"This ain't a musical, Jimmy."

"Doesn't matter. I'm a loner. I've got nothing to do with gangs."

"Not this time. You know what the fighting's about?"

"I could give a shit, Eddie."

"Just listen, it's important."

Jimmy rolled his eyes and slouched, indicating he would tolerate Eddie's story.

"See, the Mid-City Marauders made a play for the Valley and caught the Roscoe Street Boys with their pants down. By the time the Roscoes started defending their turf, the Marauders had them outgunned and surrounded. And now all the smaller gangs are jumping in, biting at the Marauders' territory while they're spread out fighting the Roscoes and making SoCal a war zone."

"Eddie, there's riots every month. That's why everybody smart left L.A., remember? As far as I'm concerned the Maurauders can kill all the Roscoe Street Boys they want as long as they stay out of my way."

"Listen, Goddamnit! The Hi-Test is *for* the Roscoes. They're cutting out. Going up to the Orbital Ring with all the rest of the assholes who can afford a better life."

A light dawned in Jimmy's mind. "That means the Maurauders..."

"...Know you're coming with a load of rocket fuel to fill up the other side. And they ain't gonna like it at all if you help the Roscoes escape before they can kill them all."

Jimmy looked down at his scuffed rattlesnake boots, made from the skin of a six-foot diamondback he had killed with his teeth, then spoke to Eddie without looking up. "Thanks for the warning. But I'll take the run just the same."

Jimmy turned and walked to his truck. He started to climb into the cab, then paused halfway in and looked the pale dispatcher straight in the eye. "You could do me a favor, though."

"Sure, Jimmy. What?"

Jimmy smiled for the first time in a month. "Call accounting and tell them to triple my rate."

Jimmy settled into the form-fitted driver's seat inside the cab. The thick door swung shut with a resounding *thunk* and a whoosh of pressurized air. He hit the ignition switch and the low whine of twin turbines cycling started below him, the vibration tickling the seat of his pants even through the giant shock mountings on the frame.

The cockpit looked more like a fighter jet's than a truck's, with computer screens and video monitors and toggle switches filling every available space. As the rig vibrated from the motors spinning up into the operational range, Jimmy hit buttons and checked systems. Everything was fine, as usual; Jimmy was rather obsessive about preventative maintenance. He preferred to deal with things before they blossomed into problems that could, say, leave him stranded in Barstow for a week waiting for a part, or turn him into a super-heated ball of gas and spread his atoms across the state. Both scenarios were distasteful to him, though the week in Barstow held a slight edge over being immolated.

The whine of the turbines turned into a high-pitched howl, and soon a green light flashed, indicating full battery power. Jimmy eased the gear shift from Neutral to Drive. There was a slight lurch as the electric motors at the end of each axle fed massive torque to the tires, then the tanker rolled out of the garage.

The trip to the refinery was uneventful. Soon Jimmy was circling the lot, bypassing the tanker trucks waiting in line to fill up with regular fuels, and heading for the isolated Hi-Test nozzles in the rear.

Jimmy could have used the elaborate system of radar, GPS, and sonar to guide the rig backwards into the refinery's loading bay, but he didn't. He killed the audio cues from the computer and did it the old fashioned way—with mirrors and skill. He wondered if he was the only driver left in the world who could back up without electronic help, but lost the thought as he felt the rear wheels bump onto the raised concrete platform that indicated the proper loading position.

The Hi-Test loading facility was automated; the fewer people around, the fewer there were to die in case of an accident. A radar-guided hose dropped to the top of Jimmy's tank and felt its way to the feeder pipe. Jimmy punched a button, signaling his permission for the loading to begin, and the volatile liquid began flowing into the tanker trailer. Internal pumps in the rig circulated liquid nitrogen through an intricate system of pipes in the tank, keeping the Hi-Test at a safe temperature.

Jimmy watched TV in the cab while he waited for the tank to fill. He usually hated television, with its endless stream of commercials and bad programming, only occasionally tuning in to an ancient reruns of "The Rockford Files" or other shows he remembered watching with his dad when he was a kid. But now he needed Intel, so he surfed through the channels.

The split screen showed four different news programs. Three broadcast celebrity gossip, while the fourth showed scenes of the local rioting. Jimmy maximized the riot coverage and learned little more from the bubble-headed reporter than what Eddie had already told him; the streets and freeways were empty except for rival gangsters shooting at each other and the occasional citizen making a break for freedom, and coming up after the break would be a story on a new diet and exercise plan that could reverse male pattern baldness in six weeks or less while helping you shed pound after pound of unwanted body fat in just minutes a day.

So much for Intel.

Jimmy dumped the TV and thought about calling up a satellite map of the region, but turned the monitor off instead. He knew where he was going. And if Eddie was right, so did the gangsters. There was no use trying to sneak into the Valley. Jimmy was going to do the run the way he did everything: head on.

There was a *clunk* from the rear as the robot hose disconnected from his tanks. A series of flashing green signals indicated the load was sealed and cooled and ready to go. Jimmy dropped the transmission into gear and headed for the 405 Freeway, the truck now a gurgling 20,000 gallon bomb.

Other than the occasional emergency vehicle, Jimmy had the eight lanes of freeway to himself. As he cruised north through Torrance the elevation of the roadway gave him a commanding view of the Los Angeles basin. Columns of smoke and fire dotted the landscape from the South Bay up into the jagged spine of mountains that ran to the ocean. It was a gorgeous place, he thought. Too bad people had to come along and ruin it for the animals.

The rioting was seemingly everywhere, and since firetrucks were nothing more than bright red targets for meth-happy snipers, the few firefighters left in the area pretty much stayed in their station houses playing cards, eating chicken wings, and waiting for armored escorts to take them to the most important blazes, like hospitals, schools, or any mansion above Sunset in Beverly Hills. Nobody blamed them. You had to either have a screw loose or be heavily armed to go outside these days.

Or both.

Like Jimmy.

He played with the computer as he drove, running the truck though another series of system checks. Some people might have called Jimmy's repetition obsessive; he just called it *making damn good and sure.*

A crackling sound interrupted him. One of his radio speakers blared to life. "Jimmy. Partner. What are you doing out driving on a day like this?"

Jimmy knew the voice instantly; it was Andy, his old over-the-road driving partner. They had worked together for years, plying the concrete trails of North America in an endless marathon of pay-by-the-mile bulk cargo hauling, constantly in motion and never quite finding the finish line to a race they hadn't even consciously entered. Andy had been the one to quit, the break in the partnership coming at about the same time Jimmy decided to make shorter, much more profitable runs. Andy chose a safer job than running the Hi-Test. He became a cop.

Jimmy punched a button on the radio to return the call. "Just another little milk run, Andy."

"Yeah? Well, you're gonna curdle your cream if you let people sneak up on you like this."

Jimmy looked out his window to the mirror and saw Andy's police car cruising behind him on the left, hovering just on the edge of his blind spot. The car looked more like a tank, thick armour mated to bulletproof glass, all covered by metal caging and push bars. Gun ports were on either side, along with a small turret on the roof. The vehicle was impressive and powerful, but looked silly next to the truck. Andy grinned at him through the windshield.

Jimmy glanced from the mirror to his tactical readouts. The car was invisible to his electronics. He was impressed, which said a lot.

"Not bad. I wondered when you guys were going to get your stealth package going."

"It's been going for a little while now," said Andy. "Just don't spread it around. We need every edge we can get these days."

Andy had pulled even with the truck now, and the two men glanced at each other across the whizzing pavement as they talked on the radio.

"Look, Jimmy. I thought I might be able to talk you out of this run. Why don't we pull off somewhere and get a cup of coffee."

"Sorry. I'm on a clock here."

"Come on. We could hit Delores' like the old times. They're open again, back to making those giant cinnamon rolls."

"Gotta make tracks."

"Jimmy, pull the goddamn rig over."

Jimmy looked over his shoulder, out the window and over the twenty feet of space to where Andy cruised next to him. The two locked eyes at seventy miles an hour, staring at each other instead of the road for an uncomfortable amount of time.

"Is that an order, officer?" Jimmy asked.

"What? No! I didn't mean it like that. Hell, I wouldn't pull you over if you were doing a hundred in a school zone."

"Maybe you wouldn't. But what about the Brass?"

"The Brass doesn't give a shit what you do, Jimmy. Hell, half of them want you to make the run—they even talked about giving you an escort. Figure you make it to the airport and half the felons in Southern California are going to go into orbit this afternoon. You'd be doing their job for them."

"Then why do you want to stop me so bad?"

"Are you that stupid?"

"Apparently."

It was Andy's turn to stare. "Look. I know we don't see each other much anymore. But we spent a lot of miles in that rig together. A lot of years. So let me spell it out for you. You're my friend. I don't want you to die. That do it for you?"

Jimmy watched the road for a long moment. He didn't have a lot of friends—life on the road didn't lend itself to close personal relationships—so Jimmy valued the few people he was close to. The breakup with Andy had hurt more than he wanted to admit. After a mile or so, he hit the mike button again.

"Thanks for the concern, Andy. Seriously. But I got a contract."

"The Roscoes ain't gonna sue you. They're all going to be dead by morning anyway."

Emotion welled up in Jimmy. He fought it down, but it left his voice thick. "I don't have much, Andy. You know that. I got this truck, a big insurance policy, and a couple good friends like you. And my word. I give it to someone, I keep it. I gave my word I'd get this load to the airport, and I'm going to do it. Nothing's going to stop me. Not you, not the Maurauders, not eighteen flat tires, not the Devil himself. So while I appreciate your interest, don't ask me to go back on my word."

Andy's voice was charged as well. "Stubborn son of a bitch like always. But I had to try."

"I'm not the only stubborn one here."

There was another long moment of silence as they drove northward. The 10 Freeway interchange slid past them, and ahead the 405 gleamed in the sun as it snaked into the mountains separating L.A. from the San Fernando Valley.

Finally Jimmy spoke again. "Anyway, you got nothing to worry about. I've made a few modifications to the rig since the last time you saw her. You should be worrying about the bad guys."

"I am, don't worry." Andy dropped behind the truck, then steered towards the right side of the road. He peeled away from the freeway on the Santa Monica Boulevard off-ramp. "You be careful, Jimmy."

Jimmy watched the car drop out of sight, heading for the surface streets. He was alone again on the vast highway. "I will be. I'll meet you later for that cinnamon roll."

As the voice drifted out of Andy's radio speaker both men knew he was lying.

Jimmy wasn't alone for long. Four cars pulled onto the freeway at the Wilshire on-ramp. They took up positions behind him, forming a rolling blockade on the wide road. The cars were big, powerful, beat-up old American sedans, each stuffed with at least four glowering gangsters packing automatic weapons, shotguns, and far less than friendly attitudes.

Jimmy studied the cars for a moment on the heads-up radar display projected on his windshield. With his combination of satellite data, wireless ultra-net hookup, millimeter wave radar, sonar, audio-imaging, UHD cameras, and electronic sniffers, he could see the cars from the top, bottom, front, back, could look under the hood and see what size motors they had, look in the trunk and count the empty beer cans, see how much gas was left in each tank, how much they paid per gallon, what kind of mileage they were getting, and how many miles they had to go to the next oil change. He could also read the speed and direction of the vehicles, and plot trajectories based on accumulated data about the cars' past and present performance as well as each driver's brain waves, heart rate, hormone level, driving record, and psychological profile.

Jimmy sneered as he eyeballed the gangsters in the mirror. His *tires* were worth more than their *cars*.

He squelched the computer display after a brief glance. He didn't need the technology to tell him what the gangsters were going to do: They were going to wait for his truck to slow down as it labored to climb the Sepulveda Pass, then pull alongside of him and try to shoot out his tires. The gangsters had visions in their violent, narrow minds of compressed air rushing out of gaping holes in the sidewalls while the huge rubber treads ripped off and flapped to shreds. Then they pictured the truck shuddering to a halt on the side of the road, eighteen flats gluing it to the breakdown lane. They would then screech up, surround the rig, drag Jimmy out screaming, knock back some 40s, and torture him for a while before they killed him.

This plan was doomed for a couple of reasons.

First, unlike a normal rig, Jimmy had enough horses galloping under his hood to accelerate out of a black hole with a battleship anchor tied to his bumper. So he twitched his right toe on the accelerator and the five percent grade of the freeway was effectively flattened to zero. The gangsters pondered this for a moment as the ruins of Brentwood flashed by far faster than they had planned, but decided to go for the tires after all, speed of the truck be damned.

That was their second mistake.

A car pulled up on each side of the truck, even with the rear tires of the tanker. The windows rolled down on each car and multiple gun barrels aimed at the thick rubber from close range. Jimmy watched in curious fascination; he could stop them in any number of ways, but chose to let them open fire anyway. A barrage of ten millimeter bullets and twelve gauge shotgun pellets smashed into the tires on either side of the rig. A few of the projectiles were absorbed by the gargantuan black donuts, but most simply bounced off and ricocheted back into the shooters' faces. The two cars and their occupants were ripped apart by their own bullets.

On the right, the dying gangster in the driver's seat slumped over the wheel and the car angled off the road. It smashed into a road sign, flipped in the air, and came back to earth in a snarl of twisted metal and broken bodies.

The driver on the left, blinded by the blood spurting from a gash on his head, panicked and stomped on the brakes. He was rear-ended by the car behind him, and the two cars exploded. Jimmy saw the fourth and last car swerve around the flaming wreckage and pace him at a safe distance to the rear. He could see the gangsters arguing inside, trying to figure out what to do.

Jimmy decided for them. A door opened on the top of the tanker and a turret rose into view. A gleaming military grade Gatling gun poked out of the turret. The gangsters barely had enough time to realize the truck was shooting at *them* before their car exploded, shredded by the supersonic hail of depleted uranium darts belching from the Gatling's whirling mouth. The remains of the car flipped a few times before it came to rest abutting the freeway's center divider. Blood and oil dripped onto the concrete and started their long trip to the ocean.

Jimmy drove on.

As he continued up the Sepulveda Pass, Jimmy's ever-active eyes flashed over the elaborate readouts on the dash. So far, so good; everything remained a solid green.

Small flashes on the pavement in front of him brought his attention back to the road. He was puzzled for a moment, then realized it was bullets bouncing off of the freeway, the slugs kicking up sparks and dust as they whined into the brush.

Jimmy fathomed the unseen shooters were trying to get his range. In a moment they had it; the hood and windshield shivered in a dozen places as bullets stitched across the front of the truck. The computer tracked the bullets' trajectories, reversed the path, located the origin, and flashed a wind-and-speed-adjusted targeting screen for Jimmy in case he wanted to shoot back. As usual, his Mark One Eyeballs had already seen where the shooters were an instant ahead of the electronics, but the confirmation was nice anyway.

The Mulholland overpass loomed ahead, just shy of the top of the pass. A line of dark figures dotted the soaring bridge, eighty feet above the freeway snaking below. Bright flashes indicated gunfire. Another machine-gun turret popped up, this time on the roof of the cab, but Jimmy held his finger off the trigger. The small arms of the gangsters were nothing to him; ten millimeter shells couldn't even scratch the paint, since the color of the truck was fused into the vehicle's armored shell at the factory. The windshield would hold up as well, the clear resin almost as strong as the rest of the truck.

So Jimmy held off, determined to simply drive by the Marauders' latest roadblock, saving his ammunition for the next round.

Then the windshield shattered.

The massive bullet didn't make it all the way through the glass, rather penetrating halfway and sticking in the middle of a spider web design of cracks the size of a dinner plate. Jimmy recognized the round as the type military snipers used when they wanted to leave no question as to whether their target was dead. Another fat bullet smashed into the glass, this time closer to Jimmy's face. Deeper cracks formed this time, so Jimmy decided to stop fucking around and shoot back.

Both Gatling guns on the rig roared to life, raking the bridge with devastating fire. Some gangsters flipped back from the railing, others tumbled forward and made the long drop to the pavement, but all were pierced in a dozen places or more, spraying blood as they fell.

Jimmy kept shooting until he was almost under the bridge. As he passed through the shadows underneath he punched a few more buttons. The truck shuddered as something erupted from the top of the rig with a puff of smoke, then he was out again into the sunlight and heading for the crest of the mountain.

On the bridge behind him, the sniper crawled to the edge, dragging his huge rifle along. Of the twenty gangsters who had been on the bridge moments before, he was the only one still able to move. He was bleeding badly, three holes punched into various parts of his body, but he still had enough strength left to want revenge. He was going to use his last breath to put a bullet in the tanker and blow the truck to hell.

Or so he thought.

As he leveled the heavy gun at the rear of the truck a roar reached his ears. He looked up in time to see a fat missile dart out of the sky and smash into the center of the bridge. Instead of blowing up, like the sniper expected, Jimmy's parting gift instead cracked apart. Things that looked like golf balls spurted out and began bouncing down the length of the bridge with a silly popping sound. A moment after they evenly covered the bridge, each of the lethal submunitions erupted into white hot chemical fire, turning the overpass into a raging inferno. The sniper died thinking of Putt-Putt windmills at the end of AstroTurf fairways—in Hell.

The truck blasted over the crest of the hill and Jimmy cursed. A line of parked cars blocked the freeway in front of him, and a line of trucks and SUVs were parked right behind them. Apparently the Maurauders were taking him more seriously than he thought.

For an instant Jimmy considered smashing through. He had enough speed, plenty of power, and eighteen-wheel drive. But that wouldn't be fun, he reckoned, or even remotely stylish. So he pulled the wheel to the right and the rig left the freeway, climbed an angled grassy embankment, and went around the roadblock on a dirt fire trail leading into the hills.

To say the gangsters were astonished to see the huge truck go off-road with the agility of a dirt bike would be putting it far too mildly.

Jimmy watched the gangster-covered freeway fall away on his left; the narrow fire road went more or less level here, but the 405 plunged into the valley below him. He grinned as he watched the Maurauders scrambling to chase him. This was turning into the most enjoyable run he had made in years.

The fire road turned right into the hills, and he turned with it. The dirt path was tight, and as the trailer tires skidded off the side he grabbed the auxiliary steering knob and jammed it to the right. The rear drive pod turned on its own to a better angle. The back tires bit into dirt again, the trailer remounted the road, and the rig thundered on.

Jimmy looked ahead and saw the road curve back into the hills to the left, and a tall wooden fence directly in front of him. Over the fence he could see the huge backyard of an abandoned house, and past that a wide driveway leading to a paved street beyond. Jimmy smiled and squelched the satellite map the computer was desperately trying to show him. No need for a flashlight when the end of the tunnel is in sight.

John Rosenthal loved his roses. He had spent hours in his Sherman Oaks backyard tending the thorny beauties, marveling when the buds opened up into brilliant petals. And though Rosenthal was saddened when he had to abandon his home and the flowers when he left SoCal to avoid the plague some years back, in retrospect it was good thing; he wasn't around to see Jimmy murder his children.

The truck exploded through the back fence and into the yard, blowing a rain of timbers and dirt into the air. It should have been a straight shot from the fire road, across the yard, down the driveway, and out onto the street. Should have been, yes. But the swimming pool complicated matters. It had been below his line of sight when he had looked over the fence, so he hadn't known it was there. Jimmy swerved while cursing himself for ignoring the computer. The truck narrowly missed the muck-filled pit, but he didn't miss the roses.

The speeding rig ripped through the flower bed, eighteen massive wheels grinding the blooms into the dirt. The guest house suffered the same fate, as the edge of the massive front fender caught the side of the building. The house exploded like the fence, debris clattering off the side of the tanker as it whipped by.

The driveway now impossible to get to, Jimmy aimed for the gap between the houses on the opposite side. The truck smashed through a tall hedge and Jimmy could finally see pavement ahead of him.

He saw the tree at the same instant the Low Overhead Warning klaxon started screaming in his ears. The giant oak tree loomed ahead in the yard, its thick leaves providing an oasis of shade for the front of the house. The shade was welcome, but the branch providing it wasn't. Over three feet thick and extending over Jimmy's path at a height a few inches lower than the spine of the truck, the branch wasn't welcome at all.

Jimmy liked trees almost as much as he liked his truck, so for a millisecond he considered braking. But a gut check told him he'd never slow in time. So he bowed to the physics of collisions and floored it. The huge truck accelerated across the front lawn, the tires showing as much respect to Mr. Rosenthal's brilliant green drought-resistant Kentucky bluegrass as they had to his roses, and bashed into the limb at a touch over sixty miles an hour.

For the first time, the truck met its match. Jimmy was slammed forward in his safety harness as the impact rocked the frame. The branch ripped across the top of the rig, scrunching the metal, peeling Kevlar, and popping rivets the whole way. Antennas bent and snapped off. The first Gatling turret was retracted, so the gun survived, even though it was now jammed in its mangled turret. The second cannon met the limb with a resounding screech and was ripped out by its metallic roots. As it fell to the ground, torn wires crossed and the electronic trigger circuit closed; a stream of supersonic bullets sprayed the neighborhood from the flopping barrels. One slug ripped into the rear of the tanker and punched through a nitrogen line, and a thin stream of the pressurized gas hissed into the air. The mangled truck staggered for the road.

Other than a few cracks, a small loss of bark, and a rather pissed off nest of crows, the tree was fine.

Inside the cab, Jimmy was deafened by the numerous warning buzzers clanging in his ears. The guns were offline, the rocket doors jammed shut, the cab depressurized, the satellite link and radar gone, but most importantly, the Hi-Test cooling system had sprung a leak. A virtual schematic of the coolant lines appeared, the punctured one an angry red contrasting with the normal soothing green. Jimmy took one look at the cargo tank temperature gauge and slammed on the brakes.

The truck skidded to a halt, tires digging huge furrows in the sun-softened pavement. Jimmy jumped out of the door and ran back to the middle of the trailer. He ignored the damage to the top of the truck, concentrating on an access panel near the ground. He banged the door open and revealed four round metal valves. He twisted one and the hissing from the rear of the trailer stopped. He had cut off the leak, but he had also lost a quarter of the tanker's cooling capacity. Normally it wouldn't matter, as the truck was overcooled to start with, but the tree limb had ripped the roof open, tearing away great chunks of armour and precious insulation. The hot California sun glared down on the exposed tank, and Jimmy imagined he could hear the Hi-Test bubbling inside. He angrily kicked one of the huge tires, stubbing his toe. A string of curses erupted from his mouth, but stopped when a bullet smacked off the trailer beside him.

His concern for the coolant had made him forget about the gangsters. Looking over his shoulder as he ran for the cab he saw them pouring around the edge of the house, a flood of tattooed testosterone howling for his blood. Their cars had been stopped by the wreckage in the yard, but their sneaker-covered feet still worked fine. More opened fire as they got closer, bullets zipping past Jimmy as he yanked the door shut behind him. He slammed the truck into gear and it lurched into drive, but five of the gangsters had almost caught up. They grabbed at handholds on the trailer and tried to swing on board.

The last thing Jimmy needed now was heavily armed idiots poking around in the guts of the tanker. Furiously scanning through system menus he looked for any defense he could find. Only one screen still showed full green; Jimmy instantly activated the anti-theft system.

Sensing unauthorized intruders near the truck, the thick strip of anti-personnel munitions wrapped around the rig at chest level erupted, sending thousands of metal fragments tearing through the air. The five gangsters were shredded, the small chunks that remained mixed with the shrapnel and pelted the neighborhood with gore. The others dove for cover, and by the time they got the courage to lift their heads again, Jimmy was gone.

The truck barreled down a twisting side street until it connected with the long, straight asphalt trail that was Sepulveda Boulevard. As he flashed under the 101 Freeway Jimmy breathed a sigh of relief; the mountains were behind him, and it was literally and figuratively downhill from here. The truck was defenseless, yes, and the temperature of the Hi-Test hovered a degree or two below the unstable mark, but all in all he felt good about the run. If he drove smooth and fast from here the run would be over in minutes. Though in the future he vowed to pay more attention to his instruments, it looked like another legendary notch in the belt of the Greatest Driver Alive.

The ugly stucco architecture of the Valley whipped by him at seventy miles an hour. He slowed enough to make the sharp left onto Saticoy Street, then accelerated again. He now had a straight shot to the back gate of the airport.

Jimmy kept checking his mirrors for signs of pursuit, and finally saw a stream of at least thirty cars chasing behind him. They stayed far back though, apparently unaware he couldn't shoot back. Safe for the moment, he slumped back in his chair and relaxed.

He relaxed, at least, until a stream of bullets ripped across the cab of the truck. Jimmy jumped in his seat, trying to figure out where it had come from. He looked in both mirrors, but the cars were still far behind. More shots clattered against the glass.

What the hell?

Then he saw it. The Maurauders had gotten hold of a helicopter. The Long Ranger wasn't really a combat weapon, rather a general purpose civilian aircraft that had been turned into a gunship by a sadistic entrepreneurial mechanic. But that didn't make it any less deadly. The strut-mounted fifty caliber machine guns couldn't pierce the cab's armor, but the windshield was already cracked and a stray shot could certainly punch through the exposed storage tank. It didn't help that they were shooting from above, aiming right at the Hi-Test.

Jimmy cycled through the weapons screens again, looking for anything to help him fight back. He stopped on the air defense menu, punching up a Surface to Air Missile icon. The cartoon missile glowed green on the diagram, indicating it was fully functional and ready to fly—it was the access door icon that was bathed in red. The port cover was jammed shut and no amount of button pushing was going to open it.

As the helicopter swung back around for another pass, Jimmy got an idea. He triggered the firing mechanism of the missile, the failsafe circuits keeping the frustrated engines cold as they sensed the jammed flap. But the missile was hot and ready to fire.

Reaching under the seat, Jimmy grabbed a tire iron, hit the auto-pilot button, and opened the door.

The helicopter pilot grew angry at wasting bullets on the obviously impenetrable target, but the gangster in the passenger seat kept a pistol aimed at him, so he swung the bird around for another attack. He centered the taped-on crosshairs on the truck, squinted, then almost let go of the stick in shock when he saw what was happening below. Down there, climbing on top of the truck as it sped driverless down the road, was what had to be the craziest son-of-a-bitch alive.

Jimmy clawed his way up the side of the truck. He slipped once but grabbed a stray antenna, and moments later heaved himself up on top of the cab. Completely ignoring the helicopter as well as the road rushing by, he jumped on top of the mangled sleeper unit and kneeled over the missile access doors. The wind buffeted him as he jammed the tire iron under the crinkled metal door and heaved. The Titanium stretched and a hinge popped, but the door covering the missile remained stuck.

The auto-pilot swerved left to miss a car parked in the road, throwing Jimmy off balance. He teetered for a moment, then righted himself just as the helicopter opened fire again. The bullets stitched a line across the pavement and up the side of the truck. Jimmy jumped backwards onto the trailer, and the bullets zinged through the empty air.

He landed with the exposed Hi-Test tank between his legs. For a second he was grateful for the protection he had in the small valley of ripped armour, then it dawned on him what he was sitting on. He almost thought he could hear the evil liquid hissing at him as it sloshed inside the tank. Helicopter gunship or not, Jimmy jumped back up onto the exposed top of the truck.

Grabbing the tire iron again he pushed with all his strength to free the access door. The metal groaned in protest, then gave way with a sudden snap. Jimmy tumbled forward, rolling onto the sloping hood of the truck and almost falling over the side. Behind him, the firing circuit of the missile was delighted to find the offending door was now out of the way, and the Stinger's engine roared to life. With a flash of fire it vaulted out of the truck and arched into the sky.

The gangsters in the helicopter screamed when they saw the missile roaring at them, then stopped when the pilot jerked the stick in a wild evasive maneuver and it whooshed by.

"Freaking idiot missed," the leader laughed, pointing his pistol down at Jimmy to tell the pilot to make another pass.

The pilot had learned how to fly in the Army, so he had more than a passing knowledge of missiles. He knew it was a miracle the Stinger had missed them since the weapon had more than a 90% kill ratio, and thus the odds it would miss twice were astronomical. He also knew the missile was completing a miles-wide turn and blasting a supersonic path back to meet the target that was undoubtedly glowing white hot in the simple mind of its targeting computer, i.e., his helicopter. He further knew he stood a better chance of surviving a hundred foot drop to the ground than he did by taking a three kilo warhead up his ass. So the pilot did something that would make even Jimmy proud; he clicked off his safety belt, opened the door, and jumped.

The Stinger hit a few seconds later, turning the helicopter into a white-hot ball of fire. Chunks of debris rained down on the pilot, who was nursing two broken legs and a fractured wrist on the ground below. But all things considered, he was happy with way things turned out.

Jimmy winced at the flash from the explosion and swung back into the cab. He let the auto-pilot keep driving while he strapped in and checked the gauges. The Hi-Test was three degrees above the recommended safety zone, but still relatively cool and stable. He was reasonably happy with the outcome as well.

Looking out the windshield Jimmy saw he was a hundred yards from the airport gate. Beyond it, a gleaming orbital scramjet was parked on the tarmac, surrounded by a mass of overturned cars, trucks, and dumpsters. The 300 or so heavily armed Roscoe Street Boys jumped on top of their barricades and cheered when they saw him; their savior had arrived. The mob of Maurauders surrounding them opened fire, and the Roscoes dove back under cover.

Jimmy smelled victory. He floored it and smashed through the chain link gate that blocked the entrance to the maintenance area. Flashing past open hangars he followed the access road as it curved to the right. One more turn and a hop across the tarmac and he would be pumping fuel into the belly of the rocket. He followed the pavement as it snaked back to the left and as the runways came back into view his heart nearly stopped.

A Caterpillar bulldozer was parked in the road, blocking the gate to the tarmac. If the cooling system in the tank was working right Jimmy would have considered ramming the dozer; the kinetic energy of the massive truck probably would have pushed the yellow giant out of the way and sent him down the road. But with the Hi-Test overheating, the shock of the collision would be a Very Bad Thing.

So Jimmy did the only thing he could do; he hit the brakes and whipped the wheel as hard as he could to the left, aiming the truck at a connecting road that ran in front of the bulldozer.

He almost made it.

The truck rolled to the right as he made the turn. The weight of the liquid cargo shifted, pushing the rig up on the passenger side wheels. Jimmy rode it for a hundred feet, the nine driver's side tires churning empty air, but gravity eventually won. The trailer broke free from the tractor and rolled over on its back. The tank of Hi-Test ruptured and a geyser of hell-born fluid splashed to the ground.

As the truck went past the point of no return a mercury leveling switch closed. Explosive bolts shattered an instant before a rocket motor fired, turning the cockpit into an escape pod and blasting it through the roof. Airbags inflated inside, pinning Jimmy to his seat in a high-pressure protective pillow as the pod roared into the safety of the sky.

Then the Hi-Test exploded.

Though the blast crater and the shockwave had a brief contest to see which was more spectacular, the outcome was never really in doubt. The crater was impressive, a two-hundred feet deep by five-hundred wide hole gouged out of the airport pavement in one violent instant, the concrete and dirt edges a seething bowl of plasma.

But the shockwave was even better. The dirt and rock and asphalt from the crater joined the super-heated column of air spreading from ground zero. The rapidly expanding dome of pure force raced outward at supersonic speed, smashing air, people, aircraft, buildings, trees, windows, and more with a god-like hammer. Everything within a half-mile circle of ground zero was vaporized, and everything for a mile beyond that was flattened to the ground. Hundreds of small fires sparked to life. Water spurted from shorn-off pipes. A dirty brown mushroom cloud rose into the air and towered over what was left of the airport.

The blast caught the escape pod just as its rocket ran out of fuel, punching it higher in the air. Jimmy was smashed around in spite of the protective air bags cocooning him. Temperature warning buzzers blasted in his ears as the heat wave caught up. At four thousand feet the shockwave dissipated enough to let gravity grab the pod. A parachute popped out of a rear panel, and Jimmy started the long, long float back to the ground.

The escape pod landed on top of a dumpster, smashed it flat, and rolled down the street. After a hundred feet it crunched into a building and stopped. The door hissed open, and Jimmy crawled out through the deflating air bags. He tripped in the parachute rigging and dizzily fell to the ground. Lying on his back, he kicked the pod in nauseated frustration.

"Goddamnit!!" he cursed. "Goddamnit all to hell."

He stared up at the mushroom cloud for a minute and tried to clear his head. Through ringing ears he heard a car pull up and the door open. He rose up on one arm, expecting to see one of the gangsters aiming a shotgun at his face. But what he saw was worse, for his pride anyway.

"Need a ride?" chuckled Andy.

Jimmy glared at his old partner as the cop leaned against his patrol car near the pod. "Nowhere to go," he muttered.

Andy chuckled again. "I followed your 'chute. Didn't think you were ever going to come down."

"I wish I didn't," he glowered.

"What are you all pissed about? You're a hero."

"A what?" Confused, Jimmy untangled himself from the parachute and tried to stand up. He settled for leaning on the pod until his head stopped spinning.

"I said you're a hero. The Chief's calling the Governor right now to recommend you for a medal."

"I must have got knocked around harder than I thought, 'cause you're not making a whole lot of sense."

Andy smiled and nodded towards the airport. "You just took out the two biggest gangs in the city all by yourself. No more Roscoes, no more Maurauders. You cleaned up the city and threw in a pretty epic cremation ceremony to boot. The riots are over and then some."

"What about the airport?"

"Who cares? Some asshole developer will get a trillion dollars to rebuild it and kick a billion or two back to the Mayor. And all the cool kids fly out of Santa Monica anyway."

"Yeah. That's good, I guess," Jimmy said. He still looked glum.

"Jesus, Jimmy. What's wrong with you? You pissed about your rig?"

Jimmy looked up at him, stunned that Andy didn't understand him after all these years. "I'm pissed because I didn't finish the run."

Andy stared at the mushroom cloud rising into the atmosphere for a moment, then held a computer pad out to Jimmy.

"Here."

"What's that?" Jimmy asked.

"A copy of your delivery manifest. Did you even read it?"

Jimmy shot him a dirty look. "I glanced at it."

"That's what I thought. You never did pay much attention to details."

"Get to the fucking point."

"According to this, the Roscoes asked for a load of fuel to be taken to the airport. No more, no less."

"So?"

"So they were about as dumb as you are. They didn't specify a drop point. The second you busted through the maintenance gate you were officially on airport property. And with a crater the size of the Hollywood Bowl to prove where the truck stopped..."

"I finished the run!" Jimmy exclaimed with a huge grin.

"That's right. You're still the greatest driver alive. And I'm sure you won't let me forget it."

Andy opened his door and got in. He motioned Jimmy to the other side of the patrol car. Jimmy jumped in and they sat in silence for a moment, looking out at the wreckage of the airport.

Jimmy sighed. "I may be great, but I still got to figure out how I'm going to afford another truck. There's no way the insurance company is gonna cover this one."

"I might have a solution," Andy suggested.

"No. I'm not going to quit driving."

"Relax. I wasn't going to ask you to quit. Even better. I've been authorized to offer you a position with the L.A.P.D."

"Me? A cop? No thanks. I'm not much into uniforms."

"Not as a cop. Not totally, anyway. As a driver."

"A car, even one like this, is a waste of my incredible talents."

"That's what I told the Brass. So they figured you might be a little more comfortable in the new SWAT Tactical Assault Vehicle."

"Assault Vehicle?" Jimmy's eyes lit up.

"Yeah. It's kinda like a tank on steroids. Makes your rig look like a Tonka toy. And the best part is, the city makes the payments."

Jimmy thought about it for a long minute. It would be a big step, giving up the narcotic-like call of the open road. Finally he turned to his friend.

"You got a good health plan?"

Andy smiled, revealing twin rows of gleaming white teeth. "Dental, too."

Jimmy motioned for Andy to start the car. "Drive," he said, and settled back to take a nap.

If you liked this book, please consider telling other people. Helping spread the word is a great way for readers to find new material, and for deserving writers to find new fans.

Thank you for your support.